GIRL WAITS
WITH GUN

GIRL WAITS
WITH GUN

Amy Stewart

Houghton Mifflin Harcourt

Boston   New York   2015

Library of Congress Cataloging-in-Publication Data
Stewart, Amy.
Girl waits with gun / Amy Stewart.
pages ; cm
Summary: "From the New York Times best-selling author of
The Drunken Botanist comes an enthralling novel based on
the forgotten true story of one of the nation's first female
deputy sheriffs"—Provided by publisher.
ISBN 978-0-544-40991-0 (hardcover)—ISBN 978-0-544-40961-3 (ebook)
1. Sheriffs—New Jersey—Paterson—Fiction. 2. Policewomen—
New Jersey—Hackensack—Fiction. 3. Silk Workers' Strike, Paterson,
N.J., 1913—Fiction. 4. Black Hand (United States)—History—20th
century—Fiction. 5. Organized crime—New Jersey—Fiction.
6. New Jersey—History—20th century—Fiction. I. Title.
PS3619.T49343G57 2015
813'.6—dc23
2014045223

Book design by Greta D. Sibley

Printed in the United States of America
DOC 10 9 8 7 6 5 4 3 2 1

To John Birgel and Dennis O'Dell

"I got a revolver to protect us," said Miss Constance,
"and I soon had use for it."

—*New York Times,* June 3, 1915

1

OUR TROUBLES BEGAN in the summer of 1914, the year I turned thirty-five. The Archduke of Austria had just been assassinated, the Mexicans were revolting, and absolutely nothing was happening at our house, which explains why all three of us were riding to Paterson on the most trivial of errands. Never had a larger committee been convened to make a decision about the purchase of mustard powder and the replacement of a claw hammer whose handle had split from age and misuse.

Against my better judgment I allowed Fleurette to drive. Norma was reading to us from the newspaper as she always did.

"'Man's Trousers Cause Death,'" Norma called out.

"It doesn't say that." Fleurette snorted and turned around to get a look at the paper. The reins slid out of her hands.

"It does," Norma said. "It says that a Teamster was in the habit of hanging his trousers over the gas jet at night but, being under the influence of liquor, didn't notice that the trousers smothered the flame."

"Then he died of gas poisoning, not of trousers."

"Well, the trousers—"

The low, goosey cry of a horn interrupted Norma. I turned just in time to see a black motor car barreling toward us, tearing down Hamilton and picking up speed as it crossed the intersection. Fleurette jumped up on the footboard to wave the driver off.

"Get down!" I shouted, but it was too late.

The automobile hit us broadside, its brakes shrieking. The sound of our buggy shattering was like a firecracker going off in our ears. We tumbled over in a mess of splintered wood and bent metal. Our harness mare, Dolley, faltered and went down with us. She let out a high scream, the likes of which I had never heard from a horse.

Something heavy pinned my shoulder. I reached around and found it was Norma's foot. "You're standing on me!"

"I am not. I can't even see you," Norma said.

Our wagon rocked back and forth as the motor car reversed its engine and broke free of the wreckage. I was trapped under the overturned rear seat. It was as dark as a coffin, but there was a dim shape below me that I believed to be Fleurette's arm. I didn't dare move for fear of crushing her.

From the clamor around us, I gathered that someone was trying to rock the wagon and get it upright. "Don't!" I yelled. "My sister's under the wheel." If the wheel started to turn, she'd be caught up in it.

A pair of arms the size of tree branches reached into the rubble and got hold of Norma. "Take your hands off me!" she shouted.

"He's trying to get you out," I called. With a grunt, she accepted the man's help. Norma hated to be manhandled.

Once she was free, I climbed out behind her. The man attached to the enormous arms wore an apron covered in blood. For one terrible second, I thought it was ours, then I realized he was a butcher at the meat counter across the street.

He wasn't the only one who had come running out when the automobile hit us. We were surrounded by store clerks, locksmiths, grocers, delivery boys, shoppers—in fact, most of the stores on Market Street had emptied, their occupants drawn to the spectacle we were now providing. Most of them watched from the sidewalk, but a sizable contingent surrounded the motor car, preventing its escape.

The butcher and a couple of men from the print shop, their hands black with ink, helped us raise the wagon just enough to allow Fleurette to slide clear of the wheel. As we lifted the broken panels off her, Fleurette stared up at us with wild dark eyes. She wore a dress sheathed in pink taffeta. Against the dusty road she looked like a trampled bed of roses.

"Don't move," I whispered, bending over her, but she got her arms underneath herself and sat up.

"No, no, no," said one of the printers. "We'll call for a doctor."

I looked up at the men standing in a circle around us. "She'll be fine," I said, sliding a hand over her ankle. "Go on." Some of those men looked a little too eager to help with the examination of Fleurette's legs.

They shuffled off to help two livery drivers, who had disembarked from their own wagons to tend to our mare. They freed her from the harness and she struggled to stand. The poor creature groaned and tossed her head and blew steam from her nostrils. The drivers fed her something from their pockets and that seemed to settle her.

I gave Fleurette's calf a squeeze. She howled and jerked away from me.

"Is it broken?" she asked.

I couldn't say. "Try to move it."

She screwed her face into a knot, held her breath, and gingerly bent one leg and then the other. When she was finished she let her breath go all at once and looked up at me, panting.

"That's good," I said. "Now move your ankles and your toes."

We both looked down at her feet. She was wearing the most ridiculous white calfskin boots with pink ribbons for laces.

"Are they all right?" she asked.

I put my hand on her back to steady her. "Just try to move them. First your ankle."

"I meant the boots."

That's when I knew Fleurette would survive. I unlaced the boots and promised to look after them. A much larger crowd had gathered, and Fleurette wiggled her pale-stockinged toes for her new audience.

"You'll have quite a bruise tomorrow, miss," said a lady behind us.

The seat that had trapped me a few moments ago was resting on the ground. I helped Fleurette into it and took another look at her legs. Her stockings were torn and she was scratched and bruised, but not broken to bits as I'd feared. I offered my handkerchief to press against one long and shallow cut along her ankle, but she'd already lost interest in her own injuries.

"Look at Norma," she whispered with a wicked little smile. My sister had planted herself directly in the path of the motor car to prevent the men from driving away. She did make a comical sight, a small but stocky figure in her split riding skirt of drab cotton. Norma had the broad Slavic face and thick nose of our father and our mother's sour disposition. Her mouth was set in a permanent frown and she looked on everyone with suspicion. She stared down the driver of the motor car with the kind of flat-footed resolve that came naturally to her in times of calamity.

The automobilist was a short but solidly built young man who had an overfed look about him, hinting at a privileged life. He would have been handsome if not for an indolent and spoiled aspect about his eyes and the tough set of his mouth, which suggested he was accustomed to getting his way. His face was puffy and red from the heat, but also, I suspected, from a habit of putting away a quart of beer at breakfast and a bottle of wine at night. He was dressed exceedingly well, in striped linen trousers, a silk waistcoat with polished brass buttons, and a tie as red as the blood seeping through Fleurette's stockings.

His companions tumbled out of the car and gathered around him as if standing guard. They wore the plain broadcloth suits of working men and carried themselves like rats who weren't accustomed to being spotted in the daylight. Each of them was unkempt and unshaven, and a few kept their hands in their pockets in a manner that suggested they might be reaching for their knives. I couldn't imagine where this gang of ruffians had been off to in such a hurry, but I was already beginning to regret that we had been the ones to get in their way.

The driver waved his arms and shouted for the crowd to clear the road. The other men took up his command and started yelling at the onlookers and pushing at them like drunks in a barroom brawl—all but one of them, who backed away and tried to run. He stumbled and the men in the crowd easily took hold of him. With twenty or so people blocking the way, the motor car's engine sputtered and died, but the shouting and shoving went on.

I couldn't catch Norma's eye. She was taking them in, too, the outrage draining from her face as she realized that this gang was trouble.

The shopkeepers, clerks, and drivers of other automobiles now stalled along the curb were all barking orders and pointing fingers at once.

"You're going to pay these ladies for what you did!" one yelled.

"Their horse spooked!" the driver shouted back. "They ran right in front of us!"

A ripple of dissent rose up. Everyone knew that the horse was never to blame in these collisions. A horse could watch where it was going, but an automobile with an inattentive driver could not. These boys had obviously had something on their minds besides the traffic when they roared into town.

I couldn't leave Norma to face them by herself. I gave Fleurette a firm pat to keep her planted on the buggy seat and ran around to stand next to Norma. All eyes traveled over to me. As the tallest and the oldest, I must have looked like the responsible party.

There was no one to introduce us, but it was the only way I knew to begin.

"I am Constance Kopp," I said, "and these are my sisters."

I addressed the men with all the dignity I could muster, considering that I'd just been upside down in an overturned buggy. The driver of the motor car looked pointedly away as if he couldn't be bothered to listen to me, and in fact made a great show of behaving as if I weren't standing right in front of him. I took a breath and spoke louder. "As soon as we settle on the damages, you may be on your way."

The one who had tried to run away—a tall, thin man with droopy eyes and a prominent front tooth—leaned over and whispered something to the rest of them. They appeared to be making some kind of plan. As he hobbled around to discuss the situation, I saw that his limp was caused by a wooden leg.

The driver of the automobile nodded at his friends and reached for the door handle. He was going to push through the crowd and drive off without a word! Norma started to say something but I held her back.

He pried the door open. Seeing no alternative, I ran over and slammed it shut.

This elicited a satisfied little gasp from the bystanders, who were clearly enjoying themselves. I saw no choice but to press my advantage. I stepped up and stood as tall as I possibly could, which meant that I towered above him considerably. He was about to address my collarbone, but thought better of it and lifted his chin to stare me in the face. His mouth hung open slightly, and as I watched, perfectly round beads of sweat bloomed in even rows above his lip.

"I suppose we may require a new buggy, as you seem to have smashed this one beyond repair," I said. A pin sprung loose from my hat at that moment and rang like a tiny bell as it hit the gravel. I had to force myself not to look down at it and hoped there were no other pins or fasteners working their way loose, as they could in moments of great agitation like these.

"Get offa my car, lady," he said between clenched teeth.

I glared down at him. Neither of us moved. "If you refuse to pay, then I must see your license plate," I declared.

He lifted one brow as if issuing a challenge. At that I marched around to write the plate number in a little notebook I carried in my handbag.

"Don't bother with this," Norma said from just behind me. "I don't like them looking at us."

"I don't either, but we need his name," I said in a low hiss.

"I don't care to know his name."

"But I do."

People were starting to crane their necks to hear us argue. I walked back around to the man and said, "Perhaps you'll save me the trouble of asking the state of New Jersey for your name and address."

He looked around at the crowd and, seeing no alternative, leaned toward me. He smelled of hair tonic and (as I'd suspected) liquor and the hard, metallic stench that leaked out of all the factories in town. He spat the particulars at me, releasing a wave of abdominal breath that forced me to take a step back as I wrote them down: Henry Kaufman of Kaufman Silk Dyeing Company on Putnam.

"That will do, Mr. Kaufman," I said, in a voice loud enough for the others to hear. "You'll have our invoice in a few days."

He made no answer but swung back into the driver's seat. One of his friends gave the engine a hard crank and the motor roared to life. They all climbed aboard and the car lurched ahead, clearing a path through the mob of shoppers. Men held their horses back and mothers pulled their children to the sidewalks as the motor car careened away.

Norma and I watched the dust rise up behind Henry Kaufman's tires and settle back down again.

"You let them go?" Fleurette said from her perch on our buggy's broken seat. She had assumed the pose of an audience member at a play and seemed very disappointed in our performance.

"I didn't want to spend another minute with them," Norma said. "They're the worst people I've ever seen. And look what they've done to your leg."

"Is it broken?" asked Fleurette, who knew it wasn't but loved to elicit from Norma one of her gloomy predictions.

"Oh, probably, but we can set the bone ourselves if we have to."

"I suppose my dancing career is at an end."

"Yes, I believe it is."

The livery drivers led a shaky but intact Dolley back to us. What remained of our buggy had been moved to the sidewalk, where it lay in a dozen or so pieces.

"I'm not sure it can be repaired," one of the liverymen said, "but I could send my stable boy around to the carriage shops to inquire."

"Oh, there's no need for that," Norma said. "Our brother will come and fetch it. He drives a wagon for work."

"But let's not involve Francis!" Fleurette protested. "He'll blame it on my driving."

I stepped between them, not wanting the liveryman to withdraw his offer of help while we squabbled. "Sir, if you could send your boy to my brother's place of business, I'd be very grateful." I wrote down the address of the basket importer where Francis worked.

"I'll take care of it," he said. "But how are you girls getting home?"

"Constance and I can walk," Norma said quickly, "and our little sister will ride."

I wasn't sure I could walk. I was already stiff and sore from the crash and it would be past dark by the time we got home. But I was in no mood to debate Norma, so I accepted the man's offer of a saddle for Dolley. We lifted Fleurette into place and wrapped her injured foot in a flour sack before sliding it into the stirrup. Norma took hold of Dolley's reins and we shuffled down Market, looking more like refugees from a war than three sisters out shopping for an afternoon.

Ordinarily, I would have considered getting run down by an automobile to be the worst sort of catastrophe that could befall the three of us. But this was not to be an ordinary year.

⇥ 2 ⇤

THE NEXT MORNING the sun worked past the half-curtained windows and hit the mirror on the wall opposite, casting a blinding light across my bed. Even at that early hour, the air was heavy and unbearably hot. I kicked the blanket away and tried to sit up. As soon as my feet touched the floor I knew I'd been hurt worse than I had realized. My right arm was useless, the shoulder red and hot and bruised so badly that I could hardly bear to move it. With some difficulty I opened the top buttons of my nightgown and slid out of it. I was hardly able to stand, but after a few attempts, I forced myself upright and struggled into the first dress I could find that didn't require me to raise my arm above my head.

Walking was nearly impossible. My hip felt like it had been pushed out of joint. I couldn't quite hold myself upright, and every time I put weight on my left leg, my knee cried out in pain.

This was not the soreness of a hard day's work. It felt more like the aftermath of a beating. I made my way to the hall and kept one hand on the rail as I shuffled downstairs.

I found Fleurette in the kitchen, eating a boiled egg with a spoon.

"Bonjour," she said. After Mother died last year, Fleurette took to imitating her speech mannerisms. Mother, having grown up in Vienna with a French father and an Austrian mother, spoke French and two distinct styles of German. Fleurette preferred the French for its romantic flourishes. Norma and I found the affectation tiresome, but we had conferred on it and decided to ignore it.

"Let me see your foot."

She lifted her skirt and presented a badly bandaged ankle. The cloth was stained a rusted brown. I am sorry to admit that it was a stagnation of dried blood, and not our poorly situated pins, that held the bandage in place.

"Ach. We did not take very good care of you last night."

"Je pense que c'est cassé."

"Surely not. Can't you move it? Stand up."

Fleurette didn't move. She picked at her egg cup and kept her eyes down. "Norma said to tell you that Francis—" But before she could finish, there was a rattle at the kitchen door and my brother let himself in.

"Which one of you was driving?" he said. With Mother gone, Francis had taken on the proprietary air of the man of the house, even though he'd been married and living in Hawthorne for years.

Fleurette—who looks people square in the face when she lies to them—turned to Francis and said, "Constance, of course. I'm too young to drive, and Norma was reading the paper."

"It doesn't matter who was driving," I said. "That man aimed his machine directly at us. Dolley could have been killed."

"*I* could have been killed," Fleurette said with a dramatic roll of her eyes. She shifted around in her chair to give Francis a look at the purple bruise emerging just above her knee. He turned away, embarrassed.

"She'll be fine, won't she?" he asked, and I nodded. He held the door open and gestured for me to come along for a private scolding and an examination of the wreckage he'd just delivered.

Outside was a wide and airy barn that housed Dolley, an occasional goat or pig, and a dozen or so chickens. The eaves had been extended on one side to accommodate Norma's pigeon loft. The imbalance between the two sides of the building made it seem in constant danger of losing its footing. Next to it, facing the drive, was the entrance to our root cellar. A few summers ago, Francis had laid the stone walk that led us there.

He spoke in a low voice so Fleurette couldn't listen in from the kitchen door. "Who is this man, this Harry—what was it?"

"Henry Kaufman," I said, "of Kaufman Silk Dyeing Company."

That brought him to a stop as surely as if he'd walked into a wall. He planted his feet and looked down at them with a long and loud exhale. This was a mannerism of our father's, one I had almost forgotten until Francis reached the age at which exasperation became an everyday emotion. Francis had our father's light brown hair and his pale Czech features, but where our father had managed to take a high forehead and light, intelligent eyes and make himself into something of a ruffian, Francis took the same features and composed them into those of a serious gentleman, with perfectly slicked and combed hair and a mustache that turned up neatly at the ends.

"He's a silk man? Are you sure?"

"One can hardly picture him running a factory, but that's the address he gave. He's on Putnam with all the others."

He shook his head and squinted at Norma, who had heard us coming and backed out of her pigeon loft. She took her time locking it behind her. Norma had cut her hair short this spring, insisting on doing it herself and chopping at it until her brown curls framed her face unevenly. In the last few years, she'd taken to wearing riding boots and a split skirt that fell to just above her ankles. In this costume she would climb ladders to repair a gutter or traipse down to the creek to trap a rabbit. Fleurette used to sing a little song to her that went, "Pants are made for men and not for women. Women are made for men and not for pants." Norma took offense at the song but nonetheless insisted that what she wore could not be considered pants in the least.

"You aren't hurt," I said, as she walked up. At least one of us could still move.

"My head aches terribly," she said, "from listening to Fleurette go on about how she was nearly killed yesterday. She talks too much for a girl who is almost dead."

"I wondered why she was up so early. She's been rehearsing her story for Francis."

"Listen to me, both of you," Francis said. He put a hand on each of us and led us down the drive to his wagon. "This man Kaufman. What exactly did he say?"

"As little as he could before roaring off in that machine with all his hoodlum friends," I said, as I reached up with my good arm to help Francis pull the tarpaulin off the back of his wagon. "But I let him know that he should expect—Oh."

The buggy was a horror of splintered wood and twisted metal. Until now I hadn't thought about exactly how it had looked when we left it in Paterson, but here it was, this fragile veneer of wood panels and leather and brass fittings that had done so little to shelter us from the force of Henry Kaufman's automobile.

Norma and I stared at it. It was a wonder we'd survived.

Francis removed his hat and ran a hand through his hair. "I can't be out here all the time looking after you girls."

"We haven't asked you to look after us," I said. "We only needed our buggy brought here, and that wasn't too much of a bother, was it?"

"No, but without a man around the place—"

"We haven't had a man around the place since you married!" I interrupted. "And what difference would it have made? He hit us broadside with his automobile. There was nothing you could have done."

"It doesn't matter. You shouldn't be out here by yourselves," Francis said, "especially now that you've lost your buggy. Wouldn't you rather stay in town with us?"

"I prefer not to live in a town," Norma said. "Going to town nearly got us killed yesterday, in case you've forgotten. We're much safer here."

Francis looked down at his feet again—this had been our father's way of stopping himself from saying something he didn't want to say—and worked his jaw back and forth for a minute before giving in. "All right. I'll take care of the repairs. I know a man in Hackensack who can do it. It looks bad, but

I think it can be rebuilt. The gears are fine, and most of the panels came apart at their seams."

"We can arrange for the repairs," I said, "and Henry Kaufman will pay for it."

"You can't make him pay, and you shouldn't have anything to do with him," Francis said. "You know what these men are like. Didn't you see what they did to the strikers last year?"

Francis didn't have to remind me. Everyone had seen what happened to the strikers. The mill owners got it into their heads that a worker could operate four looms at a time, instead of two, and do it for ten hours a day instead of eight. Three hundred mills shut down. Factory workers in New York City walked off the job in solidarity. The streets in Paterson were choked with outraged strikers. Even the children who worked as pickers and twisters in the mills took up their placards and marched.

The mill owners used their considerable influence to have the police turn up at rallies and arrest as many people as the jails would hold. When the police were overwhelmed, the silk men hired their own private force. That's when houses started burning down. That's when speeches were interrupted by gunshots. That's when bakeries and butchers were warned not to sell food to the strikers. Eventually the workers were too starved and defeated to do anything but return to their looms.

The silk men behaved as if they owned Paterson. But none of them had the right to run us down in the street and get away with it.

"Mr. Kaufman doesn't frighten me," I said. "He will pay what he owes."

⊰ 3 ⊱

THAT BUSINESS about us moving in with Francis began on the evening of our mother's funeral, after a supper of ham sandwiches and pickles and Bessie's lemon cake. While Norma and Fleurette washed the dishes, I sat with Francis on his back porch and watched him fill his pipe. From the lane behind the house came the sound of his children playing some game whose rules were known only to them, but which seemed to involve tossing a stick through a large metal hoop. I settled into a reed chair next to him and breathed my first calm breath of the day. It did not last.

"You know Bessie and I would love to have you girls come live with us," Francis said once he'd gotten his tobacco to smolder.

I groaned and kicked my feet up on the porch rail. "That was very unconvincing. Besides, you don't have room for the brood you've already got."

"Well, the uncles don't have room for you back in Brooklyn, either. I don't know where else you'd go."

There had been a sudden shower after the burial, but the sky had cleared while we were eating our supper. Against the gathering dark the first few stars appeared. I looked up at them and realized that on that night, and forever after, my mother would be sleeping outdoors, under the stars, under her blanket of earth. She despised dirt and rarely went outdoors, and would have been horrified by her new circumstances if she'd given any thought to it at all before buying that burial plot.

"Why do we have to go anywhere?" I said.

"You can't stay on the farm by yourselves. Three girls, all alone out there?"

"How is that so different from when Mother was alive? Are four girls any better than three?"

If Francis understood that I was teasing him, he didn't show it. He tapped his pipe and thought seriously about it for a minute. "Well, the only reason you were out there in the first place—"

I leaned over and shushed him when I heard Fleurette in the kitchen. We waited with our heads inclined toward the window, but we couldn't tell where she'd gone.

Francis lowered his voice. "All I mean to say is that she's nearly grown now. What are you going to do when she's ready to go off and get married? Live out there like a couple of old spinsters?"

The idea of Fleurette as a bride sent a jolt through my rib cage. "Marriage? She's only fourteen! Besides—" Before I could finish, Fleurette's voice sailed through the window screen.

"I'm fifteen!"

Francis rubbed his eyes and shifted around in his chair to

face me. "You girls are my responsibility now, and you should be with us. You could help Bessie around the house, and you could . . ." He trailed off, having exhausted the list of things he thought the three of us could do.

I rose to my feet, shaking out the gray-and-black tweed Fleurette had chosen as my mourning costume, and bent over Francis's chair.

"We can manage on our own," I whispered. "And if Bessie needs as much help as you say, we'll hire out Fleurette for the summer. She needs something to occupy her time."

"I'm not for hire!" Fleurette shouted.

AFTER THAT, Francis turned up every few months with another well-intentioned scheme to guarantee some sort of future for the three of us. The fact that we were unmarried and lacking an income that would keep us for life had not bothered him as much while Mother was alive. But he seemed to feel that he had inherited us when she died. He had grown into the sort of man who worried constantly over his small responsibilities: his snug little house in Hawthorne, his generous and resourceful wife, his secure employment, and his two healthy and well-behaved children. It did not seem to me that he should have any worries at all, but Francis was a man who brooded. Lacking any troubles of a more serious nature, he took to brooding over us.

Most men of his age had an unencumbered female relative or two tucked in an attic bedroom, so he must have seen it as inevitable that he would eventually take on a few as well. He did understand that we would have to be kept occupied, so his schemes always included tedious domestic employment for the three of us.

The house next door to his was put up for sale, and he suggested buying it and having us run it as a boarding house—on his behalf, of course, with the rents going to pay the mortgage. We refused, as we had no interest in becoming boarders in our own boarding house.

He then offered to hire me and Norma to tutor his children, even though they were learning their letters and numbers in school and didn't require the services of two grown women. Fleurette, he suggested, could take in work as a seamstress. When Francis talked about bringing in other people's torn and rotten clothing for repair, I just looked at him as if I'd never seen him before and wondered aloud if he remembered anything about the woman who raised him.

That's not to say that I didn't worry about what would become of us. We'd tried to find a few tenant farmers, but there was enough land for sale that no one particularly needed to rent from us. We had been forced to sell off a lot every few years just to keep going and were left with an oddly shaped thirty-acre parcel not accessible by any road but Sicomac, where the house was situated. It would be difficult to sell any more of it without building a new road right through our land, and, besides, I thought it best to keep what little land we still owned, as property seemed to be the best insurance against penury in old age.

Norma was terribly attached to the farm and refused to consider going anywhere else. She found rustic living more agreeable and, like many people who prefer the countryside, possessed a disposition that lent itself to living quite a distance from the nearest neighbor. She was distrustful of strangers, impatient of polite talk and frivolous society, indifferent to shops, theaters, and other diversions of city life, and unreasonably devoted to the few things that did interest her: her pigeons, her newspapers, and her family. She wouldn't leave the farm unless we carried her off. But Francis was right—if Fleurette was to have a future, it surely wouldn't be out in the countryside, stitching buttonholes and tossing corn to the chickens.

Something would have to be done about the three of us. I was tired of hearing my brother's ideas, but I hadn't any of my own. I did know this: a run-in with an automobile was not to be taken as evidence of our inability to look after ourselves. It was nothing but a mundane business matter and I would manage it without any assistance from Francis.

❧ 4 ❧

July 16, 1914

Misses Constance, Norma, and Fleurette Kopp
Sicomac Road
Wyckoff, New Jersey

Dear Mr. Kaufman,

I write to supply you with an accounting of
the damages inflicted upon our buggy by you and
your automobile on the afternoon of July 14. The
damages visited upon my sisters and I are considerable as well. Dear Fleurette is but fifteen
years of age and now suffers from a badly broken
foot and a dread of motor carriages which will
no doubt impede her advancement into the coming engine-powered age. But I confine myself at
present to the harm done to our buggy.

4 (four) hickory spokes @ $1 each,
   cracked: $4
1 (one) carriage lamp, smashed: $3
1 (one) whip socket, dislodged and lost in
   the commotion: $1
1 (one) oak panel, splintered to bits: $8
1 (one) complete hood assembly, bent beyond
   repair: $10
Assembly and re-attachment of disparate
   pieces: $24
Total (due in full promptly upon receipt, as
   we are at present without a buggy): $50

We appreciate your prompt payment by return
post. We remain,

      Yours in a state of caution along our town's
                ever more crowded avenues,
   Misses Constance, Norma, and Fleurette Kopp

"I am not afraid of automobiles," said Fleurette from the divan.

"Of course you are," I said. "Now, be quiet and rest your foot."

"I can rest my foot without being quiet."

"Those figures are too high," said Norma. "He won't take it seriously and he'll throw it in the trash."

"I'm including the time for a hired man to work on it," I said.

"I don't recall anything about a hired man. Read it again," said Norma.

"Don't," said Fleurette. "I'm tired of Mr. Kaufman."

"Then I'll post it."

"I'm not fifteen, either," said Fleurette.

I thought it should've been obvious to her that fifteen was a more tender age than sixteen and the violation therefore more grievous.

Fleurette grumbled and shifted in the silk peignoir she'd chosen for her convalescence. A pattern of peacock feathers ran along the collar, which she thought made her look glamorous. We'd been overindulging her since Mother's death, and I realized I would have to put a stop to that. Her taste for luxurious fabrics alone was going to ruin us.

I rose with some difficulty to get a stamp. My shoulder had calmed considerably since the collision, but every morning brought a fresh insult: an ankle that couldn't take my weight, a rib that cried out when I took a breath. Fleurette couldn't get her foot into a shoe, which made her something of an invalid. It fell to Norma to look after both of us and go out for whatever supplies we needed. Without our buggy, she had the choice of taking a long walk in hot weather to the trolley in Wyckoff, or saddling Dolley and riding her in. Naturally, she chose the latter. She'd already been as far as Paterson and back twice in the last few days, balancing a basket of pigeons on Dolley's rump and releasing them along the way.

For years Norma had been entranced with the idea of carrier pigeons and their utility in transmitting messages between people living in the countryside, or soldiers at war, or doctors wishing to monitor the progress of far-flung patients (the idea being that a doctor would leave several pigeons with his patient, to be dispatched at intervals with reports of the patient's progress). Telegraph and telephone wires would never stretch far enough to reach everyone who needed to send a message, she reasoned, and could not be trusted for the transmission of private information anyway, because the operator was privy to every word. But a properly trained and equipped pigeon, released hundreds of miles away, would fly a direct course at great speed, through storms or enemy fire, to bring a message home.

To prove this point, Norma was in the habit of taking her pigeons as far away from home as she could and sending them back with tiny missives strapped to their legs. Having no news of any importance to relate to us so soon after leaving the house, she sent us newspaper clippings instead. Norma read half a dozen papers every day and took it as her moral obligation to have an opinion on all the doings in northern New Jersey, not to mention New York and the rest of the world. She spent the better part of every evening with her newspapers, stashing clippings in drawers all over the house for future use. It was not unusual for one of us to go looking for the sugar or a pincushion and instead find an announcement titled "Diplomat's Wife Impaled on Fence."

She rigged up a tripwire in the pigeon loft so that a bell would ring near our front door when a bird arrived carrying the news of the day, as selected by Norma for its dramatic nature or the instruction it might offer. Variations on "Girl Fined for Disorderly Housekeeping" arrived any time I failed to do my part of the washing up. "Large Percentage of Women Recklessly Follow Prevailing Fashions Without Knowing Why" was delivered after Norma objected to Fleurette's silk tunic embroidered with birds of paradise, her attempt to copy the fashions of Paris. "The Morals of a Woman Are Read in Her Gowns" came the next ominous message.

Fleurette devised a way to get revenge by replacing each objectionable headline with one of her own and leaving it for Norma to find. Norma would discover "Piles Quickly Cured at Home" tied to her pigeon's leg band, or "Imbecile Sister Reported Missing."

Although Mother hated the birds and wouldn't go near the pigeon loft, she had encouraged Norma's interest in them, believing that girls should have hobbies that kept them entertained and close to home. She made no secret of the fact that she hoped raising baby birds would encourage a mothering instinct in Norma that would lead her to marriage and children. Exactly how Norma would find a husband, living out in the countryside as we did, was never explained. And Mother seemed oblivious to the fact that Norma was so opinionated, so argumentative, and so set in her ways that no man would ever dare take up with her. It didn't help that Norma had all the girlish charm of a boulder and had never shown the slightest interest in romantic love or child rearing. Mother had been right that pigeons made a good pastime, but Norma was in no danger of becoming engaged as a result.

At least Norma had some satisfactory means of occupying herself. I found the demands of farm life to be dull and unnecessarily difficult. When Francis married and moved into town several years ago, Norma happily took charge of the barn and its occupants. Fleurette kept up with the sewing and the washing, and the three of us took turns at cooking. I was left with the disagreeable task of weeding and watering the vegetable garden. I hated spending all that time bent over in the dirt for a basket of wormy cabbages. All I ever wished for was a good clean job in an office and a salary that would allow me to purchase a cabbage if I wanted one, which I didn't think I would.

There was a time when I tried to find a life for myself away from the farm. First I sent away for a course to study to be a nurse, but Mother, with her dread of filth and disease, was so horrified by the idea that I had to put it aside. Then I took up a course in law, having heard that there was a woman lawyer in New Brunswick and thinking I could petition to join her firm. Believing this line of work would force me into close quarters with criminals and drunks, Mother was even less pleased. I completed my coursework nonetheless, but when the time came to send it back to New York and request the next lesson, my papers were gone. Mother would not admit to it, but I knew she took them.

Now I was starting to wonder if I would live my whole life out here. I worried that I was destined to die in the same bed my mother had died in, leaving behind nothing but a cellar full of parsnips and uneven rows of stitches along cuffs and collars that nobody even remembered me making.

WE WAITED A WEEK for a response to our letter. There was enough nursing to keep me occupied, and to make me wish I'd taken that medical course. Twice a day I washed and bandaged Fleurette's foot, hardly daring to press too hard against it to feel for broken bones. She insisted that we not send for Dr. Winter, a musty old man with watery eyes and hands that shook as they reached for his patients' unclothed limbs. I didn't blame her for wanting to keep him away. But all I could do was clean her scrapes and scratches and require her to rest. This meant that I also had to bring her meals on a tray and answer a little bell she'd found in our sewing basket and kept on hand to ring whenever she was thirsty or tired or bored, which was most of the time.

The only place I could go to escape the sound of that bell was Mother's old room, which stood exactly as it had on the day she died, with her robe still hanging on the closet door and her hairbrush still on the dresser, a few wiry white hairs rising from it.

For months I couldn't go into her room at all. But lately I'd taken to slipping in when I wouldn't be noticed, and sitting on the edge of her bed the way I did when she was sick. During the last few days of her life her eyes would often flutter open, seeing nothing, and remain locked in a gaze that never shifted. I had to put a mirror to her mouth to make sure she was still breathing. I spent hours on the edge of that bed, watching her drift close to death and rise away from it, over and over.

The bed, which had belonged to her mother, was an old-fashioned heavy antique brought over from Austria, with rosettes of carved walnut along the headboard that served no purpose other than to gather dust. As I sat gingerly on the edge, the sheets crackling with starch, I realized that no one had been in to clean in months. It was Fleurette's job to dust, which explains why it accumulated in our house the way it did.

The walls were papered in a pale green and white pattern of chrysanthemums that had faded terribly and started to lift away, revealing cracked plaster and horsehair. Something would have to be done about this room. Even Mother—with her dread of change and her attachment to tradition and the heavy dark rituals of grief—would surely not object to me dismantling this shrine to her final years and making something useful of it. But I couldn't bring myself to do it yet. For years I just wanted to be free of her, and now I found myself clinging to the only traces of her that remained.

Fleurette always addressed Mother in French, but I knew that Mother preferred the German of her girlhood in Austria. I would never hear the language spoken in this house again if I didn't continue to whisper it to her.

"Mama, wär es nicht endlich Zeit, dass wir was mit Deinem Zimmer machen?"

I received no answer. Perhaps Mother didn't care what happened to her room. I took a deep breath. Her violet-scented powder still hung in the air. From somewhere downstairs a door slammed, and Fleurette, having given up on her bell, hollered my name.

It had always been Mother's responsibility to answer to Fleurette's demands. *"Geh amal nachschaun, was sie will?"* I asked her.

But Mother didn't volunteer to go. I rose and closed the door quietly behind me.

⭤ 5 ⭤

"TRY THE PLUMS," Fleurette said at breakfast a few days later.

Norma ignored her and kept her eyes on her newspaper.

"Just one. Just a bite." Fleurette took her butter knife and cut out a perfect triangle of toast and plum preserves. She slid it onto Norma's plate.

"Look," she whispered. *"C'est tout violet."*

Norma rattled her newspaper and put it between herself and the offending toast.

"That's more red than purple," I said, sitting down across from them. "You'll never win at this."

Fleurette giggled and took her toast back.

The long-standing and largely one-sided feud between Norma and Fleurette over the regal hue of their breakfast condiments began years ago, when Norma absentmindedly reached for a jar of pickled red cabbage and spooned it onto her toast. After the initial shock, she found that she liked it a great deal and continued to eat it, every morning, for the rest of her life thus far. Fleurette was only seven or eight when this began and couldn't understand how anyone could eat such a disagreeable food for breakfast. She asked Norma about it so often that one day Norma finally said, "Because it's purple, of course. Didn't you know that eating purple food at breakfast increases one's height by two inches over a lifetime? It's why we're all so much taller than you."

She waved her newspaper around as if to suggest that she'd read it from a place of authority, adding, "If only there was anything more purple than pickled cabbage, I'd eat that instead."

Fleurette didn't know how to tell when Norma was making a joke — none of us did, really, even all these years later — and took the challenge seriously, presenting Norma with any purple food she could find in the morning: jams and preserves, violet pastilles, blueberries and grapes. Every now and then, she resumed the old feud again out of habit. But so far, she'd failed. Not even plum preserves could match the brilliance of Norma's cabbage.

That's just how it was with Norma: once she approved of a thing, she adopted it to the exclusion of everything else. If she believed pickled cabbage and toast to be the best breakfast, it would be a betrayal of her principles to eat jam and porridge. If a pair of boots suited her, they became the only style she wore. I'd only ever seen one book on her nightstand (*The Practical Pigeon: A Complete Treatise on Training, Breeding, Flying and Uses of Winged Messengers*) and suspected that she had read it hundreds of times, having found none better.

At breakfast I read aloud my second letter to Henry Kaufman. Before I got past the salutation, Norma interrupted.

"I don't like this Kaufman," she said.

"Well, of course you don't like him," Fleurette said. "None of us do."

"What I mean to say is that I don't like us writing letters to him," Norma said. "We shouldn't be carrying on a correspondence with a man like that."

"It's an invoice, not a correspondence," I said. "And this will be the last one. I'll go and collect from him myself if he doesn't reply."

"But do you not agree with me that we shouldn't . . ."

"Norma! He owes us the money." Fifty dollars was no small sum to us. We lived on about six hundred a year, and because we were relying mostly on savings, that fifty dollars took one month of independence away from our dwindling funds. I rattled the paper and began again.

July 23, 1914

Misses Constance, Norma, and Fleurette Kopp
Sicomac Road
Wyckoff, New Jersey

Dear Mr. Kaufman,

I trust you have received our invoice for the damages inflicted upon our buggy as a result of the collision with your automobile on July 14. The amount owed remains the same. The buggy remains in a state of disrepair. Anticipating that you are a busy man whose bookkeeper undoubtedly falls behind in his work when business is brisk, I will present myself at your place of business next Tuesday

to collect in full if we have not yet received the
fifty dollars owed. Until then, I remain,

Yours in a state of cautious expectation,
Miss Constance Kopp

"It's best not to criticize a man's bookkeeper," Norma said
without looking up from her newspaper.

"I was only offering an explanation for his failure to respond."

"You wouldn't like that, if you were his bookkeeper." She
noticed a strand of pickled cabbage on the back of her hand
and flicked it onto her plate.

"I wouldn't like much of anything if I were Mr. Kaufman's
bookkeeper," I said, signing my name to the letter.

I MAILED THE LETTER on a Thursday. When no reply arrived by the morning post on Tuesday, I readied myself for a
visit to Paterson.

"Are we going to town?" Fleurette said when she saw me
in my hat.

"I am," I said. "I have business to do. You're not well
enough yet."

"But I haven't left the house in ages." She flopped into a
stuffed chair in our sitting room. She'd wrapped herself in a
Japanese shawl and pinned her hair into a complex arrangement of cascading glossy curls, held together somehow by an
enormous red silk poppy. The bandage had just come off her
foot, and to celebrate her newly liberated appendage, she was
wearing ballet slippers.

"Read a book," I said. "Help Norma in the kitchen if you're feeling so much better."

More moaning. More flopping about on the chair. I wished for the hundredth time that we had treated Fleurette less like a curiosity, an exotic bird nesting in our chimney, and more like a child in need of instruction.

I left her to issue her protests to an empty room and went outside to saddle Dolley for the trip into town. Dolley was not happy to see me coming. I was built like a farmer, even taller and broader than my brother. I looked ridiculous on a horse. But there would be no other way to get around until our buggy was repaired.

Norma had been in the barn all morning, mucking out the chicken coop and spreading fresh straw in the horse stall. It smelled of sweet, dry grass. She'd given Dolley a good brushing and was checking her hooves when I walked in. She ran a hand down the mare's leg until the hoof lifted off the ground for inspection. Animals instinctively trusted Norma. She'd held every sort of claw or hoof or paw.

"I spoke to that boy at the dairy who fixes their wagons," Norma said when she saw me. "He says it can be put back together. He'll come over in the evenings and do the job."

I didn't say anything. I pulled the saddle off the wall and Norma helped me cinch it into place.

"Mr. Kaufman isn't going to pay, and we'll still have to get our buggy repaired," Norma said. "That boy has all the tools, and he's just down the road."

There was no point in arguing over it. Living this far out of town was dull enough without a means of escape. We couldn't all ride Dolley. "All right. Have him keep a record of his expenses," I said, "and make sure it comes to fifty dollars."

Norma finished her inspection of Dolley's hooves and walked her out of the barn. "We don't go around demanding money from strange men," she said, as she watched me hoist myself up.

"This is an exception," I said.

"Well, then we shouldn't make exceptions," Norma replied, and trudged off to pump water for the chickens.

THE KAUFMAN SILK DYEING COMPANY sat along the railroad tracks among a string of other dyers, warpers, and winders, bleach works, jacquard card cutters, and suppliers of dyestuffs and intermediates—all housed in low brick buildings that turned their backs to the street. The windows sat high enough off the ground to prevent anyone from looking in, but I could hear the sounds of industry from within: the clattering of machines, the sloshing of dye in tubs, and voices calling to one another in German, Italian, French, Polish—every language but English.

Delivery wagons had worn deep ruts in the street. Dolley picked her way around them, and I watched the small signs stenciled across the metal doors at each factory until we came to Henry Kaufman's. I heaved myself out of the saddle without any finesse and lashed Dolley to a post. She tossed her head and snorted to let me know she was happy to see me go.

Inside, the coppery sulfuric stench of the dyes hit me with such force that I had to close my eyes and grope blindly for a handkerchief. I coughed and choked and fought the urge to take a deep breath, not wanting to draw any more of it into my lungs. I couldn't swallow and my vision was so clouded with tears that I could hardly make out the dim figures around me. I almost backed out the door and went home.

Finally I composed myself and saw that I was standing at the edge of a factory floor, looking down a row of enormous troughs, with two or three men attending to each of them. Steam rose up from the troughs and floated to the broad wooden beams overhead. The dye lay in bright pools at the workers' feet, and to protect their feet they wore wooden clogs stained in shades of deep midnight blue and a bright pink the color of peppermint candy. Everywhere the dye met another color it turned a blackish gray. It took two men to hoist the skeins of silk out of the troughs on their metal poles, and when they did, the dye ran down their arms and into their shirtsleeves. A troupe of girls and young boys pushed brooms around the edges of the room, sloshing the runoff into drains, and a few of them wheeled carts piled high with raw silk. Off to one side, a row of wringers were in constant motion, clattering and groaning as the workers fed the wet skeins through them.

A few men looked up at me through the steam but no one said anything. To my right was a long, windowed wall dividing the office from the factory floor. I lifted my skirt and walked over to try the door but it was locked. Through one of the windows, a secretary looked up from her desk and seemed to be considering what to do with me. Finally she rose and led me in.

"I'm sorry to bother you," I said. "I'm here to see Mr. Henry Kaufman."

She ushered me through the door and closed it quickly behind us, which seemed to have more to do with keeping the malicious odor out than an eagerness to invite me in.

"Your name?" She spoke with a brisk efficiency. She wore a smartly tailored navy suit with a long plain skirt and a trim jacket, and her hair was tied in a tight bun. After resuming her post behind the desk, she looked at me over the top of delicate gold spectacles and waited for me to explain myself.

I said my name and told her that I had come to deliver an invoice for damages to our buggy. She held her hand out as if she was in the habit of receiving such invoices daily. I gave it to her and she laid it across her blotter, smoothed the folds, and read it slowly. Then she looked up at me with an expression that I could not read. It might have been sorrow or shock or deep skepticism.

"Henry did this," she said, mostly to herself.

"He claimed that our horse ran in front of him, but everyone along Market saw the accident, and he is most certainly the one who ran into us."

She waved her hand to silence me. "I don't doubt your story. Are you sure this took place on the fourteenth?"

She glanced up at me and I nodded.

With a sigh she handed the letter back to me. "He was supposed to meet with our banker. He told me a tire burst."

She dropped her head into her hands and muttered something I couldn't hear.

"Forgive me for saying—"

"Oh," she interrupted, "you're forgiven. What is it?"

"With the company he was keeping, I don't believe he was on his way to visit a banker."

She gave another long, aggrieved exhalation and pushed herself to her feet. "Have you any brothers, Miss Kopp?"

"Just one," I said.

"Is yours as much trouble as mine?"

"Henry Kaufman is your brother?" I said. "I'm sorry. I thought you were the secretary."

37

"I am, according to the letterhead. Marion Garfinkel. My husband's Ed Garfinkel. We're in town from Pittsburgh to try to sort out the mess Henry's made of our factory." Before I could say another word, she turned and yelled in the direction of a closed door across the room.

"Henry!"

In addition to her desk, there were three others, all occupied by young women working at typewriters and ledger books. The girls ducked down when she shouted. The door didn't open.

Through gritted teeth she muttered, "If he ignores me one more time—" and marched over to his office. Without turning around to look at me again, she called, "Stay there."

She rapped at the door and rattled the knob. When it didn't open, she fumbled around for a ring of keys at her waist and let herself in. "Henry, there's a girl out here who says—" Then the door slammed behind her, and I heard nothing but muffled shouting.

I fidgeted with my handbag and tried to ignore the curious glances of the other girls. Dolley had been waiting unattended long enough, and I just wanted to hand him my invoice and leave. The shouting had ceased from inside Henry Kaufman's office. I picked up my letter from Mrs. Garfinkel's desk and crossed the room, giving the door a quiet knock.

It swung open. Marion appeared to be on her way out, but she stepped aside and swept her arm into the room, inviting me to enter, her lips pinched together in a kind of forced smile.

"My brother doesn't recall the incident," she said crisply.

"But I—"

"Tell him yourself, then."

I had the uneasy feeling that I was being sent in to prove a point, although I couldn't imagine what that point might be. I took one hesitant step inside and Marion slammed the door behind me. I could hear her shoes clicking across the floor as she hurried to her station.

Behind an enormous oak desk sat Henry Kaufman in yet another elegant suit, his hair slicked back the way men wore it if they were going out for the evening. But with that round, soft face, he looked more like a child trying to dress like his father. He couldn't have been much younger than me—thirty, perhaps—but he had the pampered manner of a boy who had been too long at boarding school. He would've seemed entirely harmless if there hadn't been a cold distance in his eyes and an angry set to his mouth. Here in this factory, he seemed like a man who didn't want what he had, but also didn't have exactly what he wanted.

And in leather chairs all around the room were his friends, his unsavory, no-good friends. There was the droopy-eyed man with the wooden leg, slumped over in a brown suit that was two sizes too big for him, and a beefy character with arms like stovepipes and the broadest set of chins I'd ever seen. The rest were lean and angular types who each seemed to have lost something in a fight: one lacked a third finger on his left hand, one was missing a patch of hair above his ear, and another wore a milky glass eye. They all held cards in their hands, and a bottle of whiskey sat on the table between them.

I wanted out of that room.

"Oh, you're the one," Henry Kaufman said. "She came in here talking about a girl wanting money and I told her it could have been half of New Jersey."

The other men snickered and drew on their cigarettes.

I stood a little straighter and looked down at him with what I hoped was a calm and dignified air. "Then you remember me. I am Constance Kopp, and—"

"And these are your sisters," he sneered. "Or haven't you brought them along? Who is the youngest one? Fleurette?"

I felt a little sick when he said her name. "We haven't had a reply to our letters," I said, "so I've brought you another one. You owe us fifty dollars for the damages to our buggy, and I will take payment now."

He didn't accept the letter I held out for him, so I stepped forward and dropped it on his desk.

"I'll just speak to your father about this," he said. "Is his business here in Paterson? Or does he . . ." He picked up the envelope and examined our return address. "Or does he work on your farm in Wyckoff?"

He had our address. I should have asked him to make payment at our bank. In spite of the heat, I went very cold.

"You live on Sicomac Road? Down by the dairy?"

He came around the desk and stood right in front of me, easing his shoulder between me and the doorway, drawing a low whistle from one of the men. Henry Kaufman may have been a head shorter than me, but he was stout and powerfully built. He smelled of whiskey, and again of hair tonic and his own factory.

"I'm sure I can find it," he said in a low voice. "When I get there, tell me, through which window may I find Miss Fleurette's bedroom?"

He looked over at his friends and they laughed. There was a roar in my ears and suddenly he was very small and far away. I grabbed his shoulders and threw him against the wall, hard enough that the back of his skull cracked the plaster.

"Don't you dare," I said. I'd gathered his lapels up in my fists without realizing I'd done it. From the corner of my eye, I could see the other men rising to their feet.

A thin trickle of blood smeared the wall. There was a shuffle behind me and I could feel someone breathing over my shoulder.

"If you'd like to pick a fight with a man your own size," he said quietly, "I'll send one over."

My hands flew away from him as if they'd touched a hot pan. Before the other men could get hold of me I was out the door and running past the secretaries. Marion rose from her desk and called out to me, but I didn't answer.

I pushed the door open and fell out onto the factory floor, running straight into a slender red-haired girl carrying a steaming tray of fabric. She dropped the tray and emerald-green dye ran down the front of her apron. We slid around in a puddle of it, and then someone shouted in Polish and the girl grabbed my arm to stay upright, but I shook her off and ran for the door without once looking back.

Outside, I grabbed Dolley's bridle and dragged her a few blocks away before stopping to catch my breath. My palms were slick with sweat and my head floated away from my neck like a balloon tethered by a string. Little pinpricks of light swam in front of me. I swallowed to push down the bile rising up in my throat, and then forced myself to focus on the shop across the street, a place called Gurney's that sold boilers and ranges. "WE MAKE IT HOT FOR YOU" read the sign in the window, next to another sign announcing that the shop was closed for vacation because Paterson was hot enough already.

An engine rattled around the corner and I pulled Dolley toward me. Would they come after me? I held my breath and waited, but the machine rumbled past and its driver didn't even turn to look at me.

I tried to imagine how I would tell Norma and Fleurette what had happened.

He said your name, I would say to Fleurette. *He asked about your bedroom.*

And to Norma: *He said he wanted to speak to our father.*

I could still feel the men in that room coming up behind me and a hand reaching for my shoulder.

⤞ 6 ⤝

HAD MY MOTHER BEEN ALIVE, none of this would have happened. We didn't go marching into factories to demand payment from strange men. In fact, we hardly ever went anywhere. Mother didn't even like to go out shopping. When we lived in Brooklyn, she had almost everything delivered, and when we moved to the countryside, it became Francis's responsibility to ride into town and get things for us.

My mother named me after her, but I was never like her. She was Constance Clementine Kopp and I was Constance Amélie, my middle name being her mother's name. Francis was her firstborn, but having grown up with four brothers, a boy was unremarkable to her. She was waiting for a girl: a girl she could wrap inside her cloistered world, a girl who would sit next to her and work at needlepoint and keep her secrets and pretend not to hear the door when someone knocked.

She lived most of her life in this country, but she was never an American and she didn't trust Americans or American ways. Her parents left Vienna when she was sixteen, like so many of the middle class did in the wake of the revolution of

1848. My grandfather—an educated man, a chemist—liked to say that he brought his family here to give them a more stable and certain future, and to keep his boys out of the endless wars with France and Italy, but my grandmother once whispered that they moved to get away from the Jews. "After they got to leave the ghettos they could live anywhere," she hissed, and glanced out the window as if she suspected they were moving to Brooklyn, too, which of course they were.

My mother married my father, Frank Kopp, at the age of twenty. He was what my grandparents called Bohemian, which meant that he was Czech, but in some convoluted way having to do with the outcomes of wars still being fought in those distant countries, they had decided that he was practically Austrian. They were relieved he wasn't a Jew, and even though my mother had met him in New York, he wasn't an American. On the grounds of what he was not, my grandparents allowed him to marry their daughter.

He was a wine merchant when they married, but he failed at that and became a bartender, and when that occupation didn't agree with him, he was only a drunk. My mother forced him out of the house many times, but he didn't leave for good until I was about ten. After that we saw him so infrequently that people began to think that Mother was a widow, an idea she encouraged. When we left Brooklyn she didn't tell him where we'd gone, and as far as I knew, he'd never tried to find out.

Secrets and deception were my mother's specialty. She invented new birth dates for herself whenever it suited her to lie about her age. She mistrusted authorities and never quite believed she had a right to live here. There must have been some record of her entrance to this country, but she knew nothing about it and claimed not to be a citizen. She possessed no identification, no marriage license, and no birth certificates for any of us, having birthed us at home and breathed not a word of it to any official. She had a dread of doctors, tax collectors, census-takers, inspectors, newspaper reporters, and the police—particularly the police.

She believed that Americans were crude and uncivilized, and tried instead to raise us as good Austrians, insisting that we speak her own peculiar blend of French and German, and engaging us in the tedious practices of lace-making and decorative painting in an effort to keep us indoors and away from the other children in the neighborhood.

As a result, there was not a bread tin or a sewing box in our Brooklyn apartment that hadn't been painted with a spray of roses and then covered with a doily. Our home was a dark and crowded museum of our mother's Viennese girlhood. Her faded needlepoint hung on the wall alongside oil portraits of unnamed ancestors and a china doll in a glass case that wore the hair of her long-dead grandmother. A miniature porcelain tea set—each dish edged in gold and hand-painted with delicate toadflax and fern—sat inside a mahogany breakfront alongside a collection of miniature glass animals: elephants and lions, fish and sea monsters. We were forbidden to touch them.

She never opened the door for strangers. She read salacious newspaper stories to me and Norma as we worked at our sewing, hoping, I suppose, that with each stitch her shocking morality tales would teach us the dangers that a knock at the door could bring. I can't look at our childhood samplers without remembering the disgraceful fate of Laura Smith, age seventeen, who was lured away from her home by the grocer and ruined by him, or that of thirteen-year-old Lena Luefschuetz, found dead for reasons having to do with her "undesirable companions." A girl named Amelia was arrested for "going into a hallway with an Italian" and was detained as a witness for two weeks, which prevented her from boarding a steamship that would have carried her back to the bosom of her family in Germany and away from the horrors that a city like New York could visit upon a young girl. *"Arme Amelia, so weit weg von ihrer Familie,"* Mother would say under her breath. Amelia lived constantly in her prayers.

For weeks we followed the story of a girl arrested for waywardness after her mother called the police and demanded that they take her away. Her own mother! The girl had been out past her curfew, which, we were shocked to learn, was ten o'clock. The girl claimed that the door was locked and her mother would not let her in, so she had no choice but to ride her bicycle all night long. A trial was held in which her cyclometer was presented as evidence. It showed that she had traveled fifty miles. A church pastor testified on her behalf, as did a Sunday school teacher. The magistrate seemed inclined to let the girl go until her mother held up a letter the girl had written to "a young physician in Manhattan." (Mother read this in a grim tone, suggesting that nothing good could come of correspondence with physicians.) The magistrate read the letter, gave the girl a shocked and stern look, and committed her to the Wayside Home until she turned twenty-one.

If Mother knew what that letter contained, she wouldn't tell us. All she wanted us to understand was that in America, letters were dangerous, as were hallways, bicycles, doctors, and Italians. We could be locked up for any of it, and ruined.

She would have been terrified by our accident, not just because of our injuries and the damage to the buggy, but because it left us so exposed. The thought of the three of us thrown into a heap on Market Street, a crowd gathered around us, everyone watching, everyone wondering who we were—Mother dedicated her life to avoiding that very thing.

And now I had gotten into a fistfight with a factory owner. If my mother had nightmares, this would have been one of them.

⇥ 7 ⇤

FLEURETTE AND NORMA didn't look up when I walked in. They were engaged in a game of preference, with Fleurette holding two of the three hands.

"Oh, good," Fleurette said when she saw me. "Come and take Mother's place."

"You're bidding for Mother?" I said, dropping into a chair across from them. Fleurette was on the divan with a pillow propped up next to her in the place of a third player. Norma was seated across from her with her own hand, wearing a look of high skepticism.

"No, she's bidding for a pillow," Norma said, "and I have begun to suspect that the pillow is cheating."

"Constance wasn't here," Fleurette said. "We'll never have a threesome if you're always running off by yourself like that."

"I'm not always running off," I said.

"Did Mr. Kaufman pay?" Fleurette asked.

I had decided that Fleurette shouldn't know what had happened. She was an excitable girl, prone to vivid dreams and

48

wild ideas. If she thought we had an enemy, she'd keep me up half the night with elaborate cloak-and-dagger schemes.

"Mr. Kaufman has received the invoice," was all I said.

Norma raised an eyebrow at me and put down her cards. "It's nearly dinnertime. Constance and I will finish the noodles."

"Don't cut them into squares!" Fleurette called as we left for the kitchen. "They taste better as triangles."

On the kitchen table Norma had rolled out the noodles for *Krautfleckerl* and laid a wet towel across the dough. When we were girls in Brooklyn the entire building knew what the Kopp family was having for dinner when the odor of onions, vinegar, caraway, and cabbage filled the hallway.

"It's what Fleurette wanted," Norma said, before I could ask why she was making a hot cabbage dish on a sweltering summer evening. "She was missing Mother all day, and you weren't here to do anything about it."

"It was good of you to play cards with her." I took a knife and began cutting the noodles. Norma watched me warily from the stove.

"What are you doing?" she asked when I made the first cut.

"Triangles."

"You're making a mess of them. Just cut them the way we always do and let Fleurette make her own triangles."

"But she doesn't want it that way. I thought we were making this for her."

Norma reached for the knife. "I'll cut the noodles. You do the cabbage."

I pushed her away and sliced a row of perfect squares. "Well, you're right about Henry Kaufman," I said. "He is the most ill-mannered young man I've ever met. And that gang of thugs he runs around with! What's a businessman doing with a crowd like that?"

Norma dropped the noodles into the pot, and a cloud of steam rose up around her. The curls at the back of her neck were slick against her skin. Without turning around, she said, "He was not so happy to see you?"

"No, he was not. I don't expect we'll be getting any money out of him."

She banged her spoon against the pot and turned around, waving it at me. "It's just as well that we forget about Henry Kaufman. I've got that boy working on the buggy. He brought over an old runabout the dairy isn't using. We can ride that until ours is finished."

I took a breath and tried to summon the nerve to tell her what had happened. But the air sailed right back out of my mouth the way it came in, and no words followed. What was the point in revisiting the entire awful encounter?

"That's just fine," I said at last. "I'd like to forget about it."

Through the kitchen window I could see the neighbor's pigs pacing in their pen. I tossed our kitchen scraps to them, a small service that earned us a flitch of bacon in the fall. The pigs were still some weeks away from slaughter, but already their bellies dragged in the mud as they staggered around, calling out in their guttural pig language.

I dropped the pitted stalk of the cabbage into a bowl and looked around for something else to feed them.

"Take the potato peelings," Norma said, and I did, walking them across the road in the unrelenting heat. The cicadas whined from some distant grove, and the crickets in the tall grass around the dairy pond raised their own chorus, which was not a song at all but just the dull scraping of a hundred blades against each other.

The pigs grunted and shuffled toward the fence when they saw me coming with my bowl of scraps. With the drone of the countryside all around me, I didn't notice Henry Kaufman's motor car until it was nearly on top of me.

He was driving and there were three men with him. The setting sun kept me from making out their faces, but I thought I could see the young man with the droopy eyes gaping at me, his mouth half open, his front tooth jutting out in a look of perpetual, confounded surprise, and the great hulking figure of the man with the stovepipe arms next to him. The car fired and coughed as if it was about to die, then roared again and swerved right at me. I fell back into the weeds. One of the men leaned out and yelled, "Take your pick, Henry! Which one of these girls do you want?"

Another one laughed and said something I couldn't hear.

"The French girl. What was she—"

Another mutter, and then he did the most intolerable thing. He shouted her name down our drive, as if he knew her, as if he knew anything about us at all.

"Fleurette! That's the one! Here, girly!" and then there was nothing but rough and drunken laughter and the thunder of the engine and dust everywhere. A bottle flew out the back of the car and hit a rock, shattering to pieces as the men disappeared down Sicomac Road.

The bowl slipped out of my hand. I watched the sand-colored cloud of dust settle back into the road, and then the air was still. Even the crickets had been shocked into silence. I stood and tried to pick the burrs and foxtails out of my skirt, but my fingers trembled and wouldn't take hold of them.

Across the way Norma stood in the half-opened front door, Mother's old kitchen apron tied crookedly over her riding clothes. Fleurette perched on her toes and peered around her to get a better view. They looked like those fuzzy figures in a picture postcard, frozen in place, staring out from some world that no longer existed.

⋈ 8 ⊱

THE THREE OF US retreated to my bedroom. Our dinner was forgotten and the noodles were a sticky mess in their pot. Fleurette was red-cheeked and wild-eyed. Norma was as grim as I'd ever seen her. She kept her eyes on the floor, and her breath came out noisily as she worked up to whatever she was going to say.

"How did he find us?" Fleurette asked, bouncing on my bed.

"I wish you'd stop fidgeting," Norma said.

"I can't. How does he know my name?"

They both looked up at me expectantly, Fleurette eager for the rest of the story, and Norma dreading it.

"Well—the letters. I put our address on them and our names."

Norma tied a knot in a loose piece of piping around her knees. Fleurette considered it a waste of her talents to make undergarments for us, when a complete set could be purchased so inexpensively from the catalogs, but Norma had grown attached to a particular style of nainsook chemise that was no longer offered. She wore them until they frayed at the hems and then had to bribe Fleurette to make her a new one.

"Don't pull on it," Fleurette whispered. Norma pulled her hands away but kept her eyes on the fraying edge.

"I'll go to the police tomorrow," I said.

Norma snorted. "I take a dim view of the police in this county."

"What do you know about them? We've never so much as spoken to a police officer."

"I read the papers. They can't even catch a pickpocket. Do you remember just last week, at the train station—"

"Norma," I said, giving a great sigh of exasperation, which was what I so often did after saying her name. "It's a simple matter for the police. He has wrecked our buggy and refuses to pay, and now he's harassing us."

"And why is that?" Norma said.

"Why is he harassing us? You saw the crowd of hooligans he runs around with. They probably have nothing better to do. They—"

Norma raised one eyebrow at me, a particular talent of hers that she deployed whenever she wanted to assign blame.

"You don't think I'm at fault!" I cried. "If he'd been any kind of gentleman, he would have paid the damages straightaway. All I've done is to try to collect what we were owed."

Fleurette had been looking back and forth between the two of us like a spectator at a tennis match. But she couldn't stay silent any longer. "Where does Mr. Kaufman live? Let's go to his house tonight. We can all wear disguises, and we'll wait until he's gone to bed, and—"

Norma shushed her and put her hand over mine. "I don't think you know how you look sometimes," she said, patting me in a show of sympathy.

I pulled my hand away. "How I look?"

"At the accident. You towered over him, and you shoved that car door closed so he couldn't get in. How do you think that made him appear to his friends?"

"Like a fool," I said.

"He is a fool," Fleurette added.

"And what about today? Were his friends with him again?"

"Oh, they run in a pack," I said. "They're like wild dogs."

"And by any chance did you make Henry Kaufman look like a fool again today?" Norma asked, her voice still quiet and steady. "In front of all those wild dogs?"

I closed my eyes and pictured his head hitting the plaster, a detail I was now glad I hadn't shared with Norma. "But that's no reason to come after us. He's the one who ran us down."

"I don't believe he sees it that way."

"Well, it's nice of you to take his side," I snapped, and tugged at my bedcovers, dislodging Norma. Hunger got the better of Fleurette, and she persuaded Norma to go downstairs with her to see what they could salvage from our ruined dinner. I stayed in bed, feeling that I deserved to be sent upstairs without my supper. The very idea of food turned my stomach anyway. I was made nauseous by the idea of drunken lunatics charging at us in motor cars and strange men hurling threats at Fleurette.

Fleurette, who had seen so little of the world, who Mother kept even more carefully hidden away than her other girls.

Fleurette was like a little jewel, small and bright and easy to steal. And now, with me in charge of her welfare for only a year, these men were driving by the house and shouting at her.

What was I to do? Mother would have wanted me to put up the storm shutters and bar the doors and hide in the root cellar every time an automobile drove by. Norma, who saw the farm as some sort of fortress designed to keep the rest of the world at bay, would have agreed. But I was tired of hiding out here in the country.

Francis would have wanted me to sell the farm and move in with him, where we could all be properly supervised. But I wasn't about to become one of those women who serves out a life term as her brother's housekeeper.

The only way I could fall asleep was to tell myself that I was making too much of the situation. I had made one small miscalculation in confronting Mr. Kaufman and had brought a little trouble our way as a result. It would not happen again.

THE NEXT MORNING, Norma and I sat down with Fleurette and warned her to be wary of automobiles driving past our house and to stay away from unfamiliar men in all circumstances.

"You two sound like Mother," Fleurette said, rolling her eyes. She still had the long dark lashes that some children are born with, and she had a habit of fluttering them at us dismissively.

"This time it's real," I said. "This time it's serious."

"Mother thought everything was serious."

I didn't appreciate being compared to my mother, but Mr. Kaufman did seem to pose a fresh new danger. "Promise me,"

I said. "No automobiles. No strange men. We must stay away from him until he forgets all about us."

She promised. "But we're still going to Paterson next week, aren't we?"

I looked over at Norma for an explanation. She reached into the basket next to her chair and pulled out yesterday's newspaper.

"I might have seen something about a moving picture concern coming to town," she said, thumbing through the pages. "They're going to film a motor car running into a trolley as part of a safety campaign."

"I think we've had enough of motor cars running into things," I said.

"Oh, we have to go," Fleurette said, jumping up from her chair. She wore an outlandishly large pale pink dahlia in her hair. It seemed to be placed purposefully next to her face as if to offer a comparison. "Norma promised you'd take me."

Norma kept her face behind the paper. "I would go myself, but I couldn't possibly. You know I take my pigeons out on Thursdays."

"You take them out on Wednesday and Friday, too," I said, "and on Monday and Saturday. Tuesdays are—"

"They dislike any change to their routine," Norma said. "It would put them out of joint."

"Well, I can't go, either," I said, although I didn't have a reason.

Fleurette tugged at my arm the way she used to when she was a little girl. "But what if they're looking for actresses?"

"It's a crash," I said. "What use would they have for an actress?"

"I have experience with crashes," she said.

"I don't think they'd want you for a safety campaign."

"Please," she said. "Norma said you would. She said you had nothing else to do but keep me entertained."

"Norma!" I tried to snatch the paper away from her, but she wouldn't let it go.

"And after that terrible fright I had yesterday," Fleurette said, working her eyebrows into a sorrowful little knot. "Wouldn't an afternoon out do me good?"

She leaned over and pursed her lips at me in that droll, beguiling way she had. The girl was unbearably pretty and knew it. Sometimes I wanted to pick her up and squeeze her until she could hardly breathe. Whether that impulse grew out of love or rage I could not say.

THE ACCIDENT was to be staged at the corner of Main Street and Market. Norma helped us hitch Dolley to the runabout we had on loan from the dairy. Its seat was only just wide enough for the two of us.

"You see, I couldn't have gone anyway," Norma said with evident relief.

The questions began as soon as we rolled onto Sicomac Road.

"What sort of part do you think they'd have for a young girl?" Fleurette asked.

"We're only going to watch."

"I could play the part of the victim with her leg crushed under the wheel."

"You are not going to be in the pictures."

"You don't know that."

I kept pointedly quiet, but it didn't matter since she hadn't been listening to me anyway.

"At least let me drive."

"After what happened last time?"

We continued in this fashion until we reached Paterson and rode over the river and past the great hulking Lambert Castle, one of those foolish medieval follies built by American industrialists after their first trip abroad. This particular industrialist, a silk man named Catholina Lambert, was still occupying his folly, after having seen his wife and all but one of their eight children off to the graveyard, most of them lost to consumption or childhood fevers or a kick to the head by a horse. I heard that he married his wife's sister, herself a widow, and that they spent their days in the marble atrium gazing up at the enormous dark oil portraits of other, more distant castles, and of moldy forests, and of the Lambert ancestors. The terrace offered an expansive view of New York City, but apparently the occupants of the castle didn't care to look at the view, for no one ever saw them outdoors.

Fleurette fell silent as we rode under the shadow of the castle. When she was a child and misbehaved, we used to threaten to send her there to work in the kitchen. She believed us. She believed everything we told her until she turned fourteen. The castle held enormous power over Fleurette—and over everyone in town, really. No one could stand to go near the place.

"Who lives over here?" Fleurette said, once we had put the castle behind us.

"All the silk men do," I said.

From our vantage point on the hill, we could see the mills and factories clustered together at the edge of Paterson's downtown, casting their shadows into the Passaic River. Narrow brick stacks discharged coal smoke into the air, where it formed a permanent gray cloud. The river dwindled to a trickle this time of year, leaving nothing but mud and boulders and puddles visited by mosquitoes. The mill owners preferred to live a comfortable distance away from their red-bricked empire, so they retreated to this cool, quiet neighborhood with its canopy of elms and wide, sloping streets.

"You're taking a very roundabout way into town," Fleurette said, fidgeting with her hat.

"We're early," I said. "I thought we could ride around the park."

"Well, I wanted to get there early!" Fleurette protested. "I wanted to have a chance to meet the director!"

"I know you did," I said, slowing Dolley to a leisurely walk under the elms.

PATERSON was a city of industry. Every schoolchild read the story about Alexander Hamilton and his Society for Establishing Useful Manufactures, conceived for the purpose of harnessing the powers of the Great Falls of the Passaic River and building along its banks a national manufactory. Although things did not go as Hamilton had planned at first, Paterson did eventually grow into a city of steel mills and, later, silk mills. The factories produced locomotives, Colt revolvers, and, most recently, hair ribbons and yardage. But all industry ceased when a motion picture concern came to town.

As Fleurette rushed to the intersection of Market and Main, dragging me behind her, we passed banks that had closed for the afternoon, grocers who had locked their fruit stands, and jewelry stores with shutters over their windows. Businessmen in pinstriped suits stood on the sidewalk as if they had no business to attend to. Schoolteachers crowded into the street with their young charges. Police officers pushed the crowd aside, only to get a better look for themselves.

Fleurette couldn't see above anyone's head, so I let her climb the stairs of the library (closed until further notice) and perch atop a lamppost pedestal. She wrapped her arm around the post and craned her neck to see. In a peach-colored afternoon dress that flowed and swirled around her and her hair in dark glossy waves around her shoulders, she looked like Liberty with her torch. I stood below and watched with alarm as young men took their eyes off the proceedings down the street and grinned up at her instead. She kept her chin high, but I saw her glancing down at her admirers and wished I'd taken the post with her to discourage their interest.

The intersection had been cleared as if for a duel. One of Paterson's older trolley cars sat on the tracks, awaiting its fate. An enormous black motor car lurked on the other side of the intersection, half a block away, its engine growling. A wooden platform had been built for the camera, which stood all alone on its three-legged stand.

Finally the motor car's engine roared and a conductor jumped into the trolley and waved to the crowd. Everyone yelled back and fluttered their handkerchiefs at him. The driver of the motor car stood and waved to even more applause. Then they both settled down and a hush fell over the crowd.

The cameraman gave a nod. Someone raised a megaphone and counted down.

"Three. Two. One. Go!"

Over gasps and screams from the audience, the trolley rolled along its tracks and the motor car came at it broadside, picking up speed, just as Henry Kaufman had. The conductor looked out with an exaggerated expression of fear, which drew a laugh from the audience just as the car plowed into the trolley. It rocked back and forth. The conductor's expression grew more alarmed, and finally, with one last push from the motor car, it collapsed on its side, its wheels spinning.

Cheers erupted from the crowd. Fleurette was jumping up and down and clapping madly. Policemen, firemen, and a doctor with his medical bag all ran to the trolley, but the conductor emerged, victorious, shaking his fists in the air. All around me, people were congratulating one another as if they'd had some role in the outcome.

I turned to look for Fleurette, but at that moment I felt a hand on my sleeve. It was the red-haired girl from the factory.

"You don't remember me," she shouted, straining to be heard over the crowd. She was younger than I'd first realized—not much older than Fleurette—and would have been pretty if she hadn't spent her life in a dye shop. Her hair was thin and dull, her mouth pinched, and there was a burn mark on her neck and another one like it on the back of her hand, both of them quite brown, suggesting an accident that occurred years ago. Her fingers bore the gray stains that accumulated from the dye.

"I do," I said. "I made you spill all that dye. I'm sorry." I stepped back and took my arm away from her. There was nothing on the library's pedestal but a lamppost. Fleurette had left her spot.

"It's nothing to be sorry for," she said. "We can't help but spill dye. Every day my apron's a different color."

The people in the crowd were pushing past me like a school of fish.

"Please excuse me," I said. "I'm looking for my sister."

I broke away from the crowd and backed into the street

so I could get a better look at the library steps. It was nothing but a sea of hats, and all of a sudden I couldn't remember which hat Fleurette had worn. Now I was thinking about Henry Kaufman, too, and watching the side streets to make sure I didn't see a black motor car roll away with a young girl in the passenger's seat.

By the time I saw Fleurette, she was almost upon me, still smiling, still glowing, still bouncing on her toes. I grabbed her and pulled her roughly to me, looking over the top of her head as I did. She tried to push away from me but I wouldn't let her.

A voice behind me whispered, "Is she the one?"

I spun around but kept one arm wrapped around Fleurette's neck. It was the girl from the factory again.

"Is this her?" she asked. "I knew it couldn't have been you."

Fleurette wriggled away from me to get a better look at her. "Who are you?"

She took a deep breath and settled her shoulders. "I'm Lucy Blake. I work in Henry Kaufman's factory. Is there another child? You can tell me."

"Another child?" Fleurette screwed up her face and looked back and forth between the two of us. The girl's meaning was starting to dawn on me.

"I had a boy," Lucy said. "Bobby. But he's gone."

"I beg your pardon, Miss Blake," I said, pulling Fleurette away from her. "There's been a misunderstanding. I went to see Mr. Kaufman about the payment of an invoice."

Lucy gave Fleurette another quick glance. "Do you mean that she isn't—"

I shook my head, horrified by the idea of Fleurette having anyone's child, much less Henry Kaufman's.

"What boy?" Fleurette asked breathlessly. "Where has he gone?"

Lucy looked at Fleurette with teary eyes. The story tumbled out before I could think to stop it. "I don't know," she said, her voice wavering. "I never asked Henry for anything until we went out on strike. I just wanted enough money to feed Bobby. Nothing for me! I only needed milk and bread. But Henry was furious. He thought I was trying to trick him into giving me a share of the family business."

"That sounds like him," I said in spite of myself. I didn't want Fleurette to hear any of this, but I was growing outraged on the girl's behalf.

She sniffed and nodded. "He knew there was a baby. I mean, I hid it as long as I could, but he saw me every day. He knew. I told him all I wanted was to keep my job—nothing from him! He's not fit to be a father."

"Of course not," I said quickly.

"But when I asked him for help through the strike, he acted as if I were threatening extortion! He wouldn't give me a dime. So I had to send Bobby away in the children's evacuation."

"You sent your baby away?" Fleurette said. "How could you?"

"Fleurette! What choice did she have?" The strikers' children left Paterson by the wagonload last year, bound for New York City, where families sympathetic to the strike had agreed to take care of them until their parents were back at work and could afford to feed them again. We had all seen the pictures in the paper of them leaving, those doleful children with notes pinned to their collars.

"All the other children came back, except mine," Lucy

said, grabbing at my hands. "I think Henry had something to do with it, don't you?"

I shook her hands off, tripping over my skirt as I fell away from her. I felt as though I'd been pushed out of a window. Henry Kaufman was a sluggard and a scoundrel, but a kidnapper?

"I couldn't possibly know," I said. "Haven't you been to the police?"

A man carrying a stack of hatboxes jostled me as he walked by. I jumped and pulled Fleurette back to the library steps. Lucy Blake looked nervously around and followed.

"I can't," she whispered, grabbing my wrist and leaning up to my ear. "If I go to the police, he'll make sure I disappear, too. That's what he told me."

Why was she was telling me this? I could hardly look at her, but I couldn't move, either. Fleurette, crushed against me, watched her with wide, dark eyes.

"He's getting so much worse," she continued. "When he first took over the factory, he wasn't so terrible. He could be nice when he wanted to, especially with the girls."

I put a hand over Fleurette's ear. "Lots of men can be nice to girls."

Fleurette pulled away. "I can hear you!"

"But he's horrible now," Lucy said. "He'd rather run with that gang of his than run the factory. They do nothing but drink whiskey and plot their little schemes. They're always going out to get revenge or to teach someone a lesson. You wouldn't believe the fights they get into, even with each other."

"What about his sister?" I said. "She seems sensible enough."

Lucy shook her head. "She's disgusted with the whole mess. Her family has all sorts of mills, and this is the only one that's in trouble. She and Mr. Garfinkel have been sent in to get Henry straightened out, but she can't do anything with him either."

"But surely she could help you?"

"I tried. Mrs. Garfinkel wants nothing to do with my situation. And it isn't that she doesn't believe me. I had a few things of Henry's—some notes he left me and . . ." She glanced at Fleurette, who had never listened so carefully to anyone in her life. "Well, some personal things of his. She knows Bobby is her nephew. But I'm just one more problem as far as she's concerned—" Her voice broke again, and she brought a handkerchief up to her eyes. "She told me not to mention it again and not to involve the police in her family's affairs."

"Why would you work for those people?" Fleurette said.

"Hush," I told her.

"I can't go anywhere else," Lucy said. "All the mills keep blacklists. I'm to stay quiet if I want any job in town. And I keep hoping I'll hear something about Bobby. When you walked in last week, I thought you might know of a similar situation. I thought we could help each other. I've been looking for you."

All at once it came to me that if this girl was in so much trouble with Henry Kaufman, Fleurette and I shouldn't be seen on the streets with her. "I'm sorry, Miss Blake, but our situation is quite different. I hope you . . . I mean . . . just look after yourself." I took Fleurette's arm and turned to walk away.

"Watch out for him," she called after us. "He won't stop. Once you cross him, he doesn't forget."

Something about her story was bothering me. I halted in the middle of the sidewalk and turned around. She was standing all alone in front of the library, watching us go.

"Lucy, what about the people in New York who were keeping your baby? What do they say?"

"That's just it," Lucy said. "They're gone, too."

⊰ 9 ⊱

FLEURETTE GOT TO DRIVE HOME. She nosed the run-about along Paterson's crowded streets while I stared straight ahead, trying to shake off the peculiar feeling that had taken hold of me since we broke free of Lucy Blake.

Something had shifted, in some subtle way I couldn't put a name to. The everyday rush of shoppers and carriages and motor cars and shopkeepers and delivery boys, once so familiar to me, now seemed foreign and vaguely threatening. I watched three men push a wagon with an enormous wooden crate perched atop it. They had to hold it on all sides to keep it from crashing over as it rolled by. What it contained I couldn't see, but all at once I was suspicious of it. What were they hiding: Ammunition? A bank vault? A missing person? Across the street, a woman walked out of her shop with a bucket that she discharged into the gutter. I shuddered and wondered what foul mess she was trying to scrub away. A girl about Fleurette's age stepped in front of our horse with a baby-shaped bundle pressed against her chest, and all I could think was: *Whose child is that? Where are you taking it?*

Fleurette pushed Dolley onward, keeping quiet until we reached the edge of town. Then she said, "Did Mr. Kaufman really do all those things?"

"I don't know."

"Do you think she was lying?"

"It doesn't seem that way."

"Shouldn't she go to the police?"

"Fleurette! Please." I was exhausted and irritated. I wanted nothing more than to lie down in a cool dark room and close my eyes. Fleurette was holding Dolley back, making her plod along, dragging out our journey. A milk truck passed us, then a wagon overloaded with traveling trunks and furniture.

"Are we ever going to get home?" I asked her.

"Not until you tell me what this is all about."

"I don't know anything more than you do."

"Why would she take up with a man like that?"

I sighed and shook my head. "All the usual reasons."

"Because she was in love?"

"Maybe."

"And she thought he would marry her?"

"Quite possibly."

"I don't see how anyone could marry a man like that."

I thought about that for a minute. "Maybe he wasn't always that bad. Maybe he used to be different."

"Did you used to be different?" Fleurette asked.

I didn't answer that.

WE RETURNED HOME to find Bessie in the sitting room with Norma. She had dropped by, she declared, to deliver a strawberry cake she'd won in an auction to benefit the library, but I suspected that Francis wanted a woman's opinion on how we were managing. Norma appeared to have passed the inspection because Bessie was getting ready to leave when we arrived. She rose from her chair when she saw me and pulled me affectionately to her. She was a cheerful, plump woman with a wide, generous smile and the kind of brown hair that turned red in the summer. As she leaned toward me, she murmured, "Your brother worries about you. He just doesn't know how to show it."

"Sending over a strawberry cake is a fine start," I said, giving her shoulder a squeeze.

"You know that was my idea." Turning to Fleurette, she said, "Have you really been watching a picture get made all day?"

Fleurette began a lively and elaborate report in which she not only managed to keep our meeting with Lucy Blake a secret, but invented an afternoon's worth of activities to explain the length of our absence, including an actual derailed streetcar that forced a lengthy detour, an impromptu turn through the piano shop to hear a demonstration of new sheet music, and an encounter with a street vendor selling green African parrots from an enormous brass cage. The parrots spoke French, she said, and a little Dutch, but when asked their nationality would reply in a chorus, "We're Spanish!" The man selling them could offer no explanation for that. He merely laughed and shrugged and offered Fleurette a good price if she would take two.

The ease with which these small, meaningless lies unraveled from her tongue astonished me. Who taught her to fabricate such stories? I could hardly look at Norma while Fleurette spun those outlandish tales. For once Norma seemed not at all suspicious of the story being told to her, and Bessie was completely taken in by it, leaving us with a wave of her hand and shaking her head over the idea of parrots with French accents. It made me wonder how often I, too, had let Fleurette fool me.

ALL EVENING I tried to push Lucy out of my mind, but her predicament tugged at me. I couldn't stop thinking about the possibility that somewhere, at the center of this mess, that girl's child was missing.

Norma knocked at my bedroom door that night just as I was getting into bed. She sat on the edge of the mattress, one leg tucked under her and the other stretched out alongside me. She smelled of milk soap from her bath, and rice powder, and her hair was all wet curls, each one lifting individually as it dried in the warm night air.

She had a way of pursing her lips when she had something serious to say. I knew better than to ask directly and just waited to hear what it was.

"Green African parrots?" she asked.

"What about them?"

"Where did Fleurette get the story about the man selling green parrots on the street? You didn't expect me to believe that, did you?"

I had to smile. "No. I was surprised that you did."

"Well, I didn't." Norma looked down and smoothed the wrinkles out of the bedspread. "This has to do with Henry Kaufman, doesn't it?"

"Well—in a way, yes. It does."

"I can't believe you would take Fleurette to see that man. We hardly let her out of the house for years, and now you're parading her in front of a criminal. Why would you—"

"But it wasn't Mr. Kaufman. It was a girl from the factory."

"We don't know any girls from factories."

"I saw her when I went to Mr. Kaufman's office, and we ran into her on the sidewalk today. She . . . she thought I was in a different sort of trouble with him."

"Different sort of trouble?" she said, looking up and fixing those sharp eyes on me. "How many different sorts of trouble does Mr. Kaufman have to offer?"

"The girl, whose name is Lucy—"

"Don't tell me her name."

"I don't have to tell you any of this."

"No, tell me. What about her?"

"She had a baby."

"Oh. And she asked for your expertise?" Norma raised an eyebrow at me.

"Norma! The baby's gone missing. Lucy thinks Mr. Kaufman had something to do with it."

"Why would he care about a factory girl and her baby?"

"It's his child."

Norma ran her fingers through her wet hair. "Mr. Kaufman's morals sink lower with every passing day. By Wednesday, he'll be a murderer."

"Lucy thinks he's kidnapped the boy, so I suppose—"

"Do you not agree with me," Norma said, stretching out on my coverlet and putting her (blessedly clean) feet against my pillow, "that a man who carries on with factory girls and then kidnaps their children is the sort of man with whom the Kopp sisters would rather not become better acquainted?"

"I do," I said, "but don't you think it's terrible what happened to that girl?"

Norma propped herself up on an elbow to get a better look at me. "I do think it's terrible what happens to girls who get themselves into trouble. But we've had enough trouble already."

"I just feel that someone should try to help her."

"That feeling will pass." She rolled off my bed and stood over me, her arms crossed. "Francis and Bessie are having us over for a roast. I told her you'd do the peas."

"Nobody likes my peas," I said.

"But we like having you *do* them," she said. "Now, go to sleep and don't think about that girl anymore and I won't either." This seemed to be a satisfactory conclusion to her, so she slipped out and closed the door gently, leaving me alone in the dark, willing myself not to think about Lucy Blake.

⌐ 10 ⌐

IN BROOKLYN our only excursions out of the house, apart
from school, were to dancing lessons at the Rivers' Academy,
where our uncle Charles worked as an accompanist. Because
he was willing to keep an eye on us, Norma, Francis, and I
were made to spend most of our afternoons there, enduring
minuets and fancy dress tableaux, lumbering through polkas
and tarantellas, memorizing marches, and sitting in the corner folding crepe flowers for headdresses while the younger
children had their turn in front of the mirrors.

Francis also took lessons on the zither from our uncle. On
recital days he would stand, shaking, on the stage, and pick
out a solo while Norma and I danced a wooden duet next to
him. Being the tallest girl in the class, I was once dressed as
Uncle Sam and placed in the center of the stage while forty-
five girls, each portraying a different state, danced around
me. Norma refused to choose a state. Wyoming was forced
upon her. She wore a linen dress the color of sand and spread
her arms wide to convey the vastness and futility of a place
she could not imagine and did not wish to.

It was after one of those dancing lessons that I met the Singer man for the first time. In those days we lived on the top floor of a building with a rear entrance for delivery men and a front entrance for everyone else. Salesmen used to ring the bell in spite of the signs telling them not to. They sold silver polish and washing powder, pencils and notions, books by subscription and even fruit tree saplings. I used to watch the man with the bundle of twigs over his shoulder going up and down our street, finding no takers for his black cherries and Cox's apples. Only the most unlucky fruit tree peddler would be assigned Brooklyn as a territory. But a sewing machine salesman had an easier time of it.

The salesmen would ring the bell until someone let them in. Eventually their footsteps would approach our door, and then the knock would come, and my mother's hands would descend upon the heads of her daughters, a signal to remain quiet and perfectly still until the threat had passed.

Salesmen were dirty, she told us. They sold inferior goods that no store would offer. They preyed on lonely shut-ins and the feeble-minded. They only wanted in so they could come back and burgle our home while we were away. And they carried fleas.

I knew that couldn't be right. I went to school with girls who got their hair ribbons from a traveling salesman, and their kid shoes. I'd seen the sheet music man stop in at the dance academy to offer new songs for sale. A man selling tonics and remedies poured me a sample one winter when he heard me coughing on the sidewalk. (I ran away, but only because I was afraid my mother would catch me talking to him.) So I understood that salesmen were not as dangerous as my mother believed, but I didn't dare contradict her, and Norma didn't either.

This is why we were so astonished to come home from the dance academy one day and find a Singer salesman in our mother's parlor, demonstrating a new electric motor. Mother looked at us like one of the terrified kidnapping victims she read about in the newspaper. The Singer man just rose to his feet and smiled.

Having only just turned eighteen, I was too old for dancing lessons, but Norma, at the age of fourteen, was finishing her last year and had convinced me to go along and help with the younger children so that she wouldn't have to face it alone. She was embarrassed to be seen in her pleated skirt and bloomers, so she ran past the Singer man and slammed the door to our bedroom. That left me face-to-face with him.

"*Sholem aleykhem*," he said quietly, as if my mother weren't in the room. "I am here on behalf of the Singer Sewing Machine Company. How do you do?"

He was a Jew. I had heard Yiddish spoken on the street, but never under our own roof. I stared past him at my mother, who sat frozen on the divan. How had she allowed this to happen?

He spoke to me again in that soft voice. "And you must be one of Mrs. Kopp's lovely daughters."

From his accent, I could tell he'd only been in the country a short while, but already he'd learned good English.

When I didn't say anything, he added, "I met your mother just as she was stepping out the door to hang her washing. I'd been next door showing Mrs. Fritz the benefits of our newest model. Your mother was kind enough to let me demonstrate it again here in your parlor."

My mother? Kind? He must have put a spell on her.

"I am Constance Kopp," I said at last. "Please excuse my sister. I'm afraid she's overly tired from her exertions at dancing class."

The Singer man was half a head taller than I was, which was already a rarity for me at that age. He had chocolate-brown eyes and a head of thick black hair that parted in the middle and flopped across his forehead. He looked down at me through gold-rimmed spectacles that gave him the appearance of a scholar.

"You are not tired from dancing class?"

"I don't take the class anymore. I'm too old for it."

"A girl is never too old to dance."

He was one of those men who perpetually smiled and whose face had become agreeably lined because of it. I knew I shouldn't smile back at him, but I did.

At last my mother found her voice. "My daughter does not like to dance."

Without turning away from me, he said, "But she took the lessons."

"Dancing lessons are good for girls." Mother rose and marched between us to the door and held it open. Seeing that he hadn't moved, she added, "She does not like to sew, either."

At last he turned around to retrieve his sample bag and the model of the electric motor. He gave me a polite nod and something more — a wink? — as he walked to the door.

"Perhaps she would like a lesson," the Singer man said, deploying one of his warm and generous grins on my mother from the hallway. "I offer instruction on all of our machines."

My mother closed the door on him and I turned so she

couldn't see the rush of blood to my face. At that moment I wondered if she had been right all along. Maybe young girls really did face threats to their virtue every day in America, even in their own homes, even from traveling salesmen carrying nothing but order books and sample cases.

THE NEXT TIME the Singer man knocked on our door, I was the one who let him in.

I'd refused to take Norma to dancing lessons any longer. Mother wouldn't let her go alone, so every Wednesday and Saturday the two of them rode the trolley to the dance academy, leaving me at home to start supper. Francis was working as a stock clerk for a hardware store, which meant that I found myself with the unexpected luxury of an empty apartment twice a week.

That afternoon I'd been very lazy, reading a book on the divan and neglecting the roast I was supposed to cook for dinner. It was an unusually mild day for November, and I had opened all the windows, pushing aside the heavy tapestry curtains to let in the high, clear breeze.

I had adopted Mother's habit of never answering a knock at the door—all of us had—but this one came so softly that it seemed harmless. I was at the door before I had time to think about what I was doing.

The Singer man's eyes crinkled when he smiled. "I hoped I'd find you at home, Miss Kopp."

Something happened to my limbs. They were frozen in place but also fully charged, as if a great river were rushing through them. He was inside with the door closed behind him before I could move. Now I knew how he'd gotten past my mother on his first visit. He had a way of gliding through a door as if every home were his own and he'd been expected for hours.

The Singer man put his case on the table and released its latches. The sides fell open to reveal a polished black machine.

"It's our newest model. I wanted you to see it first. I thought it might persuade you to take more of an interest in your sewing."

Nothing could make me take an interest in sewing, but for reasons I didn't understand, I nodded anyway and sat next to him and watched as he unrolled his fabric samples and bobbins. Each length of cloth had been stitched before, hemmed and pleated and taken apart again, exhibiting the traces of every sewing lesson he'd ever given.

I have a vivid memory of a piece of gingham rolling under the machine, and of a feeling just below my heart like a bird had hatched and was struggling to get out. It rose up into my throat and I swallowed to keep it down. Some part of me was aware that time was passing and that Mother and Norma were due home, but I could hardly breathe, much less rouse myself to look at the clock.

The Singer man possessed the long, thin fingers of a musician. He could handle the slimmest grade of thread and make the most minute adjustments to his machine the way one tunes an instrument. Those fingers brushed across mine to guide a piece of fresh silk under the needle, leaving a row of fine blue stitches more perfect and precise than anything my mother had ever attempted.

The lesson went on for an hour, ending just ten minutes before Norma and Mother returned. He left as silently as he came and our flat showed no sign that he'd been there. When he was gone, I stood in the middle of the empty room, wondering if I'd only imagined him.

I can't say that I learned anything. I was in no position to purchase one of his machines and he must have known it. That night, as we waited for the roast to finish, I said nothing about how I'd spent the afternoon. It was the first secret I'd ever kept from my family.

⇥ 11 ⇤

OVER THE NEXT FEW DAYS, Norma and I did not speak of Henry Kaufman or Lucy Blake. But Fleurette could think of little else, and she took any opportunity to pull me aside and tell her outlandish ideas to me.

"What if the boy is to be the heir to the Kaufman fortune, and he has been smuggled off to Russia, where he will never know his true heritage?" she asked one day in the languid hours of late afternoon, when Norma was out with her pigeons and we had retreated to our cool, dim sitting room to read. "He could be another *dauphin perdu*."

"We don't have princes in America," I said. "And why would he be taken to Russia?"

She put a finger purposefully on her pointed little chin as she thought about it. "The Bolsheviks. They took him to New York in the evacuation, and then they found out he was a silk man's son, and they put him on a ship to Russia to be raised as a revolutionary."

I put my book down, as Fleurette's story was vastly more interesting. "And will he return someday?"

"Yes," she said, stretching her arms above her head and yawning. "At eighteen, when he becomes a man, he'll claim his fortune from his father, who will be very old by then—"

"Not so terribly old," I corrected her.

"Oh yes, very old, fifty or so, and the *dauphin* will return to Paterson—"

"I'd like to think Mr. Kaufman will have been run out of Paterson by then."

She cleared her throat theatrically to discourage further interruptions. "He'll return and find his father, *wherever he may be,* and claim his fortune, and then hand his money out to all the workers in the factory, and Mr. Kaufman will scream and shout, but he'll be penniless and his workers will all go home in the middle of the day with their pockets full."

"But what about Lucy? Shouldn't she get something?"

"He'll have a palace built in Russia for her, and they'll return together so she can be queen of the Bolsheviks." Fleurette slapped her own book shut to signal the end of the story.

"I'm fairly certain the Bolsheviks don't want a queen."

"Well, she should get to be queen of *something* in the end."

ALL OF FLEURETTE'S STORIES about Lucy Blake involved hidden treasures, dramatic rescues, and glorious escapes to exotic locales, which were always populated with peacocks and black swans, those being, in her mind, the *accoutrements* of the royal class.

But Lucy Blake wasn't a character in a fairy tale. And her baby was not a *dauphin perdu,* but the illegitimate child of a factory girl, lost in a city of millions.

Although I worried over her predicament and wondered about the mess Henry Kaufman had made of her life and his own, those matters were, in some ways, still an abstraction to me. To my way of thinking, I'd had an accidental encounter with a man who was certainly not a fine citizen and possibly a criminal—but the entire affair was on its way to becoming a memory, a bizarre story that Fleurette would embroider and Norma would file away as a cautionary tale, but that would have no bearing on our lives henceforth. I didn't even think of Henry Kaufman as a man who went out and did things every day—who combed his hair and ate his lunch and drank in saloons with his friends and quarreled with his sister. In my mind, Henry Kaufman existed only in those moments when I had seen him, and the rest of the time he was still and quiet, like a marionette hung backstage by his strings, motionless until someone took him up and sent him skittering back to life.

What I couldn't fathom—what I hadn't considered, really—was that we continued to exist in his mind. He wasn't a marionette on a post, and he hadn't forgotten about us. He was always out there, doing whatever it was that Henry Kaufman did, and I had failed to appreciate the fact that sometimes what Henry Kaufman did was think about us.

This was at last made clear to me late one Tuesday night, when I found myself inexplicably awake, jolted out of a bizarre dream about Lucy and a bright green swan swimming in the dye tubs at Mr. Kaufman's factory. The sound that had awoken me was an engine rattling outside my bedroom window.

I sat up and clutched a pillow to me, having nothing else to protect me from whatever was coming. There was a flash of light through the window and then the glass shattered, sending shards flying around me. Something heavy hit the bed and I screamed.

From outside the window came the sound of tires spinning in the gravel and a motor car roaring away.

I had the shaky, nauseated feeling that comes from being thrown so suddenly from sleep. I gathered my blankets around me as protection against whatever had hit my bed. My fingers skipped around, past the broken glass, and there it was.

A brick. There was a piece of string around it, and paper tucked underneath.

Then Fleurette was in the room, and Norma's footsteps were close behind. The window with its mouth of jagged glass gaped at us.

"Get down on the floor," I whispered. I rolled out of bed and risked a step across the shattered remains of my window, which clinked and glittered across the floor. I peeked outside, but the road was dark and vacant, as if nothing had happened.

Norma and Fleurette were crouched down in their nightgowns, staring up at me, their arms wrapped across their knees.

"It was him, wasn't it?" Fleurette said. "He's back."

I nodded. "I think so."

We waited a second and then Norma rose and lit a lamp. She lifted the paper away from the brick and unfolded it gingerly, as if something might fly out of it.

Madam:
    Stay away from H. Kaufman and his place of
business. This time we warn you. Soon we shoot.
We use gun on you, we use more bullets, we
get you.
                                 H. K. friend

She passed it to me and then to Fleurette. The note was written in childish block letters, like a right-handed man writing with his left hand.

"Shoot?" Fleurette said. "Does he really mean to shoot at us?"

I looked out the window again. The trees whispered in the dark and an owl made a muffled cry. I was still half inside that dream of the factory and the swan, and I had the strangest feeling that Mr. Kaufman had come after me because I had dared to dream about him. "Surely not," I said. "He hardly knows us."

A breeze rose and lifted the curtain away from the broken window. All three of us jumped.

"I thought it was a man climbing in," Fleurette said, her hand over her throat.

"You can't sleep in here," Norma said to me. "Not with the window like that."

I took the brick and knocked the rest of the glass out of the pane. Outside was nothing but the dark barn and the empty lane. "I'll be fine," I said, although I wasn't at all sure I would be. "It's only a prank, meant to frighten us and nothing more."

"Let me read the note again," Fleurette said, reaching for it.

"I don't want you brooding over it all night long and having nightmares."

"Just let me see it."

I held it above my head. "No! We should all go back to our beds, and we'll talk about it in the morning."

She leaned against me. "What would Mother make of all this?"

I smoothed Fleurette's hair, not daring to look at Norma over the top of her head. "I don't know what she would have done," I said. "Nothing like this ever happened to her. But I know what she would say to you."

"Really? What?"

"Geh ins Bett."

"All right! I'm going."

Norma leaned against the door frame and watched Fleurette return to her bedroom. Then she slipped back into my room and closed the door behind her.

"How can you be so certain that Mr. Kaufman does not intend to shoot us," she began, "when he wrote a letter stating exactly the opposite and went to the trouble to break a window to deliver it?"

"I'm not certain of anything," I said. "I just didn't want Fleurette to work herself into a pitch in the middle of the night."

Norma sat down next to me on the bed and picked up bits of broken glass, dropping them into her cupped hand. "I suppose this is how we'll live now, behind boarded windows with strange men throwing bricks at us. If only we had a basement, we could move into it and never go out at all."

"It was only a prank, and I don't think they'll do it again," I said. "We've given them no cause to." Next to my pillow I found a chip of window glass the size of a penny with a little white paint on it.

"Well, of course *we* haven't given them cause," Norma said, "but you have. Men don't like to admit when they've done something wrong, and they particularly don't like strange ladies coming around demanding payment in compensation for their wrongdoing."

"That's not a reason to shoot at us."

"It's not a reason for a sensible person to shoot at us," she said. "If Mr. Kaufman were sensible, he wouldn't have run us down in the first place. In fact, he never would have bought one of those machines." The auto industry had a formidable foe in Norma, who believed self-propelled vehicles to be a path to lawlessness and social chaos. Mr. Kaufman was only strengthening her argument.

"Well, it's a matter for the police now. I'll go and see them in the morning."

"You won't find the police to be any help at all. They won't arrest him, and if they go and ask him questions, he'll only get more agitated, and I don't want to know what he'll do then."

There was a footstep in the hall. Fleurette pushed open the door and flopped down on my bed. Norma leapt up so as not to spill her handful of glass. "Go back to sleep," I said.

"But, Constance. I just realized."

"What?"

"Lucy was telling the truth. He goes after anyone who crosses him and he doesn't stop."

"I would hardly say that we're the ones who crossed him." But I remembered the way I'd pushed him against the wall. He'd looked like a trapped animal. And what do animals do when they're cornered?

"If this is how he treats us, what has he done to Lucy?" She put her head on my pillow and looked at me pleadingly.

I shook my head. "I don't know. I can't imagine."

"What are you going to do about that girl and her baby?"

"Well, there's nothing at all I can do, especially now that we're having bricks thrown at us."

"But if you don't, who will?"

I leaned over and put my chin on Fleurette's head. Norma looked down at the two of us and drew in her breath as if in preparation for another speech on the inadvisability of having anything to do with the matter, but the words wouldn't come or she decided not to say them. She opened her hand above my waste bin and the slivers of glass fell down like rain.

⊰ 12 ⊱

A LATE SUMMER STORM blew through Hackensack the next morning and washed the dust off the buildings. By the time I got to town, the sun had pushed away the clouds and the city smelled of clean hay and wet stone. The sour, ripe heat of summer had lifted. I climbed the courthouse steps under the heady influence of this shift in the season, and stood just inside the door to let the perspiration dry behind my collar before I approached the girl at the receptionist's desk.

"I am here to file charges against a man," I said. "It's a criminal matter."

"Is this man your—" She pursed her rosebud lips and I suppose she thought about the word "husband" in relation to me and decided against it.

"He is a man who committed a crime," I said. "Have I come to the right place?"

She gave me a look of prim disapproval but directed me to an office and told me to speak to whatever detective I found there. I marched past her desk and through the high and bright rotunda, where the muffled noises from the court-rooms met in the center and circulated, lifting a contentious and quarrelsome murmur to the stained-glass dome above. The door to the prosecutor's office was closed. I pushed my way in without knocking.

Seated at the desk was a slump-shouldered man with a face the exact shape and texture of an egg. His eyes were a jaundiced yellow, and his lips pointed down in a deep V shape, giving the impression of a permanent and immovable frown. The plate on his desk read simply "DETECTIVE."

He was talking to a man in a brown suit. I couldn't see the other man—his back was turned—but the detective re-garded him with an expression of profound disgust, the way one might look at a tramp carrying a colony of fleas under his coat. He jumped to his feet when he saw me, clearly relieved by the interruption.

"Good morning, miss," he said. "I am Detective Courter. How may I—"

"I'd like to file a criminal complaint," I said.

The other man rose and turned to face me. He was not a tramp, just a man in a plain suit and a bow tie. He wore a mustache that seemed too wide for his face, bringing to mind a boy in his father's clothes. He looked at me through mourn-fully dark and deep-set eyes.

"Sheriff Robert Heath," he said. "How do you do?"

I introduced myself and explained the purpose of my visit. As I did so, Sheriff Heath stepped aside to yield the floor to Detective Courter. I addressed my concerns to the detective but could not help glancing at the sheriff, who watched the exchange with a half-suppressed smile.

Upon hearing my account, Detective Courter glanced at the sheriff and then sat down at his desk and squinted at the threatening note I'd presented to him.

"Miss, did you say the accident took place over in Paterson? Isn't that a matter for Passaic County?"

"Yes," I said, "but I live here in Bergen County, and he's harassed us twice at our house." The truth was that I'd chosen Hackensack over Paterson because I hoped that the police in Hackensack would be less sympathetic to the silk men than those in Paterson, a city dominated by the industry.

"It appears, Miss Kopp," he said, not moving his eyes from the paper, "that this is a matter for you to settle directly with him. If he's damaged your buggy, simply write out the charges and send them to him." He raised his eyes to me at last, elevating one eyebrow in a manner that suggested that he'd just brought the matter to an entirely satisfying conclusion.

I took a seat across from the detective, leaned toward him, and spoke slowly and quietly.

"After Henry Kaufman plowed his automobile through a crowd of people on Market Street and destroyed our buggy, he drove past our house with three other men and shouted vulgarities at my younger sister. He then hurled a brick and this letter through my bedroom window in the middle of the night." I paused to give him time to write this down, as would be the custom when a citizen comes to the courthouse to make a complaint. He did not write anything down, and in fact did not appear to possess a pen or any writing paper. But I continued.

"I have sent Mr. Kaufman an invoice, which he refuses to pay. Now I wish to file a complaint. He has committed a series of criminal actions against us with no provocation whatsoever."

Mr. Courter looked up at the sheriff, who gave him a nod of acknowledgment but said nothing. He looked back at the letter and then up at the ceiling. Discovering no answer stamped in tin above him, his glance fell back to me. At last another idea came to him.

"Now, Miss Kopp," he said. "With whom did you file the report?"

"I have come to file the report with you," I said.

"Well—ah—yes. But the officer at the scene. What officer took down a report of the damages to your buggy?"

"There was no officer. I was surprised that not a single constable came to our aid. But a few men from the shops helped us right our horse, and I took down Mr. Kaufman's name and address so that I might forward him a bill for the damages."

He seemed to consider my reply. "Well, we only investigate the accident reports that come to us from the officers, Miss Kopp. If no report was taken, there's nothing I can do."

It was my turn to consider him. I rose from my chair and looked down at him. His head was covered in thick black strands glistening with oil. It reminded me of Mr. Kaufman's. They seemed, all at once, like the same man.

"My sister Fleurette is but thirteen years of age," I said, loud enough to cause him to jerk his neck back and look up at me. "She has been threatened twice by a dangerous criminal." I grabbed the letter and snapped it once again under his nose. "You know as well as I do what can happen to young girls. It is your duty to stop this man."

Detective Courter, I am sad to say, reacted to my speech

with a fit of giggles. He leaned back, his shoulders shaking and his eyes wet. At last he seemed to come out of it and realize that I was still standing over him.

"Are you suggesting," he said, "that this man might run off with your sister rather than pay a fifty-dollar bill for damages? A silk man?"

"I don't see what difference his profession could make. Are you prepared to take my complaint?"

The sheriff coughed quietly in the corner. Detective Courter glared at him. After a few more delays and equivocations, the detective managed to find a pen and I returned to my seat. I repeated the entire story and watched him copy it down. I left out the most unpleasant bits of my encounter with Henry Kaufman in his office, and did not mention Lucy Blake and her claims about the kidnapped child. I didn't trust Detective Courter to handle the girl's situation with any sensitivity.

While he wrote, I looked around the office. It was a fine room, lined with good oak panels and lit by brass lamps with milk-glass shades suspended from the ceiling, clearly designed for pursuits more honorable than those that were at present taking place within it. Along one wall ran a bank of cabinets fitted with bookshelves, drawers for files, and cubbyholes for messages, all empty. The room had been furnished with two desks for the detectives and a secretarial stand equipped with a typewriter and a telephone, but from the accumulation of dust I could see there was no secretary to operate them. I couldn't imagine they could keep a woman in that position for long. I certainly wouldn't have wanted to work for a man like Mr. Courter.

At the end of my recitation, I glanced at the page he had filled with notes and satisfied myself that it was accurate.

"Well," he said, closing the book and brushing off his hands as if he'd just completed a long day's work. "That takes care of it. Thank you for bringing this to our attention." He stood to see me out.

I kept my seat. He sank uncertainly back to his. "When can I expect to hear from you, Detective?" I asked.

He opened the ledger again as if he hoped to find the answer written there. "Ah—yes. Well, we have your case on file, and if any other incidents should arise—"

"I expect that there will be no more incidents. I expect you to pursue charges against Mr. Kaufman and put a stop to this unwarranted harassment of my family!" I said, rising to my feet at last.

Some change came over Detective Courter when I spoke to him like that. He looked up at me coldly. A vein throbbed on his temple and his eye twitched slightly. "I will speak to the prosecutor," he said slowly.

"And what are we to do if he comes back?"

He looked over at Sheriff Heath, who was staring at his feet. "Haven't you anyone to look after the three of you?" Mr. Courter said with mock concern. "A father or an uncle? A brother, even?"

It had grown very stifling and I decided I couldn't stay in that room another minute. I spun around and left without another glance at either of them.

I WAS STANDING on the courthouse steps trying to catch my breath when I heard—or rather felt—Sheriff Heath behind me. I spun around to face him. He was a tall man, tall enough to look me squarely in the eye.

"I take it this is your first visit to the prosecutor's office," he said.

"It is," I said. "I won't waste my time here again."

He smiled. The sun had been gaining strength all morning and now it struck his face, highlighting the composition of lines and angles around his eyes. There was a kindness about him and a sort of sober warmth and decency, which struck me as unusual for a man in public service in New Jersey.

"I'll speak to Mr. Kaufman. If he gives you any more trouble, come see me."

"I didn't realize your duties extended beyond running the prison and chasing down poultry thieves."

"Poultry thieves do fall under my jurisdiction, Miss Kopp, but so do gangs throwing bricks through windows. Besides, I've had trouble with Kaufman before. May I see the note?"

I offered it to him. "What kind of trouble?"

"During the strikes. The silk men had their own ideas about how to keep order. He had his friends following my men around to make sure we didn't go too easy on the strikers. I didn't appreciate it."

He squinted at the letter and shook his head. "I wouldn't mind a chance to go after that bunch. I suspect they're up to more than just chasing you and your sisters around."

"What do you mean?"

"The usual things. Smuggling liquor. Gambling. Blackmail. They're all thugs and con men, that crowd. A note like this is just the kind of thing they do. Has he tried to shake you down for money?"

"No! Why would he? He's the one who owes us money!"

"You must understand that this is just a game for them."

"Well, it's a cruel game," I said. "And why didn't you say anything back there?"

He shrugged. "You saw what Courter was like. He's not going to take on that gang. The prosecutor's office can be very friendly with the factory owners. But don't worry. Mr. Kaufman doesn't have any friends in the Sheriff's Department."

"Well, that isn't all he's done. I talked to one of the girls who works for him—"

"One of the girls?" He gave me another one of those amused half-smiles. "When did you talk to the girls?"

"It was one particular girl. I just bumped into her. This girl got into some trouble, and it was Mr. Kaufman who . . ." I wasn't sure how to say it, but Sheriff Heath seemed to catch my meaning.

"I'm afraid that is outside my jurisdiction, Miss Kopp."

"But now the child has gone missing, and she thinks Mr. Kaufman is behind it."

The sheriff frowned and cocked his head to the side. "Who's the girl?"

"Well . . ." I took a step back. "What are you going to do if I tell you? I don't want to get her into any more trouble."

Just then a man in a deputy's uniform came running around the corner from the jailhouse, calling the sheriff.

"I can't do anything unless I know who she is," he said. "Have her come and talk to me herself if she wants help."

"But I—"

The deputy ran up to us, wheezing, and said, "They just brought him in."

Sheriff Heath looked at him in surprise. "Already? Well, Miss Kopp," he said, extending his hand. I almost never shook hands with a man, but I removed my glove and slid my palm into his. His hand was warm and dry and I gripped it rather tightly. He laughed a little as he released me. "Not to worry. Mr. Kaufman is no longer your concern. If he bothers you again, come tell me right away. You can telephone me at the Hackensack jail any time of the day or night. And tell that girl to come see me. Will you do that?"

Before I could answer he was gone, trotting down the courthouse steps with his deputy. They spoke excitedly as they walked away from me, already caught up in some far more important matter. I watched them disappear into the side entrance to the jail, and the most inexplicable sorrow and longing settled in around me.

A train rattled in the distance and its whistle announced the next stop. It was leaving for Paterson, where Lucy Blake was working her morning shift at the factory.

I should have gone home. It was nearly time for lunch, and Norma didn't like it when one of us was not present at a meal. I hesitated for just a minute, then I picked up my skirts and ran for the train.

⫷ 13 ⫸

I ARRIVED IN PATERSON an hour before the noon whistle. Along Broadway a group of boys were taking down bunting left over from a parade to honor the mayor's birthday. In their wake came a troupe of girls selling buttons to raise money to aid victims of the fire in Salem. Three of the girls took hold of me at once, spotting an easy mark. I couldn't imagine what Fleurette would do with a set of white buttons that had been stamped with the words "SALEM SUFFERERS, 1914" in red, but I handed over fifty cents anyway and put a few in my pocketbook. The girls wandered on and I lingered outside a druggist, accepting a sample of a digestive tonic that tasted suspiciously like sugar syrup and wine. I passed the rest of the time staring into shop windows, a little queasy over what I was about to do.

Henry Kaufman's factory was just a short walk away. I paced up and down Putnam, getting close to the address and then turning back again. I was standing across the street from the ramshackle brick building as every dyer in his employ-ment emerged for lunch, all dressed in their gray smocks.

The break was nearly over by the time Lucy Blake walked out and stood in the sun, her face turned upward and her eyes closed.

"Lucy?" I called, as quietly as possible. Still, three or four men turned around and watched me approach her. Lucy took a step back and shook her head very slightly to warn me away, but it was too late. I'd made up my mind.

"Lucy, I think I can help," I said when I got closer. "About the matter we discussed."

She looked up at a row of windows at the opposite end of the building where the offices were housed. "Over here," she said, leading me around the corner.

Once we were out of sight, she said, "You shouldn't be here. What is it?"

The whistle blew and she jumped. "I've found someone who wants to talk to you," I said quickly. "About your baby. I'll go with you."

The whistle blew again. "I have to go before they lock us out," she said. "Don't come back here. You can meet me at home to-night." She gave me her address, and then she was gone.

IF I'D RETURNED HOME, Norma would have tried to talk me out of visiting Lucy, and Fleurette would have insisted on coming with me. Being unable to face either possibility, I spent the afternoon in the library and left a little after six o'clock to go see her.

Lucy lived in a neighborhood of narrow clapboard-covered row houses a few blocks off Broadway. I'd ridden past it but never had reason to stop there, as it was inhabited entirely by people who worked in the mills. Paterson was not a com-pany town, but the factory owners had been buying boarding houses and corner markets around here for years. The people who lived there paid rent to their boss, bought groceries from their boss, and went into debt to their boss if their money ran short.

I could find no house numbers along her street, so I started at the corner and counted until I found hers, an old flat-fronted two-story house whose front porch had recently gone missing. Either it had fallen off or burned, and no one had bothered to build another one. I lifted my skirt and climbed atop a pair of concrete blocks that had been placed there to allow entrance. A directory next to the door had been painted the same dull maroon as the rest of the building, as if the painter could not be bothered to stop long enough to paint around the list of people who lived inside. But someone had glued a card to the metal plate and written out the names of the occupants and their room numbers.

Lucy lived on the second floor. Finding no bell to ring and the door unlocked, I entered the dim hall and started up the stairs.

There was a crash overhead and the sound of glass breaking, then a girl's cry. I backed down and into the hall. Upstairs a door slammed and then opened again.

"Where is she?" came a man's voice.

"I don't know," a girl said. "I told you I don't know." There was another thud and I could hear her crying.

"She had no business talking to you!"

I jumped. How could I have failed to recognize that voice? I had no time to gather my thoughts before I heard his footsteps on the landing.

"You tell that Kopp girl to leave you alone," he shouted, his voice booming in the stairwell. "If I see you with her again, you'll be out on the street."

I had to move. Behind me was a door to what I hoped was a kitchen or a storeroom. It was unlocked so I opened it and backed in. Henry Kaufman pounded down the stairs just as I closed the door behind me. I looked around and realized I wasn't in a kitchen, but a lodger's room. Fortunately for me it was empty. There was an iron bed topped with a thin mattress and a ratty blanket, an oil lamp on a low table, and dingy striped wallpaper peeling off in long strips. A man's Sunday shoes sat in the corner. A yellowing newspaper wilted on a chair. My own reflection in a mirror on the wall opposite startled me—in my gray felt hat with the veil across it and my navy traveling suit, I looked like a society matron at an afternoon recital. I wished I'd worn a plainer suit of clothes. My size made me conspicuous enough.

A clock ticked somewhere nearby. There was an odor in the room, something foul and unwashed. I wanted out desperately. I waited until the footsteps passed and the front door opened and closed again, then I turned the knob quietly and I was free.

At the top of the stairs she stood like she'd been waiting for me.

"Lucy," I said. "I'm sorry."

"You shouldn't be here," she whispered. She looked tiny in her percale housedress, covered by an apron that was much too large for her and nearly wrapped around her twice. She held one corner of it in her fist and twisted the fabric around her fingers. Her cheek bore the mark of Henry Kaufman's hand, and her nose was swollen from crying.

I didn't make a move up the stairs. I wasn't sure what to do. "Is he your landlord?"

She looked surprised. "Well, yes. Of course. He owns this building and the two next door. Or his family does. He manages them now, if you call this managing."

I stood for a moment and considered that.

Lucy continued. "Mrs. Garfinkel said we could stay, even after she found out—" She looked down the stairs nervously as if she thought someone might hear.

"All right," I said. "Lucy, may I come up and talk to you? I'm sure he's gone, and if he does return, I'll take care of it. I can handle him."

She looked me over. "I suppose you could. You're bigger than he is, aren't you?"

Once again that sound came to me, the sharp crack when his head hit the plaster. I wasn't sorry I'd shoved him, and I thought I might like to do it again, after the way he treated this poor girl.

Lucy seemed to have calmed down, so I kept climbing and followed her to the door.

Her room was larger than that of the absent lodger downstairs, but it held two of the same type of narrow iron bed and a wardrobe as well as a dresser. The wallpaper depicted silhouettes of children rolling hoops across a lawn. There was a gold filigree border around each scene, but the gold had mostly cracked and flaked away, revealing the once-white underlay of the paper. There was no kitchen, just a wood stove topped by a hot plate and a chafing dish. The only chair was piled high with mending. Seeing nowhere to sit, I put my handbag on the edge of the nearest bed.

"That's my mother's bed," she said. "She cleans for a lady across the river. You can sit there. I'm sorry, I—" She looked around nervously, then scooped up the mending and sat in the chair, holding the bundle in her lap. She looked at me expectantly.

"I take it Mr. Kaufman saw me talking to you," I said at last.

She nodded. "I stopped for groceries on the way home, and when I got here, he was waiting. He has a passkey to the rooms."

I wondered how many other young girls lived in rooms he had passkeys to. "Well," I said, "I only came to tell you that I think something ought to be done about your son."

"I know," she said, and lapsed into tears again. "I should never have let him go with the strike mothers. I didn't know what else to do. We hadn't been paid in months, and the relief tents were always running out of food. I couldn't let him starve, could I? But you don't know what it was like, having to let him go."

I let her cry and clutch her bundle of clothes and rock back and forth as if she were soothing a baby. At that moment I could picture her pulling away from the strike mothers, not wanting to let go of her boy.

After a few minutes, she sniffed and wiped her eyes and looked at me. "I've tried to find him but it's hopeless. Everyone is gone. Everyone who had anything to do with the evacuation just disappeared."

"And you never went to the police?" I asked.

Her eyes flew open. "Oh, no! Henry would kill me if I sent the police after him."

"Well, he wouldn't—"

"No, I mean it. He would send his men after me in the middle of the night. He would burn this building right down, and me in it. You send the police after those men, and you're as good as dead."

She said it so matter-of-factly. I'm sure my heart stopped cold for two or three beats. What had I done?

"Are you sure? I know someone who would be willing to help, if only—"

She looked at me as if I were an imbecile. "Miss Kopp! If Henry has my boy—if he's put him somewhere—what do you think he will do to him when he finds out I've called in the police?"

My face must have been frozen, because she leaned over and peered at me. "Did you hear me?"

I nodded numbly.

"I don't know why you're here," she said, "but if all you have to offer is a call to the police, then I'm afraid you don't do me much good."

I coughed and tried to find my voice. "Well. I don't know what else I could do."

"I don't, either," she said, blinking back furious tears.

There didn't seem to be anything else to say, so I stood to leave. She made a sad sight, with her head down and her arms still wrapped around her heap of clothes to be mended.

"Before I go," I said, "why don't you just tell me what you know? Just in case I do think of something."

She raised her eyes to me and sniffed. She wasn't finished being angry at me, but in a flat voice she told me what I wanted to know. I took down the address of Regina Doyle, in whose care little Bobby had been placed. She told me that two women had taken responsibility for evacuating the children during the strike. They'd been in the papers every day last year, and I recognized their names, Sanger and Flynn. She also furnished me with a description of the baby, although it had been over a year since she'd seen him. He would be almost two years old by now. I asked her if she remembered anything from her trips to the city to try to fetch him, but she shook her head and her tears started again.

"It's no use," Lucy said. "Regina Doyle is gone. I walked up and down the street asking after her, but no one even remembers seeing her."

"She didn't leave an address with the landlord?" I asked.

She shook her head. "Nothing. One day she was just gone, along with everyone who knew her. The strike leaders who lived in that building disappeared all at once."

I heard a noise on the stairs and we both froze. The footsteps went past her door and up to the next floor. I took a long and shaky breath and told Lucy, somewhat dispiritedly, that there had to be a way to get some help for her. She shook her head and made me promise once again not to go to the police.

Having nothing else to offer, I said my goodbyes and stumbled down the narrow stairs into the glare of the setting sun. The street was strangely empty and silent but for the snap of laundry on the lines and the call of a man selling fish scraps from a wagon. It was the end of his route, so he had nothing left but porgie and the severed heads of sea bass that the housewives in the better neighborhoods hadn't wanted.

⊰ 14 ⊱

I COULD HAVE TOLD THE SINGER MAN to stop coming around. Our door had a lock. He couldn't get in unless I let him.

And I kept letting him in.

Within a few weeks it became apparent that the Singer man's long, fine fingers could handle buttons and clasps as well as a needle and thread. No man was more familiar with the ways that fabric could be bound up and taken apart than a sewing machine salesman. The first time he reached out to my neck and separated my collar from my dress I held perfectly still, surprised by how nimble and quick he could be. In the perpetual dusk of my mother's parlor, he worked at my dress like a tailor at a fitting, insisting that I stand in the middle of the room while he moved in a circle around me, releasing hooks and pushing pearl buttons through the loops my mother had stitched to hold them. He touched them lightly, as if he were merely testing their strength or checking for flaws in their design. On every visit he released another of the countless ties and latches with which we girls bound ourselves according to the fashions of 1897. It was a few weeks before he made it past the last one, but the Singer man was patient, smiling down on me as he released them. He closed his eyes like a man at prayer when he kissed me.

My mother had impressed upon me the idea that a girl should never sit alone on a divan with a man. And so we never sat on the divan. The Singer man made sure I always stood.

My knees gave out just once, but he pulled me up again.

THE SINGER MAN KNEW BEFORE I DID. He was precisely attuned to the fit of my dresses, having opened and closed them so many times that winter, even adding his own darts and pleats to make them fit better. When he saw my waist straining against his own stitches, he knew.

There was a place in New Jersey for girls like me, he said. One of the other Singer men told him about it.

Other Singer men? All at once I understood that there must have been other girls in Brooklyn taking sewing lessons from Singer men. Whatever bank of fog had been clouding my mind for the last few months cleared at the mention of other salesmen giving sewing lessons to other girls. The room came into very sharp and cold focus when he said it, and my situation was suddenly apparent to me in a way that it hadn't been before. The words describing my predicament dropped into place like type in a newspaper column.

Still I let him slip his fingers under my skirt to judge whether there was enough fabric to take it out a few inches.

I never once considered telling my mother. There was the fact of the child, and there was the fact that I'd let that man into her house again. A Jew going door-to-door, peddling the machinery of the coming century, taking her daughter apart stitch by stitch, right inside the creaky and cloistered preserve she'd built to hold us.

I didn't know what else to do but let the Singer man take me to Wyckoff and deposit me at Mrs. Florence's Country Home for Friendless and Erring Women. There was never any discussion of seeing a doctor or drinking a syrup or tossing myself down the stairs. I didn't know about any of that. I wouldn't know about it until I got to Wyckoff and the other girls told me.

So without a word, I disappeared. One summer morning I awoke in my own bed in Brooklyn as I always had, with Norma sleeping fitfully beside me, and the next morning I awoke on a wool mattress in Wyckoff, having registered under a false name the night before, presented as the unfortunate cousin of the Singer man.

I left no note behind. I took nothing with me, not even a change of clothes. In Wyckoff I would make myself a new wardrobe. As a parting gift the Singer man left me his sample machine.

⇥ 15 ⇤

THE POTATOES were heaving out of the soil. The leafy tops
had already bloomed and wilted. They'd have to be scrubbed
and packed in straw for the cellar before they turned green. I
kicked at a few of them and they lifted right out of the earth,
scattering the colonies of sow bugs hidden underneath.

Norma was brushing Dolley as I walked into the barn.
When she saw me she gave the horse a pat on the rump,
nudging her back into the stall.

"Why don't you time the pigeons today," she said, "as long
as you're out here and have so little to do."

I did have something to do, but I hadn't yet told Norma
about it. Instead I helped her saddle Dolley and led the horse
around front while she took the pigeon basket and went to
get some birds. She'd installed a pigeon clock in the loft recently, a box containing a special timer that could be stopped
when a pigeon's leg band was dropped into it. At competi-
tions the judges would open each box, start the clocks as the
birds were released, and then lock them shut. Each competi-
tor would carry the box home and wait for their pigeons to

arrive. When they flew into the loft, the band would be removed and pushed through a slot in the box to mark the time. The boxes would have to be returned to the judges to be opened, the flight times recorded, and the velocities calculated.

Norma didn't race her birds, as it would have required her to join a pigeon club and she didn't believe in associating with people on any organized basis, but she liked to keep track of their flying speeds regardless. It had become my responsibility to stand at the loft and mark the time of their return.

She gave me a starting time and I agreed to wait in her dusty and feather-lined loft with a pocket watch in my hand, while she rode to town with a watch of her own. When the hour struck, I was to start the clock and lock the box, knowing that somewhere, a few miles away, she was releasing the birds.

"I'll just go as far as Ridgewood and get my papers," Norma said. She hoisted her pigeon basket and strapped it to Dolley's saddle. From inside the basket came the shuffling of feathers and claws in what I took to be an expression of excitement on the part of the birds.

We checked our watches and conferred on the time I'd start the clock. Then she was gone, down the drive and out of sight, leaving me alone with a half-empty pigeon loft and a plot of potatoes.

I HAD JUST GONE INSIDE when Norma's pigeon bell rang.

"Ach. I've got to go get that bird."

"Go ahead," Fleurette said. She was making her favorite lunch, buttered bread with sugar, and was eager to get me out of the kitchen before I told her she shouldn't waste sugar like that. I'd been threatening to send our sugar to the Belgian soldiers if she kept spooning it onto everything she ate.

But I left her alone with the sugar bowl and ran out to stop the clock. The first pigeon to arrive had disappeared into the farthest corner of the loft, where he picked at his leg band but wouldn't let me remove it. He sat up very straight on his perch, a little opalescent feathered man, eyeing me with an expression of affront and suspicion that was uncannily similar to Norma's. I couldn't stand up straight in the loft, so after I flailed around and got my hair caught in the chicken wire and cursed the bird for its stubbornness, I backed out and stood next to the door as the next ones arrived.

Two more pigeons landed. This time I managed to wrestle the bands off their skinny legs and push them into their slots on the clock. The rest of the flock descended a few minutes later. I was back inside, trying to get the sugar bowl away from Fleurette, when Norma returned.

"How'd they do?" she said.

"The first one wouldn't come to me. He landed about a minute ahead of the others."

Norma dropped a newspaper on the table. "Your friend's in the paper," she said.

Fleurette read the headline: "Chicken Thief Goes to Bergen for Trial?"

"Let me see it." I read just enough to see that it involved Sheriff Heath. This was Norma's way of letting me know that we didn't need a chicken enforcement man involved in our affairs.

"What's the sheriff doing for us?" Fleurette asked.

"He's just going to talk a little sense into Henry Kaufman," I said.

"But Norma doesn't like him?"

"Norma doesn't know him," I said.

"Oh, but I know who he is," Norma said. "He's the one who's always begging the Board of Freeholders for more money for the prisoners."

"What do you mean, money for the prisoners?" Fleurette asked.

"The Freeholders are elected to see to it that the county is run in a businesslike manner, but Sheriff Heath is extravagant with the taxpayers' money," Norma said. "He wants to buy each of his inmates a new suit of clothes and offer them a library of books to read and give them a nice shave and a haircut, too. I'm glad the board won't let him. If he got his way, the criminals in this town would get better treatment than guests at a hotel."

"Can't you find a single polite thing to say about the man who has offered to come to our rescue?" I said.

"He hasn't rescued us yet," Norma said.

MY POTATOES had been slightly damp when I pulled them out and they were drying in the sun. As I was turning them over and brushing the dirt off them, I felt Norma come up behind me.

"You're still thinking about that girl," she said.

I didn't answer. I kept my eyes on the ground.

"We mustn't have anything more to do with Mr. Kaufman," she said. "I've told you so, and Francis agrees."

"When did you talk to Francis?"

"He stopped in yesterday when you were gone."

I stood up and brushed my hands against each other. "And you told him? About the brick? About—"

She shrugged. "Fleurette did. She couldn't resist. And I wasn't going to lie to him. He, of course, feels the whole situation is further proof that we cannot manage on our own."

"It's a bit late for that," I said. "We've been managing just fine."

Norma folded her arms and squinted at the vegetable garden and the giant stands of dandelions casting their shadows. She'd threatened many times to take over the management of the garden if I couldn't keep it tidy. I always told her she was welcome to it and that I would take any chore of hers in exchange. She hadn't accepted the offer yet, but I could tell the weeds were offending her sense of order.

"Some people eat dandelions," I said.

She sniffed. "You didn't tell me what happened with the girl."

"I thought you didn't want anything to do with it," I said.

"I don't, and you shouldn't have gone. But what did she say?"

I tried not to smile. Norma had an endless curiosity about other people's misfortunes. It was why she read so many newspapers. Something terrible was always happening to someone, somewhere, and Norma made it her business to know about it.

"There's not much to tell," I said. "Mr. Kaufman is a brute, but we already knew that. He rents his boarding houses out to young girls, and he goes around to collect rent personally every month. Which is to say—"

"Oh, please don't say it," Norma put in. "I know what that means."

"Lucy sent her boy off in the children's evacuation last year. He never returned, and the lady who was keeping him is gone. She really doesn't know anything more than that."

"She knows not to get the police involved."

"Only because she's afraid for her life," I said.

"As are we all, with Mr. Kaufman making plain his intention to shoot at us."

Dolley knocked over her bucket of oats and Norma retreated to the barn to set it upright. I trailed inside behind her. Dolley blinked calmly at us both. I put a hand on the warm flat patch between her eyes, then thumped her on the rib cage the way Norma always did. It calmed me to put my hands on her. She had a powerful heartbeat and a deep, steadfast breath like something from another time, some calmer era. I leaned against her, this enormous vanilla-colored creature who was so much sturdier than I was.

"I should do something for Lucy," I said, keeping my eyes on the horse.

"No, you shouldn't."

"I think I will. I'll just go into New York and see what I can find out. There's no harm in asking a few questions."

"No harm? After those men came to our house? And called out Fleurette's name like she's a common—"

"I know what they did," I interrupted. "But someone has to go looking for that child."

"I don't see why it has to be you," Norma said.

"Because—" I turned at last to face her. It took everything I had to look her in the eyes. "Because what if no one had gone looking for me?"

⊰ 16 ⊱

AT MRS. FLORENCE'S HOME I never spoke of my family. Most of the girls didn't. A few had run away like I had, and the rest had been deposited there by a tight-lipped, terrified mother or sister, to whom they would return some months later, having agreed upon a story about a semester in boarding school or a visit to an aunt in the distant countryside. One time an infant was left on the doorstep with no mother at all, just an envelope stuffed with money and a note promising that an aunt or uncle would come and claim it as soon as one could be persuaded to do so. No one ever did.

I tried not to think of my own mother. She'd become such an authority on the fates of wayward and vanished girls. Now I was a girl ruined by a traveling salesman and then taken away to a home in New Jersey without a word to her family. Surely that headline had already been written.

Sometimes at night I would dream of my mother at the bottom of a well, darkness all around her, the stars too distant to see. No sound but the rippling of water and the echo of her own voice against the walls. She waited for help, but none came. Week after week I returned to her in my dreams, and she was still there, so far down the well that even the sun never found her.

Did she go to the police? Did she write to our father? Did she walk the streets and ask every grocer and fruit peddler if they'd seen me? I wondered about it every night while I was away. She never spoke to me about that time, and Francis has always been too embarrassed to say much of anything about it, but eventually I got the truth from Norma. It came in scraps of whispered conversation over the years, in those rare moments when we were alone and Norma was in the mood for confidences.

I know that when they woke up and found me gone, they told themselves that I must have had a good reason to go out early in the morning, and that I would return later in the day with an explanation that, although difficult to imagine, would make sense. That night they sat up well past dark around the dim flame of a single gas lamp, knowing, I suppose, that going to bed would be an admission that there was no ordinary, everyday explanation for my disappearance, and that when they awoke in the morning, they would have passed into some new era in their lives—the era that began with the unexplained loss of one of their own, and whatever that might mean next for them. They slept in their chairs to forestall the arrival of that new day, but one by one they stole off to bed in the middle of the night, and then I was well and truly gone.

I can picture Mother in her old stuffed chair in the corner the next morning, stabbing at a piece of embroidery, her lips moving but no sound coming out. She had a way of stopping all conversation with her own grim silence. Poor Francis must've been stunned to realize that it would fall to him, as the man of the house, to bring up the delicate subject of his sister's sudden departure. (And they always thought of it as a departure, seeing no way that I could have been snatched from my bed and carried off against my will.)

Francis offered to make the usual inquiries—to the police, to the shopkeepers in the neighborhood, to the agents at the train station, and to our uncles and their wives, in case I had confided in one of them. But Mother wouldn't allow it. Her refusal told him that she had already passed judgment and decided that whatever the reason for my disappearance, it had to be something shameful, something not to be spoken of, even with the rest of the family. (She always kept my disappearance a secret from her brothers, and later they would refer to the time I enrolled in a secretarial college in Philadelphia. I learned to smile and agree that it had been an interesting course but that secretarial work was not for me.)

Norma agreed with Francis that they should go to the police and speak to anyone in the neighborhood and do whatever else was in their power to bring about my return. Mother was absolute in her opposition, and it was this, I believe, that caused something to break between the two of them. Norma realized, with a sudden cold shock, that if she herself disappeared, Mother would not go looking for her, either. And Norma was bold enough to say this out loud.

"You would do nothing? You would just let me go?"

This was the only part of the story Norma ever told me in any detail. She was still hurt by it years later. Mother had taken Norma's chin forcefully in her hand and said, "You would never disappear. You would never treat me like that."

That's when Norma understood what Mother had really intended with her newspaper stories of disgraced girls. They were a warning of not just what could happen to us out in the wide and unruly world, but also of what would happen if we tried to come home again.

Then my brother heard about another girl who had been visited by a sewing machine salesman. She had vanished, too, but had come home on her own before the baby was born and confessed it all.

Francis whispered his suspicion to Norma, thinking she would deny that her sister would do any such thing. But she turned pale and reached into her sewing basket to show him an unfamiliar bobbin she'd found just a few days earlier under the china cabinet, one that didn't fit Mother's machine. They both realized at once what it meant.

Still they weren't ready to tell Mother until they could be certain. Francis had been unable to learn the name of the home to which the other girl had been sent, so it fell to Norma to write letters to every girls' home in New York, New Jersey, and Pennsylvania, and that is what she did, night after night, writing out a new copy of the letter with a description of me and the date of my disappearance and posting it every morning to a different address.

By the time her letter reached Wyckoff, the baby had been born.

⇥ 17 ⇤

THE TRAIN TO NEW YORK was so crowded that I could find no seat except one next to an old woman carrying a bag of rabbit pelts. It quickly became evident why no one else was seated next to her. A cloud of ammonia hung around the bag, as did a colony of something tiny and dreadful: gnats or, worse, lice. She didn't get off in Rutherford or any of the other stops just outside Paterson. She was bound for the city, probably aiming to deliver her rancid bundle to one of those dingy furriers at the edge of the garment district that dealt in snakeskin and small game. As soon as the train stopped for a minute, I moved to another car. Finally a boy saw me looking for a seat and gave me his.

It was a relief to get off that train and out of the station. I realized that I couldn't remember the last time I'd been to New York alone. My uncles still lived in Brooklyn with their wives and children, and sometimes they'd have us to dinner on a Sunday. Once or twice we'd taken Fleurette to a play. But it never occurred to me that I could come on my own, and I had never once been confronted by the entirety of the city, by the enormity of it, by the possibility that I could go anywhere and do anything.

I knew what I had to do at that moment. I set out for the building on East Thirtieth where Regina Doyle was believed to have lived with Lucy's baby. I rushed past the shops selling buttons and shoe leather, past the lunch counters and the grocers with their cartons of soft apples in the street, past the office buildings with gold lettering across their windows.

In a short while I arrived at the address I'd been given. It was just an ordinary brownstone in the middle of a row of similarly ordinary four-story buildings. The third-floor windows had been outfitted with flower boxes that held the russet stubs of neglected geraniums.

A woman passed me on the sidewalk and climbed the stairs. "Pardon me," I said, running up behind her. "I'm looking for someone who used to live here."

"I don't know him," she said, never turning back to look at me.

"No, I was wondering—" and then she was gone, the door slamming shut behind her before I could get hold of it.

I tried the door and found it locked. There was a row of door-bells, but I didn't recognize any of the names on the plate.

From around the corner came a delivery boy carrying packages from the butcher. I asked him if he remembered a woman named Regina Doyle living in the building and he shook his head. "Don't recall, miss," he said, never slowing down.

"But you must make deliveries here," I called, addressing his back as he walked away.

Nothing.

It hadn't occurred to me that people would refuse to answer a question put to them directly. It must have been apparent to everyone I approached that I had no real authority. I had no card, no credential, no letter of introduction. And so I stood on the street and waited for something to come to me — a witness, a clue, a better idea. Nothing did.

For lack of another plan, I took a walk around the block and stopped in a corner market, then a shoe shop, and then a bookstore, to ask after Regina Doyle and the baby. No one had heard of her. It didn't help that I had so little by way of a description of the two of them. I stopped a man peddling flowers and a girl carrying her baby brother. They didn't have a single word for me.

Down the street I located a photographer's studio, situated in a basement apartment and identified by a brass plaque on the railing. "LAMOTTE STUDIOS," it read. "PHOTOGRAPHY. ALL SUBJECTS." There was no bell to ring. I pushed the door open and found myself not in a portrait studio, as I had expected, but in a cramped office littered with paperwork and stacks upon stacks of the same kind of large brown envelope. Affixed to each one was a clasp with a red string. The strings seemed to be alive, as if they were crawling over the mess and not merely dangling from it.

If there was a lamp anywhere in the room, I couldn't find it. The only light came from the front window, which was half covered with the sort of greenish-brown moss that grew on the steps of all basement apartments out of reach of the sun.

From behind a low door a man's voice called, "Two more minutes!" I replied that I'd wait, although I wasn't sure what I was waiting for. There came the sound of water sloshing around and a switch clicking on and off again. I guessed that he was developing photographs and I was proven right when he emerged from a room with an entirely black interior. He wore the sort of rubber apron that a butcher would wear, and he smelled of a mixture of sulfur and gas. He was a short, pudgy man with thick spectacles and a badly made wig of brown hair that failed to cover his silver sideburns.

"Oh!" he said, looking up at me in surprise. "I was expecting the boy."

"What boy?"

He pushed his spectacles up his nose and leaned forward on his toes to give me a better look. "An errand boy," he said. "You are not—no, never mind. Forgive me. I am Henri La-Motte. How do you do?"

"Constance Kopp," I said. "I know the name LaMotte. *Votre famille vient-elle des Côtes-d'Armor?*"

He laughed. "Oh, no, no. I forgot my French as fast as my mother tried to teach it to me. Girls listen to their mothers. Boys don't."

"You may be right about that," I said. "My brother never spoke a word that wasn't good Brooklyn English. My mother was heartbroken that her grandchildren sounded like New Yorkers." I surprised myself. I couldn't remember the last time I'd spoken about my family to a stranger. But there was something so jovial and relaxed about Mr. LaMotte. He seemed to invite confidences.

"Well," he said. "Miss Kopp, who, judging from her name, speaks German as well as she does French—"

"Die Familie meiner Mutter stammt aus Österreich."

"Oui. Or *ja.* Are we here for language lessons, or do I have an envelope for you?"

"An envelope?" I asked, looking around at the piles of them. "No, I just wanted to ask you something. You see, I'm looking for someone . . ."

"Oh, yes," he said. "I understand. But you don't start with me."

"What?"

"The investigator calls me once you've made your arrangements."

"Investigator?"

He took a step closer to me and looked up, bemused, over the tops of his lenses.

"Yes. A detective," he said. "You wish to find someone? We take the photographs, but we only ride along with the investigators. We don't go running around on our own. They call us when they are ready for us."

"You work for detectives?" I said. "I thought this was a portrait studio."

He laughed. "Oh, I gave that up years ago. Everyone with a camera and a set of draperies runs a portrait studio. Miss Kopp, I am in the business of collecting evidence. My photographers take pictures to be furnished as exhibits at court proceedings. Or, more frequently, they take pictures that persuade people to stay out of the courts. If you'd like a portrait, I could send you—"

"Oh, no," I said, still trying to follow what he was telling me. "No, my question is about the neighborhood. I'm looking for a boy who lived on the next block."

"He didn't work for me," Mr. LaMotte said.

"No, he was—he is—a baby. A lady who lived around the corner took him in and now we can't find her." I gave her name and address.

Mr. LaMotte pursed his lips and drew in a long breath. "Oh, *mademoiselle*, you've found trouble. Did you go looking for it, or did it come to you?"

"I . . . well, I suppose it came to me."

"Then send it back!" Mr. LaMotte said, turning to pull off his rubber apron and hang it on a hook. He sat down at his desk and nearly disappeared behind the clutter. "Send it back, Miss Kopp, and go back to Brooklyn yourself. That's my advice." He picked up a pen to indicate that our conversation was over.

"I don't live in Brooklyn anymore," I said. "I live just outside Paterson now. I'm only here for the day to—"

"Paterson?" he said, looking up at me again and pushing that ridiculous hairpiece higher up his forehead so he could see past it. "Does this have something to do with the silk strikes?"

"Yes!" I said, a little too loudly. "It might. The baby was evacuated during the strikes."

He shook his head. "There were all kinds of Bolsheviks living over there during the strikes. You used to be able to hear them arguing from a block away. The police could stand right out on the sidewalk and learn every one of their plans. But they've all moved on now."

At that moment, the door opened and a boy entered. "There you are!" said Mr. LaMotte, clearly relieved by the interruption. "We have three cases for you, is that right?" The boy nodded and looked at me suspiciously.

"That's all right. Miss Kopp was just leaving. *Veuillez m'excuser, mademoiselle.* I have nothing more for you. Good day." He turned to dig through his empire of envelopes.

There was nothing to do but nod and take my leave. I wrote down my name and address and left it among the papers on his desk in case he remembered anything that might help. Then I was back on the street, puzzling over the slim bit of information the photographer had given me. I walked around the block again and stood facing Regina Doyle's building, looking up at its windows, every one of them curtained and closed.

Finally the door opened and a little boy ran out. This time I was up the stairs quick enough to catch it. I turned to say something to the child, but he was across the street and out of earshot before I could.

The door closed behind me and I stood facing a row of mailboxes in the vestibule. None of them bore the name Doyle, or any name that looked familiar to me. I could see no alternative but to go from one apartment to the next.

I rapped on the first door and got no answer. At the second apartment a girl of about ten opened the door. She held a baby on her hip. I asked if her mother was home, and the girl shook her head and gently closed the door and locked it.

I heard the music of a flute behind the next door. As I raised my hand to knock, a voice came from the stairs behind me.

"Miss! Didn't you see the sign?"

I spun around and faced an older, heavyset man in workman's clothes. He lumbered down the stairs, keeping his eyes on his feet and huffing loudly.

"A sign? No, I—"

He stopped on the bottommost step, panting.

"No solicitation. Take your pamphlets or your samples or what have you, and go on down the street. No one in this building wants to be bothered."

The flute music stopped. I supposed the flautist was listening.

"I'm not here to sell anything. I'm looking for a lady who

used to live here. Regina Doyle. She had a baby with her, but it didn't belong to her."

He stopped to consider that, then said, "Didn't belong to her? Then what was it doing here?"

"Sir, I—"

"Never mind. Don't know her. Go tell it to someone else." He waved me toward the door again. Seeing no way to get past the man and up the stairs, I wished him a good day and let myself out.

I was still standing on the steps a few minutes later when the door opened and a young man stepped out. He was so thin that his collarbone protruded through his shirt. He closed the door quietly behind him and said in a near-whisper, "Are you the one looking for Mrs. Doyle?"

"Yes. Was that you I heard playing the flute?"

He nodded and took my arm, leading me down the front steps. "I don't know where she is," he said in the same low voice, "but she was in with a whole gang of unionists. They started getting Black Hand threats and they all moved out at once."

"What kind of threats?"

He turned to look back at the building as if he was afraid someone was listening. "Usual things. Fire. Kidnapping. Then they snuck away in the middle of the night."

"Have you any idea where Mrs. Doyle might be?"

He shook his head. "Run off by the Black Hand men. That's all I know."

I thanked him and he darted back upstairs.

Was Henry Kaufman a Black Hander? The papers had been filled with stories of Black Hand crime for the last few years, most of it conducted by Italians who engaged in a trade that consisted primarily of making threats against anyone who might be in a position to pay to make the threats stop. The demands were simple and crudely worded. The usual method was to send a note promising a fire or a kidnapping unless a sum of money was paid, customarily a thousand dollars.

If the threat was kidnapping, it was usually aimed at a pretty young girl, the inference being that the girl would be sold into white slavery. A notion like that always made a father open his checkbook, no matter how much the police advised against paying them off. Any man would gladly pay a thousand dollars just to rid his mind of the idea of his child forced into prostitution.

Norma read these stories aloud to us, just like Mother used to. She was fond of shuffling between the crime page and the society page to point out that many girls, shortly after being the subject of such a threat, found themselves suddenly engaged to be married, often to an associate of the fathers who had been pressed into service. Let her husband keep her from harm, the poor father must have thought. A man can only take so much.

A wind had come up along Sixth Avenue and I had to lean into it and fight my way back to the train station. Having spent a day in the crowds and confusion of New York City, I could see the futility of this sort of search. Finding one small boy in a city of five million seemed impossible. It wasn't hard to disappear. I'd done it myself.

⇥ 18 ⇤

FLEURETTE HAD A KNACK for overhearing everything. She was small and crafty, able to slide behind a door or duck under a window without anyone noticing. She was possessed of especially fine hearing and had a musical ear that could follow the cadences of two hushed voices and pick out their meanings. There was no way to keep a secret from her in our house: she would peer through keyholes, run outside and lean against doorjambs, or climb into the attic and press her ear against the gaps in the floorboards. Even the chicken coop was not safe, as she would steal into the pigeon loft and listen through the wide planks. In fact, the only way for Norma and I to have a private conversation was to walk out to the middle of our meadow, where we could speak quietly to one another while looking in all directions to be assured that Fleurette was not creeping up on us—though as soon as she realized what we were doing, she would come running at us, and we'd have to finish our conversation in rapid-fire monosyllables to get it over with before she flopped, panting, at our feet.

When I returned home from the city, it was dark and windy and I didn't feel like walking through the meadow, so I allowed Fleurette to hear my account of the day. Norma insisted that I keep it brief, seeking only reassurance that I hadn't gotten us into any more trouble. Once she was satisfied that I had learned nothing of value and met no one who knew anything about Lucy Blake's child, she refused to allow another word to be spoken about it in her presence. Fleurette listened, wide-eyed, but didn't say anything until Norma went upstairs to bed.

"I think the flautist knows more than he let on," she said darkly. "He hears everything that goes on in that building. He seems so innocent with his music and that little blue parrot that goes everywhere with him . . ."

"He doesn't have a parrot," I said.

She cocked her head and looked at me thoughtfully. "You just didn't see it," she said. "You should've had me along. I could have snuck into his room while you were talking to him on the street. He might even have the baby. It could've been right there, under your nose, and you missed it."

"Don't imagine things," I said. "This isn't a fairy tale. It's a real baby and his mother wants him back."

Fleurette nodded. "But does Lucy really think she can keep a baby all by herself?"

"What do you mean?" I said, although I knew exactly what she meant and there was a pounding in my head as I tried to come up with an answer.

"She doesn't have a husband. She can't keep a baby. People will know."

She was stretched out on the divan and I was in the armchair next to her. Her feet were perched atop my knees, her black-stockinged toes wiggling in the air. This was nothing but a diversion to her.

I took one of those squirming feet in my hand. "I don't know how she thought she'd manage," I said, "but that is not our concern. If she won't speak to the sheriff, there's nothing more I can do for her."

"You're not going to see her again?" Fleurette sounded crushed.

"I don't know why I would," I said.

"Do you mean it's over?"

"I hope so."

"Well, what will we do now?"

ONE OF THE STRANGER EFFECTS of this business with Henry Kaufman was the way it dislodged us from our daily routines. It was as if the brick had shattered not just a window, but the carefully structured order we'd once had in our lives. Over the next few weeks Norma and Fleurette devoted themselves entirely to their own amusements, turning our household into a sort of half carnival, half menagerie. Fleurette converted the parlor into a theater, complete with a stage concealed behind a curtain of scandalous vermilion, three rows of plush seats, and an ingenious but dangerous arrangement of footlights cobbled together from all the old oil lamps placed in dark corners about the house. She put on performances nightly, most of which were attended by no one at all, but once I was horrified to walk in and find the young man from the dairy seated in the audience as if he had purchased a ticket. Fleurette was performing an Oriental dance of her own invention, accompanied by a fan of ostrich feathers she'd purchased from a street vendor in Paterson and colored a dull, vegetal pink using some sort of berry that fruited around our property. I sent the boy running out the kitchen door, warning him to make his exit quietly lest Norma hear him. I truly believe she would have gone after him with a fire iron.

Norma herself was no less of a problem. One of her pigeons had been injured on a long flight and she was nursing it back to health in her bedroom. Its foot was crushed and she kept what was left of it (the foot) in a bandage. Although she couldn't be sure, she thought that one of the toothpick-thin bones in its wing had also snapped during whatever sort of mishap had ensnared it and caused it to lose its message. ("Girl Is Sent to Reformatory" was the lost message, which she recited later to Fleurette, to no effect.) She fashioned a splint for it, but the splint kept the wing from folding back into its place, so the pigeon had a constant lopsided appearance, one wing half extended off the edge of the little tufted pillow it slept on.

She thought it might distress the pigeon to be kept locked in a room all day, far away from its customary perch in the loft, so she installed an old brass birdcage at the foot of her bed and brought in a fresh batch of pigeons every day to keep their injured flock-mate company. It didn't seem to do much good. The poor fellow slept most of the day and only occasionally opened an eye to peer at his feathered friends through the polished bars. Then, feeling that the other pigeons might be bored, Norma began conducting training exercises in her room, entreating them to fly over to a lampshade and back in exchange for a handful of bread crumbs.

She kept the birds clean—Norma was always ruthlessly sanitary when it came to her birds—so there was no odor, but there was a sound produced by their activities. One would not think that the burbling and rustling of feathers emanating from two or three captive pigeons would amount to much, but I heard it all over the house. There was a distinctly avian character about our place. I would not have been surprised if one came flying at me in the stairwell. I took to walking very carefully past her room, always prepared to duck.

Meals had become irregular events. We still had vegetables coming in from the garden, so some manner of soup was always on the stove, but Norma and Fleurette had decided to dip into it whenever they walked by rather than sit down together. Francis stopped in from time to time with one of Bessie's overloaded dinner baskets ("I don't know how that woman accidentally makes five extra pies, when I'm doing everything I can to put them away," he said), so in addition to the soup, we survived on twelve o'clock pie, Bessie's name for a dish made of leftover roast and potatoes, and her fine apple turnovers.

Washing up had also fallen out of favor. A pot got scrubbed when it was needed for something else, books and papers and other such clutter were only put away when the space was about to be used for some other activity, and the silver was never polished. Where once we had a day for airing out the beds and a day for scrubbing the floors and a day for washing clothes, now we weren't devoting any time at all to cleaning. I wouldn't have guessed that such a carefully ordered household could come apart so easily.

It had always been my responsibility to look after the money, and I continued those duties, as simple as they were. I paid the bills, watched our dwindling savings, and tried to find a way to carve off another plot of land to sell. I wondered if I could persuade Norma to take an interest in a small dairy operation of her own or to expand our flock of chickens and sell the eggs. But I knew we couldn't sell enough eggs to see us through.

In the evenings Fleurette sat with her sewing and Norma read her papers while I looked over the ledgers at my desk. There had been no sign of Henry Kaufman. Whatever Sheriff Heath had done must have worked.

ONE TUESDAY AT BREAKFAST, I decided I'd had enough of our slipshod ways and announced that we would spend the morning canning green beans and tomatoes, starting immediately and concluding at lunch, when the heat would make it too unpleasant to continue. Fleurette pouted and protested until I offered her a string of Mother's old cut-glass beads, meant to look like diamonds and emeralds, and told her that she could wear them one day for each jar of preserves we finished.

Norma disappeared early in the morning, sending a message by pigeon post that she must have been saving for this occasion: "Girl Scalded in Kitchen." Without her help the work went slowly, and we only managed three dozen jars by lunchtime. I left Fleurette to clean up and ducked out to pick up a few things in Hackensack. On the way home, I stopped in a bakery and bought a box of macaroons.

I was walking back to the trolley just as a dancing class was dismissed for the day. As the children rushed past me, the girls twirling around to hear the rustle of their skirts and the boys picking at their high, stiff collars, I wondered at the futility of teaching children to dance. What did we hope to accomplish by forcing them into those awkward pairings? They would find their way to each other on their own, without any help from their parents and their dancing teachers. And just as easily as they came together, they would come apart again.

As I was distracted by those thoughts, I didn't notice that an automobile had driven past and circled the block, rolling slowly by and coming to a stop just ahead of me. My whole body went cold at once when I saw it. I couldn't take a breath.

The passenger door opened and I looked quickly around, hoping to see someone standing nearby who could witness whatever was about to happen. It was a busy afternoon downtown, but no one seemed to be watching me.

"Miss Kopp," a voice said. "Wouldn't you like to ride with us?"

Sheriff Heath. At last I could breathe again.

He came toward me, wearing a funny crooked smile. "Were you expecting someone else?" His voice was warm and quiet.

"I do seem to run into him at the oddest times," I said.

"Maybe it would help if you stayed away from him," he said.

"I have! I haven't seen him at all!" I didn't mention the visit to Lucy's flat.

"That's good." Another one of those friendly half-smiles. He was looking at me very intently, the way you might peer into a bird's nest, hoping to find something fine and miraculous inside. I didn't know what to make of it.

"Now, won't you let us drive you home? We can talk about our friend Mr. Kaufman along the way."

We were attracting attention on the street. A mother was standing on the sidewalk with a baby on her hip, and four or five boys had gathered around the automobile. A deputy, looking rather embarrassed, emerged from the driver's seat and let the boys have a look inside.

"I suppose I'd better," I said. "Only I don't know what my sisters will make of me being driven home by the sheriff."

"I would like to speak to your sisters," he said, opening the door for me.

I wondered what performance Fleurette had rehearsed for the evening and what state of mind Norma might possibly be in.

"I'm not at all certain they're in any condition to receive visitors."

I SETTLED INTO THE BACK SEAT and started to direct the deputy to my house, but Sheriff Heath waved me away. "We know the way," he said.

"You've been there?"

"I'm keeping an eye out, that's all."

We rode along in silence for a minute.

"Whatever happened with that girl?" Sheriff Heath said. "I thought you were going to send her to me."

"She's afraid," I said. "She thinks he'll come after her if she goes to the police."

The sheriff and his deputy exchanged glances but said nothing. We were out of Hackensack by this time. The country road that led to our farm was always busy in the late afternoon as people and animals concluded their business for the day. It was not unusual to have to stop for a herd of slow-moving Guernsey cows. We passed a bakery truck headed back to the city after making its deliveries, and I realized quite abruptly that I should have thought to bring home something more substantial for dinner, as we had depleted the last basket from Bessie. We would probably be reduced to eating macaroons and boiled eggs and last summer's pickles.

"Well, I haven't forgotten your troubles with Kaufman," he said, "and I hope this takes care of it. We have a judge who will accept a complaint about the damages to your buggy. We just need you to sign a statement and appear at the courthouse to swear to its accuracy. Then the judge will order the fine and require Mr. Kaufman to stay away from you. We'll go collect the fine. You don't even have to see him. I can't say what effect any of this will have on him, but it's the best I can do."

"You . . . you filed charges? Against Henry Kaufman?"

Sheriff Heath looked at me quizzically. "Isn't that what you wanted?"

"I thought you were just going to talk to him."

"Well, I did talk to him, Miss Kopp. I told him to stay away from you and your sisters and to pay for the damage he did. Has he stayed away?"

"I think so."

"You think so?"

"Yes. He's stayed away."

"And now he's going to pay for the damages. This is how we prosecute criminals in Bergen County. Is that all right with you?"

I sighed and sat back in my seat. It didn't seem like I could refuse.

• • •

WHEN WE ARRIVED AT THE HOUSE, I led the men inside, realizing that there was a time, not long ago, when riding in a car with the sheriff, much less bringing him home with me, would have been a shocking and outrageous act. But since the collapse of the general order of our household, I thought little of it.

Norma heard me come in and walked down the stairs carrying her injured pigeon on a pillow. Her stockinged feet appeared first, and then the pillow in her arms.

"It's a good thing you're home. This requires two sets of hands. If you could just hold him while I—"

At last her face emerged from behind the banister. She stopped upon seeing the men in our front parlor. She must have recognized Sheriff Heath from the papers, because she frowned at him with the kind of deep-seated resolve that could not be summoned upon first impression. As with most people Norma disapproved of, she'd already put a great deal of effort into it and had no trouble in recalling her position.

The sheriff must have been accustomed to such treatment, because he simply introduced himself and his deputy.

Silence. Finally I said, "This is Norma. One of her carrier pigeons has been injured, and she has seen fit to move it indoors for its convalescence and to treat it like a member of the household."

The sheriff lit up at the mention of the pigeons. "One of my deputies has been asking about keeping pigeons," he said. "He thought it would be a good activity for the inmates, but my superiors don't want them at the prison. They're concerned about prisoners sending messages to their criminal associates."

I could tell that Norma was trying not to speak to the sheriff, but she couldn't help herself. "They only fly home," she said. "They're not postmen. They don't deliver along a route."

A wide grin emerged from under Heath's mustache. "I told them that myself, but . . ." and he shrugged at the pointlessness of arguing with one's superiors.

I had to admire the way he handled that. I didn't suspect for a minute that his deputy had been asking about keeping pigeons. But he said the one thing that he knew would draw her into conversation.

Norma snorted and turned to go back upstairs. "If you're looking for Fleurette," she called over her shoulder, "she went out to get some frogs."

The deputy and the sheriff looked at me with bemused astonishment. What sort of sideshow were we running here?

"When my sister was a little girl," I said, "a lady down the road used to pay her to catch frogs. Fleurette liked having an excuse to splash around in the creek. Frogs didn't bother her the way they did other girls. She'd catch a dozen in an afternoon and earn herself a little bit of money. The lady moved away a few years ago, but Fleurette still likes to go down there and get those frogs."

"You don't eat them, do you?" asked the deputy.

"I'm afraid we do," I said. "Would you like me to go down to the creek and get her? Maybe she'll sell you a frog for your dinner."

"That's all right, Miss Kopp," Sheriff Heath said, ushering his deputy out the door before he could say another word. "We've met the youngest Miss Kopp already."

"What? When was that?"

He opened the door and turned to smile at me. "We attended a matinee here in your living room recently. I believe it was the day you went to New York." He closed the door very gently in my face.

DINNER THAT NIGHT consisted of my mother's *ragoût de grenouilles*, the one dish Fleurette ever bothered to learn how to make, and only because she so loved to eat her prey. It was accompanied by a watercress salad and a lengthy scolding from me about the dangers of letting strange men into the house.

"They weren't strange men," Fleurette said between loud slurps of the sauce. "They weren't strange at all. They sat very quietly in the third row and applauded at all the right moments. I only wish they hadn't left before my encore."

I looked to Norma for reinforcement, but she'd been silent all evening. "What goes on around here when I'm away?" I said at last. "Do you just leave the front door open and let anyone walk in?"

"They aren't just anyone," said Fleurette. She pushed a strand of hair under a hat of blackish-green ravens' feathers she'd taken from Mother's closet and fixed in place with her old amber pins. I tried not to imagine what the frogs must have thought when they saw her coming in that hat. "They are sworn public officers. And apparently they are friends of yours. If you can invite them in, I don't see why I can't. Besides, they spend so much time sitting out there along the road in that stuffy automobile. They deserve to be entertained."

"You don't mean to say you saw them on our road?" Norma said, breaking her silence at last. "Right outside our house?"

Fleurette shrugged. "I thought Constance invited them," she said.

Norma stood up and dropped her bowl into the sink. "One doesn't *invite* the sheriff to sit outside with a man and a gun. If he's here, it can only mean that we are in more danger than we realized, and it's all because Constance persists in bothering Henry Kaufman."

"I haven't bothered him in some time," I said.

"You've sent the sheriff over to bother him, and that's the same thing."

"The sheriff seems to feel the danger has passed," I said. "Mr. Kaufman will be made to pay a fine and that should settle him down. We haven't seen him once since the sheriff took up the case, isn't that true?"

"You're very trusting of him," Norma said, putting on water for coffee, which she always drank after dinner. "I've said that I take a dim view of the police, and I think I'll extend that line of thinking to the sheriff, who seems not to know the most rudimentary fact about a carrier pigeon, suggesting an incurious mind. I don't think he has much to offer us, do you?"

Without waiting for an answer, she brushed her hands briskly on her skirt and went out the kitchen door to lock up the chickens. I scraped my spoon around the bottom of the bowl. Fleurette stood up, adjusting her ridiculous hat. "I've been working on a new dancing frock," she said. "Would you help me pin up the hem?"

I looked up at her, this little girl who started twirling as soon as she could walk. "Yes, of course. Go and try it on."

⇥ 19 ⇤

I DIDN'T KNOW I'd had a girl at first. All I saw was a head of black hair and the white apron of the nurse carrying her away. I had agreed to give up the child, but at that moment the wildest craving came over me. In my delirium I dreamt of mother cats biting and licking their kittens, and I imagine I would have nearly devoured that infant if only they would have given her back to me.

The doctor attending to me suspected a hemorrhage and was about to go after me with a curette. The ether cone descended but I kicked and fought it. There was a clatter of metal across the floor and a man shouting and then nothing but whiteness all around me.

I awoke hours later in the most fantastic purple darkness. It could have been the effects of the ether, but I felt weightless and clear-headed, and rose from my bed in the recovery room as lightly as steam lifting out of water. Somewhere under that roof was a child who belonged to me. The only thing in the world for me to do was to go and get it.

The night nurse dozed in her chair and didn't stir as I glided past. Not a single lamp had been left burning in the hall, but I knew the way to the nursery as if I'd walked it all my life. No squeak of the floorboard, no shuffle across the rug, no groan of the hinges alerted the nurses to my presence. I was inside the nursery with the door closed behind me, and the black-haired baby was in my arms, and the other babies—there were three more of them—wriggled and sighed and chortled up at me as if they knew exactly what I was doing.

And what did I do? I walked right out the front door with her. I took her down the long drive, which was dense with the overgrowth of climbing roses, and down the road into the cool October night, wearing only my nightgown and a pair of knitted slippers. The baby was wrapped in flannel and didn't seem to mind at all. She had a tiny pinched face like a flower that hadn't yet bloomed and lips that worked back and forth even though her eyes weren't open. Along that road I gave her a name. Fleurette Eugenie Kopp.

Eugenie for her father, Eugene. The Singer man.

In the months of my confinement, I had felt only shame when I thought of him and of what I'd allowed him to do to me. But now I was walking under a velvet-dark sky so filled with stars that I couldn't pick them apart, and the air was alive with the scent of grass and wood smoke and the sweet yeasty baby. Adding his name to hers seemed at that moment like putting a period at the end of a sentence. It was where he ended and she began.

The nurses found us in a hay barn the next morning. Of course they did. I was not the first girl to disappear in the night, and none of us, in our condition, could get far. Perhaps that's why they didn't take better precautions against us running away.

Fleurette was well and fed. She was a hungry girl, and although I'd had no instruction, there were enough natural forces at work on both of us to bring it about. The nurses sent for the wagon and brought us back to Mrs. Florence's, where Fleurette surely would have been taken from me again were it not for a letter that had arrived from Brooklyn that very morning.

October 9, 1897

```
Miss Norma Kopp
92 South 8th Street
Brooklyn, New York

Dear Mrs. Florence,

    I write to inquire after the whereabouts of
my sister, whose name is Constance Amélie Kopp,
although she may not have given that name to
you, who left a loving family on the 17 of July
to seek the care of a home such as yours. Her
mother wishes every day for her safe return and
is prepared to adopt the child, if there is one,
and raise it as the youngest member of a re-
spectable family. Any expenses incurred by her
care will be gladly repaid. She is a tall girl
of nearly six feet in height and eighteen years,
with hair more auburn than brown, eyes a light
```

hazel, a firm and decisive mouth and a tongue that speaks French and German as well as her native English.

With a word from you that such a girl is under your care, we will come promptly to collect her and express to you our endless and abiding gratitude for offering refuge to someone who must have been rendered so insensible with fright over her condition that she forgot that the most suitable home for a child of hers was the one in which she already lived.

Hoping for a joyful outcome to this most difficult trial, I am

Yours very truly,
Norma Charlotte Kopp

❧ 20 ❧

September 15, 1914

BY MY OATH I, Constance Amélie Kopp of Wyckoff,
New Jersey, swear that one Henry Kaufman, of
Paterson, New Jersey, was the owner and driver
of a certain automobile which negligently collided with a buggy in which I was seated along
with my sisters Norma Charlotte Kopp and
Fleurette Eugenie Kopp, resulting in damages to
said buggy in the amount of fifty dollars, which
Mr. Henry Kaufman has refused to pay in spite of
numerous attempts to collect the amount owed.

Sworn before the Honorable Court of
Passaic County, New Jersey,
Constance Amélie Kopp

. . .

IT HAD RAINED that morning and there were steaming brown puddles on the sidewalk. I lifted my skirt, which left me without a hand to put over my nose. Paterson had never smelled so foul after a rain. I didn't want to imagine what must have overflowed and leaked out into the gutters.

If I hadn't looked up before we began climbing the courthouse steps, I would have run right into Henry Kaufman. He had his feet planted on the top step, and he stood with his hands in his pockets and his hat pushed back on his forehead, with all the lazy confidence of the idle rich. With him were two of his men: the one with the glass eye, and the enormous one with shoulders as broad as snowplows. A third man stood nearby, puffing desperately on a pipe. He was tall and thin, with curly hair that tended toward red, and gold spectacles.

Sheriff Heath saw them just after I did. He took my arm and steered me away from them.

"John," he said to the curly-haired man as we passed.

"Sheriff," the man said.

Those two words were enough to catch Henry Kaufman's attention. "Is she under arrest, Sheriff?" he called after us. "Because she's been harassing me at my place of business. Let the record show . . ."

Sheriff Heath pushed me through the courthouse door amid the laughter and back-slapping of Mr. Kaufman and his friends. I was relieved to feel the door close behind me. Inside, the courthouse lobby was cool and quiet.

"I thought he wouldn't be here," I said.

"I didn't think he would. He's up to something. I don't know how he roped a lawyer into this."

"That was his lawyer?" I asked.

The sheriff nodded and led me down a corridor lined on

both sides with men in shabby worsted suits or overalls. There was hardly enough room for us to get past.

Someone bumped into me and I nearly fell against the sheriff. "What is this?"

"It's the last of the charges against the silk strikers."

"A year later?"

"They were charged with unlawful assemblage and sentenced to hard labor, but never served their sentences," he said in a low voice. "Now there are rumors of another strike, and the police chief issued new warrants for all of them, just to discourage them from striking again. Today they had to appear or be arrested. Fortunately for them, they're going before one of the only judges who is at all sympathetic to their cause."

"You mean that he's not a friend of the silk men. Which is why we're going to see him."

He smiled. "That's the general idea." He took me down a side corridor away from the crowd. At an unmarked door he stopped and said, "Remember, this isn't a trial. Just swear to your statement and sign when the judge asks you to. That's all we're here to do."

I nodded and he held the door open. Just inside was a row of men, their backs to us. The sheriff cleared his throat and they turned and parted. The courtroom was as noisy as a carnival, with a clerk barking orders and spectators shouting and grumbling. Every seat in the gallery was taken, and there was hardly a spot around the edge of the room that wasn't occupied by a mill worker leaning against a wall and waiting his turn.

"I didn't know I'd have to do this in front of anyone," I whispered to the sheriff.

"It's a full docket," he said. "You'll be next." He gave a salute to the clerk, who nodded and whispered to the judge. The judge—a jowly, watery-eyed old man with white whiskers sprouting from his cheeks and ears—called out, "All right, Bob, bring her here."

The sheriff took my arm and led me to the front of the room. He handed the paper to the judge, who fumbled with his spectacles and read it to himself in a low mumble. Then he looked up at me.

"Is this all true?"

I looked at Sheriff Heath, who just nodded. "Yes, Your Honor," I said.

"And this man—Henry Kaufman—he's been given ample opportunity to pay the charges?"

"He has," said the sheriff.

"And is he here today?" The judge looked around the courtroom.

There was a shuffling sound from across the room and the curly-headed man stepped out of the crowd. He pulled a pipe out of his mouth to speak.

"Your Honor."

The judge looked around and found him. "John? You're not involved in this mess, are you?"

"I'm afraid I am." He seemed sad to admit it. "I have represented the Kaufman family's business interests for many years, and recently Mr. Henry Kaufman has engaged me to handle his personal affairs as well."

Sheriff Heath sighed and shook his head. The attorney stepped forward and the two of them exchanged polite nods.

"If Your Honor will permit it, my client begs the court to hear his statement."

148

"Where is your client?" the judge said.

The attorney cleared his throat. "My client prefers to wait outside due to the—ah—due to the interests of the parties—ah—other proceedings taking place today in Your Honor's court that might—"

"Never mind," said the judge. "Quickly. I was promised this was a simple matter."

"May it please the court," the lawyer said, pulling a piece of paper from his coat pocket and unfolding it. "The statement"—and here he glanced meaningfully at Sheriff Heath—"which I am obligated to read on my client's behalf in spite of counsel to the contrary offered as a matter of—"

The judge groaned. "Read it."

The lawyer rattled the paper, adjusted his stance, and began. "Mr. Henry Kaufman, of Kaufman Silk Dyeing Company of Paterson, New Jersey—"

The chatter in the room got louder as the mill workers realized that the man in question was a factory owner. No wonder Henry Kaufman didn't want to show his face.

"That's enough!" shouted the judge. The room quieted. "Go on, John."

The lawyer looked nervously around and repeated the opening line to himself before continuing in a monotone. "Hereby refutes all charges leveled against him pertaining to an incident on the fourteenth day of July, in the year 1914, in which a buggy under the control of the three Kopp sisters did willfully collide with Mr. Kaufman's automobile, inflicting substantial damage on said automobile, and, further, Mr. Kaufman alleges that Miss Constance Kopp is a unionist and anarchist sympathizer who has harassed him at his place of business and spoken to his workers with the intention of inciting strikes and riots among a peaceable workforce, and that said harassment has disrupted production at his factory and inflicted—"

At the mention of strikes and disruption of peaceable workplaces, another rumble went through the crowd, with several men standing to get a better look at me.

The judge rapped his gavel and a bailiff walked among the rows of benches, urging the men back to their seats.

"That's enough, John," the judge said. "Bring it here."

The lawyer handed it over and leapt quickly back as if he were afraid of getting hit with the gavel himself. After reading it, the judge looked up at me. "Miss Kopp. Are you a unionist?"

I was too surprised to say anything. He leaned closer and squinted at me.

"Are you one of those Wobblies? An anarchist sympathizer? A Bolshevik? That's what it says here."

This brought a round of laughter from the crowd. When it died down, I said, "No, sir. I only went to see Mr. Kaufman to collect on the amount owed. And we did not willfully collide—"

"That's fine, thank you," the judge said. He turned to the lawyer. "She doesn't look like much of an anarchist sympathizer to me, John."

"No, Your Honor."

"Is the statement made up entirely of fabricated nonsense, or just that bit?"

The lawyer opened his mouth to answer but then seemed to think better of it and closed it again.

"I thought as much. Now, Miss Kopp. Come here and sign your statement." He passed the paper across to me. I climbed the steps into the witness stand. He handed me his pen and

I signed my name. His hand trembled and his fingers had a bluish cast to them. I wondered how a man his age withstood the chaos and tumult of the courtroom every day.

"Thank you," I said quietly, sliding the paper back across his desk.

"Don't thank me for any of this," the judge said. "Looks like a whole lot of trouble to me." Then he leaned over again to address the sheriff.

"I'm ordering a fifty-dollar fine. It's up to you to collect it, Bob. And keep Miss Kopp and Mr. Kaufman away from each other. It appears they don't get along."

Sheriff Heath nodded grimly. "Yes, Your Honor."

"And next time, take your routine matters to another courtroom."

The mill workers laughed and some of them applauded. The judge pounded his gavel until they stopped.

WE STEPPED OUT into the bright noonday light and confronted the usual lunchtime rush on Main Street. "I'm sorry about that nonsense," the sheriff shouted above the rumble of traffic. "Mr. Kaufman might not know better, but his attorney should have. He's probably wishing he'd never heard of the Kaufman family."

"It's all right," I said. "I'm just glad it's over."

An automobile had stalled at the corner and its driver was standing over it, using his hat to fan the smoke billowing from the engine. No one could get around him, and the other drivers were honking and yelling. A large wagon pulled by two draft horses was trapped in the middle of the street, and the horses were trying without success to back away from the noise.

"What a mess," the sheriff said. "Wait here, Miss Kopp. I'll just go find a constable."

He ran into the crowd and I backed under the awning of a shoe shop until he reappeared, his coat over his arm, his shirt-sleeves rolled up. "Forgive me, Miss Kopp," he said, panting a little. "We just had to push him out of the way. Now, listen." He took my arm and led me down the street. "Don't pay any attention to those ridiculous claims. They weren't formal charges and they never will be. I saw this sort of thing during the strikes last year. These men call everyone they don't like a Bolshevik and an anarchist. They get their lawyers to write up all manner of absurd accusations in hopes of confusing the matter and tying up the courts. But it won't work. Not this time."

We crossed at the corner of Grand and a swarm of school-children, all running after an ice cart, separated us in the middle of the street. I reached the other side first and felt an arm at my elbow. Thinking it was the sheriff, I turned around and found myself staring into a milky glass eye.

"No more police."

He gave my arm a sharp twist that threw me off my balance, and by the time I regained my footing, I was face-to-face with Sheriff Heath and the man was gone.

⋖ 21 ⋗

THE SENSATION of that man's fingers digging into my elbow stayed with me all evening. I couldn't bring myself to tell Norma and Fleurette about it. I'd promised them that this day in court would put an end to our troubles with Mr. Kaufman, and I didn't know how to admit how wrong I'd been.

Sheriff Heath tried to tell me not to worry. He said that Henry Kaufman wouldn't be foolish enough to bother us again now that a judge had ordered him to stay away. I told him it would be a mistake to underestimate Mr. Kaufman's capacity for foolish and reckless behavior.

It didn't take long to find out which of us was right. I'd just settled down to sleep when a window shattered down the hall. I thought I heard a man laugh, but I might have dreamed it.

The three of us staggered out of bed toward one another. There was no moon and it was impossibly dark. I could barely see their faces in front of me.

"Whose window did they break?" Norma said. "It wasn't mine."

It took a minute for each of us to understand that none of our bedroom windows had been broken. Once we realized that, we all ran for Mother's room, half forgetting that she didn't occupy it anymore.

Norma was the first to find a lamp and light it. She made Fleurette go back to her room and put on shoes before she walked in. I found it very irritating that Norma had taken charge of the situation. Bricks coming through windows were my responsibility.

By the time Fleurette returned, Norma had the letter in her hand. She looked at me with an expression that I cannot properly describe. It was as if she had never met me, as if I were a complete stranger, standing in her mother's bedroom in the middle of the night.

"Is this how Sheriff Heath protects us?"

I didn't say a word. Norma read the letter to herself and handed it to me.

Madam:

You are here given warning not to sue H. K. for if you do you will suffer for we his friends will get square with you, we watched you in court house, if you make him spend any more money we will trap you or burn you. Don't give letter to police if you do you be sorry.

H. K. friends

We each read it twice, passing it around in the small circle where we stood among the broken glass. The brick had landed on the bureau, shattered a mirror, and knocked off a lacquered box of straight pins. They were splayed around us on the floor like slivers of ice.

Before any of us could say a word, we heard a motor in the distance. The roar grew louder and I yelled, "Get down!" just before another window shattered and a second brick barreled to the floor, breaking in half when it hit. Fleurette screamed that she was cut and I ran to her, crouching low in case the men were still outside. But the tires skidded in the drive and the motor car rumbled away. Fleurette fell against me.

"Are you hurt?" I said.

"I . . . I don't know. I felt something hit my head."

Norma moved the lamp closer, and I looked her over but found no cuts and only a few shards of glass in her hair. I reached for the brush on the dresser, but Fleurette said no.

"Not Mother's brush. Just leave it the way it was."

I set the brush down and smoothed Fleurette's hair with my fingers. "I don't think you're hurt," I said. "I think you're all right."

Norma pulled the lamp away and it was only then that I saw the note tied to the second brick. She read it and held it out to me without a word.

Dear Miss Florette,

Have you ever been to Chicago? We believe a girl of your talents would find a nice place for herself with no trouble at all. Maybe we bring you with us next time we go. Are you ready for an adventure? Ha! Ha!

—H. K. & Co

Fleurette, still leaning on my shoulder, took hold of the letter and read it under her breath.

"Chicago? Why am I going to Chicago?"

Norma raised an eyebrow, waiting for me to explain it.

"'A girl of your talents,'" she read. "What do they mean by that? They don't know me. Do they mean my dancing, or singing, or . . ."

I took a deep breath, looking to Norma for help. Finding none, I blurted it out. "This is a kidnapping threat. They're not talking about putting you on the stage in Chicago. They're talking about taking you to Chicago and selling you."

She scrunched her face up in that childish way she had. "Sell? What do you mean, sell? How would you—" and then she stopped. She sat up and wrapped her arms around her chest. We'd all read about white slavery in the papers, but I didn't know how much of it she understood.

"They drug you," I said quietly. "They grab you and cover your nose with chloroform and take you somewhere. There are men who will pay . . . who, ah, will pay for . . . that. For you."

Fleurette pulled away from me and stood with her fists tucked under her arms, looking down at her feet and the irregular pattern that the broken bits of Mother's mirror made on the floor. She was possessed of the kind of fine, pouty features that could be so easily shattered, and I watched the corners of her lips drop and tremble as the truth came to her. "But that's not what this is," she said in a whisper. "They're not serious, are they?"

I shook my head. "I don't know. I think Henry Kaufman is very dangerous. I think our buggy collided with the wrong man."

For a minute we just stood where we were and considered that. In the dark Mother's old room was quite beautiful. The chrysanthemums on the wallpaper glowed like distant jellyfish in the sea. Near the window was a lamp fringed in glass beads that she'd brought with her from Vienna. A breeze came in and pushed them against each other, making the faintly musical sound of bells ringing someplace far away. Her filmy dressing gown still hung on the closet door and it lifted and swayed like a woman dancing. At that moment it looked like a stage set, not a home where ordinary people lived. I could imagine stagehands wheeling it all away, leaving us with nothing but a black floor and a backdrop.

"Well," I said at last. "You can't sleep alone tonight. I've got the biggest bed. You'll sleep with me."

"What about Norma?" Fleurette said.

Norma hadn't said a word since she read the letter. I wasn't sure she'd taken a breath. Her voice came out in a croak.

"I suppose we have no choice but to hunker down like soldiers in a trench. I'll make a bed for myself on the floor."

And that's what we did. Fleurette climbed straight into my bed. Norma went to get some blankets and while she was gone, I went looking for Francis's old hunting rifle. It had been years since I'd fired it, and I'd been aiming at rabbits, not at strange men in automobiles.

"What do you intend to do with that?" Norma asked when she returned.

"It does us no good in the back of a closet," I said. I leaned it against the window.

Norma settled down on her pile of blankets. "Why don't you put yourself in front of Fleurette so she doesn't catch the next round of flying glass?"

She was already half asleep in the middle of my bed. I rolled her to the side away from the window. She moaned and kicked but moved over.

I settled in next to her. Fleurette was so small that my body made a wall around her. Her rib cage rose and fell against me.

Norma nodded in the darkness. "You'll be the one they hit. That seems fair."

This time I had to agree with Norma. She turned to look again at the rifle, and then she put her head down, but I don't think she slept. I didn't either.

❧ 22 ❧

IT WAS NORMA who decided that we should live in Wyckoff. Mother was unable to make a plan of any kind. She was
so astonished to learn that Francis and Norma had not only
found me, but had made a commitment on her behalf to raise
her newly discovered granddaughter as her own child, that
she was rendered speechless and nearly paralyzed. Upon ar-
riving in Wyckoff she stood on the porch at Mrs. Florence's,
with Norma next to her (while Francis waited in the carriage
at the end of the drive, as they were all unsure as to whether
a man should even approach the house), but she could not
raise her hand to knock. It fell again to Norma to take charge
of the situation, gaining entrance to the house and asking to
see her sisters.

Already Fleurette was her sister. There would not be a single moment in Fleurette's life in which she was to be treated
as my daughter. Norma had arranged for Mother to sign adoption papers making Fleurette hers, and great care was taken
to make sure that my name would never be found in Mrs.
Florence's files—only the false name I'd given when I arrived.

The letter Norma had written was returned to her. Only a few nurses knew our secret, and they were accustomed to forgetting any details not written in the files, to best protect the interests of the child. An illegitimate girl might never marry, might never have a family of her own, might be cast out of any social circle she attempted to enter. The nurses understood this better than the families did. They assured Norma that no one would ever be told the circumstances of the child's birth, not even Fleurette herself.

Once my mother signed the papers, Fleurette was taken directly from the nursery and handed to her. A few minutes later a nurse came for me, and that's how I found her: seated in an armchair in Mrs. Florence's office, baby in her arms, Norma looking over her shoulder. When I walked in, they both looked up at me with identical expressions of curiosity and shock, but then Fleurette made some sound and their eyes went back to her. I perched on a high-backed chair and watched while they fussed over her.

I'd been so relieved when I learned that Norma had found me and that I'd be keeping my child, but now a stone sank to the bottom of my stomach. I wasn't really keeping her. They were keeping me, that was all.

We couldn't go back to Brooklyn. Girls of eighteen could not disappear for months and return at the same time that a baby was brought into the family without attracting suspicion and gossip. Francis rented a suite of rooms for us in Paterson and planned to return to Brooklyn for our things as soon as we settled on a place to live. Philadelphia was under consideration, as was Boston, with the idea that Francis could easily find work and Norma could finish school. Mother had her inheritance, so we were not without resources.

I believe we would have gone to Philadelphia or Boston had Norma not overheard, as we were leaving, a conversation between two of the nurses about a farm nearby. The man had moved out west and was eager to complete a sale. Norma made a note of the location and as we rode past Sicomac Road, asked Francis to turn and take a look at it.

There it was: the wide and gabled farmhouse, the barn, the pen for animals, the meadow that led to a creek lined in willows. Across the road the neighbor's cows moaned amiably. The drive was overgrown in weeds and the paint had flaked off the house, but Norma saw something there. She got out and took a walk around the barn and then around the house, and stood looking over the fields at the trees in the distance. When she returned to us—Mother, cradling Fleurette, with me sitting alongside, and Francis at the reins—she had already made up her mind.

"No one would know us here," she said to Mother. "And we'd be away from that filthy, crowded city." She glanced meaningfully at me, as if to suggest that filthy cities themselves were to blame for what had happened.

Mother nodded slowly. "When you children were small, I always wanted to bring you to the country. Your father would never agree to it."

Before Francis could object, she added, "Francis, you could fix up the farmhouse, and once that was done, I'm sure you could find work in Paterson."

"And what would you do?" I asked Norma. Everyone turned to look at me as if they'd forgotten I was there.

Norma smiled and looked back at the barn. "I'd get a goat and maybe some pigs. And I believe I might like to keep birds of some sort."

⇥ 23 ⇤

I MUST HAVE DOZED OFF around sunrise. I had been dreaming about a flock of messenger pigeons circling the roof in the early gray light before dawn, carrying slips of paper in their beaks and dropping them down on us. "Chicken Thieves Send Kidnapping Threat" arrived first, then "Police on Lookout for Brother's Hunting Rifle." Fleurette caught one in the air and held it out to me. "Sisters on War Footing," it read.

By the time I awoke the morning was half over. I sat up in bed and wondered if it had all been a nightmare—the brick shattering the window, the note threatening to take Fleurette from us. Then I saw the rifle leaning against the wall and knew I hadn't dreamed it.

A door opened downstairs and I followed the sound into our kitchen. Sheriff Heath had apparently just arrived and was holding his hat in his hand in the manner of a man about to deliver a speech. Norma and Fleurette were standing next to the kitchen table, each with a hand on the back of her chair. No one was saying a word. They were holding their postures as models do in a tableau. "Sisters Awaiting Rescue," it could have been called.

I leaned around the tableau in hopes that someone had left some coffee on the stove for me. They hadn't.

The sheriff's eyes were even darker and more deeply sunk into their sockets. His hair was matted to the side of his head and, as far as I could tell, he was wearing the same brown suit I'd last seen him in.

"You look like you've had even less sleep than we have," I said.

He grimaced and reached up to smooth his hair. "I suppose so," he said. "I was called out in the middle of the night to pull Henry Kaufman's automobile out of a ditch just up the road."

"I don't know why you didn't just leave it there," Norma said.

"Where was Mr. Kaufman?" Fleurette asked.

"He must have run off. We counted four men's footprints in the mud. I sent one of my men to watch your house, but we never saw him."

"That's because he visited us first," Norma said, "and treated us to his latest literary efforts."

"I was afraid of that. How was it delivered?"

"Again by brick," I said, "but this time he aimed for our mother's old room."

Sheriff Heath looked disappointed. "Smart man," he said. Then he saw our surprised expressions and apologized. "I mean that he's avoided using the post. If he mailed them we'd be able to charge him with a federal crime. He knows what he's doing. Could I see the letter?"

"There were two of them," I said. I thought I'd left them upstairs, but Norma pulled the letters out of her pocket. He gestured for her to set them on the table, then he sat down. We took our seats around him as he bent over the crumpled papers.

"Ladies, I'm going to teach you a little detective work." Fleurette sat straighter in her chair. This was precisely the wrong sort of excitement for a girl of her temperament. Without taking his eyes off the letters, he continued. "The first rule of crime scene investigation is to keep your hands off the evidence. If we're lucky we can take up a fingerprint, but not if yours are on top of it."

Norma was not a woman who appreciated having her mistakes pointed out to her. "You wished us to leave the letter on the floor and go peacefully back to bed, having no idea of its contents?" she said stiffly.

"Not at all," he answered, still scrutinizing the letters. "Just use a pair of gloves, a handkerchief, a corner of your skirt to pick it up. Anything will do."

After he finished reading, he slid a finger underneath and lifted both of the letters with calm and steady hands to make sure nothing was written on the back.

"I don't like it," he said, looking up at us at last. "It's got all the marks of a Black Hand letter."

"Black Hand?" Norma and I said at once.

"This is what they do," he said. "They start small, with vague threats. Maybe they break a window or fire a shot in the air, to let their victims know they're serious. Then the threats get more specific as to kidnapping and arson. There's always a warning not to go to the police."

"How clever we were to ignore their advice," Norma declared.

"Your sister was right to call for me and to stand up for herself," he said. "Most people wouldn't. That's why we don't see many of these early letters. But then comes a demand for money, and by that time the victims are too scared to do anything but pay."

"Are you saying that Henry Kaufman is a Black Hander?" I asked. "He's not even Italian."

"Not necessarily," the sheriff said. "These letters have been in the papers so much that anyone can copy their style. They're just imitating what they read. When did this happen?"

I shook my head. "I'm so sorry, Mr. Heath, but I don't think any of us thought to look at a clock. It was the dark of night and we were all so deeply asleep when it happened. There was a bit of confusion because—"

"It was a quarter past two," Norma said.

We all looked at her in surprise.

"I checked the clock when I went to get my blankets. Constance was too busy messing around with that rifle to notice what time it was."

Sheriff Heath sat back in his chair to regard Norma from a distance. "A rifle? What were you girls planning to do with a rifle?"

Norma sniffed. "She was planning to protect her sisters. What were you doing?"

He looked at me and back at Norma, perhaps trying to figure out where he stood with each of us. Then he pushed his chair back and asked if he could go upstairs to view the crime scene. Norma told him he could not, and I told him he could.

She shoved her chair away from the table and went out the kitchen door without a word. I took the sheriff upstairs and Fleurette followed.

Norma had knocked the glass out of the windows in our mother's room, swept up the broken mirror and the pins, and wedged boards into the empty panes. The bricks sat carefully in the center of the dresser, like trinkets put on display, the way one might exhibit a starfish taken from the beach.

Sheriff Heath looked around for a minute, glanced out the window, and tested the boards to be sure they were secure. His hat brushed against a little chandelier above the bed and made him duck. I was embarrassed for him to see Mother's things, the way we'd left them. There was a faint smell of gasoline about him that seemed to take up all the air in the room.

"I'll take the bricks," he said, wrapping a handkerchief around them. Then he looked down at Fleurette.

"Did they let you read that letter?" he asked.

I started to defend myself. "Had I known what it said—"

He held out a hand to stop me. "It's all right. It was directed at her. She should know."

Fleurette was leaning in the doorway. He put his hands on her shoulders, the way a father might, and she straightened up in surprise. It startled me, too, to see a man handle her like that. She bit her lip and looked up at him with wide, wet eyes.

"These men are serious," he said in a low voice. "They're not playing a game. I'm going to do everything I can to keep them away from you, and you're going to stay away from them. Understand?"

She nodded and took a deep gulp of air. He kept hold of her shoulders. I was standing behind him and found myself watching the way the back of his neck lifted away from his collar as he bent to speak to her. "I don't want you to leave the front door unlocked. I don't want you to sleep with the windows open. I don't want you going down to the creek by yourself, and for that matter I don't want you to even go to the barn by yourself. If you're going to town, you take someone with you, and you watch out. All right?"

She could barely answer. "All right."

I thought he was finished, but he wasn't. He kept talking to her with that same mixture of paternal warmth and sternness that Fleurette had so rarely heard from anyone. Even Francis had never spoken to her quite like that.

"Keep your eyes down around strangers. Don't talk to anyone you don't know. Don't open the door for salesmen or delivery boys, unless you're expecting them. Can you do that?"

Fleurette was staring at him, mesmerized.

"Can you?"

She nodded. "Yes."

"You will stay off streetcars and trains. Don't have lunch or stop for any reason in a hotel. No hotels."

"No hotels," she whispered.

"And listen to your sisters and do what they say. If I'm going to put my men in harm's way for you, you mustn't do anything that makes their job more difficult or dangerous."

She took it all in with tremulous, wide-eyed surprise. At last he let go of her shoulders and said, "I'm going to take a walk outside and speak to your sisters now. I want you to keep yourself busy in here and don't try to follow us."

We left her in Mother's room and walked downstairs together. He let himself out through the kitchen door and I followed him. Norma was in the pigeon loft feeding her birds.

She took her time, enjoying making us wait. Sheriff Heath tried to ask a few polite questions about carrier pigeons, but she gave him disgruntled silence in response. When she was finished with her work, she shook a canvas apron off her neck and hung it on a nail outside the loft. She looked at us expectantly, but still she refused to speak.

"All right," Sheriff Heath said. "Come with me."

We followed him out to his car, which was parked near the end of our drive. He reached in the back seat and took out a wooden case. Then he straightened and looked around him, surveying the house with its shuttered windows, the old misshapen barn, the neighbor's hogs in their pen across the way, and our unmowed pasture with the river and the willow trees beyond it. Down the road the dairy cows lowed and slapped their tails against their flanks.

"Would you ladies mind a walk to the creek?" he said.

Norma and I followed him across the pasture, matching his long strides. In a few minutes we were standing under a copse of willow trees, their branches whip-thin and starting to shed leaves. Sheriff Heath scrambled down to the creek bed and set his case down. He straightened up to look back toward the house. "You can't see much of the house from down here," he said, mostly to himself.

Then he unlocked the case and we saw that he had two dark blue revolvers with him.

"Do both of you know how to shoot that rifle?" he asked.

"It belongs to our brother," I said. "We can fire it, but just to scare something off. I don't think I could hit anything."

"We could hit Mr. Kaufman, if it came to that," Norma said. That made the sheriff laugh.

"I hope you won't have to," he said. "Now, why don't you come try this one?"

Norma stood next to him and looked down the length of the creek. With the leaves coming off the trees, we could see all the way down to the end of our property line and into the woods beyond.

"Now, listen," Sheriff Heath said, with the same stern tenderness he'd shown to Fleurette. "You see the one red tree down there? The maple coming out right where the creek makes that bend?"

Norma nodded.

"Just below that is a big rock. A big white boulder really shining in the sun. Do you see it?"

Again she nodded.

He lifted a revolver from the case and opened the chamber to check the ammunition. Then he swung it closed and pressed the butt of it into her hand. He kept his hand over hers and raised it to the white rock.

"Use the notch on the top to get it in your sights," he said in a low voice. He was standing so close that he could talk right in her ear. "See the blade at the end of the barrel? Like a half a penny. Use that to line it up."

She nodded and aimed.

"That's good," he said. "Put one foot behind the other like this. Steady feet. Steady hand. Strong arm. Bend your elbow just a little. That's it."

Without turning her head, Norma shifted her eyes just enough to meet his. He brought his hand up to pull back the hammer, but before he could, she cocked it with her thumb, looked back at the rock, and fired a shot.

The explosion echoed up and down the length of the creek. I felt it hammer my chest, like another heart beating next to mine. There was the smell of something burning and a ringing in my ears. I couldn't tell if she'd hit the rock, but she'd fired it to Sheriff Heath's satisfaction.

She was still aiming the gun straight up the creek when he reached around and took it out of her hand. "That's good," he said. "Thank you." Then, turning to me, "Miss Kopp?"

Norma took a few steps back and folded her arms. I'd never seen her fire a revolver before and she seemed awfully satisfied with herself for having pulled it off.

It was my turn next. The sheriff took my right hand by the wrist and raised it. My fingers curled instinctively around his. He smiled and said, "Don't hold on to me. Hold on to the gun."

When he pressed the revolver into my palm, it was heavier than I expected and warm from having just been fired. I tried to keep my hand from shaking.

He stepped back and gave me the same instructions he had given to Norma. "Aim straight for that white rock. Plant your feet first. Strong arms. Steady hands. When you're ready—"

Before he could say another word I pulled the hammer back and squeezed the trigger. I must've hit the treetops, not the rock, because a flock of starlings raised a cry and circled in the sky before landing some distance away.

"That's all right," he said quickly. "That's just fine. Now you know what to expect. Fire it once more, and this time think about holding steady when it kicks. Use your sights."

I squared my stance and aimed the barrel straight at that rock, squinting at the notch and the narrow half-moon at the end of the barrel that were my guides, and fired. I don't think

I hit the rock, but I managed to keep the gun level. Then I stood holding the revolver straight out until Sheriff Heath took it from me.

He pulled three bullets out of his pocket and reloaded it, then bent down to lock it back in its case. After that he stood and offered the case to me.

"There's one for each of you," he said. "Don't let Miss Fleurette handle them. I'd rather she didn't even see them. Keep them near you at night, but don't put them under your pillows, and don't tuck them into your clothing. You're not to fire directly at anyone. If those men come back, aim in their general direction but shoot into the trees. You're just trying to scare them off. Understand?"

Norma nodded and climbed up and out of the creek bed. Sheriff Heath followed, then leaned down to offer his hand to me.

I didn't need it, but I took it.

⇥ 24 ⇤

AFTER THAT, Fleurette ceased her theatrical performances, and Norma returned her injured bird to the loft. Its wing had mostly healed but its delivery career was at an end. Fleurette, who hated chores and usually refused to do them, became remarkably obedient following her talk with the sheriff. She patched a hole in the coop where mice were getting in to steal the chickens' feed, and she painted the fence around the vegetable garden and cleared a patch for spring peas.

Sheriff Heath had his men watching the house, but they weren't there all the time. They would stop late at night on their way home from tending to some other criminal matter. I grew accustomed to the sound of an automobile idling in the road after midnight. This was why the sheriff warned us not to fire directly at anyone. He was afraid we'd shoot his own deputies. They seemed to understand that too, because they never stopped in front of our house. They always rolled a few yards past our driveway and parked in a wide, bare spot under an oak tree.

I thought a lot about Lucy going to work every day in the

dye factory and taking the wages she earned and handing them back to Mr. Kaufman in rent. And I pictured that baby, wherever he was. He'd be learning to talk by now. Someone would be calling to him with their hands outstretched the way people do with little children, but what name they called him I didn't know.

I did wish there was something I could do for Lucy. But it seemed like every advance I made against Henry Kaufman invited another brick through our window.

"WHO IS HENRI LAMOTTE?" Fleurette said one afternoon as she brought in the mail.

"Let me see it," I said.

"Not until you tell me who he is."

"Is the letter addressed to me?"

"I don't know. It's addressed to Miss Kopp. It might be for me."

She stood over my chair with the envelope in her hand. "You've already opened it, haven't you?" I said.

She held it out to me reluctantly. "It could've been for any one of us."

"You know better," I said.

October 1, 1914

Henri LaMotte, Proprietor
LaMotte Studios

Dear Miss Kopp,

I have found some photographs that may be of interest to you. They were taken last year at the building that was the subject of your inquiry.

One of my men had been engaged to photograph the
goings-on at that address for several weeks, but
the attorney who hired us never paid for his pictures. I had forgotten that we had them until
they reappeared just now. If you want them, I
will hold them for you until Tuesday. After that
I must destroy them. We prefer not to become a
repository for unclaimed photographic evidence,
although I have apparently let my standards slip.
I shall right the ship and sail on!

Au revoir,

Henri LaMotte

"What does it mean? Photographic evidence of what?"

I looked around to see if Norma was within earshot. She
must have been outside. I read the letter again.

"It has to do with Lucy," I said at last.

Fleurette gasped and slid into my armchair, half perching on
the arm and half sitting in my lap. She hadn't done that in years.

"We've found a clue, haven't we?" Fleurette breathed into
my ear.

There was a sugary smell that hung around Fleurette, like
the crumb tarts we used to bake when she was a little girl. I
closed my eyes and the memory of it came over me. I used
to tell her that she was good enough to eat, and she would
shriek and run to Mother in mock horror.

She twisted around to look at me directly. "Would these
pictures help her get her baby back?"

"I don't know," I said. "I'll forward the letter to her. She
can decide what to do about it."

Fleurette jumped out of my lap. "But there's no time! He said you have to come and get them Tuesday. That's tomorrow. We have to take this to her now."

I shook my head. "You heard what the sheriff said. We have to be very careful around strangers."

"But she isn't a stranger," Fleurette said. "Just go over there and drop it in her mailbox."

I turned the envelope over in my hands. "I don't think I should," I said. "I believe Norma's right this time. We need to stay out of Henry Kaufman's business."

"But don't you care about that poor girl?" Fleurette said, a little desperation in her voice. "Try to imagine for one minute what it would be like to be a young mother and lose your baby like that. How would you feel?"

I bit the inside of my lip. She'd never come this close to the truth, and I didn't want her getting any closer. I'd made my own kind of peace with the past and was not eager to reckon with it again.

But Fleurette was right. Lucy was living with a kind of loss I had never known.

"Don't tell Norma where I'm going," I said.

⊰ 25 ⊱

ALONG LUCY'S STREET the windows of the old boarding houses were smudged with smoke and steam. Someone was boiling coffee, someone was scorching the bottom of a pot of soup, and someone was frying a fish. In front of one house, a woman in a brown dress bent over a patch of overgrown greens, searching among the tough stalks and seed heads for a few leaves that were still tender enough to eat.

I had put Mr. LaMotte's letter into an envelope of my own with a note of explanation, hoping to leave it in Lucy's mailbox and run off before anyone saw me. But when I tried to open the front door to Lucy's building, it wobbled and fell down, landing in the dark hallway with a bang. It had been torn off its hinges and propped up to cover the entrance.

I backed into the weedy front yard and looked up. One of the windows on the second floor had been boarded over. There were no signs of life in the building—no washing on the clothesline, no lights or curtains in the windows, no clatter of dishes or smell of dinner on the stove. Then, as I leaned closer to risk a peek through the gaping doorway, the odor hit me. Fire.

I jumped back as if the building were still burning. A woman across the street swept her porch and watched me. Three boys played with a ball on the corner, and when it bounced against the street it gave an eerie and empty echo.

A low fence between Lucy's building and the one next door had been knocked down. I stepped over it and walked around to the rear of the house, which was entirely scorched. Blackened timbers had begun to disintegrate in the autumn wind and rain, and the windows were nothing but holes offering admittance to birds and squirrels.

Where a back door might have once stood, there was nothing but a cement threshold and the burnt end of a wooden post. I took a step inside and kicked away a cracked glass doorknob and the blistered lid of an enameled pot. The rattle they made echoed around the hollow and charred interior. Even the staircase was gone. The remains of the bannister hung uselessly from the second floor.

If Lucy had been home, I didn't see how she could have made it out alive. Everyone on the upper floors would have been trapped.

I don't remember running to the trolley, but I was on board and halfway to Hackensack before I could hold my hands steady again. At the courthouse I asked to speak to Sheriff Heath.

"He just left," the girl at the reception desk said.

"A deputy, then," I said, pushing my hair back under my hat. I was still sweating from my race away from Lucy's. "I was to come here if—if something happened. Give them my name. It's Constance Kopp."

With as bored and indifferent an air as she could muster, the girl went and whispered something to the guard standing on the courthouse steps. "Wait here," she said, and the guard walked down the steps and around to the jail.

A few minutes later, a gray-haired man in a deputy's uniform walked in. "Deputy Morris, miss," he said. He looked at the receptionist, who was watching us curiously. "This way, please."

He took my arm and we walked down the corridor, where no one could hear us. "Sheriff Heath has been helping me and my sisters with some trouble we had," I said.

"Yes, miss. I've been by on patrol a few times. Has he bothered you again?"

I shook my head. "It's something else. It's about a fire over in Paterson. Sometime in the last few weeks. A boarding house on Summer. Did you hear about it?"

He thought for a minute. "I might have. What about it?"

"A friend of mine could have been there. Did everyone get out?"

He shook his head. "I don't know, miss. It wouldn't be a matter for the sheriff over here in Bergen County."

"But can't you find out?"

He looked down the hall at the receptionist. "I'd have to ask her to telephone."

"Couldn't you, Mr. Morris? Please?"

He laughed, but not unkindly. "Begging doesn't suit you, Miss Kopp."

FLEURETTE WAS SURPRISED to see me come downstairs the next morning in a hat and a traveling coat. She was sitting on the floor in the parlor, sorting through a box of buttons to find a matched set for a dress she was working on.

"Where are we going?" she said, jumping to her feet.

"You're staying here," I said. "I'm going into the city. I'll be back by suppertime."

"The city! Without me?" She stamped her foot and the buttons scattered across the rug. What a child she could be when she didn't get her way! I swallowed my irritation and bent down to speak to her in a low voice.

"You know I can't take you. You heard what the sheriff said. No train stations, no strangers, no strange places."

She pushed the buttons around with her toe. "You're going to go and get those pictures yourself, aren't you?" she said.

"I'm going to try. Now, I wish you'd be a good girl and stay here and do what we ask you to do."

"I've done everything you've asked me to do!" she cried. "You and Norma and the sheriff. When do I get to do anything for myself again?" She threw herself on the divan and buried her face in the cushion, sobbing.

What now? I only needed a few hours away, but I managed to set off a full-blown tantrum just by walking past Fleurette. I sighed and looked out the window. Norma was out there raking leaves. I knew she wanted to get away, too. It was unpleasant to be confined to the house for so long. We were living such queer and isolated lives out here by ourselves.

I sat down next to Fleurette and put my hand on her back the way I used to when she was a little girl. Into the pillow she said, "And next week is my birthday and what are we going to do about that?"

"It is? Are you going to be fifteen or sixteen?"

She gave me a little punch in the leg. "Seventeen. You know that."

"Already? Well, you're right. We should take you somewhere."

She sniffed and sat up. Her eyes looked like the clear night sky when she cried. "Where?" she asked.

"Anywhere you want to go. As long as the sheriff agrees."

"You'll ask him?"

"I will."

LUCY DIDN'T DIE IN THE FIRE. No one did. It started in the rear corner of the house—I could picture Henry Kaufman and his friends sneaking around with a bucket of kerosene—but the man living downstairs smelled it right away and ran upstairs to wake the others. He must have been the one whose room I'd backed into when I went to see Lucy. It had seemed like such a drab and miserable little room, but the man who lived in it had done something heroic. I wondered where he'd gone. I wondered where any of them had gone. Deputy Morris hadn't been able to tell me that. With Lucy's whereabouts unknown, I had no choice but to go to Mr. LaMotte's myself before he threw the pictures away.

The train got me into New York by noon. There was a tearoom near the station where ladies could have lunch, so I stopped there first and ate a ham salad sandwich and a pineapple ring with a cherry on top. There was coconut cake for dessert. I wasn't hungry anymore, but I'd grown tired of our farm cooking and couldn't resist something as exotic as coconut. I ordered a slice and drank a cup of coffee with it. The buttons on my dress were about to pop, I'd stuffed myself so. I was glad for the long walk to Mr. LaMotte's studio.

He was sitting at his desk, looking as if he'd been waiting for me. "Miss Kopp!" he exclaimed, jumping to his feet as I walked in. "Just in time."

I took a step forward and knocked a pile of envelopes off a

chair. "Pardon me," I said, crouching down to retrieve them. The envelopes were blank except for a name written in light pencil on the front of each one: *Wapole, Dowd, Kurtz, Wood.* They didn't seem to be in any particular order, so I scooped them up and returned them to the chair.

"Not to worry," he said. "They have a tendency to leap out at a person. Can't be helped." I thought that it could be helped with the employment of a filing cabinet and a secretary to file them, but I didn't say so.

"I hope I haven't kept you waiting," I said. "Your letter only just arrived yesterday, so I didn't have time to reply."

He cocked his head to the left and looked at me over the tops of his spectacles. "Oh, yes, the photographs. I have them here, and I would be most happy to let you look through them. But first I have a favor to ask of you."

Before he could continue, the door opened and a mountain of a man pushed his way into the tiny office. He wore the largest wool overcoat I'd ever seen on a person, and a black hat that a small child could have hidden inside. A shadow fell across his face, but I could see an enormous mustache above lips the size of sausages, and two bulging chins. "Is this her?" he asked in a growl that could only come from the Bronx.

Mr. LaMotte rushed around to stand between us. "Mr. Hopper! I wasn't expecting you so soon. Please let me introduce you to Miss Kopp."

I extended my hand and found it gripped roughly by something that felt like a catcher's mitt.

"How do you do?" I said. "I didn't realize I was expected."

"You're not here about the job?" the man grunted.

Mr. LaMotte waved his hands to silence us. "I was just getting around to that," he said. "Miss Kopp, I wonder if you might do a favor for my associate Mr. Hopper. You see, from time to time, we have need of a girl photographer, and—"

"A photographer?" I said, taking a step back and overturning yet another pile of envelopes. "I don't know a thing about photography. I'm only here because you said—"

"I said I'd be willing to do you a favor," Mr. LaMotte said, having regained his calm. "Now I'm asking you to do a favor for me. This gentleman would like you to pay a visit to a hotel for ladies just off Fifth Avenue."

"Pay a visit to a hotel?" Sheriff Heath had only just warned us to stay away from hotels. "I couldn't possibly."

"We only want you to inquire about the rooms and ask to see one with a rear-facing window on an upper floor. They'll give you a key and send you up by yourself. Just go and take a photograph of the room, and get a picture of whatever you can see from the window. Then return the key to the desk and bring the camera back here to me. I'll have your photographs waiting."

Before I could compose an answer, Mr. LaMotte added, "You look like a woman who can handle herself, Miss Kopp."

"Well, I—"

"Please be assured that we are not asking you to be involved in anything disreputable. The matter we are investigating concerns only a witness to a crime. We must confirm certain details of her story by attesting to the layout of the room and the view from the window. Nothing more. We would go ourselves, but they will only permit ladies upstairs, and I have none in my employment at present."

Mr. Hopper was breathing in that way that large men breathed, as if fueled by a boiler room instead of a pair of lungs. He still hadn't removed his hat. I couldn't get a good look at his face.

"Is Mr. Hopper one of your—"

"Associates. He handles investigations for several of the better attorneys in Manhattan. His reputation is beyond question. He enjoys the high regard of both the police and officers of the court."

Mr. Hopper made a sound that could have been a grunt of agreement. We both looked at him, but when he said nothing, Mr. LaMotte continued.

"He will accompany you to the hotel and bring you back here as soon as your work is completed. I assure you it won't take but an hour, and that is only if you enjoy a leisurely stroll up Fifth Avenue and visit some of our fine shops along the way."

Now Mr. Hopper chortled—a noise that sounded more like the eruption of a minor volcano—at the idea of enjoying a leisurely stroll with me.

I was too astonished to take offense. Never in my life had I been thrown into so many unexpected situations in such a short time. Mr. LaMotte took my silence for acquiescence and wasted no time in getting a camera in my hands. It was a little box camera that had been rigged to resemble a ladies' handbag. I admired the soft Italian leather handle and the fine tweed covering the box. This was a well-made instrument. As soon as it was in my hands, I decided that I should have one of my own someday.

"Hold it against yourself, just like that," Mr. LaMotte said. "There's nothing to it. This little lever slides across to open the shutter. Just go slowly, until you feel it engage on the other side. Then wind the key until the next number appears. You have eight pictures. Please do use them all. I must develop the film immediately, so a half-used roll doesn't save me anything. Get as much light as you can in the room and hold the camera perfectly still. Is that all clear? You can do that, can't you?"

He smiled up at me with genuine fondness, the way one might regard a niece one was bringing into the family business. I couldn't help but return the smile.

"It is, Mr. LaMotte. It's perfectly clear. But why are you asking me to do this? Surely if you need a girl photographer, you can find one in this city."

He stepped back and studied me for a minute. "You look capable, Miss Kopp. You are—forgive me for saying—substantial."

I saw no reason to take offense at that.

"And serious," he added quickly. "You seem like you could handle any sort of trouble that might—not that there will be any trouble, it's just . . . well—"

"It's all right," I said. "I'll be fine." With that I slid the camera's strap over my wrist and looked in the direction of the towering figure that was Mr. Hopper. He hadn't made a move. He was just waiting. I had a feeling that in his line of work, he spent a good deal of time waiting. "Shall we go?"

Mr. Hopper opened the door and pressed himself against it to make room for me to pass. He smelled of tobacco and wintergreen. Soon we were out in the pale October sunlight, marching toward Fifth Avenue like two soldiers.

He was not a man for conversation, but that suited me just fine. I made a point of not looking in a single shop window so he would not think I was the kind of girl who wanted to fritter away time trying on hats or squealing over bracelets. I don't know why it mattered to me what Mr. Hopper thought. I had not gone looking for a job as a girl photographer, but now that I had it, I intended to do it right.

When we rounded the corner on Fifth Avenue, a gust of wind caught us and made the going more difficult. The avenues were like canyons, the buildings funneling wind straight through them. I tucked the camera under my coat and buttoned up the collar.

Mr. Hopper only looked back once to make sure that I could keep up. I could.

The hotel for ladies, called the Mandarin, was located across the avenue, along a shabby block in the Thirties. It was just an ordinary six-story building with a pair of glass doors and a green canopy above them. A doorman stood outside under a brass gas lamp.

We walked swiftly past the hotel to the next corner. There Mr. Hopper stopped and told me he would wait for me. He pushed his hat back and looked down at me.

"All right, miss?"

His disposition was not unkind. He had deep brown eyes and a younger, softer face than I had first realized. He was probably the sort of man who terrified people without meaning to.

"I'm just fine," I said, and I meant it. I strode confidently back to the hotel. The doorman tipped his hat and opened the door.

The lobby was about what I'd have expected for a small hotel catering to a female clientele. The tiled floor was covered in red Oriental rugs. The walls were paneled along the lower half and papered in a pattern of green and gold ferns along the upper half. There were old gas lamps on the wall that matched the one outside, and a mahogany desk staffed by a porter and a prim older woman dressed in a smart blue velvet dress with brass buttons down the front. To the right was a sitting room where the guests could meet their male visitors.

I presented myself at the desk and did what Mr. LaMotte asked. He was right. There was no trouble about getting a key to go and inspect a room before reserving it. There was a room available on the sixth floor with rear-facing windows, the woman told me, and one on the fifth floor with a view to Fifth Avenue. I didn't need that one but she seemed to want me to consider it, so I took the keys for both.

The porter came around the desk to accompany me upstairs. I tried to make some excuse as to why I preferred to go on my own, but just then I was rescued by a mother and her three daughters emerging from the elevator and demanding the porter's assistance with their luggage. I smiled, ever the gracious guest.

"Please don't worry about me," I said. "I won't be but a minute." Before he could say anything I dashed up the stairs and out of sight.

I took a look at every floor as I went, and they were all the same—red carpets, oak paneling, and gold-striped wallpaper. It looked like a clean and decent hotel. On the sixth floor I found the room and let myself in. There was not much to see, just a brass bed topped with a white coverlet, a nightstand outfitted with a mirror and washbasin, and a small desk furnished with an ink blotter and writing paper. In one corner was a stand for luggage and a coat rack.

The layout of the room seemed not at all unusual to me, but I stood in the corner and took a picture. Then I pointed it at the window and took another one while I looked across the alley at the blackened brick coated with decades of coal dust. The gap between the hotel and the building across from it was nothing more than an empty space where people might have tossed their garbage or the contents of their chamber pots. I wondered what the mysterious witness had seen, and what had been hurled into that dark place.

There were only a few windows on the building opposite, just the sort of small utilitarian windows that would be placed in a stairway to illuminate it. I didn't know what about that view might have interested Mr. LaMotte. I had six pictures left, so I took two looking down, one to the left and one to the right. Then I held it straight out at eye level and did the same thing, and then I pointed it up at the rooftops and once again took a picture in each direction.

I stopped on the fifth floor to see that room, too, even though I had no particular reason to. I could see why the lady at the desk offered it to me. It was a much larger room, more like a suite, and it must have fetched a higher price. It was furnished with a larger desk and two overstuffed chairs arranged around a small tiled fireplace. A pair of wide floor-to-ceiling windows looked across to Fifth Avenue. I went to the windows and the sight of the avenue from above made something catch in my throat. If I wasn't looking down on the busiest place in the world, I was a few blocks from it. A river of people moved below me, identifiable only by their hats and scarves. An endless parade of buildings marched up to Central Park and down in the other direction to Wall Street. New buildings were going up all around, each in a race to get closer to the clouds, with their scaffolding silhouetted like bare tree limbs against the October sky.

There, in that room, I felt like I was at the center of something. I was someplace that mattered. And that made me feel like I was someone who mattered.

I liked that room very much. I wanted to rent it on the spot.

I returned the key and inquired about the rates for the room on the fifth floor. The woman behind the desk smiled and handed me a rate card. "I thought that one would suit you," she said.

Mr. Hopper was waiting where he said he would be. I assured him that I'd had no trouble getting the pictures, and we walked back to the studio in silence. When we arrived, he opened the door for me, but he did not go inside.

"Good day, Miss Kopp. I'm on to my next job. I'll leave you to yours."

With that he disappeared into the street.

Mr. LaMotte took the camera from me and set it in his darkroom. He returned with a fat envelope in his hands. "Your wages, miss," he said. "Take them with you. I've got to close shop and attend to matters of my own." He turned and started rummaging through a desk drawer.

I thanked him and tucked the envelope under my coat. I started to leave, but I couldn't resist asking him. "Mr. La-Motte?"

He looked up as if he was surprised that I was still there. "Yes?"

"What did the lady see?"

"Lady? What lady?"

"The one in the hotel."

He shook his head and came around the desk, peering up at me kindly. "Miss Kopp. I'm going to give you a piece of advice that will serve you well if you continue in this line of work."

"Line of work?"

"Whatever you want to call this little investigation you're conducting."

I reddened. "All right."

"The less anyone knows, the better. If you have nothing to tell, you won't have to worry about being questioned."

"I see."

"I mean it. Put up a barrier between your witnesses, your victims, your investigators, your prosecutors, your attorneys, and your friends and enemies at the newspaper. Don't let anyone know a single thing they don't have to know. And do your best to keep them from talking to each other." He made a series of chopping motions with his hands. "You see? Walls. I am putting a wall between you and the lady in the hotel. If you don't know about her, you can't tell anyone if they ask."

He turned back to his desk. Without looking up at me again, he said, "The fewer people who know what that lady saw, the better. My girl photographer in particular does not need to know."

I'm not your girl photographer, I thought. But I didn't say it. I took my pictures and left for the train station. Mr. La-Motte followed and locked the door behind us, hurrying off in the other direction with still more envelopes under his arm.

❧ 26 ❧

I COULDN'T LOOK at the photographs on the train. There were far too many people on board, all jostling for seats and all rushing to get home in time for supper, just as I was. I clutched the package and held on as we roared out of the city and back into Paterson. The train rattled and shook and swayed on its tracks, racing toward the station like a runaway horse.

In Paterson all the passengers had to get off and switch cars. I stepped out in the middle of the crowd and waited for it to disperse. Once the platform was empty, I took a seat on a bench and opened the envelope. Inside was a stack of over a hundred prints. Mr. LaMotte's name was printed nowhere on the prints or on the envelope. The only mark was the name *Ward* in light pencil.

The pictures had been taken over several weeks in the summer, from a vantage point just across the street from the address in question. I could see time passing on the face of the building. As the weeks wore on, the geraniums in the window boxes on the third floor leafed out and bloomed.

Then the windows opened, and bed sheets came outside to dry.

I was near the bottom of the pile when I heard a muffled cough behind me and jumped up. Sheriff Heath had been looking over my shoulder.

"What are you doing here?" I felt like I'd been caught doing something wrong.

"I'm an officer of the law, Miss Kopp," he said. "I don't have to account for my whereabouts. But you do. I thought you were home looking after your sisters. Fleurette told me where you'd gone. She said she was frightened to be left alone."

I pushed the photographs back in their envelope and tucked it under my arm. "She wasn't frightened—she just wanted to come along. Norma is perfectly capable of watching Fleurette for an afternoon. I had business in the city."

"What kind of business?"

"It doesn't concern you."

He frowned, but it was the false frown of someone who was only pretending to be hurt. "I have something for you," he said, reaching into his vest pocket. "Mr. Kaufman has paid his fine."

He handed me a roll of bills. I put the money in my handbag and dropped down to the bench again, suddenly exhausted. "Well. His debt is paid. This takes care of it."

He sat next to me. The train had pulled out of the station and we were alone on the platform. "I hope so. He wasn't happy about paying the fine, but he had little choice. It was due and I could have arrested him."

"That must have been a pleasant visit."

"It was not. His sister was there this time."

"So you've met Mrs. Garfinkel?"

He nodded. "She was not at all pleased to see me. She wants to keep her family's name out of the papers. She handed me two hundred dollars and said that she hoped this would be the end to Henry's legal troubles."

"Two hundred! But the fine was only fifty. You don't mean—"

He nodded. I stared at him, then reached for the roll in my handbag.

"Miss Kopp! I didn't take it."

"Of course you didn't."

He smiled and put his head down, then looked over at me from under the brim of his hat. "A sheriff can always find a way to put extra money in his pocket. I'm not that type of sheriff. Now, let's have a look at those pictures."

I thought about what Mr. LaMotte had said about putting up walls between the parties in an investigation. But I didn't want to argue about it, and I was fairly certain that the photographs held no clues anyway. I handed the envelope to Sheriff Heath and told him where I'd gotten them.

He thumbed through the pictures. In one of them an old woman with a cane stopped at the entrance but did not go inside, in another two boys ran upstairs for dinner, and several showed the same man returning home from work in a bellman's uniform.

"I don't recognize any of them," he said. "This doesn't have anything to do with that boarding house fire you were asking Morris about, does it?"

"I shouldn't say."

The sheriff sat still for a minute, looking at the empty train tracks. A piece of waxed paper from the delicatessen next to the station had rolled onto the tracks, and a gray rat ran out from under the platform to inspect it.

Finally he handed the envelope to me. "Well, may I drive you home, Miss Kopp?"

THE SHOPS IN PATERSON were due to close at any minute. Shoppers were dashing across the street with parcels in their arms, ignoring the line of motor cars shuddering and wheezing as they lurched in a slow and unsteady line. Green window shades came down at the bank as we rode past, and the grocer brought in his cart of onions from the sidewalk. A newsboy pushed the last of the evening edition into the hands of men rushing from their offices to catch the trolley home. The windows in the library went dim. Darkness chased us out of town.

The sheriff drove along in silence, his lips moving but no sound coming out. I stayed quiet as he seemed to be puzzling something out. By now it was almost completely dark. He said he wanted to pull over and check the headlamps before we drove into the country.

I got out of the car when he did. It felt good to stand along the side of the road with grass under my feet and breathe in the sharp, cold night air. I felt as though I had lived someone else's life all day, and now I was returning to my own.

Sheriff Heath bent down and squinted at the headlamps, then walked around to my side of the car and leaned against it, his hands in his pockets.

"This girl's afraid of the police, but she'll speak to you," he said. "A stranger."

"You're a stranger too," I said.

He looked out along the tops of the trees. "We always have trouble getting women to talk to us."

"They don't have any trouble talking to me."

"But that does us no good if you won't tell me about it," the sheriff said.

A black motor car took a bend in the road a little too fast and kicked gravel and dust at us. It was enough to spook me and I stumbled back into the grass. He took my elbow.

"It just caught me by surprise," I said, brushing off my dress. "But that reminds me. It's Fleurette's birthday soon. Do you think we could take her to town for the day?"

He thought about it for a minute. "Just keep an eye on her, and take your revolver. Don't go to Paterson. I don't want you running into him."

I agreed.

"Then go ahead. We'll drive by the house while you're gone."

"Doesn't the sheriff have better things to do than watch for prowlers in the countryside?"

He looked at me in surprise. "My mother always said things like that."

"I don't suppose I know your mother."

"She passed away last year."

He opened the door and I took my seat. "I'm sorry," I said. "Mine did too. I didn't know we had that in common."

He started the engine again and drove us a ways down the road, then said, "She had very definite ideas about a sheriff's duties, as did my father, although he didn't live long enough to see me in office."

"What was he like?"

"Oh, just ask any old-timer about Doc Heath. Twenty or thirty years ago, he ran Hackensack. He was the fire chief and the town druggist and the dentist."

"All at once?"

"My mother always wanted him to pick one and quit the others, but he never would. She's a Gamewell—the fire alarm company."

"That's her family's business?"

"Oh, yes. And every man who marries a Gamewell girl becomes a fire chief in some city or another so he can go around having fire alarms installed. But my father learned a little dentistry in the War between the States and couldn't help but do that, too. Then he became a justice of the peace—"

"A fourth profession!"

The sheriff nodded. "He used to brag about how he sent more people to jail, married more couples, and pulled more teeth than any man in New Jersey."

"You take after him, then," I said. "And are there more sheriffs and fire chiefs in the family?"

"Oh, no. My brothers are company men."

"I suspect you have sisters, too."

He nodded. "There were ten of us."

"Ten!"

"Only five lived. I was the first one to live."

I turned to the window and watched the trunks of the trees and the fence posts roll past us and disappear from view. "Your poor mother."

"She was . . ." He faltered, and then said, "Yes, she had a trying time."

"Well, I suspect your father would have liked to have seen you in office."

He shook his head and said, "I don't know what he would have thought. He was a lock-them-up-and-throw-away-the-key man. He didn't like any of my ideas about reforming the

jails. If he were alive, he'd be down at the Board of Freeholders meeting every Tuesday night, complaining about my expenses like the rest of them do."

"Then you're still arguing with him, aren't you?" I said.

"I suppose I'm still arguing with his ideas." After a pause
he added, "I know one thing he would've liked."

"What's that?"

"To see Henry Kaufman arrested. Doc Heath despised
drunkenness and laziness, and he couldn't tolerate anyone
harassing a lady."

"Well. Neither can I."

⊰ 27 ⊱

WHEN I PROMISED FLEURETTE I'd take her anywhere for her birthday, I meant that I would take her to her choice of shops in some nearby city. But she wanted to go to the seashore. "We didn't go at all this summer," she said. "Everyone says it's going to be the coldest winter in years. We should go just once before it gets too dreadful."

On the morning of her birthday, the sun streamed into our windows and got us all out of bed early. Even though there was a chill in the air, it was the sort of day meant to be spent outdoors. Norma rushed outside to get the buggy ready. Fleurette packed a blanket and three Chinese parasols, along with a bundle of silk scarves whose purpose I could not determine. I made chopped liver sandwiches and potato salad, and packed an apple for each of us and six hard-boiled eggs. We drank our coffee and ate our toast standing around the kitchen table. It seemed a waste of time to sit when we had somewhere to go.

We left Dolley at the stables next to the train station. We'd decided to go to the bathing beach at New Rochelle, where our uncle Frederick used to run a beer garden in the summer. It was nothing more than a tent in a gravel lot, but that was all the beach-going crowd wanted anyway. He'd set out benches and folding chairs and serve Austrian beer and sausages. The beer was his own recipe. "I make one kind," he used to tell his customers. "Cold."

When Francis, Norma, and I were children, we weren't allowed inside the beer garden. Mother would sit at a table nearest the beach with her knitting bag or a piece of embroidery and talk with her brother's wife and a few of our other female relations. We would run back and forth in the sand, collecting bits of driftwood and broken shells and arranging them around her feet like some kind of offering.

By the time Fleurette was a little girl, Norma and I were too old to play at the beach, but we went back occasionally for her sake. She talked about it as if we had a tradition of going every summer, but I couldn't remember the last time we'd taken her there. Our uncle had long ago given up the beer garden, being too old to manage it himself and having no sons to help him.

The train was nearly empty on the way to New Rochelle. From the station it was only a short walk to the beach. Fleurette ran on ahead while Norma and I lagged behind, carrying our lunch and the bag of parasols and scarves.

"It's odd to be here without Mother," Norma said under her breath.

At the water's edge, Fleurette kicked off her shoes and, before Norma or I could tell her not to, reached under her skirt to roll her stockings down. She stuffed them in her shoes and ran into the waves. We watched her from the edge of the boardwalk, not sure if we should follow or set a more dignified example.

From a distance, she still looked like a little girl. She dashed into the water with her skirt lifted to her knees and shrieked when the waves leapt up at her.

"She's going to ruin that silk," I said.

"It isn't silk," Norma said. "It's one of those new fabrics meant to be worn in the water. She's been working on it all week."

"She has? I didn't notice."

"She works fast," Norma said. "She has a natural talent."

FLEURETTE'S INTEREST IN SEWING never struck any of us as unusual until the day, when she was about eight years old, that she found the Singer man's sample machine in my closet and carried it down, sitting on the stairs and dragging it in her lap.

"Can't I use this one, *maman?*" she asked, pulling it across the floor like a puppy she wanted to adopt.

Mother looked up from the lace collar she was adding to a pinafore. "Where did you find another—" she said, then her face went blank.

Norma put her newspaper down and stared at the machine. They both very deliberately did not look at me.

She ran to Mother, throwing herself across her lap. "Constance had it," she said. "But Constance hates to sew. I want to make you an apron. *S'il te plait, laisse-moi essayer.*"

Mother smoothed Fleurette's hair absently and looked over at the machine.

"It's the wrong kind for a little girl," she said, her voice even and tightly controlled. "We will take it to Paterson and trade it for one that suits you. A Franklin, maybe. Not a Singer."

Without a glance at me, she pushed Fleurette off her lap, picked up the Singer man's machine, and walked outside with it. The next day, she and Fleurette went to town and returned with a new black Franklin decorated with an Egyptian phoenix and scarab motif and mounted in an oak cabinet. Francis had just married and moved to Hawthorne, so his bedroom became Fleurette's sewing room.

Within a year she was making her own play clothes, copying the styles in the ladies' pages of the newspaper. By the time she was twelve she'd moved on to fancy frocks and nightgowns. And now, it appeared, she was stitching bathing costumes as soon as the idea for a visit to the seashore occurred to her.

NORMA SPREAD OUT THE BLANKET along the short wall between the sand and the boardwalk and we sat down together. Fleurette yelled for us to come and join her but we waved her on and looked out at the expanse of flat slate-blue water. The waves had subsided and Fleurette took to kicking the ocean to get it moving again. A trio of seagulls circled and landed next to her. Finding herself with an audience, she splashed even more vigorously, which excited the gulls and prompted them to do a dance, shaking out their wings in the droplets of water she made rain down on them.

The sun warmed the little rock wall and we leaned against it. Norma closed her eyes and tilted her face up to the sky. "Isn't it nice to be on our own, without any armed deputies watching over us?" She sat up and looked around. "Or has Sheriff Heath followed us here and concealed himself inside a bathing tent? I thought I saw one of them move a minute ago."

"We're perfectly safe," I said, "and I take it as a good sign that we've seen nothing of Henry Kaufman lately."

Norma frowned. She rarely took anything as a good sign. "Don't you agree," she said, in the lilting musical voice that she used for her most sweeping proclamations, "that it would be best if the three of us stayed entirely away from that business with the factory girl and made no more secret trips to New York City that we don't tell the others about? Meaning, of course, that you in particular—"

"Yes, I realize that you're speaking of me in particular. I suppose Fleurette told you all about it, which means that I don't need to." A pinch of sand had worked its way under my collar and I sat up to brush it away.

"Fleurette loves secrets because she enjoys telling people things they aren't supposed to know. I prefer to tell people the things they *are* supposed to know," Norma said.

"You're very good at it," I answered.

"I have always thought so."

I felt something on my neck again and sat up to brush it off. When I did, I realized that a colony of tiny black ants resided inside a crevice in the rock wall and had organized themselves to make an advance upon our dinner basket. Norma and I stood up and shook the ants off our blanket, and found a better place for ourselves a few yards away.

"This hasn't been good for Fleurette," Norma continued when we'd settled back down. "She talks of nothing else. All those mysterious trips and secret letters. She's far too excitable for something like this."

"We should find something more substantial to occupy her

time," I said. "Then she won't think about it so much. I don't want her working as a common seamstress. Maybe we could find a stenography course, or . . ." I realized I hadn't any ideas about an occupation for Fleurette.

"She'd never do the lessons," Norma said, "and even if she did, what then? We can't let her go off to an office every day. I can only imagine what she'd get up to."

I turned to look Norma squarely in the face. There was sand all over us, and some of it had landed on her eyelashes and the fine hair above her lip. "She'll have to go off on her own someday," I said. "Won't she?"

Norma shook her head. "I'd rather not think about it."

"But surely she's thinking about it," I said. "She's seventeen now. She's almost as old as I was when—"

"All the more reason to keep her at home," Norma said briskly, "if only we can keep strange men from driving by and calling after her. Do you think we can do that?"

I was tired of being lectured about Henry Kaufman. I stood up to get a better look at the ocean. At the end of the beach a group of girls about Fleurette's age sat on their wide striped blankets. They wore the sort of bathing costume we wouldn't let Fleurette have, the kind with divided skirts and a drawstring that lifted the hem up into bloomers for swimming. The idea was that girls would wait until they'd gone in the water to lift their skirts, but these girls hadn't and we knew Fleurette wouldn't either. Instead they drew them up as high as they would go and splayed their legs in the sunshine. Their blankets were arrayed in a starfish pattern so that their heads met in the middle. They were leaning in close, whispering to one another, their legs wiggling like a pale multi-limbed sea creature washed up onshore.

"We've come all this way. We should dip our toes in the water," I said.

The beach was almost silver, shimmering in the sunlight like a mirror. It had grown unexpectedly warm since our arrival, and all at once it felt more like August than October. I pulled the laces out of my shoes and—after looking around to make sure no one was watching—rolled off my stockings. The pleasure of immersing my bare feet in the warm sand made me shiver. Norma gave a little half-smile of surrender and soon she was barefoot, too. Once Fleurette saw us, she ran up and took us both by the hands, dragging us to the water. For an hour we splashed and kicked at the sand and chased the seagulls like any ordinary family at the beach.

We spread out our picnic and two boys came around selling lemonade and pretzels. Fleurette wanted us to buy something in honor of her birthday, so we did. We ate our pretzels in the sand and then stretched out on our backs to look up at the sky. The little waves barely made a sound at all when they patted the shore. The gulls whooshed down next to us to inspect our empty lemonade bottles and lifted off again. I must have fallen asleep, because the next time I looked around, Fleurette had left us and gone to stand by herself and look across Long Island Sound toward the distant and endless Atlantic.

❧ 28 ❧

AT FIRST, there was no point in pretending that the baby wasn't mine. Fleurette's bassinet stayed in my bedroom for the first year so that I could nurse her and get up with her in the middle of the night. But during the day, Mother took her from me.

"She has to learn to come to me," she said.

I knew she was right. I knew that, years later, Fleurette couldn't have an inexplicable bond with one sister that she didn't have with the other. The girl needed to grow up with one mother, and it had already been decided who that mother would be. So my mother was the one who held her and fussed over her and decided how to dress her and when to bathe her.

She only handed the baby to me when it was feeding time. I would take her into the pantry and crouch down on a little stool we'd put there for that purpose. It was just the two of us in the dark, surrounded by tins of baking soda and break-fast tea. Fleurette would look up at me through enormous black, uncomprehending eyes as she fed. She was looking at her mother, as any baby would when it nursed. With her eyes open but her mind unformed, she was witnessing the great secret of her life, one that she was supposed to forget, and would forget.

In those moments I felt like I'd stolen her. If she fell asleep I would sit and hold her, matching my breath to hers there among the preserves and pickled beans, counting the minutes until my mother's footsteps would come across the floor and the door would open.

"You know better," she would say, and take her from me.

Norma wasn't particularly interested in the baby. She was a teenager, still finishing school in Ridgewood, and happily occupied with farm chores in her spare time. She and Francis bought a pair of goats, they built a chicken coop and figured out how to raise a flock, and they put up a fence to keep the deer away from the vegetable garden. The two of them kept so busy that no one even noticed that they'd built a pigeon loft as well. It wasn't until an incubator appeared in the kitchen that we realized what Norma had in mind.

Baby pigeons were far more interesting to her than baby humans, but she took her turns with Fleurette anyway, sitting with her on the kitchen floor and watching the gray fledglings hop around in their crate of wood and straw. Sometimes Norma would take one of the baby birds firmly in her hand and hold it out to Fleurette, its legs splayed and its wings pinned behind it. Fleurette would reach one finger out to the bird's downy undercarriage and laugh uproariously.

Everything made Fleurette laugh. She was at the very center of a world created just for her, and she knew it.

⊰ 29 ⊱

NIGHT CLOUDS OBSCURED THE MOON over our house. We maneuvered down the drive in total darkness. Fleurette had fallen asleep on the ride home and slumped over against me, warm and heavy. Norma brought Dolley to a stop and was about to jump out and check on her birds when I saw it.

Our front door was open.

We both reached for Fleurette at the same time, which made her squeal.

"Shhhhh." I felt around under her feet for the picnic basket, where I'd hidden the revolvers. Fleurette caught a glimpse of them and gasped.

"What are those?"

I backed out of the buggy and took her chin in my hand. Her eyes were wide open now and frantic. "Be very quiet," I whispered. "If anything happens, go straight for the dairy and pound on the door until they let you in." She nodded. I pressed Dolley's reins into her hands.

Norma had stepped out on the other side of the buggy. I

tilted my head in the direction of the open door. We advanced toward it and she took a gun from me. We were almost to the porch when, from the other side of the house, the kitchen door burst open and half a dozen men scrambled out into the black night.

I chased after them, stopping just long enough to get them in my sights and fire.

The shot exploded across the meadow and sent a flock of crows screeching into the sky. By now the men had reached a bank of trees along the road and I could hardly see them. I took up my skirts and ran, but then came the kick of an automobile starting and the sound of tires grinding in the dirt.

By the time I reached the road, the black bulk had sputtered and motored away. I fired again and again into the darkness it left behind.

Gunpowder smoke and dust drifted around me in a cloud. It took a minute to clear, but once it did I took a deep breath and willed my hands to stop shaking. Only then did I turn to look back at our darkened house, and the dim figure of our horse in front. I couldn't see Norma or Fleurette.

I'd left them alone.

I ran back down the drive and Norma met me at the buggy. Both of us reached for Fleurette at once, as if we needed to feel her pulse.

"I didn't dare shoot once you started to run," Norma said.

"That's fine," I said. "I think they're gone."

We started to lift Fleurette out of the buggy, but she shook her head and stayed planted on her seat.

"We can't go in," she whispered. "What if he's waiting for us?"

"Who?" I asked.

"H-Henry Kaufman."

Norma and I both laughed at once, but it was a nervous, trembling laugh. "He never goes anywhere without that gang of his," I said. "If he was here, he ran out with the rest of them."

I turned to the open front door and shouted. "Did you hear that, Henry Kaufman? If you were here, you're gone now!" I fired my gun in the air, high over the house, to make my point. Norma flinched and Fleurette covered her ears, but I didn't care. I'd had enough of Henry Kaufman and I refused to be afraid of walking into my own house.

"Let's go." I stepped inside, feeling bold from the gunfire still ringing in my ears. Norma picked up our porch lamp and lit it as we went in.

Our grandfather clock was overturned in the foyer, surrounded by a mess of broken glass. We picked our way across it, stumbling over magazines splayed open and scarves and hats that should have been on our coat rack. Norma lifted the lamp, and it was only then that we understood. The house had been ransacked. Every piece of furniture in the parlor was piled in the middle of the room: upended chairs, overturned tables, desks with the drawers knocked out of them, and the divan, standing awkwardly on its end. Pictures had been torn from the walls and thrown into the pile, the glass broken out of the frames. Vases and lamps and even the contents of a knitting basket were strewn about.

The occasional table near the door, where we kept our mail, had been thrown into the drawing room, atop another pile of furniture. Books had been pulled from their shelves, and a potted rubber tree that I would have thought too heavy to move was on its side, surrounded by dirt and broken ceramic. Even the rug was rolled up into the rough, uneven pyramid made by our things.

"Did they take anything?" Fleurette asked at last.

I shook my head. "I don't think so. I think they were only trying to—"

By then we'd reached the sitting room, and all three of us smelled it at once. Smoke.

This time Norma ran on ahead, reaching the kitchen first and shouting for us to bring a blanket. Seeing nothing we could readily extract from the mess around us, we followed her in. They had started a fire on our kitchen table, setting flame to the newspapers we'd left there that morning. There was nothing left of them but dry and drifting ashes, and a few corners still curling and flickering. Now the lace table-cloth was giving way, each filament glowing orange before crumbling to black. The flames cast a weird light around the kitchen and the smoke drifted to the ceiling like a miniature storm cloud.

I pulled my coat off and Norma and I slammed it down on the table and beat at it while Fleurette drew a bucket of water. Soon there was nothing but a soggy pile of tweed and ashes on the table, along with the broken remains of the crumb-covered plates we'd left there that morning.

The three of us dropped into our chairs, panting and coughing a little, staring at the mess in front of us. The intruders had left the kitchen door open when they'd fled. It had a tendency to close on its own, but it was still open just enough to let in a draft of cold air. Our eyes wandered over to it.

There was a metal can just outside the kitchen door. Fleurette started to ask what it was, but I already knew.

"Kerosene. They were building a bonfire."

SOMEONE HAD TO CHECK THE BEDROOMS UPSTAIRS. After a moment of indecision over who should go—we were too exhausted and confused to think clearly—we walked through the downstairs rooms together, locking doors and windows as we went. Norma and I each kept a revolver pointed in a different direction.

"Where did you get those?" Fleurette asked.

"Sheriff Heath," I said quietly, out of the side of my mouth.

"Why would he give you . . ." And she trailed off as the answer occurred to her.

"Because of this," Norma said grimly. "Because he knew something like this might happen."

Once I was sure no one was hidden downstairs, I left them standing by the front door and ran up, pounding the stairs as loud as I could to announce my arrival, rapping my gun on each door before I entered. But our bedrooms were empty and untouched. Fleurette's chemise still dangled from the bedpost where she'd left it. Norma's treatise on pigeons was open on her nightstand. The thought of those men running through our rooms, touching our things, sent another jolt through me and my knees almost buckled.

Downstairs, Norma and Fleurette had already begun to sort through the mess and try to make sense of what happened. "Norma found a box of matches outside the kitchen door," Fleurette called to me, "and they're not the kind we use. She thinks they heard us ride up and didn't have time for the kerosene, but threw a match on the table before they left anyway."

I nodded, my arms crossed over my chest. "It must've been something like that."

Norma came in from the parlor with a man's overcoat hooked over one finger. She held it out at arm's length. "They left this behind."

Fleurette reached for it. "Can a coat have fingerprints?"

"I don't think so," I said. "Maybe the buttons. But let's be careful."

Fleurette took it from Norma and held it up in the dim light of the porch lamp. It was a thick wool coat, navy blue, lined in silk the color of rhubarb. There were leather tabs at the cuffs and collar, and buttons that must have been made of brass but looked like gold. It might have been hand sewn: as we leaned in, we saw no label advertising a department store or even the city of manufacture.

It was a beautiful piece of work, something worn by a man who appreciated fine tailoring. But it was also quietly terrifying to have the shape of the man who had been in our house suspended there from Fleurette's arms. I took it from her and found a place for it on our coat rack. We all stepped back and watched it like it might turn on us.

Something on the coat gleamed and caught the light. It was a gold stick pin topped by a diamond.

"Just the sort of thing a vain man would wear," Norma said.

We took up the lantern and made another turn around the wreckage. We found a handkerchief that didn't belong to us, and a man's gold ring. I couldn't see a jeweler's mark, but I held it carefully by the edges, hoping it might yield a fingerprint.

"We'll take this to the sheriff tomorrow," I said. "There's nothing more we can do tonight."

"We can't possibly stay here!" Norma said.

"Where do you expect us to go? I'm not about to wake up Francis at this hour. He'll never let us move back in here if he finds out about this."

Fleurette shuffled across the floor, kicking away the pieces of a ruby cut-glass bowl we'd always believed unbreakable. When she reached the stairs, she called over her shoulder, "I can't look at this mess any longer. If they come back, you two can just shoot at them and we'll clean it all up tomorrow."

"Get in my bed," I said.

When she was gone, Norma whispered, "I won't sleep in this house."

"I don't intend to sleep. But there's nowhere to go, unless you'd like to ride into Hackensack and ask the sheriff to take us into the jail for the night."

Norma deliberated over that for a minute. "If it's to be a choice between Francis and the Hackensack jail, I suppose we'll manage for one night."

We made one more check of the doors and windows together, then climbed the stairs and took up the same positions we'd occupied before. I wrapped myself around Fleurette, and Norma spread out her blankets under the window. The rifle leaned against the wall again, but this time Norma settled down with a revolver next to her, and I did too. Fleurette curled into a tight ball and stared at the wall. At some point in the early morning, her eyes closed. I listened to her breathe for hours.

⇥ 30 ⇤

THIS TIME WHEN I WENT TO TOWN, no one stayed at home. We were up at the first light and packed a few valuables and keepsakes into the buggy in case the men returned while we were gone. I rolled the intruder's coat into a pillowcase, along with the ring, stickpin, and the matches we'd found. It made me queasy to touch all of it, but no one else would.

Fleurette tried to take the reins but I wouldn't let her on the grounds that I didn't know who we might be passing on the road. So Norma drove and I sat with my arm around Fleurette and my hand over my handbag with the revolver tucked inside. Along the way every black automobile looked suspicious to me. An engine misfired and I pushed Fleurette to the floor, eliciting a yelp of protest.

"Stop it!" she said. "He's not going to come after us on the street in front of everybody."

"He has before," I said.

"Stop it anyway," Norma said over her shoulder. "You'll give me a nervous fit if you keep jumping around like that."

I didn't say anything for the rest of the drive, but I slid my hand in my bag anyway. I found the cold weight of the revolver calming.

We arrived at the jail in Hackensack before nine o'clock. It was a new building and a decidedly odd one, designed, according to the Board of Freeholders' wishes, to look like a medieval fortress with turrets and tiny windows of the sort one might use to shoot a cannon at attacking armies. The Hackensack River ran alongside it like a moat. The edifice had been mocked in the papers as being a waste of taxpayers' money and looking more like a playhouse for schoolboys than a serious building with a public purpose.

And like most medieval fortresses (I supposed, not having visited any others), it did not feature an expansive and welcoming entrance. We walked around the building once, unsure which of the locked, windowless doors were intended for our use. At last I shrugged, climbed some stairs, and pounded on the door that looked most promising.

A harried, red-cheeked woman in a yellow apron answered the door. A perfect angel of a baby sat on her hip, its face framed in blond curls. I took a step back in surprise.

"Oh," I said. "We meant to go to the prison. We're here to see Sheriff Heath. Did I . . ." and I trailed off, looking up at the building for some clue as to where I might have gone wrong.

"This is the prison," she said brusquely. "And it also happens to be my home."

She looked so affronted by this that I thought she expected an apology from me, but I wasn't sure what I'd done.

Fleurette started to say something. Before she got us into

even more trouble, I said, "I'm so sorry to disturb you. We're here on an urgent matter for the sheriff."

The baby was starting to squirm in the cold air. She closed the door slightly so that he was behind the door and out of the wind. "I know," she said. "He saw you coming from the third floor and called down. He'll be here soon as he can."

Again she stared at us. Her mouth was a hard blank line.

Realizing that we weren't going to be invited in, I said, "Where would you like us to wait?"

At that she exhaled a tired and exasperated sigh, looked out at the empty drive that ringed the prison, and pushed the door open. "I suppose you'll come in. The great minds who designed this building seemed to have forgotten about a public entrance or a waiting room."

We followed her inside. To my surprise, the room was furnished like an ordinary living room, with overstuffed chairs and a fireplace and children's toys strewn about.

"It looks like someone lives here!" Fleurette said.

I turned to tell her to be quiet, but the woman said sharply, "A lot of people live here, most of them thieves and murderers. But you're in the sheriff's living quarters. I am Mrs. Heath."

Mrs. Heath? I hadn't given any thought at all to the sheriff's wife, but if I had, I would not have pictured such an unpleasant and disagreeable woman. Although I couldn't imagine what sort of woman would want to keep up a home and children on the ground floor of this cold, stone structure.

"Pleased to meet you," I said, trying out a smile that wasn't returned. "I am Constance Kopp, and these are my sisters, Norma and Fleurette."

The baby squirmed out of her grasp. She set him down and gave me a long look as she stood up. Then she glanced at Norma and scrutinized Fleurette, who was especially pretty in a black velvet riding coat trimmed in rabbit fur. I should have told her to wear something more somber. We were going to a prison, not the opera.

"Bob hasn't mentioned any sisters to me," she said.

Just then I heard footsteps. To my relief, the sheriff rushed into the room. "I'm sorry about this, Cordelia," he said to his wife. She gave him no reply.

"Miss Kopp," he said, nodding at me. "This way, please."

I looked uncertainly at Norma, who was wearing a forced and unpleasant smile and clinging to Fleurette's sleeve.

"I'm sure Mrs. Heath would enjoy some company this morning," he said. It was more of an order than an invitation. We seemed to be just another disagreeable duty imposed by the sheriff upon his wife. It couldn't have been easy for her.

I followed him into a bleak corridor. He turned around to slide a metal gate in place behind us and lock it from a key on a large ring he wore on his belt. At the end of the corridor was another gate.

"David." A deputy appeared to let us in.

We stood in a tiny windowless room with a metal door opposite. It smelled of rust and turpentine wax. The deputy locked the gate behind us and then opened the door. This led us to Sheriff Heath's office.

It was a pleasant room, lined with glass-fronted bookcases and warmed by a small fireplace. I must have been holding my breath, because I let it out all at once as I sank into a chair opposite the sheriff's desk.

He didn't sit at his desk but instead took a chair next to me.

"Are you girls all right? What happened?"

I gave him the most straightforward account I could and presented him with the coat and jewelry. He lifted them out of the pillowcase and examined them slowly. "I wonder what stopped them."

"I think they heard us. If we'd come home even a few minutes later, they would have had time to pour kerosene all over everything and light quite a bonfire."

"My deputy rode past yesterday, but he didn't see anything. They must have come after he left." He sat back in his chair and looked up at the ceiling. "I wish we'd caught him," he said, mostly to himself. "That was our chance. Well, just be sure—"

"Wait," I said. "That isn't all he's done." A prickly sort of fear came over me as I realized that the fire at Lucy's had to be connected to what had happened at our house. "You remember the girl I told you about?"

He sighed. "Miss Kopp, I wish you would—"

"Listen! That was the boarding house in Paterson. He set that fire. He went after her first, then he came after us."

"What makes you think he set that one?"

"He'd already threatened to. She told me herself. She was terrified of him."

"But Kaufman's family owns that building. Are you telling me he burned down his own building just to scare off a girl?"

"He might have," I said. It sounded preposterous when he said it like that, but I knew it to be true.

"But you still won't give me the girl's name."

"I mustn't. I promised her."

Sheriff Heath stood and paced around the room. He put his hands in his pockets and kept his head down, as if the answers were written on the leather uppers of his boots. "I'll talk to the fire chief. And I'll work on the evidence we've got. I'll send my men around to the jewelers in town, and I know a tailor who might be able to help with the coat. Maybe the matchbox has a fingerprint. Then we'll have a case for the prosecutor."

"But what are we to do while you're out speaking to tailors? Turn our home into a bunker? Guard it in shifts? Keep one revolver pointed at the road at all times?"

He squeezed his eyes shut and ran a hand through his hair. "No. I'll do that. Take your sisters home and I'll be there as soon as I can."

Just then the door opened and a guard looked in. "They're ready for you, sir."

Sheriff Heath nodded and the guard backed out silently.

"Ready for what?" I asked.

"I'm sorry, Miss Kopp. It's a bad day at the prison. We found a man dead in his cell after Sunday services. I've got to speak to the inmates."

"Oh! I—"

"There isn't anything to say about it. Go home and look after your sisters."

There was something lost and uncertain in his face. He opened the door and the guard took me away.

⤙ 31 ⤚

WE TOOK OUR TIME putting the rooms back together, having decided to polish the floors and wash down the walls first.
Fleurette read about a way to take the bruises out of furniture by covering them in damp brown paper and applying a
hot iron until the dent rose to the surface. It seemed hopeless to try—every table and chair and breakfront was pitted
and scratched—but she had a new iron and was eager to put
it to use. Norma and I shoved the heaviest pieces back into
place, and she ministered to the upholstery and wood. We
dusted the books and put away the pictures whose frames had
broken, having decided that we'd grown tired of looking at
them anyway. The glass globes had been smashed out of every
lamp, but they'd grown too stained with smoke to clean, and
we were glad to replace them. When we were finished, the
rooms were brighter and airier than they'd ever been.

That week the charred body of a magazine illustrator was
found in what remained of a home in Harrington Park. A bur-
glar was suspected until the dead man's wife confessed to
Sheriff Heath that she'd run off to New York and her husband

had threatened to burn the house down if she didn't return. A few days later a woman drank poison on the courthouse steps because her employer would not give her the time off to see her children. The prisoners in Sheriff Heath's jail saw her collapse from their windows and shouted to him to save her. He carried her to his office and she died there, asking the sheriff to take care of her children when she was gone. The next day he resumed more mundane duties, arresting a girl for unlawful cohabitation and serving a foreclosure notice to a widow.

All of this was diligently cataloged in the newspaper. Reporters must have followed the sheriff everywhere. I wondered why they didn't follow him to our house. Perhaps they thought nothing of interest happened this far out in the country.

He drove down Sicomac Road twice a day to pick up a deputy and deposit another one. Sometimes he would park his automobile in our drive and wait for me to join him for a walk around the property. We would circle the barn, then make a wider loop around the house, and he would show me how to look for footprints and tire impressions. We'd walk out to the end of the drive and look up and down the road. If there was any news, he'd give it.

"You were right," he said one day, after about a week of this.

"About what?" We had just finished making our rounds of the house and barn.

"The boarding house. The fire chief in Paterson believes it was arson. Didn't you say you'd met Mr. Kaufman's sister?"

"Yes, Marion Garfinkel. She mostly runs the place, I think."

"Then I want you to come with me."

• • •

SHERIFF HEATH TELEPHONED IN ADVANCE and persuaded Mrs. Garfinkel to arrange a meeting with the two of
us. He wanted me along on the grounds that she'd met me
before and might be more willing to cooperate in an investigation if one of Henry Kaufman's victims was sitting across
from her. She was reluctant to see us but agreed after Sheriff
Heath said that he would only offer a private, quiet meeting
once, and after that he would simply turn up unannounced
with a full force of deputies and wouldn't be able to help it if
a few reporters followed along.

"Come first thing in the morning," she'd said. "Henry
never gets in before noon anymore."

Deputy Morris drove us to the factory but left us at the
corner. "It's a friendly visit," Sheriff Heath said. "I don't want
her to see the sheriff's wagon in front of her factory." He put
his badge in his pocket.

Work had already begun for the day. The floor was still dry,
but the first skeins were going into the dye troughs, and there
would be a lake of pigment sloshing down the drains by the time
we left. I was prepared this time with a handkerchief for my
nose, but the odor wasn't as strong this early in the morning.

Marion Garfinkel was waiting for us at the door to the offices. "We can use Henry's office," she said, and led us there,
past the clerks at their typewriters. With their eyes on us, she
called out, "Girls, I'll be in a sales meeting."

The odor of stale cigarette smoke and spilled whiskey was
even worse than that of the dye vats. Marion groaned and
asked the sheriff to help work one of the levers that would
open the tall windows.

"He keeps these windows closed because he's convinced
someone is listening in on him," Marion said. "If he'd spend

half as much time thinking about the factory as he spends scheming with those friends of his, I wouldn't be here."

She dropped into the wide leather chair behind his desk and gestured for us to sit. There were playing cards and ashtrays all over the table in the middle of the room, along with brass cartridge casings, which Sheriff Heath regarded with interest but did not touch. He pulled two chairs away from the table for us and turned them to face the desk.

"All right," Marion said when we were settled. "You've got your meeting. Let's do this quickly."

"Will your husband be joining us?" the sheriff said.

"He had business at our mill in Pittsburgh. Honestly, he'd rather I took care of this place. He hates dye shops, and he's not too fond of Henry."

"Will you be taking over for your brother?" he asked.

She made a dismissive little shrug and said, "I hope not. My father thought that Henry would shape up if he was put in charge of a factory and given control of its finances. But to be honest, the elder Mr. Kaufman has grown quite feeble, and the rest of us have been taking over the family's operations. I drew the short straw and was sent here to do something about Henry."

"What do you plan to do?"

"Well, Henry's got to go, and the only way to get him to leave is to cut off the money. But I need my father's signature for that. We're still working on it," she said with a tight smile. "Is that why you're here? To hear about our family's difficulties?"

Sheriff Heath held his hat in his lap and fingered the brim. "I don't mean to pry, Mrs. Garfinkel," he said. "This concerns a criminal matter. We'd like your help."

She glanced at me over the top of her glasses. "Henry paid his fine. Didn't that take care of it?"

"I'm afraid he has continued to harass Miss Kopp and her sisters. But today we—"

"Forgive me, Sheriff, but I can't be responsible for anything my brother does outside of these four walls. My husband and I are only interested in getting this factory back on a profitable footing and getting Henry—well, finding some solution to the problem of Henry, which, to be honest, has been this family's most pressing problem for longer than I care to remember." She looked up at the patch of sky just visible through the open window. "Since his fifth birthday, now that I think about it," she said, mostly to herself.

Seeing an opportunity, I leaned forward and said, "How much trouble can a boy get into on his fifth birthday?"

She turned sharply back to me. "He can set a fire in the cellar and try to push his brother down an air shaft."

"All in one day," the sheriff said quietly.

"All in one day. He should have been sent off to reform school, but oh, no. We can't have the Kaufman name associated with a school for troubled boys. No, it's always been so much better to just—"

She seemed all at once to remember to whom she was talking, and she stopped. "What is it, Sheriff? I'm sure we all have work to do this morning."

The sheriff was still considering the hat in his lap. "The matter I'm investigating," he said, "concerns a fire."

She groaned and leaned back in her chair. "The boarding house. I know. Our family's owned a whole row of them for years, and they've been nothing but trouble. I'm surprised we haven't had a grease fire before now. My husband's planning to sell them all off."

"Who told you it was a grease fire?" Sheriff Heath said.

"Well, Henry said he spoke to the fire chief and . . ." She stopped in midsentence, her mouth hanging open. "Henry."

With a sharp look from the sheriff, I stayed quiet. After a minute she began straightening the papers on the desk and said, "But there's no evidence of that, is there? And who would set fire to his own property?" She said it with the contemplative air of a lawyer considering a legal defense.

"I understand your brother had trouble with a girl who lived in that building. Miss Kopp said she worked here. Will she be here today?"

I froze. What was he doing?

Marion looked back and forth between the two of us, but before she said a word, I could tell our interview was over.

"I don't know what Miss Kopp thinks she knows, or what business it is of hers," she said crisply. "Lucy Blake is no longer in our employ. She left without notice and will not receive a reference. She'd been harassing my brother and, frankly, it's better that she's gone."

I cringed. I'd kept my promise and never given the sheriff Lucy's name, but I'd given him too much other information. Now he knew.

"I've been told a child is missing," the sheriff continued.

At that Marion rose to her feet and we reluctantly followed suit. "That girl only wanted our family's money. It was extortion, that was all. If there ever was a child—and I never saw one—it's probably better off wherever it is now."

She marched to the door and held it open. Sheriff Heath

followed and took hold of it gently, closing it again. He spoke so softly that even I had to lean over to hear.

"Someone attempted a bonfire at the home of the Kopp sisters last week. I came by only to ask your brother's whereabouts on that evening and the evening the boarding house burned. Your cooperation would let us handle this matter quietly."

There was a twitch at the corner of her mouth and I thought she might be considering it. But then she opened the door again.

"Thank you so much for your visit," she sang out for the benefit of the typists. "We won't be needing any."

⇥ 32 ⇤

"I WISH YOU WOULDN'T have brought Lucy Blake into this," I said as Deputy Morris drove us back to Wyckoff.

"I needed the girl's name," the sheriff said calmly. "She's a part of this mess. I can't help any of you if I don't know what's going on."

"She made me swear I wouldn't go to the police."

"But we can help her if she'll let us," the sheriff said. "If she'd only come to us when the baby was born, we could have petitioned a judge to have Kaufman declared the father. He would have been made to pay. We've done it before."

"I don't think a scared young factory girl would have gone running to the sheriff in the middle of the strikes, even if she had known," I said.

"Well. She shouldn't be so afraid of us," he said. "And you wanted me to know her name. You always did."

He was right, but I wasn't going to say it.

"Now she's a missing person," he continued. "Doesn't that change things? Wouldn't she have wanted you to do something if she turned up missing?"

"What are you going to do?" I asked.

"We'll take a description from you and we'll start looking," he said. "And we'll bring Henry Kaufman in as soon as I can get the prosecutor to agree on some charges."

"Do you mean you have to ask that man for permission before you bring an arsonist and kidnapper in for questioning? What was his name? Courter?"

"No," said the sheriff. "It's worse than that. I have to ask his boss."

When we rolled into the drive, Norma and Fleurette were standing outside with one of the deputies. "We have a letter," Fleurette called to us before we were even out of the car. She was bouncing up and down on her toes the way she did when she was excited. I was beginning to think Norma was right. Fleurette did see this as another installment in a Sunday serial.

Sheriff Heath rushed over and took the envelope from his deputy. "Did he mail it?" he said, holding it lightly by the edges.

He had, which the sheriff considered good news, because it meant that he could take it to a man at the post office assigned to work on Black Hand letters and other such threats sent through the mail.

I read it over his shoulder.

Madam,

You make mistake to bring police in. We settle this ourselves. If you insist on prosecuting Henry Kaufman you will be sorry, for we will blow up your home.

This time we get you, when you run, us shoot you before you pass us in field or street.

—H. K. & Friends

Sheriff Heath looked out at the road and my eyes followed his. Anything could come hurling down that road at us. I'd always felt so secluded in the countryside, so isolated. This is where we'd gone to hide. But we weren't hidden anymore.

Fleurette crossed her arms over her chest and hopped up and down to get warm. The day had grown gray and damp, and the chill was getting into our bones. Norma put an arm around her and rubbed her shoulders.

"I'll put a guard here around the clock," the sheriff said, his eyes still on the empty road. "We'll be able to see them coming. I don't want you to worry. The next time they turn up out here, they'll all be arrested."

But he also told us to stay away from windows, and to keep buckets of water around the house in case we had to put out a fire, and to keep our revolvers nearby, even during the day.

So that's the way it would be. We were under siege.

WINTER WAS CLOSING IN ON US. By the first week of November, we'd already had a few snow flurries. In the morning we had to sprinkle salt on the porch stoop to keep from slipping, and every day we chipped the ice out of Dolley's water trough. Our chickens went through an early molt, shedding their feathers so rapidly that in the morning we'd find the floor of their pen covered in them and think that one of them had been slaughtered by a fox in the night. Francis arranged for a boy to bring us a cord of firewood, knowing that we wouldn't make it to Christmas if it stayed this cold.

The willow trees down by the creek were encased in ice at sunrise. When I walked out to the meadow, I could hear those thin, whip-like branches jangling against each other like the glass on a chandelier. I worried about the deputies stationed out there in the cold, and finally got them to accept a camp stove to furnish some small measure of heat.

It was a few weeks before Henry Kaufman made good on his threat. I awoke to the sound of ice cracking under someone's feet, but I had been so deeply asleep that at first I didn't understand what was happening. But then a twig snapped and I heard a man's soft cursing. In a second I was out of bed and crouched under the window. The revolver was so cold that it was a shock to wrap my hand around it.

I raised my eyes to the windowsill. The glass was covered in a fine, crystalline lacework of ice. I had to stand a little taller to find a spot that was clear enough to see through. From my bedroom I had a view of the meadow and the dead, dry vegetable garden. I could see only a corner of the barn. No light came from its window. I didn't know if the deputy was watching or not.

Seeing no one in the yard, I lowered myself back to the floor and wondered if I should wake Norma and Fleurette. We had only just started sleeping in our own bedrooms again a few nights ago. Now I wish we'd rigged up a bell to signal one another.

I slid my window open a few inches, and as I did, I again heard the crack of ice under someone's feet. I risked another look through the glass. He saw me just as I saw him. His gun was already drawn. I pushed my revolver through the narrow opening and fired.

The bullet hit a tree and he shot up at me. There was a small shudder when the bullet hit the house. A second later I heard the groan of the barn door swinging open. I couldn't shoot again without endangering the deputy. I dropped below the window and waited.

When the man didn't return fire, I stood alongside the window and peeked out. He was running down the drive, a short and stocky figure in a coat and hat. I couldn't say for certain that it was Henry Kaufman, but nothing about his appearance gave me reason to believe it wasn't.

A car met him at the end of our drive and roared away. It was only after the road was empty that I saw the deputy chasing after him, fast but not fast enough.

SHERIFF HEATH WAS ANGRY with his deputy for letting the man get away, but I forgave him. We could see from the footprints in the ice that our intruder had approached the house from the other side, staying away from the barn so as not to alert the deputy stationed there. Even if he had dozed off for a few minutes (an accusation from Sheriff Heath that he denied), it would have been difficult to get up and out of the barn in time to react. The entire confrontation only took a minute.

"Wouldn't this be a very good time to arrest the man and put an end to all this?" Norma said when the sheriff stopped in the next morning.

"We're still trying to make the case to the prosecutor," he said.

"But Constance saw him!" Fleurette said. She was sitting at the kitchen table spooning sugar on her toast. The sheriff, Norma, and I were standing in an awkward half-circle around her.

"She thinks she saw him," Sheriff Heath said. "And I think she did, too. But we have no proof."

"If only she'd shot him," Norma said, "we'd have excellent proof in the form of a frozen corpse in the drive."

"What about the coat and the stickpin and the ring? All those things they left behind?" I asked.

He shook his head. "I've sent my men around to every tailor and jeweler in town. No one recognizes them. The coat was made by a very good private tailor, and the jewelry has no marks. We couldn't get a print from the matchbox."

"And the letters?" I said.

"I've got someone at the post office working on that. I know it isn't any comfort, but we're doing everything we can."

"So is Henry Kaufman," Norma said.

After that, there were two deputies on duty, and the three of us went back to sleeping in the same room. We chose Mother's room because it squarely faced the barn and the road, making it more difficult for someone to sneak up to it. The bullet that had been fired at the house remained lodged in the siding. The wood was sturdy enough to protect us, so we weren't worried about anyone shooting at us through the walls. Our house was powerfully built of wide, thick timbers. It wasn't meant to withstand the ammunition of gangsters, but it seemed to be serving that purpose just fine.

All the same, we moved every piece of furniture in Mother's room to the outside wall. Any bullets coming at us would have to get through the shingles, the crossbeams, and Mother's oak chiffonier.

⇥ 33 ⇤

WE TRULY HAD GONE BACK INTO HIDING. There was the same sense of dread, of fear, of an ever-present danger pressing in from the outside world, that had hung about the house when we first moved to Wyckoff. I remembered the weight of it from last time, and the sense that I had brought this down upon us all.

Except that then we had a baby to distract us. Now we had a bored seventeen-year-old and a platoon of deputies stationed in our barn on twelve-hour shifts.

Norma scoured the newspaper every day for hints about what Kaufman and his gang might be up to. "There was a raid on a gambling parlor last night," she would say. "Maybe he got swept up in that." Any story about an automobile running someone down got her attention, for we knew him to be a dangerous driver. And if there was a fire—any kind of fire at all, even a kitchen fire started accidentally by a maid—Norma cut it out and left it for the sheriff to see.

"Not knowing his whereabouts is the worst of it," she said one morning. "What's he doing right now? When he's not going after us, who else do you suppose he's bothering?" Norma imagined that he had a long list of similarly situated women to harass and threaten. I said that I didn't think Henry Kaufman was capable of something as methodical as a list.

"No, I'm certain he doesn't keep a list," Norma said. "But I do wonder if he doesn't have a whole string of us he goes around and torments. I've half a mind to place an advertisement in the papers and form some kind of league."

"The Henry Kaufman Protection League," Fleurette said. Norma wrote it down.

"I want to know what he's done with Lucy Blake," said Fleurette. "Maybe he's got her and the baby hidden in the basement. Has anyone gone to look?"

Norma rattled her newspaper to signal her displeasure with the subject of Lucy Blake. But the girl's story played like a moving picture in Fleurette's head, and it was impossible to get her to stop talking about it.

"Why can't the sheriff find her?" Fleurette continued. "Wouldn't someone have seen her? They should ask at the train stations. Or we could put a notice in the paper about her. Haven't they done any of that? A girl can't just vanish."

"Oh, girls can vanish," Norma said without looking up at us.

IT WAS A WEEK before the next letter arrived. What prompted him to send it I couldn't imagine. We had hardly stepped foot outside, much less gone anywhere near him or his factory. I imagined Henry Kaufman's mind working like one of those swirling, sucking whirlpools that formed without warning at the bottom of the Passaic Falls. They'd arise from nothing and then spin around until something flew out of them—a piece of driftwood, a rubber ball, an old shoe. This was Henry Kaufman, spinning like a dervish until another demented letter came hurling out at us.

This one arrived once again by mail. It was delivered in the afternoon just before Sheriff Heath stopped in to pick up a deputy.

Madam: This is a last warning to you. We git this time the whole bunch of you, we lay for you. We know you and when we get you be sorry for we finish you.
    Good-by

                     Your time has come soon
                            —H. K. & Friends

"Last warning?" I said. "What does he want from us? Warning before what?"

Sheriff Heath sat down on the divan and closed his eyes for a minute. He looked terrible. His eyes were bloodshot and rimmed in dark veins the color of a bruise. As he held the letter, his hands trembled. He looked smaller somehow, as if he'd shrunk inside his overcoat.

"Sheriff Heath," I said, suddenly worried. "You don't look well." Why hadn't I noticed it before?

He gave a shuddering, chesty laugh that sent him into a coughing fit.

"Strange men are firing guns at your house and you're asking after my health?"

I was about to offer him coffee when we heard a bang and a scream from the meadow. The sheriff dropped the letter and was out the door before I could even make sense of what I'd heard.

Norma had been in the pigeon loft. I saw her running to the creek and Fleurette struggling across the meadow, where none of us should have been alone.

Norma got to her first. Fleurette was crying and pushing at her. Norma tried to hold her but then realized that she only wanted to get to the house. They turned and ran together, slipping in the mud and half-melted snow. Sheriff Heath reached her before I did. He pointed his two deputies in the direction of the creek bed and corralled us into the house.

Fleurette wore a black wool skirt that was soaked through with water and splattered with mud. If she had been wearing a hat, it was gone. She kept covering her face and turning away from us. It was impossible to get a word out of her.

Sheriff Heath saw that he could do nothing for a girl in this condition. He told us to take her upstairs and get her settled down. He would watch the house and wait for word from his deputies.

We took Fleurette to Mother's fortress-like bedroom, where at last she started to calm down. She let us pull off her wet clothes and wash her face and dress her in a nightgown and a flannel robe of Mother's. I found no scratches on her, just mud and grass. Once she was propped up in bed with us on either side of her, she was finally able to speak.

"Two men," she said. "I could barely see them through the trees. They were standing in the creek bed, like they were waiting for me."

"What did they do to you?" I said.

She wrapped her arms around her chest. "They fired at me and I ran."

"And you're sure you're not hurt?" I wanted to pull up her nightgown and check every part of her, her knees and elbows and the tiny dip between her shoulders, but she held tightly to the blankets and wouldn't let me.

"What were you doing down at the creek?" Norma asked.

Fleurette looked from Norma to me and back again, her chin trembling. "The water pump was stuck. I just went to get water for the washing. I thought everyone could see me."

The water pump did have a tendency to stick in the winter. We resorted to melting buckets of snow or bringing up water from the creek when we couldn't get it moving.

"But there were three men standing about with nothing to do," Norma said, "and one of us could have given it a try as well. You know we can usually get it going again. Why didn't you just ask someone for help?"

"That's enough," I said. "Sheriff Heath is waiting downstairs for a word from you. Can you describe these men?"

She shook her head and sunk deeper under the covers. "They wore long overcoats and hats with the brims turned down. They were tall men, taller than Mr. Kaufman, I think."

"And they were standing right in the creek? In the water?"

"They were on the flat rock I use to get across."

I ran my hand along her forehead and she closed her eyes. Her hair formed a perfect half-circle of brilliant inky black on the pillow. "Stay here and rest. We'll be downstairs with the sheriff."

Sheriff Heath and his deputies were standing outside in a tight circle, stamping their feet and talking in low voices. The men had parked an automobile in our neighbor's field on the other side of the creek and driven off in it. There was nothing but the ruts of tires in the dirt by the time the deputies got there.

We told them what little we had learned from Fleurette. It seemed most likely that the men had been crossing the creek to get closer to the house when she surprised them.

The sky had cleared a little that afternoon and lit up the frozen ground. Sheriff Heath raised a hand to shield his eyes from the glare and squinted at me. "They're getting bolder," he said. "They'll slip up soon enough. This is almost at an end. But I can't have the three of you running around in the woods and splashing in the creek. You have to do as we ask and stay where we can protect you."

Norma and I just nodded. We were going to have to take turns watching Fleurette.

"Is your sister asleep?" Sheriff Heath asked.

We said that she was.

He reached under his overcoat and consulted his watch. "That's fine. Let her sleep, and then see to it that she has a good supper. I'll be back at six."

"I'm not sure it's worth the trip," I said. "I don't think she'll have anything more to say."

He squinted up at the house and back down the road and then said, "I'm coming back to give her a shooting lesson. The three of you will all carry revolvers until this is over."

And that's how we came to be standing in a meadow on a bracingly cold November night, struggling to see our fence-post targets against the gathering dark, taking one shot after another as the sheriff braced us by the shoulders and spoke steadily in our ears, slipping the revolvers out of our pale and frozen hands to reload them so that we could fire again and again and again at the menace that waited somewhere out there beyond the creek bed.

⫷ 34 ⫸

HENRY KAUFMAN AND HIS FRIENDS had been toying with
us the way a barn cat teases a fledgling fallen from its nest:
viciously, but unhurriedly. So it was with some relief that we
received, in the middle of November, his most serious and
specific threat against us.

Now, at last, we had a date and a place.

```
Madam—We demand $1000 or we will kill you. Give
Monee to girl dressed in black at the corner of
Broadway and Carroll street, Paterson, Saturday
night at eight o'clock. If you don't pay we will
fire your house and take that girl of yours. We
know your horse and wagon. We live in Paterson.
Ha ha!
                                      —H. K. & Co.
```

I read it and pushed it to the middle of the table. We all
looked at Deputy Morris, who happened to be on duty the af-

ternoon it arrived. When he didn't say anything, each of us spoke at once.

"Well," I said. "This time we'll catch him."

"A thousand dollars!" Fleurette said. "Is that what I'm worth?"

"Stop that," Norma said. "And we won't pay it."

The deputy reacted to our chorus of voices by standing up and announcing, "This is a matter for Sheriff Heath to decide. You ladies go about your business. He'll be here soon enough."

But a storm came on that night, pushing hail and freezing rain across the fields in waves. Every time we thought it had let up, another icy draft blew through. The weather must have delayed the sheriff, and there was nothing to do but wait. The deputies had been on duty for over twelve hours. I finally convinced them to come in for a bowl of soup and a hot bun. Ordinarily it was forbidden for them to dine with us, but these men had expected to be home for supper and weren't. They had to have something.

Around ten Norma and Fleurette gave up and went to bed. I stayed up and walked the dark house for another hour until at last I heard the tires of Sheriff Heath's automobile in our gravel drive.

His deputies ran out to tell him about the letter, and soon he was standing in the parlor with four of his men around him, the two that were going off duty and the two that were starting the night shift. The room was filled with the smell of wet wool and smoke from the camp stove in our barn. Sheriff Heath took a seat on the divan, placed his hat on his knees, and read the letter to himself. When he was finished, he looked up at me, searching my face for something, then read it again.

"Take a walk around back," he told his men. "Carry a lamp and check the bushes and the outbuildings. Then wait for me in the barn."

When they were gone, he said, "Sit down. I have something to ask you."

"What is it?"

"Just—sit."

I dropped down next to him and waited. He rubbed his eyes and held his forehead in his hands, breathing so quietly that I thought he had fallen asleep right in front of me. At last he pulled his hands away and turned to look at me, his eyes watery and red.

He swallowed hard. "Miss Kopp. I've tried everything in my power to stop this man. I've followed him around town, I've watched his house, I've spoken to his sister and his business associates, and, for that matter, I've spoken to him. I've tried to build a case for the prosecutor but they fight me on it. They've never charged a factory owner with any kind of crime and they're not inclined to start now. The Kaufmans are a powerful family. They own mills in three states. They can get all the silk men behind them."

He waited to make sure I understood. I nodded, and he continued.

"I've also devoted more deputies to your protection than the sheriff's office can readily afford. The Freeholders fight with me over every invoice I submit to them. They make it nearly impossible for me to get my men paid. So far I've been able to hide the expense, but if they find out how much they are spending on this one case, I'll be held to account."

"I'm so sorry," I said. "I didn't realize—"

He held up his hand to silence me. "That's not your concern. What does concern you is the fact that we need to bring this matter to a resolution quickly. We cannot spend the rest of the winter lying in wait."

Once again he paused and waited for my agreement. I nodded and he went on.

"This letter gives us an opportunity. I would like you to go to Paterson on Saturday night as the letter instructs. You will carry your revolver and I will post men all around you. We will make sure nothing happens to you. But we must try to catch this girl in black or whoever might be with her."

"Of course," I blurted out. "We have to. I can do it. I've become quite practiced with the revolver." I might have sounded a little too eager to get a shot at Henry Kaufman. The sheriff looked over at me worriedly and seemed to take a minute to make up his mind.

"All right. That's fine," he said at last. "But that's not all I want you to do."

What else could there be? I squared my shoulders and waited.

"I think we should go to the papers," he said.

"The papers? Do you mean that we should let them write about us?" Norma would not like this idea. Other people's troubles belonged in the paper for the world to read about, not ours.

"Yes. I want to let them write a story about your vigil on the street corner. You will give them a full account of what has happened, going all the way back to July. Let them report on the events of Saturday night, whatever they may be, and run their stories in the papers on Monday."

"But why would you want reporters meddling in this?"

He leaned back and rested his head against the divan. "It

will force the prosecutor to take notice," he said, his voice a little hoarse. "The Freeholders don't like to see unsolved crimes in the paper. They complain about the bills from the prosecutor's office as much as they complain about mine. They want to see that they are getting their money's worth. If the papers run this story, the prosecutor will be made to answer for his lack of action." He looked over at me. "What do you think, Miss Kopp?"

I could feel my face flush. "We've always been a very private family."

"I know. You stay out here on this country road, with acres between you and the nearest neighbor. None of you seem to belong to any social clubs. I've never seen you entertain friends or school chums or gentlemen. For whatever reason, the three of you have made up your mind to stay out of sight. I know this won't be easy for you. But I think the only way to bring these men to trial is to begin with a trial in the papers, as distasteful as that is."

The decision was mine to make, really. Norma would be opposed to it, Fleurette would beg to sit for an interview, and it would be up to me to cast the deciding vote.

"Don't you think that drawing attention to him in the papers will only provoke him?"

"I don't think Henry Kaufman could be more provoked than he is right now." Sheriff Heath pulled out his watch. "It's almost midnight. Get some sleep. You can tell me in the morning."

I nodded and he rose to leave. In spite of his fatigue, he always stood very straight. He walked stiffly to the door and then he was gone, leaving me alone in the dark with my decision.

⇥ 35 ⇤

FLEURETTE NEVER ASKED why she was schooled at home. There were no other children on Sicomac Road, and it might not have occurred to her that there was a school in town she could have attended. She simply accepted the idea that little girls do lessons under the supervision of their families. She didn't know that Mother insisted on keeping her hidden, that Mother's fear of scandal and her mistrust of paperwork and government and organizations of any kind made it impossible for her to consider sending Fleurette out of the house.

We used to argue that the school would not question a woman in her late forties with a young daughter, but Mother was convinced that someone would put the puzzle together. Although we had adoption papers, which should have made these matters easier, we had never told Fleurette that she was adopted, so the papers did us no good. This left us in a difficult position. It seemed easier—at least in Mother's mind—not to discuss it at all and to just keep the child on the farm.

To explain Fleurette's birth to the family, my uncles were given the impression that our father had returned briefly to our lives and then left again. Fleurette must have had the same general idea, although we almost never spoke of our father.

Nothing about the situation seemed odd to her, until one day when she was about nine and had been told to read aloud from a book of pioneer stories for children. She was reading about Daniel Boone. None of us were paying much attention, as the sound of Fleurette reading her lessons aloud was such a familiar part of our day that we only pretended to listen as we went about our work.

I was balancing our ledger books and had my back to Fleurette as she read, "'At last they turned to go home, when suddenly two fierce-looking Indians sprang out of the woods and seized the boat.'" I looked over at Mother, alarmed, but she was intent on her needlepoint and didn't seem to hear. Mother thought nothing of letting children read the most terrifying tales of ogres and witches and adventures gone terribly wrong. It was one of our points of disagreement about Fleurette's upbringing.

"'Betsey fought with her own oar,'" Fleurette was saying, "'but it did no good: the Indians carried them off through the woods.'"

I put down my pencil and made ready to say something. Fleurette was a sensitive and imaginative child. She'd be up half the night after a story like this.

"'Betsey reached up and broke the bushes as she passed along. She knew that her father would look for her, and she hoped that he might follow her by seeing the broken bushes.'"

That was enough. "Mother, don't you think—"

Mother looked up, but before I could finish, Fleurette had closed her book and was standing in front of her. "Where is our father, *maman?*"

"What have you been reading?" she said, fumbling with her needlepoint.

"Pioneer stories," I said. "I was about to say that they're too much for a little girl."

"Don't we have a father?" Fleurette said, climbing into Mother's lap. "Doesn't Francis have a father?"

Mother pushed her back to the floor and smoothed her skirt. "Of course," she said. "Everyone has a father."

"Where is he?"

Mother looked at me for help. But she was the one who refused to speak of our father, and who seemed determined to make sure that he never heard about Fleurette and never knew where we lived.

"I'm afraid he's . . ."

I shook my head. It seemed unfair to Frank Kopp to say that he was dead. She'd called herself a widow before, but never in front of Fleurette. Besides, the man could appear at our front door someday, and what a shock that would be!

"Gone?" Fleurette said. "Gone to fight the Indians?"

Mother smiled and patted her hand. "That's right, *chéri.* He's very brave."

I couldn't believe how easily she lied to the child. Then again, what else would she have said?

"Is he coming back?"

"I'm afraid not. He's gone very far."

IN SOME WAYS, we all raised Fleurette. She was a wild and unpredictable child who was as happy stomping through the creek in search of frogs as she was in a dancing frock on a make-believe stage. It required the attention of all three of us—and Francis, before he married—just to keep her working at her lessons and her chores. As she got older, Mother couldn't match Fleurette's energy and abdicated more and more of the responsibility for bringing her up to me and Norma.

But for the first ten or twelve years of the girl's life, I stood by and watched my mother raise her. When she had a fever, Mother took care of her. On her birthday, Mother planned the party. And if she skinned her knee or got chased by one of the roosters, it was Mother she ran to with her tears.

It was never me. Fleurette never needed a thing from me — until now. I would stand on the corner with a gun all night if that's what it took to keep those men away from her.

⤐ 36 ⤏

"MISS KOPP, is it your assertion that the attack was entirely unprovoked?"

I sat at a table placed in Sheriff Heath's office for my use. He had wanted the reporters to come to the courthouse so he could parade them right past the prosecutor's office. But every room at the courthouse was occupied. The reporters milled around in the hall until the sheriff was satisfied that they'd attracted enough attention, and then he walked them across the lawn to the prison.

After a brief introduction from Sheriff Heath, I told my story in as straightforward a manner as possible. Every small newspaper in Passaic and Bergen County had sent a reporter. Many of the larger papers had news bureaus nearby, so reporters from New York, Philadelphia, Newark, and Trenton papers were present too.

The men sat quietly and scribbled notes as I gave a short and carefully rehearsed account of the events. But as soon as I finished, they unleashed a volley of questions that I was entirely unprepared to answer.

"Miss, had you ever fired a gun before Sheriff Heath gave you lessons?"

"How do three girls manage the running of a household on their own? Is there not an uncle or some other male relation who could take you in?"

"Haven't any of you received a proposal of marriage in all these years?"

I looked to Sheriff Heath for help. He'd been reclining in a chair behind his own desk, appearing entirely relaxed, as if he spent every afternoon being questioned by twenty reporters. But when I caught his eye, he jumped to his feet and took over.

"The Kopp sisters do just fine on their own," he said. "They live in the countryside and already knew how to handle a hunting rifle, and have proven quite competent with a revolver. And of course the attack was unprovoked, Simon. How would three girls in a buggy incite an oncoming automobile to plow directly into them?"

A rumble of laughter went through the room, then it fell silent as the reporters scribbled in their notebooks.

"I believe that answers your questions," Sheriff Heath said, returning to his seat.

A brawny Italian man in the back of the room said, "No, sir, I didn't get an answer to my question about marriage proposals."

I jumped up before Sheriff Heath could. These reporters needed to see that I could speak for myself. "The presence or absence of suitors in the lives of the Kopp sisters has no bearing on this matter," I told them, "and I see no men here today who would stand a chance with any one of us."

That got loud, appreciative guffaws from the men and a grin from the sheriff.

The questions lasted only a few more minutes, and then Sheriff Heath briefed the reporters on his role in the investigation and the lack of cooperation from the prosecutor's office. He gave them the particulars about the meeting with the woman in black planned for the following night, and distributed handwritten copies of the threatening letter so that they could reproduce it in full in their papers. He had arranged for any reporters who wished to be present on Saturday night to assemble in a garage on Broadway just a few blocks away from the meeting place. They were warned to arrive early and remain hidden until released by the sheriff or one of his deputies.

Every man in the room seemed eager to go along. There was a current of excitement in the air. It was the anticipation of a pack of hunting dogs waiting to be turned loose on their prey, or the nervous excitement of a posse rounded up in the night to go after a horse thief. Even I felt it.

But as soon as the reporters left, Sheriff Heath turned somber again. "This is only a game to them," he said. "I'll need to station a deputy at the garage to keep them from rushing out and bungling the whole operation." He stood to open the door for me. "But that's not your concern. Get some rest and be ready for tomorrow. Dress warmly and wear sturdy shoes. Bring a handbag for your weapon. I'll call for you at seven."

He'd polished his badge and put on a fresh collar. When I stood at the door, I could smell the dry, chalky laundry starch his wife used. "Thank you for coming to my aid. With the reporters, I mean. I'm not used to being interrogated like that."

He gave me the briefest of smiles and then said, "You did just fine, Miss Kopp. You gave it right back to them. They just wanted to see if you can handle yourself, and you can."

⇥ 37 ⇤

"SHOULDN'T I BE THE ONE to meet the girl and give her the money?" Fleurette said.

"No one is giving anyone money," I answered. "We are not about to take their demands seriously. The only item of value I'll be carrying is a revolver."

I was sitting on Fleurette's bed, watching her search her wardrobe for the proper ensemble in which to rendezvous with a blackmailer. She produced a cape with a fur collar and red velvet lining, and a hat that had a hidden pocket in the band.

"That cape would look ridiculous on me," I said, "and, besides, the sheriff wants me in dark, sensible clothes. It's going to be freezing tonight, and who knows how long I'll be standing out there."

Fleurette wrapped the cape around her own shoulders. I had to admit that it suited her. She looked like a woman of mystery, someone who might carry a thousand dollars to a lady in black and live to tell about it. She fixed her bright and lively eyes on me.

"Would you shoot her?" she asked.

"Who?"

"The girl in black. The one who's coming to collect the money. Would you fire at her?"

"No! I'm not going to shoot a girl who's been roped into this mess. Besides, the sheriff and his deputies will be all around me. All I have to do is stand in a conspicuous location and wait."

Fleurette twirled around and the cape flew about like a wild bird coming to land on her shoulders. "I would do a much better job of standing in a conspicuous location," she said.

I smiled. "I know you would."

Norma walked in, eyeing the frivolous garments Fleurette had thrown on the bed.

"You aren't wearing any of that," she said.

"Of course not," I said.

"I don't see why we bother employing deputies if the women of this community have to go out and catch their own criminals."

"They can't do this without me. You know that."

Norma frowned and crossed the room to look through a pile of handbags that Fleurette had tossed on a chair. She discarded a fringed teardrop-shaped bag of yellow silk, a beaded purse made to look like a butterfly, and a velvet pouch meant to hold binoculars at the theater. "These won't do for carrying a revolver," she said. "You'd get all tangled up in these frills if you needed to fire it."

"I won't need to fire it. Why are you two so convinced that I'm going out to gun down an innocent girl tonight?"

Norma looked at me sorrowfully, as if it pained her to see how little I understood about my own situation.

"He wouldn't have you carry it if he didn't think you might need it."

I'D BEEN PACING THE HOUSE for an hour by the time I heard the sheriff's tires in the drive. There were two deputies riding along, and two more would stay with Norma and Fleurette. Before he let me in the car, Sheriff Heath asked to have a look at my shoes to make sure I could run in them. I lifted my skirt and he looked down, then gave me a half-smile when he saw that I was wearing the boots I usually wear to muck out the barn.

"Good girl," he said quietly.

He reached for my handbag—a sensible leather traveling bag we'd found in Mother's closet—and inspected its contents. It was empty save for the revolver, which he pulled out and checked for bullets.

"You have nothing else of value? No jewelry around your neck or combs in your hair? No money tucked away?"

He was standing so close to me that I thought he might start rifling through my coat pockets.

"Nothing at all."

We gave each other a level stare. I had the feeling he was sizing me up one last time.

"All right," he said. "Then let's go."

No one said a word on the drive to Paterson. We parked at City Hall, several blocks away from the meeting place. We disembarked and I stood shivering in the garage, looking around at the ghostly old timbers and wondering what these walls had seen over the years. Had they ever watched anyone do what I was about to do?

"We can't get too close without attracting attention," Sheriff Heath explained. "You'll walk from here."

"From here!" Never in my life had I walked down a city street at night unaccompanied. But I regretted saying it. Sheriff Heath looked worried suddenly, as if he just realized he'd made a mistake in asking me to do this.

"I'll be fine," I said quickly.

He shook his head. "No. You're right. Someone should be with you. Here's what I'll do. I'll send my men with you, but they'll each walk one block over. Morris will stay a block to the east, on Fair, and English will walk a block to the west on Van Houten. I've got a deputy stationed on Auburn in front of the garage where the reporters are. He knows to watch out for you. You'll pass him on the way, but you'll walk on the opposite side of the street, and you won't look at him or signal to him unless you're in trouble."

I agreed to that and the three of us set out for Broadway. Deputy Morris went first and cut to the left, which would take him down a narrow street occupied mostly by cobblers and tailors and other such shops whose doors had closed hours ago. Deputy English waited a few minutes and then followed him, cutting over to the right to walk down a street populated with small churches and a girls' school. When Sheriff Heath gave me the nod, I left too, but he called after me in a whisper.

"Miss Kopp!"

I turned around. He was standing by himself in the entrance to the garage, his hands stuffed in his overcoat.

"You won't know where I am tonight. You won't be able to see me. But I'll be watching every minute. I won't take my eyes off you."

I swallowed the mixture of dread and apprehension welling up inside of me, then nodded and set off for Broadway.

The streets were dark, but not entirely empty. Four young couples went running past me, laughing and calling out to one another, maybe on their way to a dance. A few workmen walked silently along, the ends of their cigarettes glowing and bobbing like fireflies.

Paterson's downtown ended just past Straight Street, giving way to three-story apartment buildings meant mostly for people who worked in the shops. Each one had an identical patch of grass in the front and a little flower bed that held geraniums in the summer and mounds of dirty snow in the winter. Smoke rose from the chimneys, and sometimes I could catch the smell of someone's dinner: a pork chop in a pan, onions and sausage stewing over a burner.

Sheriff Heath's men stayed just ahead of me. Every time I reached an intersection, I caught a glimpse of them crossing the same street one block away. As I approached Auburn, the deputy stationed there ducked into a doorway's shadows. I was careful not to look directly at him, and I made a point of not looking up at any of the windows around him to see if the reporters were watching me.

I arrived at Broadway and Carroll sooner than I'd expected and stood for a few minutes on each corner, studying the layout of the streets and the walkways, looking for an escape route, or a place to hide, should I require one.

On one corner stood a nondescript brick building that might have housed small offices. There were very few windows facing the street, and no lights in any of them. Across the street was a flower shop, also dark and shuttered. The corner opposite was a vacant lot, which was mowed and cleared, but strangely frightening to me for its emptiness. A vision came to me of a girl in black standing in the middle of the lot, her arms reaching out for the money she'd been promised, the dry stubble of last summer's grass and what remained of the snow all around her. It made me shiver to think about it.

I crossed the street to stand in front of a dilapidated wooden building that might have once been used as a workshop for a furniture maker or a blacksmith. It occurred to me that Sheriff Heath must have been hidden away somewhere, perhaps behind one of the building's boarded windows.

It had to be eight o'clock by now. There was no sign of a girl in black. In fact, no one had passed me on the street, and only two automobiles had driven by. I wondered what Norma and Fleurette were doing at home. Were they thinking of me this very minute? I tried to picture them, moving from window to window, watching for signs of trouble.

I'd been clutching the handbag under my arm for so long that I'd forgotten it was there. I reached in to make sure the revolver was aimed out in front of me. Just then I heard a loud bang that made me jump and nearly drop the bag. Down the street I could see one of the deputies leap out into the intersection to check on me.

It must have been a motor misfiring. I stepped out into a pool of light cast by the moon's reflection so that whoever was watching could see me.

A figure came striding up Carroll Street. In the darkness I couldn't tell if it was a man or a woman. Finally I made out the shape of a long skirt and a broad-brimmed hat.

Was that her? I couldn't tell if she was wearing black. Everything was black.

I shifted my handbag so I could feel the butt of the revolver through the leather. In spite of the cold, I was hot under my collar. A trickle of sweat ran down my chest, and another followed the same course along my spine.

As she got closer, she slowed down. Had she seen me?

I took a quick look around to make sure no one else was approaching. Several blocks away I saw two men cross the street. Somewhere a motor rattled and stalled. I noticed all the sounds I hadn't heard before: the guard dogs barking from behind the mills down on the river, the basement vents releasing hissing steam from the boilers, the distant wail of a baby who could not be comforted.

The girl got within a block of me and turned down Van Houten. She must have walked right past Deputy English. Was I expected to follow her? She'd given me no indication that I should, so I stayed at my post. Another automobile rolled by a few blocks away. There was the sound of a train whistle, then the ragged cough of a phlegmatic old man.

Finally a trio of men approached from the garage on Auburn. I recognized Sheriff Heath from the outline of his hat and his overcoat. I could also make out the figure of Deputy Morris and one of the reporters I'd met yesterday.

When they reached me, Sheriff Heath said in a low voice, "It's nine o'clock. We've waited long enough. Either they're not coming, or they spotted us and ran off."

"What about that girl on Carroll?" I asked.

He shook his head. "That wasn't her. English followed her home and talked to her. She didn't know anything about it."

I hadn't realized that I'd been holding my breath. I let it out at last. Sheriff Heath reached over and took the revolver from my handbag. "Let me carry this," he said. "You've done your job."

On the way back to the garage, he introduced me to the reporter, a man named George Pieters who worked for the Paterson paper. "George is a good friend of mine," Sheriff Heath said. "You can count on him to get the story right. I told him he could ride along with us and ask some questions on the way. You tell him whatever he wants to know. Tomorrow a bunch of them are going to come out to the house to get their interviews. They all wanted to talk to you tonight, but I told them to let you get some rest. Nobody's filing a story until tomorrow night anyway."

On the way home, the reporter asked me to explain again, in my own words, how this mess got started and what we'd done to try to stop it. He wanted to know what our house looked like when we returned home from the beach and found it in a state of preparation for a bonfire, and how I'd learned to handle a gun, and what would make a woman take the unusual step of arming herself with a revolver to protect her sisters from harm.

I looked out the window at the black night and the dim outlines of dairy barns and trees in the distance.

"My sisters and I have no one but each other," I said at last, "and if anyone should take up a handgun in their defense, I will be the one to do it."

⇥ 38 ⇤

THE PAPER WAS FOLDED on the kitchen table when I got up Monday morning. I lifted it up and saw an empty square where the headline should have been. The missing headline was returned by pigeon post a few hours later and I pasted it back in place.

GIRL WAITS WITH GUN
Miss Kopp, Annoyed for Months,
Goes to Place Named in Letter—
Home Guarded at Night

MISS CONSTANCE KOPP, who spent a large part of Saturday night under police guard waiting for the writer of Black Hand letters to appear to claim $1000 that had been demanded, said today that threatening letters were the least of the troubles that have placed the home of herself and her sisters in a virtual state of siege.

For weeks the house has been guarded night and day by armed men, but despite this the women on the place have been shot at by unknown prowlers whom Miss Kopp says come to the place in an automobile.

"One evening just after dusk I happened to look out of my bedroom window and saw a man standing near a tree not 50 feet from the house," said Constance Kopp. "He was on our property and I asked him what he wanted. There was no response, so I fired a shot through the window screen. Immediately he fired several shots back at me and I fainted from fright.

"On another occasion when Florette had gone down to the stream that runs through our land to get a pail of water, a man who was hiding in the brush nearby fired two shots at her.

"And yet, one, at least, of the County officials pooh-poohed our stories and refused to credit them.

"Why, these desperate but cowardly individuals even broke into our home one afternoon during our absence and piled up our best furniture in one room.

"None of us dare to go away from the house after dark without our revolvers, and we have a dandy magazine gun that we would love to turn loose on one of the skulking night prowlers, for that's all they are."

In response to the Black Hand letter sent to her home, Miss Kopp waited at the corner in Paterson until nine o'clock on a Saturday night but no girl dressed in black approached seeking $1000. Miss Kopp then left for her home. She had a revolver concealed in her muff and was ready to use it.

Sheriff Heath and some of his deputies patrolled the neighborhood of Broadway and Carroll Street in an automobile for an hour, closely watching Miss Kopp and all women dressed in black who passed this corner.

The Misses Kopp are attractive young women. The family is well to do. The authorities have granted the young women permission to carry revolvers.

"If we ever catch a strange man sneaking around our house after dark we will use the revolvers," said Miss Constance Kopp.

"YOU'VE NEVER FAINTED IN YOUR LIFE," Fleurette said, slapping the paper down on her sewing table. "And I'm going to write in and tell them how to spell my name."

Accounts of our ordeal ran in the *New York Tribune*, the *Sun*, the *New York Herald*, the *Philadelphia Evening Ledger*, and all the New Jersey papers. They got quite a bit wrong. One claimed that I stood on a street corner in Newark, several misspelled Fleurette's name, and all of them appended my quotes with more fanciful language. "Oh, for a Chance to Shoot at the Nasty Prowlers!" read one headline, which sent Fleurette into a fit of giggles.

"The papers have made a joke of our situation, which I knew they would do," Norma said. "I wish you would have told me you were thinking of speaking to them so I could have told you not to."

"You don't suppose Constance kept it from you intentionally, do you?" Fleurette asked, a look of mock surprise in her eyes.

Norma stirred her coffee to cool it and held the paper up again, tucking her chin down in a way that pushed the smallest roll of fat out from under her neck. It was a gesture of double-chinned disapproval that old ladies employed to great effect. I sometimes thought that Norma could not wait to reach a very elderly age and make full use of the gravity that one acquires later in life.

"There will, of course, be terrible consequences for exposing us in this manner," she said, "and I can hardly imagine what Francis will say, or poor Bessie, who has been nothing but kind to us and will have quite a shock today when she reads her paper."

"I'm surprised we haven't seen Francis already this morning," Fleurette said. "He must be saving it for Thanksgiving."

I had taken quite a chill on Saturday night and sat sniveling under an afghan reading the other papers while Fleurette let down the hem on a dress she'd outgrown. Norma finished her coffee and laced up her boots to take another batch of pigeons out for a ride. It was bitingly cold out, but the sun was shining and the roads were clear. Dolley had hardly left the barn in the last few weeks, and Norma had decided that both the horse and the pigeons needed some fresh air.

"Are you going to be well enough to travel on Thursday?" Fleurette asked as she snipped at the threads on her dress. "Because if you aren't, we're leaving you here with your own guard. I am not missing Thanksgiving."

"I'll be fine," I said, "and I certainly hope the deputies will get the day off."

"Oh, no, I'd like to bring a pair of them to dinner. Can you imagine Francis's face if we brought a police escort?"

IN FACT, Sheriff Heath was not at all willing to leave us unguarded on Thanksgiving. "I'll bet Kaufman and his gang won't take a holiday," he grumbled when he stopped by on Tuesday to deliver another deputy to our barn. We were taking our customary walk around the property. "They'll drink whiskey all day and drive around all night making a mess for my men to clean up. The holidays are the worst days of the year for us."

The wind picked up and lifted my hat. I pushed it back down over my ears.

"You shouldn't even be out in this cold," he said.

"I'm fine. I just caught a little chill. But surely your men want a day to spend with their families."

We passed the barn, where Deputy English was watching the chickens peck at the frozen stubble in their yard. He touched his hat and nodded.

"Oh, I'll give them the day off," the sheriff said. "But they'll be called in if there's a shooting or robbery, which I guarantee will happen before sundown. I'll be the one on patrol on Thursday."

"What will Mrs. Heath say to that?"

"Mrs. Heath—" He stopped and looked at me, that curious searching look that I couldn't decipher. There was something sorrowful about him all at once, but as soon as it came over him it went away again.

"Mrs. Heath is married to the Sheriff of Bergen County," he said briskly, "and she knows the sacrifice required."

⇥ 39 ⇤

I AWOKE ON THANKSGIVING MORNING to a world frozen in place. A northern storm had blown through the day before, leaving behind an unusually cold, clear sky. Every window in the house was entombed under a plate of ice. Icicles hung like daggers from the roof. There was no hope of moving the water pump, and none of us wanted to brave the frozen meadow to see if there was still water flowing in the creek. We broke icicles off the porch and melted them in the kitchen so we could wash up before we left for Francis and Bessie's. There were two jars of plum preserves left in the pantry and a nice package of salted pork from our neighbor, so we wrapped those in a tea towel and brought them along.

Sheriff Heath arrived just as we were getting ready to leave. "I wish you'd let me drive you," he said. Norma just grunted and pushed past him to harness Dolley.

"We're afraid of what Francis might think," Fleurette said.

"We are not afraid of Francis," I said. "We'll be fine. The crooks don't come out until tonight, right?"

The sheriff watched as Fleurette went to join Norma in the barn. She wore a stylish dress of reseda-green silk, gathered a little more tightly at the waist than I would have allowed had I any idea what she'd been working on.

"That girl has grown up in the time I've known her," he said.

I sighed and shook my head. "And I'm afraid the kidnapping threats have only gone to her head. She thinks she's quite the desirable little prize. I don't know what we're going to do with her."

"Keep her on the farm as long as you can," he said.

"I don't know how much longer that will be. But for today—"

"Today you should ride alongside her and keep an eye on the road. Pull down the storm curtains so no one can see you. Are you taking your revolver?"

"I am. But you don't think I'll need it?"

"I hope not."

Norma and Fleurette rode around front in the carriage. Dolley stamped at the ice and great clouds of steam came from her nostrils. I climbed up and squeezed in next to Fleurette.

"I'll drive past your brother's house a few times later today," the sheriff shouted as we turned to ride away.

I nodded and watched as he strode to the barn, a small figure in a gray and empty landscape.

FRANCIS AND BESSIE lived in a neighborhood of modest but thoroughly modern bungalows in Hawthorne. The homes were snugly built and outfitted with good plumbing and gas and new electrical wires. Each home sat next to a driveway and a garage built more for automobiles than carriages, although as we drove down the street, I saw that a few people still kept a horse stabled.

They were the first to occupy their home. After they moved in, the smell of sawdust and varnish hung about them for months. At Bessie's urging, Francis painted the house a cheerful cornflower blue and installed window boxes that sported primroses or geraniums, depending on the season. Every room blazed with electric lamps, even the children's room, and all the furniture came from Rafner's on Grand Street. Mother had been shocked to walk into their house for the first time and see that they had purchased a complete living room set, exactly as advertised in the newspaper. She'd been even more shocked when Norma pointed out that it had been listed for $195, with a charge account that offered a year to pay.

They purchased the walnut dining room set as well, which came with a china cabinet, a velvet seamless rug, and a buffet mirror. "I suppose I don't have to go down the hall to see that you bought the bedroom outfit, too," Mother had sniffed, "when we have a farmhouse full of furniture you could have taken."

But Francis and Bessie didn't want the furniture from the farmhouse, and for that I couldn't blame them. Their house was entirely new and, as Francis liked to say, "free of defects," by which he meant that it was free of gas leaks and drafts and the dark, hulking cabinets and monstrous carved chairs that represented our mother's Austrian girlhood. Theirs was an American house, a house of the twentieth century, and her old things had no place there.

Francis met us outside, unhitched Dolley, and walked her around back where she could get some water. The three of us stood on the front lawn, feeling too uncivilized to go inside. Had we really been sleeping with revolvers at our bedsides and shooting at strange men in the dark? Were we really in so much danger that the sheriff himself had to follow us around? It didn't seem like we belonged in Francis's cheerful cottage, this tidy place giving off warmth and light and the rich fragrance of Thanksgiving dinner.

The children spotted us and ran outside. The boy—whom we called Frankie to distinguish him from his father, Francis, and his grandfather, Frank—ran straight into Norma and almost knocked her over. The two of them shared a love of animals understood by no one else in the family. He led her indoors to ask her opinion about a nest of baby mice he'd uncovered in the garden. Lorraine, the older of the two, wore a dress she'd helped her mother make, and she and Fleurette fell into a conversation about collars and hemlines.

That left me on the porch by myself, taking a deep breath before I followed them inside and subjected myself to my brother's harangue.

Fortunately, it was Bessie who got to me first. She ran to me before I'd even closed the door and reached up to wrap her arms around my neck. We'd always had an unexpected sort of kinship. She was kind and infinitely patient with my brother, and she ran a good household and raised two well-behaved children. For that I admired her even if I didn't want to live the same kind of life she did. And in turn, for reasons I couldn't fathom, she treated me as if I led an adventurous and exciting life out in Wyckoff, worthy of envy and approbation.

"I'm glad to see you in one piece," she said, almost in a

whisper. "You gave us both a terrible scare. We didn't tell the children."

"Of course not," I said. "I'm sorry that you had to read it in the paper. That was thoughtless of us."

She stood back and smiled up at me, gripping my arms by the shoulders, and then leaned in again. "I've forbidden any talk of the newspapers in this house until after dinner."

Then she turned to lead me to the kitchen, adding in a low voice, "I only wish I could've taken a revolver and stood out there with you on Saturday night."

I laughed, imagining Bessie with a hand mixer in one hand and a gun in the other. "Come with me next time."

Bessie was rolling out dough on the drain board for another of what Francis called her "illustrious pies." For the next hour we worked side by side, talking of little other than the children and the weather and Bessie's volunteer work at the library. I marveled at how good it felt to be in a warm, well-appointed kitchen, enjoying such easygoing company. Maybe my life had been too rough lately. I was more relaxed in that kitchen than I had been in months.

"If you enjoy this so much, Constance, you can take over the cooking at Christmas," she said, grinning at me. "But you'll have to wait until next year. We're going to my aunt's in Boston this year. Why don't you all come with us?"

"It's too hard to leave the farm in the winter," I said. "We'll be fine on our own."

We ate our dinner in peace, with Bessie, Fleurette, and the children keeping up most of the conversation while Francis carved the birds and I passed the platters. It was a traditional Kopp family meal. Mother never did develop a taste for turkey, preferring a roasted goose or duck at the holidays. In keeping with her tradition, Bessie found a fine, fat duck and roasted a chicken as well. There were green beans and corn that she had canned last summer, pickled onions, and dinner rolls that exhaled steam when we broke them apart. The rolls were made according to a recipe of Mother's that no one other than Bessie had ever mastered. Little chips of butter, as cold as ice, had to be cut into the dough at the last possible minute, and no one else seemed to have a knack for it.

After dinner Norma and Fleurette stood to clear the table, and Francis and I stepped out on the back porch, where we could see Dolley nibbling at patches of thawed grass in the lawn. She pawed at the ground and slapped her tail around the way a person might hop up and down to keep warm.

Francis closed the door behind us and said, "I wasn't expecting to read about my sisters in the paper."

"Which paper?"

"There was more than one?" He groaned, his breath like smoke in the air.

"We made the news in New York and Philadelphia."

"No," he said sharply. "I didn't know about that."

For a minute we stood side by side in silence and let the sounds from inside the house settle in around us—the rattle of china and silver, the rush of water into a pan, the children's footsteps through every room. Francis lit his pipe and the sweet tobacco smoke drifted over to me.

I wasn't about to apologize or offer up any sort of explanation. I waited for him to say his piece.

"I didn't know you had armed men guarding the house. Most of those things in the paper—you never told me about any of that."

"I know. I should have. But what would you have done?

Bring us all here to live? What if Kaufman and his gang had followed us over here?"

He leaned on his porch railing. "Well, I should have done more. You're my responsibility."

"We are responsible for ourselves."

"And look at what a fine job you've done. What if those men at the creek had shot Fleurette?"

"But they didn't."

The door opened behind us. It was little Lorraine, sent by Bessie to ask us if we wanted coffee. We told her yes.

When she was gone, he said, "I knew it was a bad idea to leave you girls out there by yourselves. It's time to sell the farm."

I stared at him. "What do you mean? Mother meant it for us!"

"But you girls won't last out there much longer," he said. "I've been down to the bank and had a look at your account."

"You did what?" I shouted.

"Shhhhh," he said. "Listen to me. You can't keep selling off plots of land to pay the bills. What are you going to do? Mother didn't leave enough to support three girls for the rest of their lives. Within a year you're going to need some other income. And unless one of you has a husband in the wings I'm not aware of . . ."

"A husband? Now you're trying to pawn us off on a husband?"

He laughed. "I've never heard marriage described that way."

I leaned back and looked out into the approaching darkness. "Can't this wait? They're about to arrest him, and then we can put all this behind us. We'll sit down and figure something out."

Francis tilted his head and looked over at me, considering it. "All right. After Christmas. But no later than spring. That's a good time to sell a farm. It's the best thing for you. You'll see."

We sat together in uneasy silence. I heard the rattle of an automobile in the street and wondered if it was the sheriff. I didn't dare lean around the porch to look.

⚜ 40 ⚜

ARREST IN BLACK HAND LETTERS CASE
Harry Kaufman, Silk Dyer, of Paterson,
Indicted By Federal Grand Jury
for Threatening the
Misses Constance and Florette Kopp, of Wyckoff.

DEC. 3 — HARRY KAUFMAN, conducting a silk dyeing establishment in Paterson, is under arrest on a Federal indictment found in Newark, charging him with improper use of
the mails. He was released subject to bail posted by his sister,
Mrs. Marion Garfinkel of Pittsburgh.

Detective Francis A. Butler, who investigated the case
upon receiving the sensational story of Miss Constance Kopp,
of Wyckoff, made the arrest, and the indictment was the outcome of his inquiry.

The *Evening Record* last week told of the lively experi-
ences of the Misses Kopp, all of which followed their encounter with Kaufman in Paterson nearly six months ago, when

his auto crashed into their buggy. Kaufman refused to pay $50 for the damage done, and the suit was instituted.

Constance Kopp says anonymous letters began to arrive, threatening all sorts of disaster if they continued the suit against Kaufman. Armed men began to prowl around the house after dark, and shots were fired to terrorize the family and even at members of the family.

County Detectives Blauvelt and Courter, Prosecutor Wright, Assistant Prosecutor Zabriskie, Judge Seufert, and the Franklin Township Committee have all been working on this unusual case and the trial will no doubt prove particularly interesting.

Sheriff Heath has provided an armed guard at the Kopp home for some time past.

"WHO ARE ALL THESE PEOPLE?" I asked, setting down the newspaper and looking up at Sheriff Heath, who stood beaming at me along with Deputy Morris and Deputy English. Fleurette and Norma sat next to me on the divan, reading over my shoulder. Norma reached out with her scissors for the headline, but I batted her hand away. "Detective Blauvelt and Prosecutor Zabriskie and Detective Butler? I've never seen any of those men in my life. And since when has the Franklin Township Committee been involved? I thought they went after horse thieves."

Sheriff Heath grinned and pulled up a chair. "I believe you just learned an important lesson about law enforcement in Bergen County. My men do the hard work of chasing after thieves and shooting at intruders in the middle of the night. Then, as soon as a reporter turns up with a pencil and a notepad, the detectives and prosecutors leap from their desks long enough to make the arrest, serve the indictment, and make sure the papers spell their names right. That's their job, as they see it. We pay no attention to it and go about our business."

"That's no way to win reelection," Norma said. "It's no wonder you're so unpopular in the papers. All anyone ever hears are your complaints about prison conditions."

Sheriff Heath was in high spirits and couldn't be bothered by Norma's opinions. "I speak up for the people under my care," he said. "It's my duty. The voters in Bergen County can make their decision based on my actions, not the words of reporter who can't spell the name of either the criminal or his victim."

"I'd vote for you," Fleurette said.

He nodded and rose to leave. "You ladies might just get your chance."

He reminded us that Mr. Kaufman would be free until the trial. "He's been warned that if anyone comes near your house, sends you a letter, or threatens you in any way, we will arrest him again and hold him this time. His lawyer is advising him to do as we say, and so is his sister. I don't think you need us patrolling at night anymore. But we'll drive by as often as we can."

We followed the men to the door, and I opened it, letting in a blast of freezing wind. "Thank you, Sheriff. I'm sure we'll be fine. But what about Lucy Blake? Haven't you turned up anything? Hasn't anyone reported her missing?"

"We've made inquiries, but I suspect she's just run off. There's not much we can do about that."

Fleurette clung to my arm and bounced up and down on her toes. "But what about the child?" she said. "We're quite convinced Mr. Kaufman was involved."

"You don't know that," Norma said.

Sheriff Heath pulled his collar around his neck. "He claims not to know a thing about it. I'm sorry, ladies, but we've just got nothing to go on."

Norma said, "I suppose the trial will be postponed until after Christmas?"

"Christmas? Oh, no. The trial won't commence for several months. The courts are terribly behind, and Mr. Kaufman's attorney will do everything he can to delay. He has no chance of winning, so his only hope is to put it off and send his client a nice high bill every month."

"You mean he'll be free for months before he goes to jail?" I said. I couldn't imagine living in a state of uncertainty for that long.

Sheriff Heath looked at his deputies and reached around us to close the door again. In a careful, somber voice, he said, "I beg your forgiveness if I've given you the wrong impression. We don't expect him to be sentenced to any time in prison. He'll get a good steep fine, but I believe his sister will pay it. And if she does, he'll stay out of jail unless he bothers you again. That's how these cases go."

Norma put her hands on her hips, jabbing me with her elbow as she did. "Why on earth wouldn't he go to jail? Are men in this country at liberty to shoot at windows and traipse through houses starting fires with no fear of punishment?"

The sheriff started to answer. "Miss Kopp, I —"

But I cut him off. "Do you mean that you're not ever going to lock him up? He'll just be out there, doing as he pleases?

Forever? And what are we to do?" I looked down at Fleurette and tried to imagine letting her go to town by herself while Henry Kaufman remained free. How would I possibly keep her safe?

"You may feel that we can go about without any sort of protection," I said, "but I don't see how. I intend to keep my revolver, and don't be surprised if I have reason to use it."

The sheriff gave me a long and steady look. "That's fine. Keep the gun."

Was he really leaving this to me? "I'd rather put Henry Kaufman in prison and go back to sleeping through the night," I said.

"Miss Kopp. You're asking for something I can't give you. I'd hold him under my roof for the rest of his days if I could. But the truth is that I can't prove anything except threats and intimidation, misuse of the mail, and a few shots that did nothing more than break a window and scare everybody."

"And that's not enough to put him in jail?"

"He'll pay for what he did. His name will be dragged through the papers. Between the fines and the fees his attorney will charge, this will hit his family in the pocketbook. And he'll go straight to jail if he so much as looks at the three of you ever again. That's the best I can do."

There was nothing else to say. We mumbled our thanks to the men and they pushed the door open and ran against the wind to their automobile.

⇥ 41 ⇤

THE NEXT FEW WEEKS brought one of the worst ice storms in New Jersey's history. A motor car slid off an icy bridge and tumbled into the Hackensack River, sending a newly married couple to their death. A wagon taking children to a church concert got stuck in a drift of snow, and two of the boys walked five miles to get help. Their feet froze along the way. One of them lost two toes and the other lost three. The schools in Paterson closed and so did the courthouse, because so few people could get to work.

Only the mills kept going, fueled by enormous boilers and the sweat of workers who could not afford to miss a day's pay at Christmas. The sky was perpetually gray above them from the steam and smoke belched into the air at all hours. This was the busiest season, when New York demanded all the ribbon and tassels and brightly colored fabric for party dresses that the mills could produce. Even when every road in Paterson was impassable, one route from the mills to the train station remained open. They didn't miss a single shipment.

The dyers and their helpers suffered more than any other silk worker in the winter. At least the weavers could stay dry. In the unheated dye shops, the steam and drippings from the tubs froze, making the floors slick with ice. Even the workers' clothes, soaked through with dye, would freeze on the way home. That used to be Lucy, running through the icy streets after sundown, her clammy apron stuck to her skin.

If we never found her, what would become of her and her child? Sometimes at night I stood at my window and looked out at the ice on the meadow and the barn roof and thought not just of Henry Kaufman and the torment he'd brought upon us, and Lucy, and who knows how many others, but of all the madness and malfeasance in the world beyond our rutted road. I understood the haunted look Sheriff Heath so often wore. To take a stand against it—to try to save one wronged girl or put one thief or murderer behind bars—would have been like trying to stop a locomotive with a patent leather bridle. I wondered what made the sheriff think he should even try. Most men would leave it to someone else and pursue a more comfortable occupation. But Sheriff Heath sought out his office. He campaigned for it. I understood why Mrs. Heath seemed so unhappy. It could not have been an easy life.

We saw very little of him or his deputies as the year drew to an end. It was too difficult for them to get down our road. We took comfort in the fact that if the sheriff couldn't get to us, neither could any other automobile. Even the milk wagon came only twice a week. The boy driving it seemed lonely, too. He stopped to talk to us every time he went by and always accepted our invitation to come inside and get warm.

Norma and I took up our own sort of patrol, circling our

house and grounds with our revolvers plainly drawn every few hours. We went even in the hail and the snow. It was probably an unnecessary exercise, but we both needed something to do. Life was very dull without the deputies around. We had a resolution of sorts to our case, but not the satisfaction of catching Henry Kaufman in the act of any crime. I did wish he would turn up once more so I could take a shot at him.

Still, we felt freer than we had in months. I read books in bed and slept late. We played cards and took on little projects around the house. Fleurette made a new set of curtains for the kitchen, and I began to scrape off the wallpaper in Mother's bedroom.

Then another letter arrived. The envelope was typed this time, not written out by hand, so I assumed it was a bill. I didn't even open it until I sat down at my desk that night. When I saw the first line I gasped. Norma and Fleurette ran across the room to read it over my shoulder.

December 21, 1914

George Ewing
78 Albion St.
Paterson, NJ

Dear Miss Kopp,
    I overheard a deep laid conspiracy to abduct Florette. You have in some way been able to obtain the abhorrence of a dirty gang of Italians. For the time being all is O.K. Tell your girl not to answer any fake wire or phone calls to hospitals or other places. This can be settled,

and you and I and the gang the only ones to know it. Keep your head. Don't go and publish anything in the newspapers, or it will spoil our plans.

Write to me at this address if you are in agreement. Do not send the authorities because they will not find me. After I get word from you I will arrange a meeting place.

Remember! We will settle this ourselves.

Sincerely,
George Ewing

"Who is George Ewing?" Norma asked.

I shook my head. "I've never heard of him. And this is the first typewritten letter we've received. I believe we're dealing with a new criminal."

Fleurette took the letter and read it again. "Not one of these crooks can spell my name."

"The less they know about you, the better," I said. "And this isn't an invitation to a dance, so stop complaining."

"Then what is it?"

"I don't know. I'll talk to Sheriff Heath tomorrow."

"Are we to have deputies in the barn for another year?"

EVERY TIME I closed my eyes that night, I dreamed of Fleurette as a little girl, sitting alone on our parlor floor with a box of buttons. The room was dark save a lamp that cast a pool of light across her. A knock came at the door and somehow I knew, in the way one knows things in dreams that one shouldn't know, that she was being summoned to a hospital.

She jumped up, spilling her buttons across the floor. I tried to call out to her, but my mouth felt like it had been stuffed with cotton and I choked on the words. I reached for her, but my arms were so heavy I couldn't move them. She opened the door and disappeared into an explosion of light, blazing as bright as a house on fire.

I awoke choking and coughing in my dark room, a slick of sweat down my chest. I mopped it up with a sheet and untangled my legs from the covers, the heat pulsing off my skin into the frigid night air. I wanted to go check on Fleurette and Norma in their beds, but before I could move, the nightmares rose up and pulled me down again.

I remember little about the days that followed. A fever had come over me, and it seemed to rest on top of me like an enormous slumbering animal, something wild and menacing and unmoving. In my delirious state I knew that as long as I didn't wake the animal, it wouldn't hurt me. Once or twice Norma came into my room and tried to lift the blankets off to cool my skin. She told me later that I clutched at them and begged her not to disturb it, it being the creature I had imagined. She wasn't feeling well herself and lacked the strength to fight me.

Fleurette was the last to succumb. She had been nursing us both. She cooked the thinnest possible broth, nothing but hot water and salt and a chicken bone. I remember her forcing a spoon between my lips, but it made me cough and sputter, and I pushed her away.

She took to her bed before either of us were up again. There is a day or two that I cannot account for. The whole house was still and dark, the three of us each wrestling against our own fever-creatures.

Mine was the first to break. I awoke one morning with a ferocious appetite. I craved the most outlandish, impossible breakfast: a plate of fresh yellow eggs the likes of which we hadn't seen since the hens stopped laying in November, Mother's light, buttery rolls, the cherry preserves we'd not gotten around to canning last summer, and a sweet warm melon from the garden. My throat was so sore I could hardly swallow, and when I coughed I spat blood in the linen. But in spite of the pain, I would have devoured a meal like that without hesitation.

Instead I wrapped a blanket around my shoulders and made my way downstairs, keeping one shaky hand on the wall. The house must have been entirely unheated since Fleurette had taken to her bed. Even the stair rail was too cold to touch. I reached the kitchen and found that we were down to twigs and bark in the kindling basket, but I lit a fire in the stove anyway.

I found little to eat except tea and toast and the last jar of applesauce. I didn't know toast could taste that good. I thought surely the smell would wake Norma and Fleurette and lure them downstairs, but their appetites had not yet returned. I took them each a cup of tea. Norma was able to sit up and drink a little of it. But Fleurette's fever was working at her furiously. I'd never felt a face as hot as hers. I forced her covers down, but she fought for them just as I had done.

On the way downstairs a wave of dizziness came over me. I sat on the steps to steady myself. I knew I shouldn't be up yet, but I needed to get out to the barn to check on the animals and see if there was anything to eat in our root cellar. I wrapped a coat around my nightgown and pushed my bare feet into the rubber boots I'd left standing in the washing room.

But when I tried the kitchen door it wouldn't move. A drift of snow had blown against the house and frozen there, forming a wedge of ice.

I tried the front door and found it unyielding as well. Only the back door was clear of snow, though it too was frozen shut. I leaned into it and pushed it and kicked it until the stars of the nighttime sky swum around before me. It opened with a great crack and I stood panting in the thin, icy air.

Before I lost my nerve, I marched around the house to the barn. As I'd feared, Dolley and the chickens had been without water, as had Norma's pigeons. I put all my weight against the cistern pump and by some miracle got it moving. Dolley bent her enormous head to the water trough as I filled it, blinking at me through one coal-colored eye. The chickens cawed and moaned and flapped their wings until they got a drink, too. The pigeons cooed and warbled and showed no gratitude at all.

By this time, any residual warmth from my fever had dissipated and I felt distressingly light, as if I might float away or melt into the snow. I took hold of the handle to the cellar door but couldn't muster the effort to pull it open. I don't remember getting back to the house, except that there remained in my mind a picture of two bottles of cream the boy from the dairy must have just left on our porch, each of them buried in snow until only their red paper caps showed.

I slept all afternoon on the divan in my coat and boots. It wasn't until I roused myself to go to bed that I realized we had missed Christmas entirely.

⇥ 42 ⇤

THE DAY AFTER CHRISTMAS, a worker at a paper mill beat
the night watchman and stole his pay. Sheriff Heath arrested
five men and had to take into custody the eight-month-old infant belonging to one of them. I read the story to Fleurette on
the first day she was able to sit up and talk.

"I wonder what Mrs. Heath thought of having a baby
brought into the jail," she said.

"I can't imagine she would've liked it. She has her own
children to look after."

"Some people like babies."

"I know. Only I wonder where its mother was."

An image of Lucy rose suddenly before me and I flinched.
The fever had left me with the distinct impression that I was
being haunted. Lucy was one of the ghosts, Henry Kaufman
was another, along with this new man, George Ewing. I was
not yet in my right mind.

And now there was the poor night watchman at the paper
mill, beaten to death for his weekly pay. The stories in the papers

were like the old Austrian fairy tales my mother used to whisper to us at night, populated by ogres and trolls and the weak-limbed mortals who could not fight them off.

WE HADN'T REALIZED IT AT FIRST, but Norma had been the sickest of all of us. She was left with a barking cough she could not shake. Fleurette kept a pot of water on the stove and carried it to her every few hours so she could breathe the steam. She could not be left alone. I didn't dare go to see Sheriff Heath until I knew Fleurette was well enough to look after Norma for the day.

Finally on New Year's Eve, I thought the two of them would be fine on their own. The road had been cleared by then and Dolley had an easy time of it. I think she was as eager to get outside and breathe the clean air as I was. The pastures along our lane were blanketed in white, punctuated only by a few bare tree trunks reaching out of the snow as if they were gasping for breath. Black cows hunkered down between them, as cold and unmoving as rocks.

When I arrived at the jail I went directly to the door of the sheriff's residence and rang the bell. There was no answer. I rang again and gave a sharp knock. I heard no sound from within. Finally the door swung open to reveal Sheriff Heath in trousers, bare feet, his shirt untucked, and a blanket wrapped around his shoulders. His chin was ridden with stubble and his hair hung in strands from his forehead. I recognized the glassy look in his eyes.

"You're ill," I said.

He coughed and stepped aside to let me in. There were dolls and toys scattered about, and a plate with what looked like last night's dinner. It was not a sight intended for company to see. I didn't know where to look. I kept my eyes on my feet.

"We've been sick, too."

Sheriff Heath coughed and nodded in response. "Everyone has."

"We got another letter." I offered him the envelope.

He raised his eyebrows at me and took it, then stumbled backward into a chair. I sat across from him and watched him read it twice. He dabbed at his nose with a handkerchief.

Finally he put it back into the envelope and handed it to me. He tried to speak but lapsed into another coughing fit. I waited while he pushed himself out of his chair and went into the kitchen. I heard the sound of water running. He returned with a glass of water and struggled to get it down. Why wasn't his wife looking after him?

"Do you have any help? Are the children unwell too? What about Mrs. Heath?"

"All sick."

"Won't you let me look in on them?"

He waved my questions away and pointed to the letter. "Arrange a meeting."

"Are you sure? After what happened last time?"

"Different man," he croaked. "We can get this one."

I WROTE TO GEORGE EWING and a week later, I had my response. He asked to meet at the train station in Somerville. Sheriff Heath didn't like it. "A train station," he muttered when he stopped by to see the letter. "Too many escape routes. He's done this before."

"Should I ask him for another meeting place?"

"No, it's fine," he said. "I'll have men on both platforms.

Just come prepared, as you did before. Don't bring any valuables, and wear something you can run in if you have to. Oh, and I need to be able to spot you in a crowd. Wear that hat with the veil across it. You're tall enough, it'll stand out even among the men's hats."

I shifted uncomfortably in my chair.

"Forgive me," he said, stifling a ragged cough. "Mrs. Heath is always reminding me that I should never comment upon a lady's appearance. It's a hazard of the job. I'm trained to notice details."

"About women's heights or their hats?" I asked. I didn't like the idea of him noticing either.

"You wore it on Broadway that night," he said. "Don't you remember? I promised I wouldn't take my eyes off you. What else was there to do but study your hat?"

I smiled. "That must have been very dull for you."

He slid his overcoat on and opened the front door, letting in a blast of arctic air. He pulled the brim of his hat down low over his eyes.

"None of my dealings with the Kopp sisters have been dull."

⇥ 43 ⇤

ON THE MORNING OF MY MEETING with George Ewing,
I paced and fretted and watched the clock. I had on the very
same get-up I'd worn before, except for the work boots. No
one saw them in the dark on Broadway, but they'd be spotted in a train station. So I wore a sensible old pair of leather
shoes with buttons across the top. I carried the same handbag, but now it held fifty dollars in marked bills supplied to
me by Sheriff Heath. There would be no revolver this time,
he'd instructed me, on the grounds that a train station was no
place for a gun fight.

Fleurette was so intent upon coming along that I made
Norma promise to keep her under constant watch after I left.
"Sit on her if you have to," I told Norma. "I don't want her
sneaking off to the train station."

"In this weather? You think she would walk to town?" Norma's voice had only just returned. She still spoke in a croak.

"Just watch her."

At last the sheriff's wagon arrived. He brought along Deputy Morris, whom we all missed seeing in our foyer in the

afternoons, as well as his man English, who had shadowed me that night on Broadway, and another deputy, Richards. They were to take me to the train station and drive on from there. I would have a bit of a wait for the train, but they needed to get a good start for Somerville so they would be in place before I arrived. If all went as expected, they would arrest George Ewing and take him back in the wagon, and I would return by train to Ridgewood. The sheriff didn't want me to ride alongside the man who had been threatening me, even after he was under arrest, and I assured him I could make my way home on my own.

The station was surprisingly crowded that afternoon. It was the first clear day in some time. People who had been confined to their homes were getting out at last. Children raced around the platform as if it were a summer's day, and their mothers stood by indulgently, relieved to see them wearing themselves out in the fresh air. Groups of men stood about in their long black coats, stamping their feet in the cold and exhaling a mixture of steam and cigarette smoke.

Seeing all of this, Sheriff Heath turned down a side street and drove me two blocks away. He stopped in front of a newsstand.

"I don't want anyone to see you with us," he said. "Buy yourself a newspaper and circle around a few times. We'll be waiting for you in Somerville."

I stepped out and did as he asked. With a newspaper tucked under my arm, I paced the streets closest to the station and pretended to browse the shop windows. There was a hairdresser showcasing wigs she'd made from her customers' hair, and a locksmith's window with brass and iron locks gleaming like jewelry. At the pharmacy, someone had made a snowman out of rolled white bandages.

I glanced into the shop and there was Lucy Blake, standing in the doorway, staring at me. She wore a smock meant for housekeeping and a knobby red scarf of the sort an elderly aunt might knit for Christmas. When she saw me, she tried to dart out the door, but I took her elbow and pulled her back.

"Lucy? What happened to you?"

In a low voice she said, "We shouldn't talk here. I can't be seen with you."

"But you're all right," I said. "We've been looking for you. No one could find you after the fire."

"I'm fine."

"But the fire. Was it aimed at you?"

She bit her lip and blinked. Strands of hair flew about her face and she tucked them inside her hat. "I think so," she said. "He kept asking me why I'd been talking to you. And one night he just let himself in, very late, and stumbled across my mother's bed. I broke a plate over his head and he ran out. Later that night the fire started. It had to have been him."

"And everyone got out?"

"I think so. I'm fine, really. I'm taking care of some ladies now."

"What ladies?"

"Sisters. Both shut-ins. They share a house and I live downstairs and do for them. We live just up Dover Street." She pointed up the hill behind her. The homes had once been quite stately, with fish-scale shingles and widow's walks on the roof that probably gave a view all the way to New York on a clear day. Now most of them were boarding houses.

"What about your mother?"

"She took a position nearby. She does washing and mending, mostly."

I heard the rumble of the train in the distance. "I have to go," I said quickly. "Let me come back and talk to you. I've been wanting to show you some photographs I found of Regina Doyle's building. Can I bring them to you?"

She grabbed my arm. "Pictures of Bobby?"

"I don't think so," I said. "But maybe someone who was involved."

Now she was eager to see me. "When can you come?"

"Soon. And let me bring the sheriff, too. He's arrested Mr. Kaufman. I think he'd be able to help."

She shook her head. "I don't know."

The train had almost reached the station. "Think about it. Tell me, which house is yours?"

She gave me the number. The train whistled and screeched as it approached.

"I'll come and see you as soon as I can." She nodded and scurried down the street.

The train to Somerville was crowded, but the ride was blessedly brief. I squeezed into a seat and pulled out the newspaper, grateful for a distraction. As the train jerked and rocked along the tracks, I pretended to read the front page, but my thoughts were on Lucy. She'd been nearby all along. Maybe it wasn't too late to do something for her.

I put the paper down and looked out the window at the gray snow along the tracks. The telegraph wires wobbled and wove as the train rushed past. The landscape beyond them rolled by like a panorama in a theater: rows of houses turned away from the tracks, with only their laundry lines and burn barrels showing, then a stand of warehouses clad in rusted tin, then the open fields of brown stubble under snow.

I realized with a start that the next stop was Somerville and I'd hardly given George Ewing a single thought. A vein leapt up and throbbed against my collarbone and I had to put a hand over it to quiet it. I reminded myself that Sheriff Heath and his men would be waiting and watching. The station would be filled with people. I didn't know what sort of man I was looking for, but I only hoped I could outrun him or fight him if I had to.

Soon the brakes screamed, the engine exhaled a head of steam, and the conductor barked out the name of the Somerville station. I got off with a crowd of passengers and walked toward the ticket counter as if I had business to attend to, then stood around waiting for everyone to disperse.

The platform was entirely exposed to the north and the wind whistled as it went past the posts and the tin roof above me. It was nearly dark and a man was walking around lighting the old gas lamps. A few people gathered around them as if they were hoping for warmth, but the flames flickered behind glass and gave out only a thin pool of light.

I sat on a bench with my ankles crossed and my handbag in my lap. A few solitary men approached the bench, but each walked right past it. The clock in the station had just struck five. I tried not to watch it as I didn't want to look nervous. My feet bounced against the brick and I willed them to stay still.

I was staring at the ties on the tracks when a hand gripped my shoulder roughly from behind.

"Not here, Miss Kopp," a man muttered in my ear, his tobacco-stained breath on my neck. I jerked my shoulder away and rose to face him, but just as I did, a station agent blew his whistle and yelled.

"Leave the lady alone!"

I barely got a glimpse of him before he ran down the platform and out of the station, a tall, skinny figure in a baggy gray overcoat who propelled himself along with a distinctive off-center gait. It was Kaufman's friend, the one with the wooden leg.

Sheriff Heath and his deputies materialized from their posts inside the station, around the corner, and on the platform opposite. All of them ran after Ewing, leaving the station in utter silence. I was left to play the part of the astonished lady victim.

The girl running the sandwich stand rushed over with a cup of tea and a hot bun, which I saw no reason to refuse. An older gentleman came to sit with me and offered to call a doctor if I needed one. I declined, explaining that I was just taking the train to Ridgewood and would have family waiting for me there.

I finished my tea and rode the train back, then hired a cab to take me home. By the time I stood in my own drive again, it was eight o'clock. A single light burned in the kitchen. There would be a plate set aside for me, and Norma and Fleurette would be standing around anxiously. I wished I could tell them with certainty that Ewing was under arrest. I already knew what Norma would say: If Sheriff Heath couldn't catch up with a one-legged man, we were in worse trouble than we'd imagined.

⊰ 44 ⊱

THE NEXT MORNING I was helping Norma dust the chickens for mites and keeping a wary eye on the road when the sheriff's wagon pulled into our drive. It was Deputy Morris.

"I'm sorry we ran out on you last night, Miss Kopp," he said.

"Don't worry about me. Did you catch him?"

A wide smile emerged under his beard. "Of course we did. Although he goes awfully fast on that club of his. Anyway, the sheriff wants me to bring you in to view the evidence."

When we arrived, Sheriff Heath was standing over a table looking at some papers. There was the letter I had written to George Ewing to request a meeting, along with other letters addressed to him I didn't recognize. There was also a notebook with a page of scribbles, a handkerchief, and a bottle that looked like it came from a druggist.

"What's this?" I said, pointing to the bottle.

"Chloroform."

Everything went still for a minute. I took a half-step back

from the bottle as if it could reach out and poison me. Sheriff Heath pulled a chair out for me and then sat down next to me. He spoke quietly and carefully. "We believe he intended to take you to a hotel and drug you."

"A hotel? By what means would he have persuaded me to visit a hotel with him?"

He smiled. "I don't think Mr. Ewing considered who he was dealing with. But this is the way these men work. It takes nothing more than a little chloroform on a handkerchief to overpower a lady. We've seen it before."

I shook my head. "Well, he's not very bright if he thought that would work on me."

"Have a look at this." Sheriff Heath pushed the notebook toward me with the end of a pencil. I could barely make out the writing.

"What is it?"

"It appears to be his plan to kidnap Fleurette and sell her to white slavers."

"This is his plan? All written down on notepaper for anyone to read?"

"He makes it easy for us. I'm about to go interview him. That's another thing. He's claiming responsibility for all of the threats against the three of you."

"All the letters from last year? Everything Henry Kaufman did?"

He nodded. "I'm afraid so. He says he acted alone. Says he never heard of a Henry Kaufman."

"But that was him!" I protested. "With the wooden leg! I told you I've seen him with Mr. Kaufman!"

"And you're certain of that? It was the same man?"

"Of course. I told you about his front teeth, didn't I? And

the leg. How many men with wooden legs do we have running around this town?"

"I just want to be sure," he said. "Mr. Ewing was arrested in Somerset County for stripping the lighting wires from their poles with a gang of thieves, all of whom got away. I don't know if they were Kaufman's friends or not. But Mr. Ewing served his sentence in the state prison and was released right before your collision with Henry Kaufman last summer."

Just then the guard opened the door and said that the prisoner was ready to be interviewed. Sheriff Heath stood to leave. "Just be careful," he said. "Stay home and keep quiet for a while. You have your guns. We'll drive by when we can."

I didn't tell him I'd found Lucy. If she was right—if Henry Kaufman really would come after her if she ever went to the police—I didn't want to be the one who brought that down on her. She'd gotten away, even though she hadn't gone far. She could stay hidden a while longer.

SAYS HE WAS KOPP BLACK HAND "GANG"
Confession by Convict Clears
Jersey Blackmail Mystery Case

HACKENSACK, N.J. JAN. 23 —"I am alone responsible for the writing of Black Hand letters to Miss Constance Kopp, of Wyckoff, threatening to abduct her pretty sister, Florette. I had learned that the Kopp family were wealthy and I thought this was an easy way to make a bunch of coin."

This was the confession made to-day by George Ewing, an ex-convict, who was captured in the Neshanic Mountains a few days ago by Sheriff Heath, of Hackensack. A bottle of chloroform found in his pocket has led to the discovery, it is believed, of an additional plot to kidnap Florette Kopp and turn her over to "white slavers" in Chicago.

The confession ends a reign of terror that had prevailed in the Kopp home since last July, when Miss Constance Kopp started suit against Henry Kaufman, owner of a silk dyeing establishment in Paterson, to recover damages for being run down by Kaufman's auto. Black Hand letters began to reach the Kopp home, and prowling men appeared after dark, shooting at the house.

"He's claiming responsibility for all of it?" said Fleurette, grabbing the newspaper out of my hand before I could finish. "Why would he do that?"

"To keep Henry Kaufman out of trouble, I suppose," I said. "Can I have my paper back?"

But Fleurette held on to it, reading bits of it aloud but mostly mumbling to herself. "It says here that Ewing planned to entice you to a hotel and use chloroform on you," she said. "I thought I was the one being kidnapped. What does he want with you?"

"Don't talk like that," Norma said. "The fact that you've received the most threats does not make you the most popular."

"What does it make me?"

"The smallest. They are threatening you because you are the smallest and the youngest, and somehow they have the idea that we, therefore, value you the most and would pay more to get you back."

"Well, of course you would."

"Don't be so sure."

"And why would anyone write out the plan for the crime

they intend to commit and carry it around in their pocket like that?"

"You heard what Constance said. This is not the smartest criminal we've ever met."

"We haven't met many criminals. Although if this keeps up, we'll soon know every con man and Black Hander in New Jersey."

"That's enough from both of you," I said, having recovered my newspaper and finished reading the story. "All that matters now is that we caught him."

"Does this mean Henry Kaufman gets away with everything?" Norma asked.

"I don't know."

"Then it's a good thing we went to the papers so all the criminals could learn our particulars," Norma declared. "I don't know why you ever took that man's advice."

"Sheriff Heath? You didn't mind so much when he was issuing you a revolver. You didn't turn down his help then."

"I don't know what choice I had. Now what is he going to do about Mr. Ewing?"

"He'll be sent to jail for the kidnapping attempt," I said. "I have to give a statement to the prosecutor tomorrow, and then I'm going to go take care of a few other things in town." I was going to see Lucy, but I didn't want to say it.

"I'm coming with you!" Fleurette said, scrambling to her feet. "I'll wear my black crepe. I have a very serious sort of hat that would give the impression—"

I stood and took her face in my hands, forcing her to look up at me. Her cheeks were pink with excitement and her eyes were flashing. She had the face of a small, sleek animal, a mink or a fox.

"Listen to me. Under no circumstances will you ever be in the same room with George Ewing or any of his gang. Ever."

She squirmed and got away from me. "It doesn't seem like I'll ever be in the same room with anyone except the two of you," she said, pouting as only a girl of her age could do.

"I'd like that just fine."

❄ 45 ❄

THE HOUSE WAS BETTER CARED FOR than most on the block. It had recently been given a fresh coat of white paint, and it sat behind a tidy front garden fringed in a cast-iron fence. Although the garden was covered in gray slush, there were twigs and stalks standing up through the snow, suggesting the possibility of hydrangeas under the windows later on in the year, and a border of daylilies along the walk.

I gave the bell a hard twist. The smoke from some nearby chimney drifted past. The smell of wood burning made me hungry and I realized it had been a long time since breakfast.

After a while I heard a cough and the shuffling of feet. The door opened and the tiniest woman I'd ever seen stood before me. She was as frail as a bird, her small head fringed in white cottony wisps. She wore a gray dress with a collar that buttoned right under her chin, and from under her skirts appeared petite patent leather shoes that could have belonged to a schoolgirl.

She looked me up and down through china-blue eyes. "How do you do?" she said at last.

"I'm here to see Lucy Blake," I said. "I'm a friend of hers. I saw her in the market recently and she invited me to stop in."

She swept her eyes over me again, weighing the likelihood of that. "Lucy's working right now. She's helping my sister."

"I'm so sorry to bother you, Mrs.—"

"Miss Eldridge," she said. "I am the younger Miss Eldridge, by ten minutes."

I smiled. "I won't be but a minute, Miss Eldridge. I simply must ask her about an important matter. May I come inside and wait?"

The sound of footsteps coming down the stairs made Miss Eldridge turn around. Soon Lucy appeared behind her. Her eyes widened when she saw me.

"Excuse me, ma'am," Lucy said. "Just a friend of mine here to see me on a personal matter."

Before her employer could object, Lucy was out on the porch, pulling me by the wrist down the stairs to the entrance to a basement apartment.

"We can talk here," she said quietly, opening the door to a small room that appeared to have been furnished with the Eldridge sisters' cast-offs. There was a tufted red velvet settee so worn that the bare weave of the fabric showed through, and four mahogany dining chairs with embroidered cushions that looked like they could have been completed when the sisters were first learning to sew. A battered wardrobe and trunk must have contained her clothing, and a shelf above a small sink held washing powders and toiletries. A doorway at the back of the room revealed an alcove just large enough for a daybed.

There was a wood stove in one corner, but Lucy made no move to light it. She was probably given only a small quantity of fuel for the winter. With both of us crowded inside, it would soon be warm enough.

Once she closed the door, she grabbed my hands. "I've been waiting for you. Did you bring them?"

"Yes, and I want you to look at them very carefully," I said, pulling the envelope out of my pocketbook. "I hope you might recognize someone."

She turned the envelope over, holding it by the edge as if it might burn her. "What does this say?" she said, squinting at the faint writing on the outside. "Ward?"

"That must be the man who hired them to take the pictures. He never came back to pay for them, so Mr. La-Motte—that's the photographer—he offered them to me."

She slid the photographs out and looked through them, studying each face before going on to the next one. There were businessmen in suits, delivery boys, and little girls playing on the stoop. She paused for an especially long time over a picture of a woman with a bundle over her shoulder. Even if it was a baby, there was no way to know if it was hers.

After she looked at each one of them twice, she passed them back to me. "I'm sorry," she said. "I don't recognize anyone."

"Are you sure? I thought you might have seen one of them come into the factory. Some associate of Henry Kaufman's, maybe." I realized I had no idea what to do next. If the pictures were useless, then I had nothing else to offer her.

She picked at a thread coming loose from the settee. "No. But thank you for bringing them, Miss Kopp."

"I do wish you would come and talk to Sheriff Heath. I wanted to bring him here today, but now that I see your situation, I wouldn't want to raise suspicion among your employers."

She pushed her chin up defiantly. "They already know. The Misses Eldridge have lived very long lives and have seen quite a bit in their time. A girl with a baby hardly comes as a shock to them."

A little silver bell rang above Lucy's door and she stood up.

"Wait," I said, as I followed her out. "Won't you please think about going to see the sheriff? Surely he could help. Now he's arrested one of Mr. Kaufman's friends, and he's working on—"

She turned around and said, "If he puts Henry Kaufman in jail, I'll go talk to him. Not before."

"But—"

There was a hard, defeated look about her. "He set fire to his own boarding house. What would he do to this place?"

At the second ring of the bell, Lucy turned and ran up the stairs, leaving me to latch the door. The diminutive Miss Eldridge stood on the porch and watched me go.

⤳ 46 ⤶

"CAN'T YOU FIND SOMETHING TO DO?" Norma said crossly after I'd fumbled the third leg band and annoyed yet another pigeon. "I don't need your help. You're just making them nervous."

I was attempting to crowd inside the pigeon loft with her. I had to bend down to avoid tangling my hair in the chicken wire above. All twenty pigeons had retreated to a row of nesting boxes situated as far away from me as they could get. They were climbing over themselves and pecking at one another and making an agitated ruckus. Norma was giving the younger ones their first leg bands and tying on messages. "Wild Geese Never Divorce" was soon to arrive back at the loft, as was "Citizens Asked Not to Tempt Soldiers by Offering Strong Drink."

Norma reached around me and opened the door to the loft. "Go. Go and see what Fleurette's doing. Maybe she needs some help."

"She's practicing her ballet," I said, backing out of the loft as ordered.

"Then polish the doorknobs. Or go start dinner. You can do that, can't you?"

Yes. I could do that.

I pulled some carrots out of a box of sand we kept in the root cellar and took them inside. I was standing at the kitchen sink, scrubbing them and looking out the window at the barn and the barren vegetable patch we'd soon have to replant, when the crunch of wheels on gravel announced that someone was in our drive. I leaned around and saw Francis's wagon pulling up to the door, a load of baskets under an oilcloth in the back.

He jumped down and went to talk to Norma. I scrubbed my carrots a little longer than I needed to. When they were skinned bare and bright orange, I dropped them in the sink and looked around the kitchen. There was the battered old table that had survived decades of dough being pounded on it, noodles being rolled out and sliced, coffee spills, dribbles of jam and preserves, and the arguments of three girls who rarely agreed on anything but sat down together nonetheless. The black iron wood-burning stove had no place in a modern kitchen, but when we moved in, there was no source of gas or electricity, and we learned to live without it. Mother's old scalloped dishes with their pattern of moss roses sat in the cupboard, as familiar as the backs of our hands. There was nothing new in this kitchen but Fleurette's pale blue curtains, stitched all the way around in yellow piping.

I had very little love for kitchens, but I couldn't see us giving this one up.

Francis waved at me through the window as he came up to the door. He had a newspaper in his hand. He'd grown a beard over the winter and there were little flecks of gray in it. Our father used to wear a beard like that. I realized with a start that Francis was almost the same age our father was the last time I saw him.

He pounded his feet on the threshold as he came through the door. "Kopp Black Hand Gang?" he said, tossing the newspaper on the table. "What happened?"

He set his hat on the table and dropped into a chair in front of it. "I thought this was all taken care of. What's been going on out here?"

I dried my hands and sat down across from him. "I told you they were getting ready to arrest Henry Kaufman, and they did."

"Oh, I know. I read about that one in the papers, too. It's how I keep up with my sisters these days. Why didn't you tell me another man was threatening you?"

I leaned back in my chair to get a look out the window. Norma was staying very busy with her pigeons. I wasn't going to get any help from her. Fleurette had put on a recording of a Parisian ballet and I could hear her heel hit the ground each time she made a pirouette.

"What would you have done? I really do think it's over now. This man George Ewing, he was working for Mr. Kaufman. He's back in prison and—"

"But think about it, Constance," Francis said. "Whether they convict him or not doesn't matter. There will be another one after this, and another one. Don't you see? You're easy marks out here. Three girls, living all alone, wealthy as far as anyone can tell."

Rich, lonely women in the countryside. Is that how we looked to those men? I got a little queasy when I tried to see us through their eyes. "And I suppose you think we'd be safer with you."

"Of course! That's what I've been telling you all along. Move in with us and you're living in a neighborhood, not out on some dark road. We have a police officer living down the street from us, and a firefighter. Besides, I'll be there."

"Oh, you're going to protect us? I don't think Henry Kaufman and his gang would be afraid of you," I said.

"They only go after people who provoke them. And I won't."

Through the window I could see Norma strapping a basket of pigeons to Dolley's backside. She was going to ride away and leave me to handle this on my own. Fleurette's record skipped and she started it again.

He pushed his chair back and stood to leave. "You can't afford to keep this place without an income. You know I'm right about that."

He was. We'd spent hardly anything all winter, but our savings were dwindling.

"At least send Fleurette to us," Francis said. "She's the one they're after."

"Fleurette stays with me."

He bent over and said in a whisper, "Shouldn't mothers be more concerned with keeping their children safe?"

I leaned back and stared at him. "What do you think I've been doing?"

He went to the door, and I looked at the seam along the back of his coat, freshly restitched in Bessie's hand. He already had the slight stoop of a man who bore too many burdens. "Do you remember how Mother used to be when something happened on the street?" I said.

He paused and turned back to me, still aggravated.

"One time you and I were out with her," I said, "and a boy

was running past. He tripped and spilled a bag of onions all over the sidewalk. Do you remember that?"

He shook his head.

"I stopped to pick one up, but Mother yanked my arm and told me not to touch it, like it could be some kind of trick."

"She was like that," Francis said, leaning against the door. "She didn't trust anybody."

"That's right," I said. "And for years it never occurred to me that other people would stop if you dropped something, and hand it back to you. Some people—like the men who pulled our wrecked buggy off Fleurette—would run straight toward a disaster, not because they were heedless of the danger, but because they were prepared to do something about it."

Francis shrugged. "Mother had her reasons. It was a different time."

"That's exactly right," I said. "It was a different time. We don't have to hide anymore, and we don't have to run away."

Francis raised his hands in surrender. "Then don't. But you know you can always—"

"I know we can turn up on your doorstep," I said. "I thank you and Bessie for offering. But we've done just fine standing up for ourselves, and I'm glad we did."

He nodded and left. I sat in the kitchen with my eyes closed and listened to the churning of that distant French orchestra on the Victrola, and the sweep of Fleurette's slippers across our uneven parlor floor.

What I didn't say to Francis was that when Lucy grabbed me on the street in Paterson that day, I couldn't understand how anyone would take hold of a stranger and pour out their troubles. But now I realized that people did it all the time. They called for help. And some people would answer, out of a sense of duty and a sense of belonging to the world around them. That's what Sheriff Heath and his men did, lying in wait in our freezing barn, their guns drawn, to get the man who was trying to get us.

If I could give something to Fleurette—if I could give her one silent gift from a mother she didn't know she had—it would be this: the realization that we have to be a part of the world in which we live. We don't scurry away when we're in trouble, or when someone else is. We don't run and hide.

She watched Mother and learned her ways just like I did. But I hoped she would watch me too, and learn something different.

⇥ 47 ⇤

A WEEK LATER, just after dinner, a knock came at the door. I opened it to find Sheriff Heath and Deputy Morris, dripping wet on my front porch. They'd removed their overcoats and stood shivering in their vests and shirtsleeves, the fabric stuck to them like a coat of paint.

They both spoke at once. "We're so sorry to bother you, Miss Kopp," Deputy Morris said.

"Please forgive us, but could we—" Sheriff Heath began, as I opened the door wide and ushered them in.

"We realize we're barging in late," Deputy Morris began again.

"It's all right," I said. "What happened?"

Norma and Fleurette came in from the kitchen, and Norma went off to find towels and blankets for them without waiting for an explanation. Fleurette fussed over both of them, insisting that they kick off their wet shoes and stand by the fire. They crowded around the hearth. The smell of moss and river mud rose off them as their clothes warmed.

Norma returned with a stack of towels and disappeared again to heat the coffee. Fleurette added a log to the fire and settled down in front of them as if anticipating a dramatic recitation. "Do tell us everything," she said. "Were you chasing our Mr. Kaufman out of the creek? Shall we get our guns?"

Deputy Morris shook his head. "No, miss. We were after another crook tonight. A house thief. He stole some jewelry and money and gave the lady of the house a terrible fright. We rounded up some men in the neighborhood, and we've been out chasing him all afternoon, but we lost him when it got dark."

"And then you went for a swim?" Fleurette said.

"Not much of a night for a swim. The fellow we were chasing shot at the sheriff here, and we both fell backward into a creek. We were going to go straight home, but the road—"

"You've been shot?" I said around the hard thing that had leapt into my throat and lodged there.

Sheriff Heath had been looking at the fire while Deputy Morris spoke. He turned to me and said, "No. It just put a hole in my overcoat. He surprised us, that's all."

Fleurette looked up at me and frowned. "There's a tear in his vest."

"Let me see that." I moved toward him but he pulled away. I grabbed him roughly by the arms and turned him to face me. He blinked at me in surprise. "Miss Kopp, I—"

"Stop that," I said. "I think you're in shock." I picked at the tear in his vest and came away with a hand covered in blood.

"You've been shot," I said quietly, pulling him closer to get a look at the wound. "It's too dark in here. Fleurette, get some bandages and soap and things. See if we have anything that will fit a man. The sheriff's going to need another shirt."

He tried to protest. "No, we only stopped because the road—"

"Never mind about that. We're going to get a look at your shoulder right now."

Norma was coming out with coffee as I led the two men to the kitchen. She saw the blood seeping through his vest as we moved into the circle of light cast by the lamp.

"Let them have their drink," I said, "and put on some more water. Light the other side of the stove so Deputy Morris can get warm."

She did as I asked, and I pushed a protesting Sheriff Heath into a chair. Fleurette returned with the bandages and a bundle of Francis's old clothes. She helped me ease the vest off his shoulder. He groaned when we raised his arm to remove it.

"Bend over the table so we can see it in the light," I said. "We're not going to touch it. We're just going to look."

His shirt was soaked in blood across the shoulder and down the back. I lifted it carefully off his skin and Fleurette cut it away with scissors. Underneath was a wide and shallow wound obscured by half-congealed blood.

"I think you're all right," I said under my breath. "It looks like the bullet just grazed you. We'll clean it so we can see better."

He nodded but didn't look up at us. He was gripping the edge of the table with his hands, his knuckles pale.

Norma brought a towel and a bowl of hot water, and Fleurette supplied the soap. I washed the edges of the wound as carefully as I could without actually touching it. The bullet went deep enough to strip away the skin but didn't seem to expose any bone. As I cleaned it, the natural color of his skin returned, pink and white from the hot water. On his shoulder were a string of brown freckles, five of them in all.

He was breathing long, noisy breaths like a captive animal.

"Now we need to wash the wound itself," I said. "Lean back so we don't make a mess."

Without loosening his grip on the table, he eased back toward Fleurette and me. I looked down at him but he didn't meet my eyes. The hair on the top of his head had just begun to dry. Two locks lifted away from the rest.

I squeezed a trickle of water over his shoulder and Fleurette pressed a towel against him to catch it. The water ran bright red, but the wound looked clean. I peered at it closely, breathing in the metallic smell of fresh blood.

"This will have to be sewn up. It won't close on its own."

He pulled away from us and tried to cover himself with the torn remnants of his shirt. "I don't need a doctor," he said.

"Sir, I think the ladies are right," Deputy Morris said. "Shouldn't someone take a look at you tonight?"

He shook his head and tried to stand up. "I'm not going to get a doctor out of bed for this."

"Then sit down," I said, with a tone of authority in my voice that surprised him. "You're not leaving without a bandage and a clean shirt." He sat down wearily and Fleurette and I set about wrapping his shoulder. It was a difficult spot to cover properly and impossible to pin in place. Fleurette sewed a few stitches through the bandage to hold it. Then she produced our brother's old nightshirt. Sheriff Heath removed himself to the washing room to exchange his ruined shirt for Francis's. When he returned, he nodded at me.

"I need to speak to Miss Kopp for a minute."

I opened the kitchen door and he followed me down the

hall to the parlor. The fire we had fed a few minutes earlier was now blazing brightly. I encouraged Sheriff Heath to sit but instead he stood in front of it.

"I'm not quite dry," he said, leaning over the hearth. I took my seat and waited for him to speak. The room was dark except for the fire, but I didn't want to go to the bother of lighting any lamps.

"I can't get Ewing to budge," he said. "He's still claiming responsibility for all the letters and the shots fired and everything."

"All of it?"

The sheriff attempted a nod and then grimaced and laid a hand on his bandage. Behind him the flames hissed and threw sparks on the hearth. He stepped aside and the orange glow illuminated him from below. He looked like an apparition in the flickering light.

"I'm afraid so. If we can't get him to change his story, the prosecutor's going to drop all the charges against Henry Kaufman."

"But why would Mr. Ewing claim responsibility for crimes he didn't commit? He might have been in Mr. Kaufman's gang, but he didn't do it all himself. He couldn't have."

Sheriff Heath shrugged, and then winced from the pain of moving his shoulder. "Money. I think Kaufman has offered him a sum of money in exchange for confessing to crimes he did not commit. It's worth at least a thousand dollars to Kaufman, not to mention the exposure."

"Or he's threatened him."

"Maybe a little of both. I have to assume Kaufman knew that Ewing would get caught. He's the weakest animal in the pack. Easy to sacrifice."

I leaned back and closed my eyes. I couldn't believe that, after all that had happened, Henry Kaufman might get off without so much as a rebuke from the courts, simply by bribing someone else to take the blame.

"But I have one bit of good news," he said. "We're calling in a handwriting expert from New York. William Kingsley. He's an authority on the scientific study of penmanship. He's going to look at the letters and try to connect them to Kaufman."

"I don't see how that could help us," I said. "They were all printed in block lettering."

"Oh, he's got a method, even when someone tries to disguise the handwriting. He's winning cases. There's just one thing. He wants us to gather writing samples not just from Ewing and Kaufman, but from other parties involved in the case. I'd like all three of you to come down and give a sample."

"But why would we write the letters?"

"He just wants to rule out anyone who might be accused of writing the letters themselves to create a sensation."

"And would we be accused of throwing bricks through our own windows? Running down our own buggy?"

"It's only a formality."

The kitchen door opened, and Norma, Fleurette, and Deputy Morris shuffled down the hall. They looked half asleep.

"I'm sorry we kept you," I said, rising to my feet. "You must be wanting to get home."

"I thought there was some trouble with the road," Fleurette said. "Shouldn't they stay the night?"

Both men stiffened in surprise at the suggestion, as did Norma.

"Thank you, Miss Fleurette," Deputy Morris said, "but that won't be necessary. The road is very slow going because of all the ruts in it and the new moon. But now that we are warm and dry, the drive will be more tolerable."

As they went out the door, Sheriff Heath thanked Fleurette for her services as a nurse and Norma for the coffee. To me he said, "Tomorrow, Miss Kopp."

⊰ 48 ⊱

WE WERE WAITING ON THE FRONT PORCH when Sheriff
Heath arrived the next morning. The sun had come out, and
the air, while still cold, smelled damp and green.

"I don't approve of us riding around in automobiles,"
Norma said.

"I should like to learn how to drive one, and I wonder if
the sheriff would teach me," Fleurette said. "I was just looking at a charming motoring cap in one of my magazines that
I think would suit me."

"Don't bother the sheriff," I said. "He's doing us a favor by
bringing us to the station himself. I'm sure he's very busy."

Sheriff Heath brought the car to a stop in our drive and
jumped out, grinning, to open the door for me. Norma and
Fleurette settled in behind us.

"You're in high spirits for a man who was shot last night,"
I said.

"We got him. And now he faces an assault charge for
shooting at an officer of the law."

"You caught the thief after you left our house last night? In your condition?"

"Oh, not Morris and me. No, we went right home to bed. But one of the men in the posse tracked him all night and brought him in just before dawn. I deputized that fellow on the spot. We could use more like him."

"I'm sure you could."

The men from the dairy were taking advantage of the sunshine and finishing the work on the road, spreading a new layer of crushed stone and pressing it down with a roller. They stepped aside to let us through, although I know that the tires of the automobile only made the road more rutted and pitted. "We should get the county to come out and oil this road," Sheriff Heath said, half to himself. "This macadam is only good for buggies and bicycles."

"If you know a way to get the Board of Freeholders to pay for it, I'd like to hear about it."

"I wish I did. I'm fighting them for every penny right now. They put up that jail at a cost of six hundred thousand dollars but didn't finish it. I had to petition them for sanitary drains and windows that can't be picked open with common tools. There's no laundry facility and no money for me to issue uniforms to the prisoners. You can't imagine what a mess it is."

"Haven't the Freeholders seen it? Aren't any of them on your side?"

"I haven't offered them a tour," he said, smiling.

"Well, perhaps you should. Or show them some pictures. Doesn't anyone have a camera?"

"I suppose I do."

We drove along in silence for a minute. When we bounced over a large pit in the road, his face wound up in pain.

"What did the doctor have to say about your shoulder?"

He didn't look away from the road. He probably wanted to forget being subjected to the amateur nursing efforts of the Kopp household last night. Finally he said, "Mrs. Heath has examined the wound carefully and given it a fresh bandage."

"And she approves of you going right back to work today?"

"She does not."

I wondered what it must have been like for Mrs. Heath to awaken in the night and find her husband shot in the shoulder.

"I think I agree with your wife. You should have stayed home today."

He shrugged and grinned. "The criminals don't stay home, Miss Kopp. You know that. Mrs. Heath knows it too." Nothing could ruin his good mood. It was amazing to see what catching a fugitive could do for his disposition. I was cheered myself by the news.

The sheriff turned around to speak to Norma and Fleurette. "This is merely an exercise to satisfy Mr. Kingsley's rigorous method. No one suspects the Kopps of writing the letters," he said.

"I would think not," Norma said.

"His method is very scientific, the way he looks at each letter and how it's made. He can tell how hard a man presses a pen against the paper, and he knows the difference between how you write a letter at the beginning of the word or in the middle of it. He's winning all kinds of cases in New York. This is all we need to get our Mr. Kaufman convicted."

"He's not our Mr. Kaufman," Norma said.

"I think he is ours after all this time," Fleurette said. "He is our very own personal Black Hander. Most girls don't have one."

Sheriff Heath gave her a grave look. "You mustn't make a joke of this."

"We've been telling her that all along," I said. I turned to scold Fleurette yet again. "Sheriff Heath and his men sacrificed their own safety to guard our house. Don't let me hear you make light of it again, especially at the courthouse."

She shrugged and looked out the window. I wondered if we had worked too hard to protect her. She felt so utterly secure that she seemed to believe no harm could ever come to her.

As we drove into Hackensack, it seemed that the sun had brightened the spirits of the entire town. Schoolchildren were skipping rope in the playground, mothers were out walking with their babies, and shopkeepers were lingering outside their storefronts with cigarettes. I thought I could see buds breaking on the cherry trees, but that might have been my hopeful imagination.

AT THE COURTHOUSE Deputy Morris took charge of us and led us to an empty room where we were to wait our turn. "I'm afraid they're running behind," he said. "But now that the sheriff's back, I'm sure things will move along."

Still we waited for the better part of an hour. I'd brought a book, Norma had her newspaper, and Fleurette just fidgeted and complained that no one told her to bring something to keep herself occupied.

"I'm telling you now," Norma snapped at last. "When you go places, bring things to keep yourself occupied. There."

After an interminable wait, Deputy Morris returned and brought us down the long paneled corridor to the entrance to a courtroom. The door was closed and a few of Sheriff Heath's men stood guard. They looked at us nervously.

"The girls aren't to see him," one of the guards said to Deputy Morris.

"I thought he was finished."

The guard shook his head. "He's still in there yelling and pounding the table and kicking up a fuss. Never seen a man so obstinate. He's not coming to stay with us, is he?"

Deputy Morris frowned. "I don't want him under our roof any more than you do, but if a prison term is what he deserves, that's what he'll get."

"Are you talking about Henry Kaufman?" I said. "Is he in there?"

The men looked at us in surprise as if they'd forgotten all about us. From inside the room came the sound of chairs scuffing around on the floor and men arguing in low voices. One of the guards leaned against the door.

Deputy Morris gestured down the corridor. "Ladies, why don't we just go back and wait."

Just then the door burst open and the guard was knocked off his feet. Henry Kaufman pushed past him, red-faced and wild-eyed, strands of hair plastered against his forehead with sweat. I was standing in front of Fleurette. Before anyone could react, he lunged at me.

"You! You're behind this!" he roared. He rushed at me but I pushed back, shoving him against the wall just as I had the previous summer. The only reason his head didn't hit the wall with the same satisfying crack is that two officers were already on me, tugging at my shoulders and slowing my momentum.

"Take your hands off her," Morris shouted, which elicited a round of smothered laughter from the spectators. Henry Kaufman may have been the aggressor, but I had him pinned and the officers couldn't pull me away from him.

For just a second, Henry Kaufman and I stared each other down. I'd been running from this man for the better part of a year, but now I wanted him to see me. I wanted him to look into the face of the person he'd been tormenting. But although his eyes were forced in my direction, there was a black emptiness to them. They could have been two cold stones for all the humanity they revealed. He may have once been a petulant and spoiled child, but he had become a drunk and deranged man, and I saw in his face little possibility of redemption. That only made me want to shake him harder. Maybe I could knock loose whatever horrible thing was wedged inside of him.

He looked around wildly when he realized that the officers had let go of my arms. They were going to let me have him. I had gathered up his collar in one hand and used the other hand to press his shoulder against the wall.

"Not a word," I said in a low voice meant only for him. It thrilled me to have him in my grasp. I felt like a hawk about to devour a fish.

I heard a rustle behind me and looked around to see Sheriff Heath standing in the doorway, wearing an expression I could not read. No one had ever stared at me as intently as he was at that moment. He seemed to be mesmerized.

In the calmest voice I could muster, I said, "Sheriff Heath, has he given you your writing sample?"

He blinked in surprise and then smiled slowly. "He has not, Miss Kopp. He's been uncooperative."

I looked down at Mr. Kaufman, who was squirming under my grip. "Go and do what the sheriff says," I said. "I'll be waiting right here."

I gave him another hard push against the wall and shoved him toward the doorway. The sheriff clasped him on the shoulder and guided him back into the courtroom, then shot one last strange, still look at me before closing the door.

Once inside, we could hear Mr. Kaufman yell, "What's going to be done about that? I want charges brought up against that lady."

The deputies gathered around the door to hear.

Mr. Kaufman growled something unintelligible, and Sheriff Heath replied, "Now, who would ever believe that you'd have any trouble fighting off a lady, Mr. Kaufman?"

HENRY KAUFMAN did make a handwriting sample that day. When the door opened and Sheriff Heath indicated that all was well, I let Deputy Morris lead us away so we wouldn't run into him again. At last it was our turn to sit in the courtroom with the sheriff and write out our copies of the letters. I hadn't seen the letters since I had turned them over to him. It was unsettling to read them again, and even more unsettling to write out the very words that had been used to threaten us.

If you don't pay we will fire your house. We know your horse and wagon.

We will trap you or burn you.

Have you ever been to Chicago? We believe a girl of your talents would find a nice place for herself with no trouble at all.

Fleurette's hand shook a little as she wrote that line. I watched her face as she bent over the paper and I thought about all the hours Norma and I spent teaching her to write her letters. She copied out poems and stories, wrote notes to her uncles in Brooklyn, and composed messages for Norma's pigeons to carry. Mother taught her to write in French. Francis showed her what little he remembered of musical notation. As I watched her, I couldn't help but see the little girl she used to be, concentrating on her studies, not a nearly grown woman cooperating in a criminal investigation.

AS WE WALKED DOWN the courthouse steps with Deputy Morris, we met a guard holding a prisoner by the arm. It was George Ewing in shabby brown overalls. His limp was worse as he hobbled up the stairs.

I moved to put myself between him and Fleurette, and spun her around to face away from him. He'd threatened to kidnap her. I didn't even want him to see her.

Deputy Morris hurried us past him, but it was too late. Mr. Ewing shouted after us, "Is that you? Constance Kopp? And your sister?"

I froze and gripped Fleurette so she wouldn't move.

The guard shoved him through the courthouse door, but he fought to keep it open and kept shouting at me. "Miss Kopp! Don't let them send me to Trenton! Don't make me go back!"

I stood at the bottom of the stairs and looked at Deputy Morris with astonishment.

"I'm sorry about that, Miss Kopp. They shouldn't have brought him through this way. He's not supposed to see any of you."

In as calm a voice as I could muster, I said, "What was that about going to Trenton?"

Deputy Morris shrugged. "I don't know. He went in for a hearing yesterday about his sentencing. He doesn't want to go back to state prison. I guess he thought he was going to serve his time here."

"What's the difference?" I said.

"Oh, the state prison's terrible. Foul, dark, cold, overrun with rats and lice. Nobody wants to go to state prison."

"There's an easy way to stay out of prison," Norma said. "Don't break the law."

⇥ 49 ⇤

"PLEASE DON'T TELL ME that yet another man is writing threatening letters," Sheriff Heath said when I was admitted to his office the next day. "I haven't the manpower to keep the criminal element away from the Kopp sisters."

"I had an idea about George Ewing," I said.

He leaned back in his chair and laced his fingers behind his head. "Why not? No less than five of the finest legal minds in Bergen County have already reviewed the case, and several of our lesser minds have considered it as well. What's your idea?"

I said nothing but waited for him to remember his manners.

"Pardon me, Miss Kopp. Please. Go ahead."

I sat down across from him. "When he shouted at us on the courthouse steps yesterday—"

"Yes, I'm very sorry about that. We have a passageway for bringing prisoners from the jail to the courthouse, but they were doing some work there. They shouldn't have brought him around without checking to make sure you'd gone home."

"It's all right," I said. "But he said he didn't want to go back to prison in Trenton."

Sheriff Heath shrugged. "Of course he doesn't want to go to Trenton. It's the worst prison in the state."

"He likes it better here?"

"Well, it's clean, the food is edible, and we wash their clothes once in a while. We don't treat them like pigs in filth. And you know, he got beat up in Trenton. That wooden leg makes him a target."

"Then why don't you make a deal with him?" I said.

He didn't say a word, but I could see him considering the idea.

"Offer to let him serve his term here in Hackensack as long as he agrees to tell the truth," I said. "Make him promise not to claim responsibility for crimes he didn't commit."

The sheriff looked up at the ceiling. "It's not a bad thought," he said. "We haven't been able to come up with anything to offer him. It didn't even occur to us that he expected to serve his time here. Now that he knows he's going back to Trenton, maybe he would be more willing to negotiate."

"Is that something you can do? Can you fix it so he stays in Hackensack?"

He jumped to his feet. "I think so. We're still waiting for the sentencing, but we have a good judge on the case. The question is whether we can get Ewing to go along with it. Perhaps you could convince him, Miss Kopp."

I gripped the sides of my chair. "Me? Why should I talk to him?"

"He's been asking about you. He seems to be genuinely sorry for what he's done. Don't worry—there will be steel bars between you. You'll be completely safe. This time I actually can promise you that."

"Right now? But I . . ."

"Unless you haven't the nerve," he said, flashing one of his rare smiles.

"Of course I have the nerve," I muttered.

I followed him out of his office and down a corridor I hadn't seen before, into a narrow room furnished only with a row of white chairs. Along one wall was a series of small metal doors, each the size of a cupboard.

"My guard is bringing Mr. Ewing down now," the sheriff said. "I'll do most of the talking. Don't answer any personal questions."

I nodded and took a seat. He continued, "Just try to win him over and encourage him to tell the truth. Remind him that he'll be out soon and there's no need to claim responsibility for someone else's crimes."

Just then the cupboard door slid open, and I was faced with a row of metal bars and, behind them, a sleepy and surprised George Ewing.

He broke into a smile when he saw me, exposing those crooked front teeth. "Miss Kopp! I didn't think it'd be you!"

Sheriff Heath leaned around so Mr. Ewing could see him and said, "George, Miss Kopp asked especially about coming to visit with you."

The prisoner nodded vigorously, his eyes wide. He had an innocent and earnest air about him. He seemed like the kind of man who could easily be talked into wrongdoing. He was pale and gaunt, with newly shorn hair and a clean shave. His eyes were ever so slightly too far apart, and his lips trembled when he spoke, giving him a kind of stutter.

He turned back to me, leaning into the bars of the window and speaking to me in a near-whisper. "Miss Kopp. Miss

Kopp. Don't let them send me back there. Can't you say a word to the judge? Nothing too terrible happened to you and your sisters, did it? Just a bunch of threats, but you girls are all right, aren't you?"

Sheriff Heath raised his hand to stop him. "George, Miss Kopp came to me this morning with a fine idea. I wonder if you'd be willing to consider it."

He looked back and forth at us with suspicion. "I don't usually like it when the sheriff has an idea."

"I think you'll like this one," Sheriff Heath said. "What would you say if I went to the judge and asked him to let you serve your sentence here in Hackensack?"

He leaned forward and grabbed the bars. "You would do that? Sheriff, you would do that for me?"

"I think I—"

But Mr. Ewing wouldn't let him continue. "You know, I've been in a dozen jails in New Jersey, and there is not a one as fine as yours, Sheriff. I've been telling the other men. Some of them have never been to jail before, so they don't know how good they have it in here, Sheriff. It's a fine place, sir, it really is, and it would be an honor to serve my sentence here. I thank you, sir, for the invitation. I accept. I do. I accept."

"Well, that's not all there is to it, George," he said.

Mr. Ewing let go of the bars and sat back. "What else is there, Sheriff? Do I gotta pay rent? What's the catch?"

Sheriff Heath suppressed a smile. "If I could get rent from each of you, I'd have a much easier time with the Freeholders. No, George, what I need you to do is to stop taking credit for Henry Kaufman's crimes. Just tell the truth about what you did, but don't go around taking responsibility for the rest of it. Henry Kaufman's got to be punished. You need to help us with that."

Ewing filled his cheeks with air and blew them out, then raised his hands in a sign of bewilderment. "I don't know what you mean, Sheriff. Why would any man claim responsibility for a crime he didn't commit?"

"Because he was being paid to do so," I suggested.

"Paid?" George Ewing said, leaning forward in surprise. "You can get paid for that?"

"Or threatened. Did Henry Kaufman threaten to come after you if you didn't confess to the whole thing?"

He looked down at his hands and mumbled, "Something like that."

I leaned over and whispered in the sheriff's ear. "Can't we put him on a train as soon as he's served his time?" Sheriff Heath glanced at me and nodded.

"Listen, George. You just do your part. Tell the truth about this every time you're asked. You might be called to testify at Henry Kaufman's trial. Just tell them what really happened, and I'll keep you right here in Hackensack and make sure no harm comes to you. I'll even put you on a train when we set you free."

"You will?" he said.

Sheriff Heath nodded. "I'll drive you to the train station myself. I'll see that you get on safely. Where would you like to go, George?"

He sat back in his chair and let out a long breath. "Oh, boy, sheriff. I'm going to have to think about that. Can I let you know later?"

Sheriff Heath grinned. "You can let me know in six months, George."

AFTER GEORGE EWING WAS LED AWAY, the sheriff stood and called for the guard to let us out. "I have to say, Miss

Kopp. That was the best break we've had a long time. I might even go talk to John Ward. With this kind of leverage, maybe we can get a confession out of Kaufman."

"Who's John Ward?" I said, following him down the corridor.

"Kaufman's lawyer. You've seen them together."

I stopped. "Ward? Are you sure that's his name?"

Sheriff Heath turned around and frowned at me. "Of course that's his name. I've known John for years. I serve divorce papers and eviction notices for him. Although why he got mixed up with a man like Kaufman—"

"Then we've got him," I blurted out.

"Who?"

"Just—that's it. We've got him."

⊰ 50 ⊱

SHERIFF HEATH DROVE ME HOME and waited while I ran inside for the envelope. I'd hidden it in a bureau that we'd moved from my room to Mother's to barricade the windows. I stood looking at that bureau, a curiously dark, hand-painted piece of Viennese artistry, and thought how strange it was that its latest purpose had been to shield us from bullets.

I rushed down the stairs, saying not a word to Fleurette, who was at her sewing machine, or to Norma, who was completing some kind of small carpentry project in the washing room. The sheriff pulled away as soon as I was back in the car. "Wait," he said. "Let me see it."

He stopped in the middle of the road and took the envelope from me. There, in Henri LaMotte's faint handwriting, was the lawyer's name: Ward.

"I can't believe I missed this," he said. "These are the same photographs you showed me before?"

I nodded. "I didn't know who Ward was until you told me."

Without a word, he handed the envelope back to me and lifted his foot from the brake.

THE LAW FIRM OF WARD & MCGINNIS kept a suite of rooms in the Second National Bank on Colt Street, one of those monstrous brick and limestone affairs with every sort of column, dormer, tower, and Corinthian flourish known to the stone-carvers of the previous century. It had survived a fire that burned most of the city when Fleurette was a little girl, and traces of black soot were still lodged in the crevices of its scrollwork, giving it the appearance of a building that had been drawn in artist's charcoal.

I didn't know exactly what kind of law Mr. Ward practiced, but as soon as we walked into his office, I could see that he practiced it with sophistication. The walls were lined in mahogany panels that glowed and smelled faintly of furniture polish. A red carpet woven with a diamond pattern muffled the sounds of the street, and the room was lit with new electric brass chandeliers. A pair of fan palms flanked a window, rising from identical Chinese black-and-gold lacquer pots perched on tiny cast-iron claw feet.

Presiding over this stylish lobby was a girl of about twenty in a polka-dotted dress. She sat behind a dainty secretary's desk furnished with a typewriter and a telephone. She looked up at us from under a halo of honey-colored hair, and I could see at once that she was not the usual harried clerk one met in an office in Paterson. She looked more like the kind of girl who posed for the cover of *Vogue*, with enormous blue eyes, three perfect freckles alongside her nose, and lips drawn like a bow tied in red ribbon. They must have held auditions to find a girl like this one. I could not imagine that she walked into their office by chance.

"Good afternoon," she said, offering us a warm and dimpled smile.

"We've come to see Mr. Ward," Sheriff Heath said. "It's an urgent matter. Is he in?"

She lifted her elegantly drawn eyebrows. "If I could keep track of where those two are at any hour of the day, I might be able to run this place like a respectable law office."

I glanced around. "It seems respectable to me."

"Oh, it looks nice enough, but those two—"

The sound of footsteps and laughter in the hallway made the young woman jump up. The door opened and two men burst in, grinning.

"Gertie, you won't believe it," said a tall, thin man with curly hair and a pipe dangling out of his mouth. He stopped when he saw us. The man he was with—shorter, rounder, red-haired, and freckle-faced, with pale green eyes and an eager smile—came to a stop just behind him.

The girl attempted to introduce us, although I hadn't yet given our names. "Mr. Ward, I—"

He pulled his pipe from his mouth and looked me over. "Never mind, Gertie," he said, and then, correcting himself, "Miss Nolan. Bob and I are old friends. Good to see you, Sheriff," he said, taking the sheriff's hand and pumping it vigorously. "What kind of trouble am I in today?"

He grinned at me and I resisted the urge to return his smile. John Ward was not handsome, exactly, but there was something both intelligent and impish about his expression, as if he were about to tell a joke or perform a skit. From the little I'd seen of him in the courtroom, I could only imagine the kind of theatrics he was capable of putting on in front of a judge.

Once his appraisal of me was complete, he remembered his manners and introduced himself. "John Ward, miss. Attorney at law. My partner, Peter McGinnis. And you have met Miss Nolan."

"How do you do," I said. "I am Constance Kopp. I have come—"

"I thought I knew you!" Mr. Ward said, elbowing his partner in the gut. "It's the girl from that Kaufman case. All right, Petey, you go on without me."

"Hey! You're not sticking me with Mrs. Cumberland again!" Mr. McGinnis protested.

John Ward put his pipe between his teeth. "I am. Got to have a few words with Miss Kopp. This way, my dear. You can come too, Bob."

He led us across the lobby to a door bearing matching nameplates. Sheriff Heath followed silently behind me. "Petey and I share an office," he said by way of explanation as he pushed the door open. "We always have. We shared a boarding room in law school and a clerkship in Trenton, and now we even share a desk. We're like an old married couple, except Petey won't iron my shirts."

Before he closed the door, he pushed his head into the reception room and said, "Isn't that right, Petey?"

Mr. McGinnis was whispering something to Miss Nolan. He stood quickly and said, "What's that?"

"I was just telling Miss Kopp here that you won't iron my shirts, even after all I've done for you."

"I did your ironing that once, but it was an exceptional circumstance."

John Ward cackled and closed the door. "He did iron my shirt one time," he said with a note of wonder in his voice. Then, pulling out a chair for me, he added, "I'll tell you that story someday, Miss Kopp. I'd almost forgotten it myself."

I sat down gingerly, my pocketbook in my lap, and the sheriff took the seat next to me. Mr. Ward settled into a leather armchair at one end of an enormous partner's desk, then gestured to an identical chair at the other end of the desk. "That's where Petey takes his afternoon nap," he said, removing his pipe from his teeth and tapping it into a tray. "But you didn't come here for a tour of the office, did you? You're here to see if I'm going to let you beat Henry Kaufman in court again."

Sheriff Heath cleared his throat. He hadn't gotten a word in since we'd arrived, and now I wasn't sure what either of us should say. I had been prepared for a much more serious meeting.

"Well, you don't have to worry about a thing," he said before either of us could compose an answer. "I'm off the case!"

"I'm sorry?" I said. "You're off the case?"

"Your sweetheart Kaufman fired me. He's a maniac, did you know that?"

Now I couldn't help but laugh. "He's not my sweetheart!"

"I knew I could make you smile. Now, Miss Kopp." And here he leaned forward and tried without much success to arrange his features into a more serious expression. "That man put me through hell—excuse me, but he did—and I can't imagine what your year has been like. How do you suppose that sister of his puts up with him?"

"I don't think she does," I said.

He put his pipe back in his mouth and leaned back, looking up at the ceiling and propping his feet on the desk. "No, I don't suppose so. You know, they used to be such nice, quiet clients. Out-of-town family, very routine business, nothing to see. Then the old man decided that the only way to straighten out his miscreant son was to give him a factory to run. I tried to talk him out of it, Miss Kopp. I did. But he signed over the bank account, gave him the keys to the factory, everything. Said he wanted Henry to know he was serious. But the truth is, the old man's always been a little soft when it came to Henry. I've no idea why. Now Mrs. Garfinkel's come to town to try to put it all back the way it was before their father got involved. It's a real mess."

"I'm sorry," I said. "Did you say Mr. Kaufman fired you?"

"Well, you might call it a mutual agreement to part ways. You know those friends of his—they're not the most law-abiding group. Henry kept bringing them in here and asking me to defend them on some petty criminal matter. Pretty soon they were all turning up with their brothers and cousins and neighbors. Harassing Miss Nolan, stinking up the place—I finally told Henry I wasn't taking on any more criminal cases, including his. He stormed out of here and I haven't seen him since."

I shifted in my chair. "If you're not going to defend him at trial, who will?"

He laughed and swung his feet back to the floor. "Some other fool. It won't be the law firm of Ward & McGinnis, that's all I know. But I wouldn't worry, Miss Kopp. Kaufman doesn't have time to find a good attorney, and a bad one will only help your case. Mrs. Garfinkel has finally persuaded her father to give her control of the bank accounts, and I don't think Henry even turns up at the factory anymore. I don't know where he'll get the money to pay another lawyer."

Sheriff Heath cleared his throat. "If I can get a word in, John."

"Sorry, Bob. Of course. I forget myself sometimes."

The sheriff slid the envelope across the desk. "Did you, by any chance, hire a photographer to take some pictures of a building in New York?"

Mr. Ward's mouth fell open. "This is one of LaMotte's jobs!"

"You know him?" I said.

"Course I do! I use him all the time. Did I forget to pay him for these? Oh, I'll be in trouble. Why didn't Gertie take care of this?" He opened the envelope and riffled through the pictures. "Means nothing to me," he muttered, mostly to himself. "I don't know what Kaufman was after."

"So it was him!" I said.

"Oh, sure it was. This was another of his crazy schemes. I should've fired him then."

"What did he hire you to do?" the sheriff asked.

The telephone rang in the lobby and he cocked his head to listen. A knock came at the door, and Miss Nolan looked in. "It's Mrs. Ward."

He dropped his pipe back into the tray. "Not for long she isn't."

Miss Nolan and I both gave a little gasp.

"Pardon me, girls. Don't ever marry, either one of you. Can't you tell her I left with Petey?"

"She just saw him going into the Hamilton Club."

In unison they said, "And that's why she's calling."

Mr. Ward raised his hands in mock surrender. "All right. Tell her to hold the line."

Miss Nolan retreated and closed the door behind her. Mr. Ward flipped through the photographs again and looked back up at Sheriff Heath. "Where were we?"

"John," the sheriff said. "This is serious. Isn't there anything you can tell us about these?"

He pushed the envelope back across the desk. "I don't know, Bob. Like I say, he just asked me to have the building watched. I think Kaufman liked to get me caught up in his lunatic schemes, just to see what I would do. He also wanted to know what was involved with adopting a baby. Can you imagine that? Henry Kaufman with a baby?"

I jumped to my feet. "Adoption?"

Mr. Ward rose as well. "Oh, well, nothing ever came of it. I shouldn't have mentioned it at all. He just came in here asking about orphanages and paperwork. I think he was tight. He usually was."

From the other room, Miss Nolan called for him. "Mr. Ward, she's still holding the line!"

Sheriff Heath started to say something but I grabbed his arm.

"Let's go," I said.

I pulled him into the lobby. Mr. Ward followed us and took up the telephone. As we walked away, we heard him shout into the receiver.

"Peaches? Is that you?"

⊰ 51 ⊱

AS SHERIFF HEATH'S AUTOMOBILE rolled down Colt Street, I said, "Don't you see? He left him in an orphanage. That's where anyone would leave a baby he didn't want to take care of."

"How do you know so much about it?"

I paused. I wasn't about to tell him how I knew.

"People do it all the time," I said. "They drop a child off because they can't feed it, or because the father's gone to jail, or because the mother has to go away and work. They say they'll come back, but they never do. Mr. Ward said he had questions about orphanages. I bet he was just trying to figure out what he would do with a baby once he had one. Lucy was right. He didn't want to pay support, he was tired of being bothered about it, and he thought she was blackmailing him for a share of the family's money. So he took the child and left it at an orphanage for adoption. He might have even believed it was his right to do, as the boy's father."

We stopped for a train crossing. We were fifth in a line of black automobiles. Behind us, two draft horses hauling a wagon of empty wooden barrels huffed and tossed their heads at the scream the train engine made as it went by.

Once the train passed, he said, "I don't see Kaufman grabbing a baby. And what do you suggest we do? Write to every orphanage in New Jersey and New York?"

"We're not writing letters," I said quickly. "I don't think Mr. Kaufman would have gone driving around New York looking for an orphanage. He would have wanted to get out of the city. Why wouldn't he bring it right back to Paterson?"

The sheriff turned to me, puzzled. "Do you expect me to go knocking on the doors of orphanages and ask if they've got an extra boy around the place?"

"No. I'm going, too."

He didn't say anything for a few minutes as we followed the line of cars across the tracks. Then he stopped at an intersection, pushed his hat off his forehead to rub his temples, and said, "All right. We're just down the street from one of them, so we might as well go now. There's another out on McBride, and of course the orphan asylum is down on Market Street. I can't think of any others."

The days of hiding a home for girls in the countryside were over. Mrs. Florence's home in Wyckoff had been closed for years. Any sort of orphanage or home for mothers and children would be found in the city today, near the hospital and the train station.

"Well, then, we have three to visit. We could see them all this afternoon and be home for supper."

He didn't answer, but he turned down Union, and soon we were driving along Albion, a tree-lined street of older homes set back from the road. At the end of the block, we came to a wide and plainly built farmhouse with green shutters and an enormous elm in front. It looked to be a comfortable and clean place for girls in confinement and their babies, but as we reached the door, I could smell rot and mildew inside. Sitting atop that was the odor of cabbage and beans.

A handwritten sign tacked next to the door read "MRS. LIVINGSTON'S HOME FOR THE UNWED AND FRIEND-LESS. FORMERLY RESPECTABLE GIRLS ONLY. NO ADOP-TIONS OFFERED."

Sheriff Heath rang the bell and a baby wailed in response. Another child joined in, and soon there were three of them. Footsteps echoed back and forth through the front rooms of the house, but no one came to the door.

A skinny cat jumped on the porch and tumbled backward in surprise when it saw us. It hissed at us from its hiding place.

The sheriff rang the bell again and this time the footsteps came closer. A girl in a housedress answered the door. She was only a teenager, and shapeless in a way that suggested that she had recently borne a child herself. Her hair was tied carelessly at the top of her head. I fought to push back memories of my own confinement, and the way I'd hide whenever a knock came at the door. This girl seemed so brazen in comparison.

She had a rag in her hand, which she dropped when she saw the sheriff.

"How do you do, miss," he said. "I am Sheriff Robert Heath, and this is Miss Kopp. We are here to see about a child. May we speak to Mrs. Livingston?"

Without a word she closed the door and left us standing there, the cat nosing at our ankles. Sheriff Heath pushed it off the porch with his boot. He looked over at me, embarrassed. "I don't like cats."

"Neither do I."

We heard footsteps again and the door opened, this time revealing a short, squat woman with hair the color of a cast-iron pan and a disposition to match. She wore a high-necked dress the likes of which I hadn't seen since my grandmother was alive, and spectacles as thick and dusty as the windows in her old home.

"We have no business with you," she said before Sheriff Heath could get in a word. "Our girls come from good homes and the children are carefully placed with families."

She started to close the door, but the sheriff reached out and held it. "We need a word with you," he said. "It concerns a criminal matter. We wish to clear your home of any wrongdoing, but if we're unable to do that today, we'll send detectives around tomorrow. We'd like to keep it out of the papers."

Her face settled into its frown lines, but she stepped aside so we could enter. She closed the door behind us and we stood in a dark foyer next to a stack of old newspapers and a row of empty milk bottles. There were blankets and wooden toys on the stairs, cups and tiny plates on the floor, and the smell of sour milk rising from the carpet. Mrs. Florence never would have tolerated such a mess.

She looked expectantly at us. I cleared my throat and said, "We believe a man deposited a baby boy at a church home or an orphanage last year."

She shook her head. "We would have turned him away. We don't let people do that anymore. Too much trouble for us, and we have enough trouble as it is."

As if to illustrate her point, two girls of a tender age lumbered down the stairs, their bellies so swollen that no dress could hide their condition. Sheriff Heath looked quickly away. When they saw him, they turned without a word and disappeared.

"We're sorry to have disturbed you, Mrs. Livingston," I said. "Can you tell me where such a child would be taken?"

"Not to a home like mine," she said. "And not the Catholic home either. The Orphan Asylum Hospital would take him, but he'd be sent right out for adoption if no one claimed him."

THE ASYLUM WAS HOUSED in a fearsome brick building on Market Street, where it stood as a solemn reminder of the misfortunes that could be inflicted upon small children. More than one parent or vicious older sibling threatened to send little boys and girls there if they misbehaved. Such jokes were strictly banned in our household, but Fleurette knew about the place somehow, and when she was only five, she visited it in her nightmares. I remember lying awake on those nights and fighting the urge to go to her as my mother rose instead to quiet the child.

But compared to Mrs. Livingston's home, the orphan asylum was surprisingly clean and uncluttered. We entered through grand brass doors and were greeted by the smell of floor soap and the sound of a typewriter. A plump older woman sat behind the desk and stopped typing when she saw us.

"Sheriff Heath," she said, pushing her glasses up on her nose. "What a nice surprise. How are dear Cordelia and those sweet children?"

"They're just fine," he said. "May I introduce you to my associate, Miss Kopp. She's helping me with a case." Turning to me, he said, "Mrs. Griggs lived next door to us before we moved to our present living quarters."

"I'm sure Cordelia misses her kitchen," Mrs. Griggs said.

"I think she misses her neighbors even more," he said. "The inmates and guards are no company for a woman. I hope you'll come and pay her a visit."

"Oh!" she said, flustered. "At the prison? I don't think—"

"It's the safest home in Bergen County," I said. Sheriff Heath gave me a grateful look. "I've been there myself, and I can assure you that Mrs. Heath has made it quite comfortable."

"Well, perhaps I will," she said, without enthusiasm.

Sheriff Heath cleared his throat and nodded at me. I explained our purpose.

She squinted up at the two of us. "I don't remember him, but I'm not the only one who greets visitors. What does the boy look like?"

"I'm afraid we don't know," I said. "When the child was last seen, he was just a baby, and we have only the most general description."

She looked up and down the long empty hallway. There were doors on either side, the kind with glass windows and someone's name in gold lettering. "If he was here, we would have a file." After looking around again, she said, "It's almost five o'clock. I don't think anyone else will be in today. Stay here and let me go have a peek in the office."

She disappeared through a door down the corridor. Several nurses and orderlies left for the day, their coats and lunch pails over their arms. They looked at us but said nothing as they walked by.

At last Mrs. Griggs returned with a stack of folders under her arm. "Here are all the children who came in around that time. What are the names again?" she asked.

We gave her every name we could think of connected to

the case. There were a few dozen files to look through, but she paged through them quickly and shook her head.

"I'm sorry," she said. "I don't see any of those names."

"Have these children all been adopted?" I asked.

"Oh, I would think so by now, wouldn't you? Let me see." She paged through them again, placing the files in one of three stacks on her desk.

"These were returned to their families," she said, pointing to the first stack. "These were put up for adoption and placed with someone. And these are still here, or their files are incomplete. I'd have to make some inquiries to find out what happened to them."

I pointed to the second and third stacks. "May I see just the boys?"

I reached into my pocketbook for some notepaper and wrote down the names in the remaining files. There was very little information to record. In some cases it was simply a date, the age and sex of the child, and a line for whatever name people were willing to supply. I saw no Bobby or Robert or Robbie among them, nor any boy of the right age who would have been dropped off around that time.

"Are you sure these are all of them?" I said.

"All but the private placements," she answered. "Some of our records are sealed at the mother's request."

I shook my head. "The mother is the one looking for the child in this case."

Sheriff Heath rose to thank his friend and soon we were outside in the fading afternoon light. The mills had just discharged their workers, and a stream of weavers and dyers and machinists flooded Market Street, each shivering in their work clothes and trudging toward whatever kind of home they knew. Sheriff Heath drove me back to Wyckoff while I sat next to him in silence, my fingers working the edges of the page on which I had written the names of lost and orphaned children and the adults who had deposited them there for safekeeping, or whatever manner of keeping a child might expect in an asylum hospital.

"I don't like it," he said, before I got out of the car. "I don't picture Kaufman and that gang of his stealing a baby and leaving it at an orphanage. How would they even know what to do with a baby?"

I agreed. I couldn't see Henry Kaufman doing a thing like that, either. But I also couldn't believe he wasn't involved somehow.

⤐ 52 ⤏

THAT NIGHT ANOTHER SNOWFALL made Sicomac Road almost impassable again. Two of the enormous plane trees that lined the road split in half under the force of wind and ice, blocking the way until the weather cleared enough for some of the men to come out and chop them to pieces. Low spots in the road had turned into rivers when it rained and were now frozen. When the ice thawed, the ground heaved and cracked.

In the early morning, a sharp sound propelled me out of bed. Thinking it was a gunshot, I flattened myself against the wall next to the window, which was glazed with ice and impossible to see through. I was trying to force it open when Norma appeared in the doorway, already dressed and wrapped in her winter coat.

"It was a tree," she said. "It hit the barn. Get dressed."

I did as she said and met her in the kitchen, which was dark and so cold that it, too, could have been covered in ice. She handed me a pair of work gloves and a set of earmuffs.

"Watch your step," she said, and pushed the door open. "It's frozen solid out here."

I choked at the first blast of frigid air. Norma tucked her chin into her coat and trudged ahead, making little snorting sounds as she struggled to breathe. Across the drive were the severed branches of an old elm tree that lost the battle with the storm. Only its roots, just lifted out of the ground, were not covered in ice.

The barn door was entirely blocked by fallen limbs, making it impossible to get in to tend the animals. Even worse, a low corner of the roof had crumbled when the tree hit it. I could hear the chickens complaining from their roost.

"Ach. We should have done the roof last summer," I said into my coat collar.

Norma grunted. "We'll do it today."

All morning we chopped away at the tree limbs and hauled them to the woodpile. Norma took a hatchet to the smaller branches while I went after the trunk with an old and unreliable saw. It was slippery and dangerous work, with the ice shifting and melting underneath our feet and the limbs sliding out of our grasp. Once Norma slipped on the ice and fell backward, her hatchet flying out of her hand. "Get away," she yelled, but by the time I saw what I was getting away from, the hatchet had hit its mark, landing atop a fence post in the vegetable garden. I couldn't have moved anyway. The saw was embedded in the tree at that moment, and my gloves were stuck to the saw.

Fleurette took her time getting out of bed, although she must have heard us working below her window. When she finally appeared in the doorway and offered to help, we both yelled, "Coffee!" She retreated indoors and put herself to

348

good use boiling coffee, heating rolls, and frying bacon. We refused to go inside on the grounds that once we got warm, we would not want to go out again. Instead Fleurette carried our breakfast to us and kept up a steady brigade of rolls and hot drinks while we worked.

It must have been after noon by the time we cleared the branches and pushed open the barn door. A chorus of complaints rose from the animals. Dolley stamped and snuffled in her stall and the chickens answered with low cackles. Norma took her hatchet to the frozen water trough while I handed out oats and tossed cracked corn to the chickens. I sat down for just a minute to catch my breath, but as soon as I did my eyes closed and darkness crowded in.

"Get up!" Norma said. "We've got to do something about that roof, and there's more snow on the way."

More snow? I pushed myself to my feet and went to the door. Sure enough, the wind had picked up and brought a few flakes with it. I leaned against the doorway, but Norma butted me with the end of a ladder, pushing me outside.

I didn't think I could stay upright for another minute. "Norma," I said, while she set the ladder up against the side of the barn, "don't you ever wish it were easier?"

"What?"

"This," I said, gesturing at the snow and the ice and the broken limbs. "Living out here on our own like this."

She kicked at the ladder to dig it into the ground. "I've always believed that people who strive for an easy life become dull and lazy. And I don't see the point in living somewhere else, when this place already suits us so well."

"But we might have to. Francis is right. Our money's running out."

"In that case," Norma said, in a voice that suggested that the matter was closed, "it's your turn to figure things out."

"What does that mean?"

"It means that I found this place. I found you, and I found Fleurette." She looked out at the road—at the very spot where she'd stood when she first declared that we would live here, seventeen years ago. Then she turned to look at me, a kind of hard satisfaction in her eyes. "Didn't I?"

For a minute I couldn't say anything. There was just the hollow, distant sound of the wind and the gathering snowfall.

"You did," I said.

"Yes, I did. Now it's your turn. Mother's gone, so who's stopping you? Go and find yourself a little job that pays just enough to keep us. Doesn't that sound like something you'd enjoy?"

"I don't know what I'd enjoy," I said.

"I do," Norma declared. "You've had such a high time running around playing detective. Why don't you become one of those?"

She started to climb the ladder. I tried to pull her down but she shook me off. "What are you talking about?"

"There was an advertisement in the paper last week for female detectives at Wanamaker's," she said, looking down at me. "Didn't you see it? Write a letter and tell them all about yourself, and I'm sure they'll put you right in."

I stood staring up at her. She turned around and kept climbing. The hem of her split skirt, dirty from the mud and snow, brushed against me.

"Just don't let us be reduced to living with Francis."

"Wanamaker's?" I said. "In New York?"

"Take the train," she called down. "You know how to ride the train."

I looked straight ahead at the bottom rungs of the ladder and the weathered old boards of the barn behind them. Had I really just heard my sister tell me to leave the house—not once, but every day—for a job specifically designed to put me in the path of criminals? What had become of us?

"And I've got a job for you right now, if you can stop daydreaming," she said. "Hold that ladder and pass me the tools."

I handed the saw to her, then stood and watched as she chopped away at the jagged edges of the hole, letting the severed shingles drop into the chicken pen below. Once she had a clean edge to work with, I passed some odd-size chunks of wood to her, and she found a way to nail them in place. I could hear her huffing and panting above me as she worked. I was growing stiff and frozen on the ground, my boots buried once again in snow and my fingers so numb I worried they'd lose their grip on the ladder. A vision of that clean and quiet hotel on Fifth Avenue floated before me, with its white sheets and brass lamps polished by a hand I'd never see. In a place like that, I could have an egg brought to me every day, without ever once having to patch a roof on a chicken coop in the middle of winter.

All afternoon the road was empty and the surrounding pastures silent and still. Smoke drifted over from some distant neighbor's chimney, but then the wind receded and the snow fell down like a blanket, until even the smoke was snuffed out. When Norma stepped off the ladder, she wore a collar of fresh snowfall.

That night Fleurette lit the water heater and boiled some

extra water on the stove so we could both have baths, but Norma didn't want to bother with it and I wanted supper first. We sat silently in the kitchen and ate corned beef and potatoes along with the last of the morning's rolls. I never did get warm enough to do without my coat, so I sat under a mountain of wool and let the snow drip onto the floor below my chair. Norma's fingers were red and chapped from working on the roof. Fleurette offered to rub some cold cream into them, but she refused, wanting only to take tea and a bed warmer upstairs and go right to sleep. I took an extra kettle of hot water to the bathroom and left Fleurette to do the washing up.

The bath was steaming when I sank into it, drawing the blood back to my numb feet. I wiggled my toes until pinpricks of pain ran through them and the sensation returned. The tub was too small for me and I couldn't submerge myself all at once. The only way to get my knees in was to curl in a ball and turn on my side. I awoke just as the water started to cool and put myself to bed.

⇥ 53 ⇤

BY MIDNIGHT I WAS SITTING UP IN THE DARK, listening to a screech owl call to its mate, and thinking quite suddenly of Lucy. I wasn't ready to give up on the idea that the child made it back to Paterson. I saw no other way to go about it than to look into every orphan on the list, and then go to the orphanage in the next county, and the one after that. But I wasn't sure I'd ever get anywhere at that rate.

When the clock downstairs struck one, I still hadn't settled on a course of action. I might have dropped off to sleep, but when the clock chimed three I awoke again, thinking about what Sheriff Heath had said. Henry Kaufman did not seem like the kind of person who would know what to do with a baby, even for an hour, even long enough to grab him and then turn him loose again.

But Marion Garfinkel was that kind of person. She'd know what to do. She'd place him anonymously, claiming that the child was her own. If she needed to, she'd offer enough money to make sure that no one asked any questions.

What was it she told me when I asked about Lucy's child? *It's better off wherever it is now.*

And she probably believed that.

At last sleep caught up with me again and I didn't move until the chickens started cackling at daybreak. The truth was with me, as if I had known it all along.

THE SKY HAD CLEARED and the snow had hardened overnight. Dolley didn't want to be out in it any more than I did, but I nudged her along Sicomac Road anyway. A number of motor cars passed me, each of them honking and swerving and nearly running us off the road. Dolley had never been a high-strung horse, but these black and noisy machines were making a nervous animal out of her. I tried to cluck at her the way Norma did, but she didn't find it soothing.

I stabled her for a few hours in Paterson and walked over to the orphan asylum in the gray sludge that had been pushed aside by the plows. In no time at all I was at the front door, relieved to find Mrs. Griggs at her station.

She was considerably less friendly to me than she had been to Sheriff Heath. When I made my request, she frowned and said, "Shouldn't Sheriff Heath be the one asking the questions?"

I stood a little straighter and spoke in the most commanding voice I could muster.

"He requested my help on a sensitive matter. A girl got into some trouble, and the sheriff thought it best to have a lady make the more delicate inquiries. That's why he brought me here. If you feel his introduction was not satisfactory, I'll go now to Hackensack and return with him for a second one. But I know he won't be happy to be called away from the prison and his important work protecting the citizens of Bergen County simply to do again what he has already done."

She pressed her lips together in a disapproving frown. "You know I can't tell you anything about our private placements. If the mother surrenders a child, the records are sealed forever."

I knew that well enough. The same promise had been made to me. "What if a woman brought a child in and claimed to be its mother, but wasn't?"

"We'd have a look at the birth certificate. We'd ask for identification or a witness."

"But some children are born at home. They don't all have birth certificates."

"What are you looking for, exactly?" Mrs. Griggs asked.

I could tell that I wasn't going to get into those files unless I told her what I suspected. I gave her Marion Garfinkel's name, described her, and told her again the boy's age and when we thought he would have been brought in.

She wrote it all down and then scrutinized the paper in front of her. "You're suggesting the boy was kidnapped."

"It wouldn't be that unusual. Isn't it possible that someone would try a thing like that to cover up a scandal in the family?"

She searched my face thoughtfully for a minute, then rose from her desk and disappeared into the office. After a long wait she returned, clutching a folder to her bosom as if she wasn't sure she was ready to let me see it.

"We had only one private placement of a boy that age during the strikes," she said, easing gingerly back into her chair. "If this is the child you're looking for, then I believe we still have him."

I took a deep breath and dropped into the chair across from her. The realization that I might have done this—that I might have helped Lucy find her son—this sent all the blood to my cheeks and set my heart pounding.

I wasn't sure I trusted myself to speak. She set the file on her desk and ran her hands across it.

At last I said, "Is he here now? Could I see him?"

"Certainly not," she said. "If this is a matter for the sheriff, then the sheriff should come and see the child."

By then I had my breath back. "Of course he will," I said evenly. "I only wish to be sure of the situation before I ask him to take an afternoon away from his duties. Do you know anything more about the circumstances under which the boy was brought here?"

With a long and shaky sigh, Mrs. Griggs opened the file and lifted it toward her so I could not see the papers it held. After flipping through them for a few minutes, she said, "I don't remember this one, but from what I can see, it was an unusual case. A woman brought the baby to us, but had none of the papers we require—no birth certificate, no letter from a doctor, and no list of family members. She wouldn't even provide the boy's name or his last known address. She said that she'd had the baby abroad to avoid suspicion and had only just recently returned. We called him Teddy for lack of another name."

"But the mother—the woman claiming to be the mother—that was Marion Garfinkel?"

She closed the folder. "She gave a very common name and I suppose it could have been false. Our director will have to speak to the sheriff before we can say anything more about it. This may require a hearing before a judge. It's very unusual."

"But the boy is here?"

For the first time, a smile worked around the corners of her lips. "If this is the boy—and I'm not saying it is—we definitely do still have him. There are so many infants that come to us, and those are adopted first. Even a child of one or two years is hard to place."

"Mrs. Griggs, you've done a little boy and his mother a great deal of good today," I said, jumping out of my chair. "The sheriff must be told immediately. Could you place a telephone call to his office?"

She looked down at the brass phone on her desk and drummed her fingers. "I shouldn't make the call," she said. "But our director can."

She ran upstairs and, after another interminable wait, returned with an expression I couldn't read. "As I suspected, you'll have to go to a judge before a claim can be made. But first the child must be identified by its mother. Sheriff Heath said he would fetch the girl and be right over. He said you would know where to find her."

I gave her Lucy Blake's address, and she disappeared again up the wide staircase, her fingers trailing along a banister into which a row of laurel leaves had been carved. I waited the better part of an hour, with Mrs. Griggs running downstairs to tell me that Sheriff Heath was on his way, and then rushing back up to tell the nurses to get the boy ready. From her excited air I gathered that they felt quite sure that one of their charges was going home with its mother. I hope they hadn't given the boy that impression. I couldn't stand to see Lucy shake her head and tell the boy that he did not belong to her.

I paced the lobby and tried to picture Marion Garfinkel carrying a baby in. I couldn't see her without also seeing the chain of errors and misfortune that brought her here. There was Henry Kaufman's father, putting him in charge of a factory he had no ability to run. There was Henry Kaufman himself, forcing his way into Lucy's room with his own disgraceful intentions. And then Lucy, hoping—naively, perhaps stupidly—that he would face up to his obligations.

Finally, there was Marion, the expedient one, the efficient one. She saw a problem and, just as quickly, she saw its solution. It was not difficult to understand how Marion got the idea. If I were to stop a hundred women on the sidewalk in Paterson and ask them what an unmarried factory girl should do if she got herself into trouble, they would all give the same answer.

It was the answer I'd come to myself, seventeen years ago. It was the only sensible solution, and Marion Garfinkel was, I had to admit, eminently sensible.

I stopped pacing and had just sat down across from Mrs. Griggs's desk again when Sheriff Heath pushed the door open and led a trembling and tearful Lucy Blake into the halls of the Paterson Orphan Asylum Hospital.

She hadn't even taken off her apron. When she saw me, she ran across the lobby to me. "I don't know what I'll do if it isn't him," she said.

"It's all right," I said, although I wasn't sure if it was. "Be a brave girl and try not to upset the child."

Mrs. Griggs called a nurse who led us up the stairs, through a locked door, and into a short, windowless corridor. At the end of it was a door with a brass plate marked "BOYS."

She unlocked the door and pushed it open. We stepped into an enormous room with high windows and rows of iron beds on either side. Shoes and jackets and children's blocks were scattered about the room.

And in the middle of it stood one little boy.

Lucy ran for him before any of us had a moment to think. He was in her arms and smothered against her shoulder so fast that I didn't get a good look at his face. As she spun around, all I could see was black hair like his father's, wetted and combed along a neat part, and the back of the smallest blue suit I'd ever seen.

The nurse smiled and stepped back into the doorway to motion for her colleagues, who must have gathered just outside when they heard us come upstairs. Sheriff Heath bowed his head and stepped away to make room for them.

Lucy didn't stop spinning and I began to wonder if she was ever going to let the boy come up for air. They formed their own planet in the middle of the room, rotating around a sun that only they could see.

⇥ 54 ⇤

LUCY LOOSENED HER GRIP ON THE BOY. She sat down on the edge of a bed and held him in her lap. He had Mr. Kaufman's hair and round forehead, but he'd inherited Lucy's eyes and her fine Irish profile.

Sheriff Heath knelt down in front of them and held out his hand to the boy, who didn't know to shake it but gripped his fingers. He was a fine, plump boy, old enough to walk on his own, but too young to understand what was happening.

"It's nice to meet you, son," was all that Sheriff Heath could say.

I stood in the doorway and talked in a low voice with the nurses. They were willing to fix up a room so that Lucy could stay the night.

"It's better that way," one of them whispered to me. "If we make her go home without him, she could make such a fuss that the other children would hear it. We'd never get them to bed after a scene like that."

Lucy overheard us and rose from the edge of the bed, carrying the boy on her hip as if she'd been doing it every day since he was born. "The sheriff already told me he'd have to stay here tonight," she said. "It's all right. I work for two shut-ins who are expecting their supper. They've been very gracious, but I should go back to them."

"I'll get a judge to see us tomorrow, and I'll take statements from the nurses tonight so we'll be ready for his questions," Sheriff Heath said, and he and I walked downstairs and left Lucy to say her goodbyes. The news had already reached Mrs. Griggs, who was waiting for us at the bottom of the stairs.

She smiled broadly. "This doesn't happen often enough around here. The nurses are terribly pleased."

"In my years as a sheriff, I've never returned a lost child to its parents. And I didn't do it this time, either. We have Miss Kopp to thank for this one."

She nodded at me, still smiling. Then she turned back to the sheriff and said, "I suppose the story will come out before the judge tomorrow and may be in the papers."

"We hope to keep it out of the papers," he said quickly.

"Yes. I gather that the boy's father is not . . ."

"No. The father won't have anything to do with the child. But the girl is in a comfortable situation as a domestic servant for two spinsters who are willing to take in the boy. I spoke to them this afternoon, and they have agreed to sign a letter for the judge. My stenographer will get it written tonight."

"Well," she said. "If the judge is satisfied, we will be, too."

At last Lucy appeared at the top of the stairs, along with a nurse who had no doubt been sent along in case of hysterics. But Lucy's head was high and she seemed to have a firm grip on herself. She walked slowly but deliberately, and smiled bravely when she said, "I told him I had to go and make a bed for him. He's grown too much for the one I had."

The next morning, Sheriff Heath and I were waiting in front of the factory when Marion Garfinkel arrived. "If it's about the trial, you'll have to speak to Henry," she said when she saw us. "I want nothing to do with it. I told him I would pay Mr. Ward's bills, but I'm not paying another attorney. He's on his own now."

She opened the side entrance just enough to let herself in and tried to close it behind her. Sheriff Heath caught the door before she did. "We can speak here, or I can bring you to the courthouse," he said quietly.

Marion shrugged without looking back at him. "We can talk all day if you want. I'm not responsible for my brother anymore. I haven't even seen him in weeks."

We followed her across the empty factory floor. "I've taken over Henry's desk," she said, leading us into his office, which had been thoroughly cleaned and transformed from a clubhouse back into a room where business could take place.

Sheriff Heath closed the door behind him. "This concerns Lucy Blake."

She dropped into her chair and gave an elaborate shrug. "I haven't seen her either. Maybe the two of them ran off together." She picked up a letter opener and slid an envelope open.

That indifferent gesture—the flick of a knife through paper—enraged me. How could this woman sit so casually after what she had done? The sheriff had warned me to stay quiet, but I couldn't.

"We found him," I said. "Right here in Paterson, where you left him."

The letter opener dropped to her desk. She kept her eyes down. The sheriff cleared his throat and leaned forward. "A boy was left at the Paterson Orphan Asylum last year. Lucy Blake has identified the child as hers. One of the nurses at the asylum remembers when you brought in the baby. She described you perfectly last night. And your handwriting is in the file. It isn't your name, but it happens that we brought in an expert on the study of handwriting. He's helping us with the case against your brother."

She lifted her eyebrows and her lips moved, but no words came out.

"Your attorney remembers Henry asking about adopting a baby," I said. "Was it Henry's idea?"

Still Marion said nothing.

"You can make your statement here, or we will take it at the courthouse," the sheriff said.

"I have no statement to make."

"A forthright confession will help you avoid the scandal of a trial. Ask your attorney if you don't believe me. Although he tells me he isn't taking any more criminal cases."

She took in a long, trembling breath and smoothed the papers on her desk. "It might have been Henry's idea, but he wasn't involved. I couldn't trust him to keep it quiet."

I caught myself nodding in agreement. Marion was shrewd. Of the two, she made the better criminal.

"I thought it was best for the child," she continued, so quietly that I had to lean in to hear. "That girl couldn't have raised him on her own. She would have kept coming back for money. She would have dragged us through the courts eventually."

She looked up at us defiantly. "I'm expected to clean up after my brother, so I did. And surely you agree that I did that baby a favor."

I wasn't surprised to hear her say that. But I couldn't picture her sneaking into a building and grabbing the child.

"You had help," I said. "Someone created a commotion inside that building and scared off the unionists. They ran off in the middle of the night, and they never reported the baby missing. You couldn't have frightened them like that yourself."

She tilted her head to one side, and then the other, as if she was weighing her options. Finally she said, "My brother has some rather unsavory friends. But useful."

Mrs. Garfinkel walked out of the office slowly, shakily, with me on one side and Sheriff Heath on the other. She murmured a few words to one of the secretaries who was just walking in. There were two automobiles waiting outside: one to take her to jail, and another to take us to pick up Lucy Blake.

THE ARREST OF MRS. GARFINKEL mattered little to Lucy, who urged us not to press charges at all but to just return her child to her and let her get as far away from the Kaufman family as she could.

"Kidnapping is not a crime we can overlook, Miss Blake," the sheriff said. "But we expect Mrs. Garfinkel to make a full confession and avoid a trial. We should be able to keep it out of the papers. I can't guarantee that Kaufman will leave you alone, but he doesn't know where you live and we'll make sure he doesn't find out."

The hearing was conducted later that morning exactly as

Sheriff Heath said it would be. A judge greeted us in closed chambers and heard testimony from Lucy and Sheriff Heath. (I was introduced only as a friend of Lucy's and had no objection to that.) The letter from Lucy's employer was read aloud and found suitable. Prosecutor Wright stepped in long enough to say that charges had been read against Marion Garfinkel and that she would be detained until arrangements could be made about her bail. The judge heard it all and signed the order before him authorizing the orphanage to release the child to his mother.

Lucy chatted happily as we drove back to the orphanage, describing the sitting room the sisters had agreed to turn into a nursery where little Bobby could spend his days while she worked. She said that they had made substantial donations to their church's building fund years ago and had already written to the minister's wife to ask for help in securing clothing and shoes for the child. Sheriff Heath said he thought his wife might have a few things she could send over, and I offered to have Fleurette sew anything else the boy might need.

We were in high spirits when we arrived. Sheriff Heath and I stood in the lobby while Lucy ran upstairs to collect her boy.

The sheriff held his hat and ran his fingers around the brim. "I owe you an apology, Miss Kopp," he said.

"I don't think you do," I said.

"No, you did this all on your own. You went to New York and found that photographer. I missed John Ward's name on the pictures, but you remembered. And whatever made you think of going around to the orphanages—well, you put it all together very quickly. You make a good detective."

I laughed. "It appears that you and Norma agree on something. If there are any positions for lady detectives, please be sure to tell me," I said.

"What's that?" he said.

"The Kopp sisters need to find jobs or husbands, and soon," I said.

"Who says so?"

"Our bank balance says so." Lucy's feet appeared at the top of the stairs and I ran toward her. "Just don't send any suitors my way," I called back to the sheriff. "I'm trying the other route first." Lucy descended to the landing with her little boy in her arms, and they both fell against me at once, all light and laughter.

⊰ 55 ⊱

"YOU'RE NOT TAKING A JOB IN NEW YORK!" Fleurette
said, dropping the roll she'd been buttering.

"Not yet," I said. "I just wrote to them and asked about the
position."

"And what did they say?"

"They sent an immediate reply and said they were quite
desperate for extra help this spring and wondered if I'd like to
come for an interview right away. I'm going tomorrow."

Fleurette stared at Norma in horror. We had decided not to
tell Fleurette of our financial difficulties or of Francis's pres-
sure to sell the farm. We didn't want her to be angry with him.

"What are you going to do?" she asked. "Wrap presents behind the counter?"

"Oh, not at all," I said. "They're hiring store detectives."

WHEN MR. WANAMAKER first opened his store in New York,
he made much of the fact that shoppers could wander freely
through the sales floor and handle the goods themselves, an

idea that was still quite novel back in 1896. His was a glittering bazaar of velvet gloves and leather shoes and miles of ribbon and lace and tailored suits for men and every other convenience a city-dweller might want, straddling two blocks on Broadway and employing a few thousand clerks and stock boys.

He believed that prices should be written on paper tags and affixed directly to the merchandise so that his customers could see for themselves what each item cost. "If everyone is equal before God," he liked to tell his managers, "then everyone should be equal before price."

Unfortunately for Mr. Wanamaker and his Christian principles, the openness of his store invited thievery. To combat this problem, some of his clerks had become detectives, strolling around the sales floor in ordinary dress, posing as shoppers but keeping their eyes on the slim fingers and gaping pocketbooks of a new breed of genteel downtown thief. Even women stole from Wanamaker's, which meant that women had to be employed as detectives to monitor the gloves and lace and undergarments. The job was simply to walk the sales floor, as unobtrusively as possible, wearing one's own clothes, looking like an ordinary shopper. I saw no reason why I couldn't get hired to do a simple thing like that.

I WAS FIFTEEN MINUTES EARLY for my interview with Mrs. Langdon, the ladies' sales manager at Wanamaker's. I wore a wool dress of dark green that Fleurette had just finished for me. It seemed like a smart dress for a store detective—nicely tailored but comfortable, of an ordinary fabric and color that would not call attention it itself. Fleurette had declared it to be a dress for a woman who had important things to do.

I approached a girl selling scarves at a counter near the entrance and asked her where I might find Mrs. Langdon.

"Oh!" she said. "Is Annie all right?"

"Annie?"

"One of the girls. She's been missing and Mrs. Langdon said that her mother was coming in to talk to her. I thought you might have been Annie's mother."

I looked down at my suit and my high leather shoes. I did look matronly.

"I'm here to interview for a position," I said.

"You are?" The girl looked up at me, puzzled. She wore smooth ringlets of brown hair around a perfectly round face that seemed to wear a perpetual expression of surprise. She couldn't have been more than eighteen.

"Won't your husband mind?" she said.

I hadn't time to explain myself. "Perhaps I'll ask at the perfume counter."

"I'm sorry, ma'am," the girl said quickly. "Her office is upstairs and straight to the back. Through the white door without a sign on it."

I made my way past the scarves and the perfume, past the last of the winter gloves and a collection of lace for spring, past a table of sewing notions stocked with pearl buttons and a shelf of leather-bound books sold by the set. At last I reached the white door upstairs, and behind that door was Mrs. Langdon, seated at her desk.

Here, at last, was someone who wasn't eighteen. She wore a neat bun of perfectly white hair, and a crisply starched white cotton blouse to match. Everything in her office, in fact, was white: the walls, the rug, and even her furniture, all painted the color of flawless new snow.

She raised a tiny hand as I walked in to indicate that I should not interrupt her writing. I waited while she scratched her paper and blotted it, and then she turned to face me.

"I'm sorry, my dear," she said. "I'm conducting an interview at two o'clock, and I was just going out to look for the girl. Can someone else help you?"

"I . . . I am the girl," I said, realizing at once how foolish I sounded. "I mean, I am Constance Kopp. You wrote to me. About the detective position."

She made a little gasp that caught in her throat. She rose from her chair, not taking her eyes off me, and walked right up to me. Mrs. Langdon was a petite woman of hardly more than five feet in height, so when she stood in front of me, she looked directly at the button fastened across my breastbone. I took a step back so that she could look me in the eye, but she stepped forward again. I wondered if she was nearsighted. Then she walked around me, slowly, the way one takes in a statue at a museum.

I held my breath. Was this the interview?

She circled back to her desk. There was no other chair in the room, so I remained standing. "I'm sorry, my dear," she said briskly, giving me one last appraisal over the tops of her spectacles. "You won't do at all. We're looking for some-one—unobtrusive."

"Unobtrusive?" I said. "I've worn the most ordinary dress, just as you asked."

She shook her head slowly. "It isn't your dress, my dear. It's—well, we can't have a store detective who stands head and shoulders above all the other shoppers. You'll be noticed. The thieves will have no trouble describing you to each other. They do talk, you know."

I didn't know. "But my size could be an advantage," I said, trying to sound cheerful and not at all desperate. "I can see above the other ladies. And if you're trying to catch a pick-pocket, surely it would be a help to have a detective with some strength. If someone tried to run away I'd have no trouble keeping hold of them."

Mrs. Langdon gave a small, polite laugh. "My dear. We aren't hiring a police officer. I'm not looking for someone to make a scene on the sales floor. We want more of a"—and here she paused to consider her words—"a gentle presence. Watchful, but polite. Discreet."

It hadn't occurred to me that I'd be turned down after I'd come all this way. Wasn't I polite and discreet?

I let my silence hang in the air for just a second too long. Mrs. Langdon rose and opened the door.

"I don't think we're what you're looking for, my dear," she said, looking up at me with pale blue eyes. "You're better suited for something more rough and tumble."

Rough and tumble?

She patted my arm and gestured through the open door. "You'll find it."

⇥ 56 ⇤

"A GENTLE PRESENCE?" Norma said, outraged. "Are you sure that's what she said?"

"She thought I would stand out," I said. "She thought I would be too conspicuous."

"Isn't that what a store detective should be?" Fleurette asked. "How else will the thieves know to stay away?"

"It doesn't work that way." I was tired of talking about it already, and embarrassed that I'd lost a job that should have been handed to me easily.

In an effort to change the subject, Norma tossed the newspaper at me. "It appears that Sheriff Heath has won over another criminal with his kindness and hospitality."

SAVED OF PRISON TERM BY SHERIFF

GEORGE EWING OF HACKENSACK, a former convict who was indicted for using the mails to defraud victims throughout the county, was saved from being returned to state prison by Sheriff Heath of Bergen County, who said he thought the convict could be reformed.

Ewing was released from state prison after having served his part of a sentence for theft. He returned to Bergen County and led a good life, said the sheriff. Then he relapsed into his old ways and was arrested.

The sheriff took such a kind interest in him that when the case came up yesterday he appealed to the court, saying that if the prisoner were sentenced to prison he would probably never be reformed. Judge Haight then sentenced Ewing to five months in the Bergen County Jail.

"But that's good news for us!" I said. "It means that he's agreed that he won't claim responsibility for Mr. Kaufman's crimes. We can go forward with the case."

"What makes you think he won't change his mind?" Norma said.

"He agreed to tell the truth if we kept him here in Hackensack, and we've done that."

Norma raised an eyebrow at me. "A criminal has made a promise to tell the truth, and now our case against a violent and unpredictable madman depends upon him. Are you suggesting that we take this to be good news?"

"It was my idea," I said. "I told the sheriff that if Mr. Ewing really wanted to stay in the Hackensack jail, he should use that as leverage."

"Well, I knew it all along," Norma said. "You are good at something."

"What's that?"

"Telling Sheriff Heath what to do."

OVER THE NEXT FEW WEEKS, our case proceeded to trial. Prosecutor Wright called me into his office several times to go over it. The questions struck me as repetitive and unnecessary, but Mr. Wright insisted that we review every detail. Mr. Kingsley, the handwriting expert from New York, was prepared to testify that Mr. Kaufman had written the letters. He also secured a full confession from Marion Garfinkel on the basis of her false signature at the orphanage. Once she saw the way he was planning to put the evidence before a jury, she knew better than to fight the charges. She paid her own bond and was awaiting a sentence from the judge. Because the child had been returned to its mother, it was possible that she, like her brother, would face a fine rather than jail.

When the weather was finally warm enough, Francis and Bessie brought the children out to Wyckoff for what they liked to call "A Day at the Farm." Francis had instituted this tradition to teach the children the value of hard work, and Bessie went along with it to have an excuse to sit in the shade, kick off her shoes, and let the children run wild. So every year in the spring, when the hens were raising their chicks and there were baby rabbits in the field, we'd spend the day outdoors watching the children chase the animals and ruin their play clothes.

We looked forward to A Day at the Farm more than the children did because we never had to cook. Bessie always insisted that a picnic would be more fun in the countryside anyway, but we all knew the real reason: she didn't want to eat our cooking any more than we did. The chief object of the day was to make it through Bessie's wicker hampers: first the stuffed eggs and cucumber sandwiches, then the potato salad, the baked chicken, and aspic, and finally the glorious fruit tarts and peach preserves. This year they'd brought ice cream, and Fleurette made a ginger ale punch that the children drank from Mother's gilded Sèvres teacups.

We pulled every rug out of the house and spread them on the lawn, then piled on all the pillows and cushions we could find, and from that perch we dedicated ourselves to depleting Bessie's hampers. Francis was in better spirits than we'd seen him in some time. He'd shaved his beard for the summer and it gave him an air of youthfulness and lightheartedness that was not entirely in keeping with his character.

"You look better without it," Fleurette said. "You look much younger, and it's easier to know what you're thinking."

"What am I thinking right now?" Francis asked.

Fleurette pulled off the red scarf she'd wrapped around her hair and lay back on a pillow. "You're thinking of buying an automobile and teaching me to drive it," she said.

Norma groaned and said, "We've been riding around in the sheriff's wagon, and it has given Fleurette too many ideas, as I feared it would."

Little Frankie discovered something behind the barn that made him shriek, and Francis jumped up and ran to check on him.

"I hope Henry Kaufman isn't lurking back there again," Fleurette mumbled, half asleep.

I couldn't help but laugh, but Norma took offense. "We must never make a joke out of that man," she said, and, turning back to Bessie, "Please don't listen to her. Henry Kaufman is very nearly out of our lives forever."

Bessie pushed her plate away and rolled over on a pillow too, arranging her purple flowered dress around her knees. "I'm not worried about Henry Kaufman. I only ever worried about the three of you because I was sure one of you would shoot him, and then we'd have to visit you in jail."

"Sheriff Heath would never put Constance in jail," Fleurette said. "He likes her too much."

"He likes all of us," I said briskly, "and we owe him a great deal for all he's done. Although I'm sure he'll be glad when the trial is over and he can forget all about us."

Francis came jogging back carrying little Frankie under his arm like a football. Frankie was shrieking and giggling. Lorraine skipped along behind them, holding out her hands. "We found a little blind possum and now we must wash our hands," she said, seeming to leave out the most interesting part of that story. Lorraine had grown nearly a foot in the last year and was beginning to show a little of Fleurette's dramatic beauty. But today she was covered in dust and straw from the barn, and around her lips were traces of sticky jam.

"Go and wash yourselves off at the pump," Bessie said. "Ask your aunt Fleurette to help you."

Fleurette opened one eye in Lorraine's direction and let out a gasp of mock horror. She jumped to her feet and took each child by the hand, and soon they were shrieking again at the pump and splashing around in a muddy puddle, having forgotten all about getting clean.

"We were just talking about the trial," Bessie said to Francis, in a deliberate manner that suggested that she'd been instructed to find out what was going on.

Francis reached in the basket for a lemon tart and said, "What about it?" before pushing half of it into his mouth.

"It'll all be over next month," I said. "We expect a short trial and a quick conviction, and then we can all go on with our lives."

"And then what?" Francis said without looking at me.

I didn't want to have to give him an accounting of my attempts to find a position for myself. I'd ridden into New York a few times, hoping that Mr. LaMotte would have another photography assignment for me and would be willing to pay me this time. He was never there when I stopped in. I saw him on the sidewalk once, but he appeared to be arguing with a client and he waved me away.

I had even returned to Wanamaker's and wandered the sales floor, trying to pick out the girl they'd hired to be their store detective. I saw any number of pretty, petite girls in fine spring dresses circling the tables and fingering the goods, but not one of them looked capable of handling pickpockets and thieves.

There were very few positions announced in the paper either. Advertisements for bookkeepers and office clerks appeared every few weeks, but always in the men's help wanted section, never the women's. I saw vacancies for housecleaners and cooks, and the mills were always hiring, but none of that would have suited me. I could have taken a stenography course, but there were already three girls running notices each week that they were trained in stenography and looking for positions.

All of this seemed impossible to explain. "I'm looking for something suitable," I said. "A job to help make ends meet. I've been on a few interviews already."

Francis seemed poised to deliver another lecture, but Bessie put a hand on his arm and he smiled at her and settled back down in the contented manner of a well-fed husband who has submitted to his wife's charms. She patted him and said, "You girls are going to have such an adventure, I just know it. Constance will find a good place for herself, and then maybe she'll hear of something that would suit Norma. And who knows what the world has to offer Fleurette? Or what she has to offer the world?"

We all turned at once and looked toward the water pump, where Fleurette had joined the children in a contest to see who could splash the most mud on the other. Both girls had hitched their skirts up around their knees and turned on little Frankie, who had never been more delighted. He dropped into the puddle and grinned at them like the most contented pig in New Jersey.

"Let's do the world a favor," Norma said, "and not unleash Fleurette upon it quite yet."

BY MAY, there was little to do but wait for the trial. I was finally able to get a man out to put new locks on the doors and glaze the broken windows we'd boarded up. Norma expanded the size of her pigeon flock by half again, which gave her an excuse to spend most of her days in the barn fussing with the incubator and keeping the wood stove going. Fleurette took seriously the job of sewing clothes for little Bobby and soon had him outfitted with play clothes, a sailor suit, and a new suit for church. Even Norma took an interest in the boy. On the weekends she brought a basket of pigeons over to Lucy's and let him watch as she tied bright blue ribbons to their legs and released them. He laughed and clapped as they circled overhead and flew away.

I had plenty of work to do. There were tomatoes and pole beans to plant, fences to repair, and blankets and rugs to be brought outside and beaten until the dust had been driven from them. But the chores were only a distraction from our real problems. Any woman in our position would attach herself to a relation with a spare room and make herself useful. If I couldn't come up with a better idea, we would have to do the same, and soon.

And then what? Where the years ahead had once seemed vague and unknowable, amorphous in shape and indeterminate in size, after my mother died I began to see a set of decades stacked neatly in front of me like bricks. First came my thirties, already half gone, and beyond that my forties and my fifties, solid and certain. But after that, the bricks started to crumble. My grandmother died at the age of sixty-two, and my grandfather at seventy-one. Then my mother was gone, having succumbed to pneumonia after only just turning sixty herself.

When I allowed myself to think about the brevity of the time ahead of me, and the futility of spending any more of it on cooking and mending and gardening, it frightened me so much that I almost couldn't breathe.

⊰ 57 ⊱

THE TRIAL WAS SET AT LAST FOR EARLY JUNE. We were
expected in court on a Tuesday morning and hoped to be finished by Friday. Fearing that the long ride back and forth to
Newark would leave us overtired, Sheriff Heath made arrangements for us to stay at the Continental Hotel for the week. On
Monday night we rode the train to Newark with an enormous
trunk of clothes and a stack of hatboxes taller than the girl
who intended to wear them. Fleurette was delirious over the
notion of staying at a hotel and had made herself a new dress
to honor the occasion, an apricot affair that sagged strangely
at the knees in what she called a "bowling pin silhouette."

"I think you went wrong just south of the waist," Norma
said.

"It's Parisian," Fleurette said.

"That didn't come from Paris."

"It came from McCall's, by way of Paris."

Fleurette did look exquisite in the dress, and she knew
it. A porter came running the minute she appeared on the
platform and loaded a cart with our luggage. He escorted us

across the street to the hotel, where Fleurette swept into the lobby ahead of us, her head cocked slightly to show off her wide straw hat (festooned with what Norma called an "audacious" arrangement of silk roses and dyed feathers). It is no exaggeration to say that every head turned in her direction. Norma and I struggled along behind her, hot and dusty from the trip, looking every bit the part of two spinster aunts unable to keep up with their young charge.

The man at the registration desk made a little bow when he saw her. "Evening, miss. You one of Sparks's girls?"

"Sparks?"

"She's *our* girl," I said, rushing up behind her. "Miss Constance Kopp and her sisters, under arrangements made by Mr. Robert Heath."

Norma nudged me, worried, I knew, that I was about to mention the criminal trial. Norma didn't want anyone at the hotel to know that we were there in connection with the sheriff or the courthouse, believing that we would attract the attention of reporters looking for a sensational story.

"What's a Sparks girl?" Fleurette asked.

The desk clerk looked at us nervously. "My mistake, miss. Some—ah—entertainers are lodging with us for the week, and I mistook . . ." He looked down, embarrassed, and shuffled his registration cards. "Here we are! The Misses Kopp."

Just then the tallest and thinnest man I'd ever seen leaned over the desk next to us and said, in a loud and lively voice, one word: "Sparks." Fleurette had to lift the brim of her hat to stare up at him, which she did, open-mouthed. He wore a pinstriped suit made of enough yardage to clothe two ordinary men, and when he leaned over the desk to sign his name to the register, the pen looked like it might snap between his long, bony fingers.

He glanced down at the three of us and tipped his hat. "You ladies in town for the show?"

"What show?" Fleurette said, before I could stop her.

"Sparks Circus, miss. A vision of beauty and splendor, just like yourself." He winked at her and flashed a gold tooth when he grinned.

I took hold of Fleurette's shoulder, but she was effervescent by now and there was no way of stopping her.

"Are you with the circus?"

He turned to her and made a deep bow. "World's tallest man," he said, winking at her as he rose. "Haven't you heard of me?"

Fleurette was quivering. I'd never seen the girl so excited. Norma shot a worried look at me, but I just shrugged. I couldn't see how we'd get her away from him unless we picked her up and carried her off.

"Is—is everyone in the circus staying here?" she asked.

He raised an eyebrow to the desk clerk, who looked alarmed at the possibility, and said, "Only a few old friends of Mr. Cooke's. You know Mr. Cooke, don't you? Used to be a circus agent. One day he was one of us, and now he's a hotel proprietor."

Fleurette turned back to the man handling our registration. "Did you think I was with the circus?" she asked, incredulous.

The world's tallest man stepped in before the clerk could compose an answer. "A little thing like you?" he said. "We'd put you on the trapeze. How do you like heights?"

Norma couldn't stand it any longer. She took Fleurette's arm and dragged her across the lobby, leaving me to sign the register and take the key from the clerk. The circus man apologized to me but then said, "You're not quite the world's tall-est girl, but we could find something for you."

Fleurette, still straining to hear us, shouted, "My other sis-ter's got a bird act!"

Norma nearly yanked her off her feet, and they disap-peared behind a wide stone column, one of Fleurette's blue feathers sailing along behind them.

WE WERE GIVEN A SUITE of two small rooms and a pri-vate bath on the fifth floor. I was reminded immediately of the Mandarin. Although our rooms in Newark looked out not over Fifth Avenue but over Broad Street, giving us a view all the way to the courthouse where our trial would commence in the morning, they had the same cosmopolitan air about them. Both the Continental and the Mandarin furnished their hotels with the busy city-dweller in mind, offering small and well-appointed writing desks and leather armchairs for reading under the electric chandeliers.

Fleurette set about exploring our rooms as if she were snooping around someone's bedroom, opening drawers, peek-ing into the closet, lifting the sheets, and looking under the mattress. "I'd like a room just like this," she said once she'd examined every corner of it.

Norma didn't voice any opinion of the room, but dropped into a chair and pulled her shoes off with a great sigh of relief. "I wonder if we can have supper on a tray," she said wearily.

"On a tray!" Fleurette said. "In here? Aren't we going to dine downstairs with the circus?" She was already tearing through her trunk in search of a dress that would make pre-cisely the right impression on a room of circus performers. I very much hoped she didn't own such a thing.

Norma gave me a desperate look—she hated to eat in a room full of strangers and had always detested restaurants and lunchrooms—and for once I agreed with her. We needed to rest and settle our minds before the start of the trial.

"I'm sure they can send something up," I said. "Norma's right. We don't need any more excitement tonight. We have a very important job to do tomorrow."

Fleurette flopped across the bed and rolled her eyes up at the ceiling. "I think we deserve one nice evening out before we have to sit in a stuffy courtroom all day."

I sat down next to her and pulled her chin toward me. "We're not just sitting," I said. "Remember what the sheriff has told you. Our testimony will make all the difference. We have to do the best we possibly can. Don't you want to see Mr. Kaufman punished for everything he's done?"

"I suppose," Fleurette said carelessly. "Only—did you really mind so much?"

"Mind what?"

"Henry Kaufman. I mean, wasn't it the most interesting year of our lives? We learned to fire a gun and, and rode in an automobile, and you got to run around with the sheriff, and we never would have met Lucy Blake, and what about—"

"Don't talk like that," I said.

Norma groaned. "We can't let her testify. Can't we say she's too young?"

"No, really," Fleurette said, sitting up and cocking her head at me. "Can you honestly say that you wish Henry Kaufman had never run us down on Market Street? If you could do it again, would you have kept us home from Paterson that day?"

Norma shifted in her chair and she, too, was staring at me. We all knew the answer, but I wasn't about to say it.

❦ 58 ❧

CELEBRATED KOPP CASE ON
TRIAL TODAY AT NEWARK

NEWARK, June 3, 1915—Harry Kaufman, a well-known silk dyer, of Paterson, came up today for trial in the United States District Court, Newark, on an indictment charging him with sending threatening letters to Miss Constance Kopp, of Wyckoff.

Sheriff Robert N. Heath, who developed the case against Kaufman, was an important witness for the prosecution.

This case has been pending since last July and sensational testimony is expected as an outcome of the trial.

The published story of the Black Hand letters sent to Miss Kopp caused a discharged inmate of the State prison, whose home was Somerville, to add to the terror of this kind of correspondence by himself writing letters to her promising an exposure of the plot. His capture was cleverly made by Sheriff Heath. He is now serving a sentence in the Bergen County Jail.

• • •

FLEURETTE TOOK THE NEWSPAPER FROM ME, looked it over again to make sure she wasn't mentioned, and then fanned herself with it. The courtroom was hot and crowded. Not a single window could be opened for fear of the proceedings being overheard in the street.

"I intend to deliver the most sensational testimony," Fleurette said.

Sheriff Heath, who was seated just in front of us with his deputies, turned and frowned at me. This was my cue to correct Fleurette.

"You know they only say that to sell papers," I said quietly, but loud enough for the sheriff to hear. "You must give them only the plain and truthful testimony they require. Only answer questions that you are asked to you directly. And if anyone—"

"I know! You don't have to keep reminding me," she hissed.

"You don't have to keep treating this like a party game," I said, prompting a kick from Norma.

"Stop it," she whispered. "Both of you." She cast a dramatic glance behind her, and I turned to see the row of reporters waiting to write down anything we said. They had already described Fleurette as "sixteen and so attractive that she had been threatened with kidnapping" in yesterday evening's paper, a line that I knew we would hear repeated for weeks. I didn't want to give them any more salacious details.

The bailiff rose and announced the arrival of the jury. Twelve somber men filed in and took their seats behind the heavy oak partition that separated them from the rest of the courtroom. I looked them over and tried to guess at their dispositions, but their expressions revealed very little. They seemed to be ordinary men, shopkeepers or clerks. They kept their eyes on the empty chair soon to be occupied by the judge.

Once they were seated, the bailiff announced the arrival of Judge Haight, a tall and broad-shouldered man who seemed too young for his steely gray hair. Then the attorneys for each side were introduced. We were represented by United States Attorney Lynch, and Henry Kaufman by a Mr. Joelson. The judge asked Mr. Kaufman to rise and hear the charges against him.

Until then, we had not had a good look at him. He was seated a few rows ahead of us on the other side of the aisle. When he stood, I realized that he was wearing much the same sort of suit he'd had on almost a year ago when his automobile collided with our buggy. It was a finely made suit meant to flatter a vain man, with delicate pinstripes and a series of careful darts that would make even a portly man like Mr. Kaufman look trim and strong. He wore a silk vest of a somber dark blue and a pocket square to match.

He looked so small in the enormous, crowded courtroom, and strangely insignificant. He was an unimportant man who had nonetheless been the most important person in our lives for the last year.

"Mr. Kaufman," said the judge. "You are charged with sending threatening letters through the United States mail to the Misses Constance, Norma, and Fleurette Kopp. How do you respond?"

"I am not guilty, Your Honor." This brought out a murmur from the reporters. The judge cast them a sharp look.

"Please be seated, Mr. Kaufman. Attorney Lynch may call his first witness."

Sheriff Heath slid to the end of the bench and walked to the witness box to take his oath. He wore a better suit then he ordinarily did, a black serge meant for church, and a collar so stiff and high that he could hardly turn his head. He'd been to the barber just that morning for a cut and a shave that I could tell were a bit too close for his liking. His mustache was trimmed a little shorter than he usually wore it, and he looked exposed because of it.

He took his seat and began his testimony, recounting the events of the last year, beginning with our meeting that day in the prosecutor's office. His answers were as brief and colorless as they could possibly be, and the attorney's questions were carefully phrased to keep them that way.

I sat in the courtroom and watched this man, who had been a complete stranger to me a year ago, tell the story of my life. The parts he left out came back to me anyway: the nights I spent sleeping alongside Fleurette with a revolver on my nightstand, listening to her breathe and watching the unmoving but wakeful form of Norma on the floor under the window. Norma and I out in the snow, our revolvers drawn, patrolling on our own after the deputies left. And Lucy Blake, with her arms wrapped around her boy, and those of us who had a hand in his recovery standing by, delighted and a little stunned by the outcome.

The jury heard none of that, but I could hear it all in the silences between Sheriff Heath's answers.

After the sheriff had answered all of the questions put to him, Attorney Lynch dismissed him and called me to the witness stand.

I took my oath. Attorney Lynch asked me to describe the events of July 14, 1914. I didn't look at Mr. Kaufman. I looked at Fleurette, who had shown remarkable restraint in her choice of courtroom attire and made herself a fashionable but dignified skirt and shirtwaist of deep cranberry. The attorney had wanted her in pink, with bows and lace, but she'd refused, saying she was too old for such a thing. She did indeed look older, but as I spoke, I saw her as she had been that day, in her dress of rose-colored taffeta, trapped under our broken buggy with Dolley kicking and groaning alongside her.

At the attorney's prompting, I described my efforts to collect payment for the damages to the buggy and the subsequent threats and insults hurled our way.

"And what did you do in response to the threats?" Attorney Lynch said.

"I got a revolver to protect us." There was a sound from the jury—something like a gasp quickly suppressed. I turned and looked directly at them, which I had been instructed not to do. I didn't care. I wanted their full attention.

"And soon I had use for it," I told them. "A few nights later I looked from my bedroom window on the second floor and saw a man behind the house. When he raised his gun to my window, I shot at him. He returned the fire. The bullets struck the house close to the window where I was."

The jurymen stared at me. Attorney Lynch cleared his throat to draw my attention back to him.

"Please read for the jury the letter you received on November 19, 1914," he said, handing me Mr. Kaufman's letter demanding that I deliver a thousand dollars to a girl in black. I read the letter and handed it back.

"And how was this letter delivered?"

"By the United States Postal Service. You can see the postmark for yourself."

He then asked me to recount the night I spent waiting for

the girl in black and the other particulars of the case. It was exhausting to tell it all at once. Just as I thought I could not bear to answer another question, the attorney thanked me for my testimony and invited Mr. Joelson to take his turn.

"Miss Kopp," Mr. Joelson said. "My client regrets the inconvenience caused by the collision of your buggy and his automobile."

Inconvenience? He paused as if he wanted a response from me, but I'd been instructed to only answer questions. I remained silent. Did he consider everything that happened in the last year an inconvenience?

Getting no response from me, he continued, "And he considers his payment of the fine imposed by the court to be the end of the matter."

Attorney Lynch stood. "Your Honor, does Mr. Joelson have a question for Miss Kopp?"

Before the judge could speak, Mr. Joelson said, "Miss Kopp, did you ever receive a threatening letter signed with the name Henry Kaufman?"

"No, I did not."

"Did you ever receive a letter with Mr. Kaufman's return address on the envelope, or the insignia of his business on the stationery, or any other mark that would indicate that the letter had been sent by him?"

"Just the initials H. K."

"And did you ever see Mr. Kaufman fire a gun at you or your sisters?"

"I saw a dark figure matching his general description."

"What about his automobile? Did these men who threatened you ever arrive in an automobile that you could be certain belonged to Mr. Kaufman?"

"Only the first time," I said. "After that they waited until after dark."

"The first time? Which time are you referring to?" he asked with a false sense of confusion.

"The first time he drove past my house," I said evenly, looking right at Mr. Kaufman now, who quickly looked down at the table when he found my gaze on him. "He and a few other men drove past and shouted insults at Fleurette."

"Ah, yes," Mr. Joelson said with obvious and exaggerated relief. "The time he yelled out of a passing car. I thought you were referring to illegal behavior."

I opened my mouth to speak, and Attorney Lynch knocked a book off the table, making a loud bang on the bare wooden floor. This was my signal to stay quiet.

"Was that incident included in your complaint against my client, Miss Kopp?"

"I don't believe it was."

"Then you have not seen, with your own eyes, this man or his automobile involved in any of the incidents included in your complaint, is that correct?" He pointed dramatically to Henry Kaufman, who had his hands folded quietly on the table in front of him.

"Not precisely," I said.

"And you have no way of knowing if someone else was behind these alleged threats? George Ewing, for example, who I believe was the next man in line to threaten the ever-popular Kopp sisters?"

"I have no reason to believe anyone else was behind it."

"Then you are dismissed, Miss Kopp." I began to rise when he said, "Wait. There is another matter. Please take your seat again, and I do apologize for the inconvenience."

I settled back into my seat and kept my eyes on him. Attorney Lynch had warned me not to look at him if I got confused, as it would make the jury think I was looking for a signal.

"You've paid a visit to Mr. Kaufman's place of business, haven't you?" he asked.

I did my best to keep my face composed and said, "I have never paid a social call on Mr. Kaufman."

There was the sound of stifled laughter from the reporters, which the judge quickly suppressed with his gavel.

Mr. Joelson tried again. In a booming, staccato voice, he said, "What was the purpose of your visit to Mr. Kaufman's factory?"

In an equally loud voice I replied, "To collect the money owed to me for the damages to my buggy."

"And was that all?"

"To make a polite request that he refrain from harassing my family."

"And what was the result?"

"This trial is the result."

The courtroom erupted in laughter. Even the men on the jury wiped their eyes and shook their heads. The judge pounded his gavel and ordered a break for lunch.

I left with great relief for Attorney Lynch's office, where coffee and sandwiches had been brought in so we could discuss the case in private. A pretty young secretary passed the basket of sandwiches around while Attorney Lynch said, "That went as well as we could've expected. Joelson has decided he needs to offer no defense on his client's behalf as long as he can continue to get you girls on the witness stand saying that you never saw Kaufman do a thing. He wants to convince the jury that the evidence is entirely circumstantial. It's exactly what I would do if I were him."

"But it won't work, will it?" I asked.

Attorney Lynch pushed a corner of his ham sandwich into his mouth and shrugged, chewing thoughtfully. "I don't predict the future, Miss Kopp. I just make the case."

NORMA TOOK THE STAND IN THE AFTERNOON and answered the same questions that had been put to me, giving answers even briefer and more terse than my own.

"Did you see the man who threw the bricks through your window?"

"No."

"Did anyone get a look at him?"

"No."

"Not one of you could provide even the most general description?"

"No."

"Isn't that odd, for three such observant girls?"

"We were asleep."

That was the longest answer she gave. Attorney Lynch had asked her to try to soften her expression on the witness stand, but Norma frowned at Mr. Joelson and did not cast a particularly kind look upon me or Sheriff Heath when she left the stand, as if to suggest that we were equally responsible for taking her away from the farm for a week and getting her involved in a federal trial at Newark.

Fleurette took the stand late in the afternoon, looking remarkably cool and unruffled despite the long day in a hot and crowded courtroom. She'd been preparing for her role as if it were a stage debut, and I worried that she might get it in her head to improvise. But she answered Attorney Lynch's questions with a calm composure I don't think she possessed a year ago. Her hair had been carefully rolled into neatly sculpted curls, and she'd powdered her nose and arranged herself in her chair so that she sat perfectly straight, making herself as tall as she could.

"When did you first become aware that you were the target of a kidnapping plot?" Attorney Lynch asked.

"In August," she said. "We received a letter delivered by brick mail."

A few people in the courtroom tittered at her choice of words.

"Do you mean that the letter was tied to a brick and thrown through the window of your family home in Wyckoff?" he asked.

"Yes."

"Thank you. Were there other threats?"

"Yes, a few more, some sent by post."

"And what was done to protect you against those threats?"

Fleurette paused and found me in the crowd. She gave me a long and searching look.

"My sisters learned to shoot a gun," she said, with a note of wonder in her voice, as if she hadn't entirely considered it before. "And on two occasions Constance went to meet the men who were threatening me, to try to stop them."

I shivered. She was looking at me as if she were seeing me for the first time.

"That must have been very dangerous."

She thought for a minute and then, in a quiet voice, she said, "I think it was."

⚜ 59 ⚜

AFTER THE JURY WAS DISMISSED for the evening and we
turned to leave the courtroom, I saw Marion Garfinkel sitting in the back row next to a white-haired man. He had one
gnarled hand locked around the brass handle of a cane. As we
passed by, she rose and introduced her father.

"Mr. Kaufman," I said. "How do you do?"

He didn't reach for my hand and I didn't offer it. Sheriff
Heath had been standing right behind me, and with a nod
to his deputy, Norma and Fleurette were escorted out of the
room. Henry Kaufman and his attorneys had already left by a
side door. We waited until the rest of the spectators had filed
out and the four of us were alone.

"Mrs. Garfinkel," Sheriff Heath said. "We weren't expecting you. I'm sure better seats could be arranged for you and
your father tomorrow."

"That's fine, Sheriff," she said. "I don't think we'll stay for
the rest of the trial. I just wanted my father to hear for himself what Henry did to these girls."

She turned pointedly to her father, who gave a tremulous

nod and spoke in a raspy, uneven voice. "I'm afraid I've mis-judged my son's character, miss," he said. "I thought I knew the boy. It's a terrible thing to see your own child grown into someone you don't recognize."

"I suppose it would be," I said, not wanting to imagine it.

"We could add a witness to tomorrow's docket if you'd like to testify," Sheriff Heath said quietly to Mrs. Garfinkel, but she just shook her head.

"I couldn't. He's still my brother. But we won't hire an attorney to appeal the charges, and we won't pay his fine. If he's convicted, he should see the inside of a prison cell. Isn't that what we've agreed to?" She put a hand on her father's shoulder and he nodded, his head down. He wore a fine linen suit—I could see where Henry Kaufman got his taste for good tailoring—but something about him seemed shabby and defeated. I couldn't look him in the face but stared at his ears, which were red and overgrown and laced with tiny blue capillaries.

"Then we have some hope of seeing justice done this week," Sheriff Heath said. "I'm glad to see you've come around to our way of thinking."

"Yes, I realize . . ." Marion looked at her father and her voice trailed off.

We stood awkwardly for a minute, none of us knowing what to say to the other. Finally the sheriff nodded and took my arm to leave. We'd gone down the hall to join Norma and Fleurette when I heard footsteps and turned to see Marion rushing after us, having left her father in a chair outside the courtroom. When she reached us she put a hand on arm and said, "The girl. Lucy. Are she and her boy—will they be—"

"They're fine," I said. "They have a comfortable home. Lucy's a good mother."

Marion's hand tightened around me. "Of course she is," she said, with an uncharacteristic quiver to her voice. "Could you tell her—"

"I don't think I should," I said quickly. "Lucy wishes to leave things be."

She let me go and turned to look at her father, who was already nodding off in his chair. "Then I'll tell you," she said, without bringing her eyes back to mine. "If that boy ever needs a family . . ."

"He doesn't," I said. "He has one."

THAT NIGHT, we gave in to Fleurette's pleas and took our supper in the enormous dining hall that ran the length of the building. The waiters had rolled a wide green awning out over the sidewalk and set out tables for anyone who preferred the dust and noise of the street to the hushed wicker fans cooling the restaurant. We settled indoors, although Fleurette suspected that the circus performers would prefer to dine in the fresh air. She kept her eyes on the sidewalk all evening, hoping for a glimpse of them. We did see five petite but sturdy women sweep through in identical scarlet gowns, their hair arranged in a theatrical style of braids and curls held together with sparkling glass combs. Fleurette suspected them of being trick riders or magician's assistants. "Or they could be acrobats," she said. "Did you see the way they walked? Just the way they would on a tightrope." Norma and I ate our roast chicken in silence as Fleurette chattered on about her plans to run a tightrope across the meadow and begin practicing as soon as we got home. I think we were both grateful for the distraction. It was exhausting to relive the events of the last year in the courtroom, and even the notion of Fleurette dancing on a wire high above the ground seemed soothing by comparison.

There was a ladies' parlor on the second floor and a sketch room hung with paintings of sailboats and pastoral scenes of horses on mountaintops. A few young women had brought their sketchbooks and were working at copying the paintings, but we had no interest in it and instead settled in the parlor, where Fleurette had insisted that we take a cup of tea before retiring.

"We never get to sit in the ladies' parlor at home," she said as we settled into dainty armchairs arranged around a little beaded lamp on a table. There were three other groups of women seated in their own tight circles around the room, none of whom appeared to be circus performers, to Fleurette's disappointment.

"We sit in the ladies' parlor every evening at home," Norma said. "What else would you call it?"

"But there aren't other ladies there," Fleurette said. "At home it's only us."

Norma looked around at the others, all speaking in a genteel hush to their own friends. "I don't see what difference it makes," she said. "We don't wish to talk to any of them, and they don't seem to take an interest in us."

Of the three of us, Norma was the only one who was impervious to the charms of a hotel. Fleurette liked the opportunity to dress up and be seen, and I just liked living in a clean, modern building, with twice the comforts and none of the chores we faced at home.

Fleurette took as long as possible to finish her tea, but after several conspicuous yawns, Norma convinced her that it was time for bed. We had just begun to climb the stairs when

I heard Sheriff Heath's voice from a room down the hall. I told the two of them to go on and I went back to look for him.

He was just coming out of a smoking lounge at the opposite end of the hall from the ladies' parlor. He had his hat in his hand and carried the same brown coat he wore everywhere. There was a long red carpet between us and a series of tiny tables and settees.

"I didn't know you were staying here," I said as he walked toward me.

"I'm not," he said. "I was due home hours ago. Mr. Lynch kept me out too late."

"Are you all in there planning tomorrow's strategy?"

He shook his head. "We're playing cards. Don't tell Mrs. Heath."

"I didn't know the sheriff was allowed in card rooms."

"Well," he said, considering that. "It's a respectable enough card room. There are only lawyers and judges at the moment."

"Is our judge there?"

"Oh, no," he said. "But don't worry. We have a good judge. The trial's going just fine, everyone says so. And now we know that Mrs. Garfinkel won't be paying his fine, so it looks like he'll spend a little time at the state prison after all."

"The state prison? The same one George Ewing hated so much?"

A waiter came rushing by with a cart covered in a white cloth, and the sheriff and I backed into an alcove off the hall to get out of his way. He gestured to one of the little velvet settees. I sat down and he settled in across from me.

"That's the one," he said. "And by the way, I'm bringing Ewing in with me tomorrow. We still expect him to testify against Kaufman. If I tell him that Kaufman's going to serve his sentence in Trenton, that will be all the more reason for Mr. Ewing to do everything he can to stay with me in Hackensack."

I leaned back and regarded Sheriff Heath in the dim light. We'd been talking about catching and convicting Henry Kaufman for so long that it hardly seemed possible that it was all about to end.

"I hate to admit it," I said, more to fill the silence than anything else, "but I do feel sorry for the elder Mr. Kaufman. It must be a terrible thing to watch one's son on trial."

"And one's daughter," he said. "Although I couldn't tell how much Mrs. Garfinkel had told her father about the kidnapping charge."

"Nor could I. Will she go to jail, too?"

"I won't know for a few more weeks. We're still working on charging the men who helped her. I'd rather put them in jail than Mrs. Garfinkel."

"So would I," I said.

We sat in silence for another minute or two, but as there was nothing to look at in the alcove besides one another, I began to fidget and then realized that Norma and Fleurette would wonder why I'd taken so long. I rose suddenly, knocking my head on the low ceiling above us, and backed out into the hall. Sheriff Heath followed. He walked with me to the wide central staircase, where I would go up to our room and he would go down. The situation must have struck us both as odd, because we laughed at the same time and then the sheriff said, "Tomorrow, Miss Kopp," and jogged down the stairs, two at a time, waving over his shoulder as he crossed the carpeted lobby with its blazing chandeliers and went out into the warm blue night.

⤚ 60 ⤙

OVER THE NEXT TWO DAYS, the trial proceeded just as we'd
hoped it would. Mr. Kingsley's handwriting analysis was accepted by the judge as thoroughly scientific. Mr. Kaufman's
only hope—that he could persuade George Ewing to confess
to the threatening letters and gunshots in exchange for some
sort of bribe—fell apart when Mr. Ewing took the stand and
gave a simple and truthful account of his role in the attacks
against us. He acknowledged that he'd been in the car on
the day of our buggy accident and that he'd been with Mr.
Kaufman and some other men on a few other occasions,
but said that he hadn't written any letters except the last
ones, which contained his signature, and had never taken a
shot at our house or thrown a brick through our window. He
said that Mr. Kaufman had coerced him into writing those
final letters with the idea that they would shift the blame
for the entire mess. He added that when he was caught, Mr.
Kaufman threatened him harm if he didn't take responsibility for everything.

Henry Kaufman took the stand in his defense but had little to say beyond his denial of the charges.

"Do you admit to having caused your motor car to collide with a buggy driven by the Misses Kopp on July 14 of last year?" Attorney Lynch asked.

"I do," he said, "and I have paid my fine." He spoke woodenly, as if he had memorized the answers. He was paler than when I'd last seen him and a bit thinner. He was no longer a man who looked like he was about to explode. I wondered if his attorney had persuaded him to reduce his drinking before the trial.

"Do you admit to driving to the Kopp home in Wyckoff to harass them and shoot at them after the collision?"

"I do not."

"Are you the writer of the threatening letters sent to the Misses Kopp from August to November of last year?"

"I am not."

"Mr. Kaufman," Attorney Lynch said, approaching the witness stand with a sheaf of papers, "did you not provide these handwriting samples to the sheriff's office, which were used to positively match your handwriting to that of the writer of the letters?"

Mr. Kaufman leaned forward and squinted at the paper. "I admit to writing the name 'Constance Kopp' at the suggestion of the sheriff, but the rest of it was coerced."

"Coerced?" said Attorney Lynch with a smile. "By what means were you coerced?"

Mr. Kaufman looked around until he found me. "She was there!" he said, rising and pointing at me. "She trapped me and forced me to write out handwriting samples against my will."

The men in the jury box smiled.

"Forced you?" Attorney Lynch said, taking a step back in amazement. "By what means does a lady like Miss Kopp force a grown man to do anything he doesn't want to do?"

Mr. Kaufman looked down and mumbled something.

"Could you repeat that for the jury?" Attorney Lynch asked.

He looked up and said, in a loud, plain voice, "She's not a regular lady."

AFTER HIS TESTIMONY CONCLUDED, the jury took only two and a half hours to convict Henry Kaufman. He was fined one thousand dollars and, having no means of paying the fine, was taken into custody. Mrs. Garfinkel and her father hadn't returned for the conclusion of the trial, and none of Mr. Kaufman's associates had made an appearance, either. When he was led away, there was no one to say goodbye to him.

The verdict was read at two-thirty in the afternoon. By three o'clock we were standing in front of the courthouse saying our goodbyes to the sheriff, his deputies, and the attorneys. The reporters were trying to get Fleurette's attention, but Sheriff Heath put Deputy Morris by her side to keep them away.

It was a perfect summer afternoon, with a jewel-blue sky above us and clouds that looked like they had been painted on. A breeze had risen to push the heat out of Newark's fetid streets, and a willow tree planted alongside the courthouse waved its drooping branches, whispering like the rush of water. Everything looked cleaner and brighter than it had when the trial began. The granite courthouse behind us, the rows of brick offices and shops across the street, and the trolleys running along their tracks, all seemed to speak of a crisp and orderly world in which people could walk the streets in peace. The attorneys and deputies laughed and joked with one another, and they, too, seemed younger and brighter in the light of a favorable verdict and a clear June day.

We said all the thanks we could think to say and a silence fell over the group. Norma and Fleurette turned to walk to the train station. Sheriff Heath took me by the arm and led me away from them. We walked down the stairs, and then he stopped and turned to me.

"You had more of a role in this than anyone in that court-room knew," he said.

"Oh—" I looked at him in surprise. "Well. We all did our part."

The sun glared on the white steps and he squinted at me with that half-smile, half-frown I still hadn't learned to read.

"What you did will serve you well in your new occupa-tion," he said.

I laughed. "Occupation? I have no occupation. That's just the trouble. If we—"

He didn't let me finish. "Miss Kopp. I think you'd make a fine deputy."

"Deputy?"

"Deputy sheriff."

My throat went dry. I had to swallow before I spoke. "I don't understand."

He smiled and looked down at his feet, then raised his eyes to mine.

"I'm offering you a job, Miss Kopp."

Historical and Source Notes, Acknowledgments

THIS IS A WORK OF HISTORICAL FICTION based on real events and real people. My task as a writer was to take the public record—pieced together from newspaper articles, genealogical records, court documents, and other sources—and invent the rest of the story. All of the major events described in the novel actually happened, with a few notable exceptions: There was no Lucy Blake, which means that every part of the story connected with her—the missing child, Constance's trips to New York, and the scenes at the orphanage—are all fiction. (It is true, however, that children were sent away to live with "strike mothers" during the silk strikes, and that some of those children did not return.) Although Henry Kaufman did have a secretary named M. Garfinkel, the character of Marion Garfinkel is fictional. Another significant difference is that Mrs. Kopp, Norma and Constance's mother, died a few years later than she does in my version of events. Also, to my knowledge, Norma Kopp had no interest in pigeons.

Everything else happened more or less as I described it. I

invented dialogue, personalities, backstories, and scenes that helped piece together the stories behind the events described in the public record. Most of the people who appear here as secondary characters—people such as Bessie Kopp, John Courter, John Ward, Peter McGinnis, and Cordelia Heath—are also real people who led lives that I know little about. The personality traits, ambitions, and actions I ascribed to them are my own embellishments to the few facts I do know about them.

The circumstances surrounding Fleurette's birth are not entirely known, but the basic facts—the identity of her mother and father, the relevant dates, and the fact that Fleurette grew up not knowing the truth—have been verified through court documents and interviews with Fleurette's son.

I used real letters and newspaper articles in the book to help anchor the story in reality. I'd like to acknowledge the following sources for text that I reproduced word for word, or with very slight modifications:

The incidents described on pages 45–46 are all sourced from *New York Times* articles in the 1890s.

The filming of the trolley car accident (page 60) actually happened in Paterson around the time of the Kopp sisters' accident with Henry Kaufman.

The text of the letters from Henry Kaufman on pages 84, 154, 227, 234, and 238 come from court records of the original indictment and multiple newspaper accounts, with slight modifications.

The other crimes Sheriff Heath dealt with, as described on pages 219–20, all actually occurred and were sourced from Hackensack newspapers of the day.

The story that Fleurette read on page 244 came from

Stories of Pioneer Life: For Young Readers by
Florence Bass, published in 1900.

The headline "Girl Waits with Gun" (page 258) came
from the *Philadelphia Sun* article that ran on
November 23, 1914, but most of the text comes from
two similar stories that each ran in the Philadelphia
Evening-Ledger, one titled "Oh, for a Chance to
Shoot at the Nasty Prowlers!" (November 21, 1914)
and the other titled "Girl, Armed, Waits for Black
Handers on Street Corner" (November 23, 1914).

"Arrest in Black Hand Letters Case" (page 271) ran in
the *Bergen Evening-Record* on December 3, 1914,
although I added a line about the fictional Marion
Garfinkel posting bail.

The text of the letter from George Ewing dated
December 21, 1914 (pages 278–79) was printed in
several newspaper accounts, including one in the
Bergen Evening-News on January 23, 1915.

The story of the night watchman beaten to death (page
283) ran in the *New York Times* on December 27,
1914, under the headline "Held in Murder Inquiry."

"Says He Was Kopp Black Hand 'Gang'" (pages 295–96)
ran in the *New York Tribune* on January 23, 1915.

"Saved of Prison Term by Sheriff" (pages 372–73)
appeared in the *Trenton Evening Times* on March 8,
1915.

"Celebrated Kopp Case on Trial Today at Newark" (page
385) appeared in the *Bergen Evening-Record* on June
3, 1915.

"Kopp Sisters Tell of Death Threats," from the *New York
Times,* June 3, 1915, is the source of Constance's

quote in the epigraph and some of her dialogue
during the trial (page 389).

The headlines Norma cut out of the paper and sent by
pigeon post were all actual headlines from Paterson-
area newspapers of the day.

Passaic and Bergen County history buffs will notice that I
took a few liberties with geography, train schedules, streetcar
routes, and other such details. What can I say? This is a work
of fiction, and sometimes the story takes over. If my characters started riding over a bridge, I let them, even if no bridge
existed at that place.

I'd like to thank the following people for their help with
the research: Maria Hopper, genealogist extraordinaire; Jona-
than Rapoport; and the staff and volunteers at the Ridgewood
Public Library, Paterson Public Library, Hackensack Public Library, Hawthorne Historical Society, Bergen County Historical
Society, and the Passaic County Historical Society at Lambert
Castle. Extra heaps of thanks go to Inspector Mickey Bradley
at the Bergen County Sheriff's Office for an impromptu tour
of the old jail and Sheriff Heath's living quarters, as well as his
willingness to preserve and share Heath's photographs.

Most of all, heartfelt thanks go to Dennis and Deanne
O'Dell, John Birgel (father and son), and members of the Heath
and Ward families for their willingness to talk about their ancestors with a complete stranger and to share their stories.

My retelling of the Kopp sisters' story owes its life to four
people who believed in it as much as I did: my husband, Scott
Brown; my first reader, Masie Cochran; my agent, Michelle
Tessler; and my editor, Andrea Schulz. Thanks to everyone at
HMH for giving Constance, Norma, and Fleurette a home.